My Hellion, My Heart

LORDS OF ESSEX

My Hellion, My Heart

LORDS OF ESSEX

AMALIE HOWARD
&
ANGIE MORGAN

Entangled Publishing, LLC
2614 South Timberline Road
Suite 109
Fort Collins, CO 80525
Visit our website at www.entangledpublishing.com.

Select Historical is an imprint of Entangled Publishing, LLC.

Edited by Alethea Spiridon
Cover design by Liz Pelletier
Cover art from Period Images and iStock

Manufactured in the United States of America

First Edition July 2017

For our husbands, who put up with all the madness.

Chapter One

Princess Irina Volkonsky ignored the scandalized glances and hushed whispers of French society's crème de la crème as she downed the last of Lord Deroche's whiskey. Savoring the bite of the liquor on her lips, she returned his glass and nodded to the ballroom floor where partners were lining up for the next dance.

"Shall we?"

"Again?" Deroche asked with a low laugh. "Three dances? You'll ruin my spotless reputation, and I will be forced to offer my hand like the rest of these enamored whelps."

Irina eyed him from over her fan and flashed him a sultry smile. "Let's call a spade a spade, Deroche—you are well and truly ensnared by my charms."

"Quite," he said. The way his lips shaped the word made her eyes settle there for a moment. Those lips had been on her knuckles—and then on her mouth—moments before in an alcove on the balcony where they had retired for some air. Despite his play at sarcasm, Irina knew he wanted far more than a few kisses. She, however, did not.

"And you should know by now that I don't care for such silly rules." She stifled a derisive snort as they took their places for the set. "If two dances suggest special attention, and three imply I'm off the marriage mart, then heaven help us should we dance a fourth. I'd likely be impregnated."

"You don't mince words, do you?" His dark eyes met hers, widening slightly at her provocative and entirely deliberate response.

"Why should I? Gentlemen aren't encumbered by such restraint." Irina fluttered her eyelashes and peered up at him, the demure look at odds with her direct speech. She hadn't shocked him, Irina knew. Her unconventional opinions seemed to amuse Deroche. "And honestly, it's just so tiring the way people soften the blow when one straightforward word will do. In this case, an immaculate conception."

An answering smile curved her companion's lips. "Then I shall endeavor to solicit such a dance. Though I must warn you, my methods are hardly *immaculate*."

Despite the heated flush that rose to her cheeks, Irina couldn't stop the laughter that bubbled in her throat. Unlike most of his peers, Deroche was good fun, but even with his diverting company, it seemed as though this season was shaping up to be exactly like the last: boring, lackluster, and a complete disaster. Irina was simply making the most of what was left of it.

She glanced over his shoulder as they paired for a rousing quadrille, feeling the burn of dozens of eyes upon them. It wasn't that she didn't want to wrangle an offer from Lord Deroche; she simply did not want to have to turn him down. Her guardians in Paris, Lord and Lady Marceau, close friends to her sister's in-laws, the Earl and Countess of Dinsmore, had turned down no less than seven offers on her behalf since the start of the season.

Notwithstanding her title and her fortune, she'd been declared an Original, an Incomparable, and all manner of ludicrous names meant to awe and excite. Rich and eligible bachelors fawned at her feet, but none of them came remotely close to taking her fancy. Take Lord Deroche, for example. He was a fine specimen of the perfect catch—wealthy, titled, and devilishly handsome. But something was missing.

Something was always missing.

Deep down, Irina knew she was being unreasonable. She would eventually have to marry *someone*. Her coming out in St. Petersburg the year before had resulted in a dozen rejected proposals, and by the end of this season in Paris, she knew that some of the monikers she'd received during her first would return to torment her. *Ice princess*, *stone heart*, and her favorite, *cold fish*. She jutted her chin as the music began. No matter. She would weather this season as well.

By the end of the set her heart was racing and her earlier thoughts had vanished. She thanked Lord Deroche for the dance and, rejecting his wicked invitation for a fourth, retired to the ladies' salon. While she'd enjoyed the innuendo and his attentions, Irina did not want to play games with someone as dissolute as Deroche. She'd likely end up with her skirts over her head and her already spare reputation in tatters. And as much as she claimed not to care for the precious thoughts of the beau monde, Irina still had her sister's position to consider, if not her own. Lana was now a respected viscountess in English society, and from the tone of her last letter, she was not pleased with reports of Irina's latest vagaries.

A trio of pastel-wrapped debutantes twittered as she walked past them toward a pair of empty armchairs. Irina paid them no mind as she sat. Her recent behavior was scandalous she knew, and despite her social standing, associating with her would be viewed as foolish. As a result, she was surprised when she was joined by a red-cheeked lady drowning in layers of aquamarine tulle.

The woman fanned herself vigorously and smoothed tendrils of fiery red hair that had escaped the jeweled combs at her temples. "I loathe the quadrille," she announced with dramatic flair as she signaled for a glass of champagne from a nearby footman. "It does absolutely nothing for my complexion."

Irina recognized her as Lady Lyon, an English countess close to her own age who had only recently married. No English rose, Lady Lyon was known more for her bawdy humor than her beauty, and though their paths had crossed before, they had never exchanged more than a few words.

Irina smiled and nodded her head in greeting. "Lady Lyon."

"Please," she said with an exaggerated eye roll before draining the contents of her flute. "No more titles. Countess this, lady that. Call me Gwen. And I shall call you Irina."

Irina suppressed another smile. It was clear that the countess was shockingly into her cups, which would explain why she had voluntarily sat in the first place. And the use of given names after what could hardly be called an introduction was unheard of. Such a breach of stuffy etiquette suited Irina immensely. "Lady Lyon...*Gwen*...are you well?"

The countess's pale blue eyes swung to hers. "Why wouldn't I be?" She waved her glass and added, "Oh, you mean this? Not to worry, my mother was Irish."

As if that explained everything.

At that moment, Irina realized she had found an unlikely kindred spirit.

"So?" Gwen asked, leaning forward in a conspiratorial fashion. "Deroche, eh? I hear he's made of gold — everywhere it counts. Good catch."

Irina laughed to herself at her suggestive wink. Three dances had indeed been enough to insinuate an interest in marriage. "I hate to disappoint, but no. Lord Deroche is a passing entertainment, nothing more."

Gwen stared at her circumspectly, something like interest dawning in her eyes. "Are you ever in London?"

"I haven't been as of late, but my sister does live there, as well as in Essex."

"Ah yes, Lady Northridge. Lovely woman." She grinned. "I used to fancy your brother-in-law. Thankfully, North did not return my affections, otherwise he would have been ruined for any other woman."

A reformed rake, Irina knew her brother-in-law had had an active past. He'd conceived a child with one of his mistresses and a few years later, had fallen in love with Irina's sister, who had taken the child in as her own. Though she missed Lana and had seen her in St. Petersburg months before, Irina hadn't set foot in England since she'd left four years ago. Her throat tightened painfully. There was a reason for it. One she refused to entertain at the moment. She drew a calming breath.

Gwen stood, her cheeks still violently flushed. "Well, I suppose I should go find my husband. No telling what trouble he has gotten himself into by now." She peered down at Irina. "I like you. You should visit me in London next spring. Lord Lyon gives the most marvelous midseason ball."

"I have no plans to—"

Gwen cut her off with an airy wave. "No plans? Wonderful, then I must insist."

The young countess swirled away in a whirlwind of blue-green skirts. It wasn't often that Irina met another female who left her feeling bewildered. She was usually the culprit of such mayhem.

Smoothing her hair and her dress, Irina exited the retiring room. Lost in thought about Gwen's invitation and what returning to London would mean, she almost crashed into a gentleman's back.

"Oh, please excuse me," she said, the blunder one more potential thing for people to chide her for.

"It is I who should apologize to a lady of such mesmerizing beauty," the gentleman said, turning to fawn over her gloved hand. "You are an Incomparable. The Ultimate. The Prize. The Toast of Paris and Thief of All Hearts."

"Max, you wretch!" Irina shook her head and swatted at her childhood friend as he pressed melodramatic kisses to her knuckles. Distant cousins, they had been close as children and had reconnected at the start of the season in Paris. In a few short weeks, they had become inseparable.

"I should have pushed you down just now. Where have you been all night?" she asked. "I've been looking for you."

He arched a slim, golden eyebrow. "Didn't seem like you were looking for me. Deroche, I hear?"

Irina groaned. "What is *wrong* with people? We danced, that is all."

"Four times I was told."

"Three, and my best friend deserted me, so what choice did I have?" Irina eyed her longtime friend, noting his tousled blond hair and bee-stung lips. Her eyes narrowed, and she lowered her voice. "And where exactly have you been, Lord Remisov?"

"Remi," he said, handing her a glass of champagne and escorting her to a quiet corner of the massive ballroom. "And none of your business."

It wasn't any of her business. She knew the type of lovers Max favored, and none of them were ever appropriate. Women, men, young, old, beau monde, demimonde, it didn't matter. It was some kind of defiance, she knew, against the rules of his stringent father. Max was sowing his wild oats, so to speak, and had been for a while, leaving a trail of broken hearts across the Continent, from St. Petersburg to Paris.

"Max, you really should think about settling down. You have more than enough variety to choose from."

"As do you, my sweet, and yet I don't see you settling."

She shook her head. "That's different."

"How so?" He sipped his champagne. "I've heard you turned down seven suitors."

"I am a princess," she grumbled. "With standards."

"Size doesn't matter," Max said sagely.

Irina swallowed her shocked giggle. "Someone will hear you," she said, blushing fiercely. "And that's not what I meant."

"Surely there is a gentleman here who has taken your fancy. There has to be someone you can fall in love with."

Irina's mood sobered. "Alas, falling in love is not as easy as the romance books make it out to be. Most of the men here want only one thing—a beautiful face or an enticing body to warm their beds. They care naught for a woman's mind." She took a sip of the champagne and grimaced. She didn't know how Max enjoyed its frothy taste; she'd much prefer a good whiskey like the one she'd pilfered from Lord Deroche earlier. "A woman's place is to be seen and not heard. Poppycock, if you ask me."

"Which would be torture for you, I expect."

"What would?" she asked, distracted by the sight of Deroche escorting a gorgeous blonde to the terrace. It supported her earlier assessment that men were only out for one thing. It didn't surprise her that Deroche would seek it elsewhere. Still, it stung. Slightly.

"Not being able to speak."

She grinned at Max's insult. "You know me too well." She linked her arm in his. "Why can't I fall in love with someone like you? Handsome, when not rolling in stable barns. Clever and witty. And someone whose company I genuinely enjoy." With a sigh, she added, "Perhaps I will have better luck in

London."

"London?" he asked with a surprised look. "I thought you hated the place."

"I do. It's gloomy and stodgy, but my sister's last letter made me feel guilty for being away for so long. I feel I should spend some time there."

Her heart doubled its pace at the decision she'd just made. She would go to London. *A decision made is a decision kept.* It was something her father had said numerous times when she and Lana had been young and still happily growing up in St. Petersburg. Many years had passed since her mother and father had died, but there was always a little prick of pain whenever she thought of them. Seeing Lana would help soothe it away.

She had just given birth to little Kate at the start of Irina's first season and had been unable to act as chaperone, and earlier this season Irina had decided upon Paris considering Lana was again increasing. Sadly, a letter had arrived at the Marceau's home two weeks before with horrible news: Lana had lost the babe. She'd been only less than two months into the pregnancy, but Lana and Gray were devastated. They already had three children in addition to Gray's daughter, Sofia, and from Lana's letters they were the center of their world. Irina had always known her sister would be a naturally wonderful mother, and had, admittedly, greatly missed feeling the glow of her care and attention. Now that Irina was older, she longed to do the same for her older sister. Going to London for the following season would be good for them both.

Swallowing hard, Irina wondered if she'd see *him*.

From her correspondence with Lana, Irina knew the Earl of Langlevit had not yet married. Once she was in London, their paths would undoubtedly cross. He was an earl, after all. He'd be at balls and soirees and dinners, and as his handsome, unforgettable face forged its way into her brain once again, Irina imagined how she would react. She would be cool and aloof, a princess to the core. He would take her hand and brush his lips across her fingers. The image was so visceral, so *real*, that the mere thought of it made her breath hitch painfully in her lungs.

"Or perhaps not," she said, draining the vile champagne and rethinking just how dedicated she was to her father's old saying about decisions made and kept. "Perhaps a second season in Paris may be best."

"No," Max said. "London sounds fetching. I haven't been there in years, either. It will be a new start for both of us. And just think…after the two seasons you've had, the gentlemen there will be vying for your hand. You'll have your pick of the litter." He waved a dramatic arm, warming to the subject. "The competition will be so fierce that men will bet fortunes on whom you will choose."

"Now you're being silly."

"I am not," he replied with an affronted look.

She laughed. "Well then, if that's the case, I can assure you that entire fortunes will be wagered and lost."

Irina had not accepted any offers for the past two years for a reason, and it was as unshakable a reason as it was a secret. As she'd expected, not one potential suitor had come close to the image of the man who held her heart in his keeping… who had held it there for the better part of four years despite her own good sense. No other man could compare to the Earl of Langlevit.

Not that he knew, of course.

She and the earl had crossed paths once during her first season in St. Petersburg. The Gorchev's soiree had been a crush, and yet he had still managed to be the only person in attendance she seemed to be able to see. Irina had not expected Henry to be there; she hadn't even known he was in the city. And just as quickly as a swell of pleasure and hope had filled her chest and spiked her pulse, it had been extinguished. Langlevit had bowed, made the necessary pleasantries, and had hardly looked her in the eye before moving on across the ballroom.

He'd kept his distance for the remainder of the evening. Seeing her again after so many years had meant nothing to him. Clearly, the Earl of Langlevit still thought of her as a child, as his mother's ward. He would never see her as otherwise—not as a woman, and not as marriageable material. It had chafed her pride to no end when he'd left the soiree with not one, but *two* unattached ladies of her acquaintance. The rumors about him being a profligate had run wild, but they had done little to temper the fire of her affection for him. In fact, the knowledge had made it burn brighter.

She'd imagined and reimagined scenes of when they would next meet. She'd seduce him thoroughly and lead him on a merry chase, whereupon he'd fall madly in love with her. But their paths hadn't crossed since. Her fevered imaginings had become nothing but a dearth of hopeless wishes.

"I wonder how much they'd wager?" Max asked.

Irina turned back to him. "For what?"

"For your hand in marriage."

She stared at him and shook her head. "Betting on a woman's hand? You can't be serious."

"Why not? You're a princess, Irina, and you've a reputation as…well…"

"Don't say it, Max."

"An iceberg," he finished. She pinched his arm. "What? You love me for my honest summarizations."

She sighed and held back a laugh. He was right. His blunt honesty was a gift. Most of the time.

"I am also of the male species and rather competitive," he went on, finishing his flute of champagne. "Being well schooled in how competitive men think, I am quite certain that if there is a wager concerning who can melt Princess Iceberg's heart, it will be a lucrative one. The more money in the pot, the more attention you'll receive." He leaned in close. "Think about it. They'll be mad for you."

Irina did, and her pricked pride flared to life. "They are all money-greedy goats."

And it would be a game for the goats, nothing more. But isn't that what the whole season was?

"Vying for a lady's hand in marriage and winning her dowry is the game every man is playing, isn't it?" she asked.

"Yes, but the women make it so plain whom they intend to choose. There is no risk involved for the men," he answered.

"What is going on inside that scheming head of yours, Max?" she asked, seeing the glint of excitement in his eyes.

"Just an idea to spice up the season next year," he replied. "Imagine…men attending every social function with the goal of winning your attention."

She narrowed her eyes on her friend. "Because there would be money in it for them?"

"And a challenge they would not normally have," he answered, cocking his head. "Of course, they needn't know what I do: that you won't have any of them."

Not unless the Earl of Langlevit were to enter the game. He wouldn't, though. She had no illusions that it would capture his attention, if such a farce even came to fruition. But if Max were right, she would have London in the palm of her hand while she was there. Perhaps the recalcitrant earl would be forced to take notice of her then. And if he didn't, at least it would be an entertaining diversion before she returned to St. Petersburg.

Irina lifted her nearly empty flute high and toasted her friend. "You may be onto something, Max."

Chapter Two

It was barely noon, but Henry James Radcliffe, Earl of Langlevit, was already inside his bedroom, a glass of Scotch in one hand and his eyes hitched on two women removing each other's dresses. The curtains were drawn to block both the bright sunshine and any possible view from the street below. No passing lady or gentleman need glimpse the lewd display currently unfolding in the earl's bedroom. The show was meant for him, and him alone. And usually it worked.

Henry shifted in his wide leather chair, the small fire in the hearth behind him warming the back of his neck and causing small beads of sweat to form on his temple. The moment Camilla and Mary had been led inside Henry's room, they had dropped their fur-lined capes and started to laugh. Neither woman had bothered to wear a chemise or petticoat underneath her muslin gown, and by all appearances it looked as though they had each dampened the thin white muslin as well. Their breasts and legs and the rosy areolas of their nipples had stood out in stark clarity through the sheer fabric. Poor Marbury, Henry's faithful and close-lipped valet, had definitely gotten an eyeful before he'd been able to shut the bedroom door. These women had traveled across London, all the way from The Cock and the Crown, where Henry's missive had been delivered earlier that morning, practically naked.

It was not the first time women from the gaming hell had done so. These two, however, he'd asked for specifically. Brunettes with dark blue eyes. Tall and willowy. Willing and able to serve his needs however he wanted.

He'd felt the stirrings in his groin and the hard thump of his pulse as the two women had sauntered across the room toward him, slow enough for him to look his fill. When they'd touched him, however, their hands running over his chest and stomach, he'd felt a whisper of panic.

It wasn't working.

He'd sent them a few paces toward his bed and told them to give him a show. He just needed a few minutes to get his mind right. To let it go blank and serene. Once it did, the rapid beating of his heart would slow and that restless, nameless feeling of something invisible nipping at his heels would go away. He would pour himself into these women, let them drain him of every thought and every sound, until he was blissfully empty. And if he was extremely lucky, he'd also manage to erase the image of the beautiful face that had haunted him for the last two years.

"Are you paying attention, my lord?" Mary asked.

Henry looked at her and realized he had not been. Instead, he'd been staring at the carpet the two women were standing upon with their bare feet.

"Of course," he said, lying, and swallowed the remainder of his drink.

Camilla grinned at him as she ran her skilled hands over Mary's curved hips. It had taken them less than five minutes to artfully strip one another bare, and now they stood before him expectantly.

His heart was still racing, his mind whirling, and for Christ's sake, he wished he wasn't in bloody London. *Hartstone.* That was where he longed to be right then—utterly alone, breathing clean, quiet air. But he'd left his Essex estate weeks ago to come to town and sit dutifully in the House of Lords, and there wasn't a damn breath of fresh anything, least of all air, to be had.

He knew he should get up from his chair and cross the room, that he should touch Camilla and Mary and let them distract him as best they could, the way the women from The Cock and the Crown usually did. It wouldn't be enough.

When had it started to not be enough?

St. Petersburg, murmured the irritating, know-it-all voice in his head. Henry didn't understand how or why spending less than one minute in Princess Irina Volkonsky's presence two years before had affected him so completely. She had been nearly unrecognizable at first. Gone was the coltish fourteen-year-old he recalled, replaced by a startling beauty with noticeable curves and swells and…and he had acted like an utter buffoon.

Henry clenched his teeth at the memory, as he did every time he thought of it. Of his lack of good graces and what had been an utter loss of the ability to speak. Irina had not crossed his mind for so long—years, perhaps. Ignorant of her identity, it had been her laugh—a rich, bold, and unabashed sound— that had drawn his attention from across the ballroom. It was her confidence and the beguiling glimpse of bare shoulders in a silk gown he'd wanted to remove with his teeth that had ultimately held it.

The attraction had been immediate. Raw and visceral,

and it had taken him completely by surprise. He'd sought no introduction, striding toward her like a man possessed with one singular objective—to stake his claim. But then she'd turned, laughter glimmering in those deep-violet eyes, and his world toppled inward as recognition landed on him like an avalanche.

Princess Irina Volkonsky.

His mother's bloody *ward*. In hindsight, he'd done the only thing he could: resort to extreme courtesy while his blood simmered and his groin tightened ignominiously at the full, unobstructed view of her. Good Lord, she'd taken his breath away.

On the cusp of womanhood, she had grown into those long limbs, which now supported her with grace and poise. Her face had held a gamine quality, dominated by mesmerizing eyes that had deepened and matured. And that luscious mouth of hers…devil take him, it had caused him to swell more. What had he been thinking? She was a goddamned child. Could he have sunk any lower in depravity? Discomfited, he'd grappled for something to say like a stuttering oaf. And then, furious with himself, he'd shut up for good. He'd felt uncomfortably warm, and his clothes had suddenly felt ill-fitting, his cravat too tight.

Much like right now.

What in hell was wrong with him? Two women stood before him, ready for the taking, wanting only to give him pleasure, and Henry felt nothing but hollow panic. Perhaps he'd been too clear in what he'd demanded. Too precise. He should have asked for blondes, redheads, anything but what now seemed like pale imitations of the female he craved. And all because of one brief, silly line he'd read a week ago in the gossip column in the *Times*, one his tortured brain had replayed over and over about a certain visiting princess.

His breath hissed from clamped lips.

In the drop of silence, and with Camilla and Mary exchanging a worried glance, he heard the slam of the doorknocker two stories below. Stevens would answer the door, and whomever it was would leave their card. It would be among the others Stevens would present to Henry in the salver at luncheon. There was no reason for him to stand and excuse himself so that he could see who was calling.

And yet he did.

The women stared at him, their eyebrows raised in surprise.

"I'm sorry," Henry said. More was needed. Something coy and playful, and perhaps reassuring. He should go to them, tap them both on the backside and thank them for their brief diversion. But again, it felt as if simple speech was beyond his grasp. "If you'll excuse me," was all he managed to get out before going to the door and exiting into the corridor.

Once there, Henry gulped in air and felt the shake of his hands. He'd just left them standing there, naked. What kind of man was he to turn down an invitation to tup two women at once?

Deranged, the voice murmured again.

Henry pushed it away and straightened his collar. His cravat was still loose, but who the devil cared? He was in his own home. Though at the moment he felt a stranger to everything around him.

His butler's voice drifted up the open, twisting stairwell from the foyer below. Henry glanced over the banister as he descended, saw the black-and-white tiled floor and Stevens's shiny, bald pate as he dropped the calling card into the silver salver set upon the credenza.

"Who was it?" Henry asked as he came down the last flight of carpeted steps.

Stevens turned and took a crisp bow before answering. "A footman from her ladyship, Lady Langlevit's residence, my lord."

He extended the salver to Henry, who spotted his mother's familiar cardstock easily. The pale pink color with spring green embossing never failed to amuse him. The Countess of Langlevit was just shy of her fiftieth birthday, and yet she insisted on the kind of calling card a blushing debutante would choose. She had aged well, and only ever having borne one child, had kept a girlish sort of figure he supposed, but those were not the things that made his mother appear young. It was her bright presence. Her smile. She was like an eternal springtime, and there was not a soul in London who did not adore her. Including her wretched son.

Of course, that did not mean he was eager to answer her summons. Henry knew exactly what she wanted to discuss, and it weighed on him. It was his birthday, his thirtieth, which meant one thing to the Earl of Langlevit: he needed to marry and perform his filial duty to produce the next heir. It was not a request made by a woman yearning for grandchildren, but a necessity stated within the letters patent attached to the Langlevit title, issued by none other than the tyrannical King Charles I.

Henry did not want children. Nor did he want a wife. However, thanks to an archaic stipulation written into the Langlevit title, he *required* both. For the past six generations, every Earl of Langlevit had been held to the unusually rigid requirement of marrying by the last day of his thirtieth year and getting to work producing an heir or suffer being stripped of the title, all holdings, and inheritance. And for the past six generations, every Earl of Langlevit had likely tried to figure a way to wriggle free from the restriction, one that was unlike anything found in the letters patent of other peerages.

Two hundred or so years ago, King Charles, who had a penchant for ruling as his own conscience saw fit, granted a peerage to a friend—a friend he wished to see married. Most specifically, to the king's own cousin. Charles awarded the man an earldom with the precondition that he marry by age thirty, or else the title and holdings would revert to the Crown. The monarch's exact language did not release future heirs to the earldom from that one precondition, however, and so every heir since had been forced to meet the requirement.

It was absolutely preposterous, Henry thought, but it was also irreversible.

After his father's death seven years ago, Henry had become earl—and the countdown had begun. He'd known he could not simply sit back and allow the Crown to revoke his family's legacy, not when his mother depended upon the income of her late husband, and not when the tenants working and living upon Langlevit lands depended upon him for their security. A title in abeyance would spell uncertainty and possible disaster for them. Henry had a duty to them all, just as the previous earls had. It was marriage. Not the guillotine.

No. Henry would heed the rules of his inheritance and marry. Though he'd waited until the last minute, it remained his responsibility. His duty. With the season getting underway, there would be a pool of prospects in town, but Henry had already come to a decision. He could not abide the endless balls and dances and crowds, and then the game of calling on the young woman he selected, plying her with flowers and making small, polite conversation in the hopes that she would accept him and not the several other young men vying for her hand. Just the thought of it exhausted him and made his pulse leaden.

Hell, he couldn't even make it through an encounter with two nude women in his own bedchamber.

What Henry wanted was to propose to a woman who would not require the romancing a debutante would expect. What he wanted was a woman who would answer him quickly and be amenable to a simple and fast ceremony.

What he needed was a widow, and he knew just the one: Lady Carmichael, the widow of one of Henry's closest childhood friends in Essex. It had been two years since John had died, and Rose was alone in Breckenham with a young son and about to cease half-mourning. The timing was right.

If she were to accept his written proposal, which he had sent to her home near Breckenham two days prior, he would break ties with the light-skirts he often sent for while in London, like the two upstairs. Town, with its noise, crowds, social requirements, and close quarters, always caused a buildup of tension and panic deep inside of him. Henry hated it. Fought it. Tried to reason with it. But there was only one thing that helped to silence the noise: the base act of sexual release. No emotion attached, no conversation, no pleasant company. Just sex.

Thinking of Rose in such a way, as a means of release, made him feel slightly ill. But if he had to marry, he'd rather it be to someone he trusted. Someone who knew him…who didn't have to be warned about his erratic behavior, or of the night terrors brought on by ghastly memories that he could never escape. Along with the countess and a select few in the War Office, Rose and John had been the only ones who knew the truth of what he had endured while he'd been held captive in France. As far as sexual release, he would secure a discreet mistress—he simply couldn't fathom using Rose that way.

Henry had broached the marriage requirement with her twice before. Once, long before she and John had married, and she had laughingly promised that should they both be unattached by the time they were thirty, she would consider it. Then she and John had fallen in love. After John's death, Rose had claimed she would never marry again. She didn't need to. John's estate provided more than enough for her and their young son.

The second time was eight months ago, when Henry had

called upon her to check in on his godson, William. Rose had been the one to bring up the subject.

"Your time is running out, you know," she had told him, bouncing William, who was the spitting image of John, on her lap, while they sat in the garden.

"I won't be a fit husband to anyone, Rose, you know that."

She had clasped his hand and squeezed. "You're robbing yourself of the chance to be happy."

"Happiness is an illusion."

"And you are a cynic, my lord." She shook her head. "There has to be a young lady out there for you."

Henry's voice was quiet. "No blushing deb deserves a man like me."

"Yes, I've heard about the type of company you prefer," she said with a sidelong glance that had held no judgment, only a measure of concern. "Perhaps you should consider widening your prospects."

He hadn't shared her enthusiasm, but had struck upon an idea as he'd watched her with William. He had no interest in widening his prospects. There was no other woman he felt more at ease with than Rose. Theirs could be a marriage of friendship. Of convenience. *If* she would have him.

The relief he'd felt that day had been instantaneous, and he'd left Rose and William with the idea percolating in the back of his mind. The damned stipulation in the letters patent made no mention of when an heir had to be conceived. Perhaps, as time went on, he and Rose might be easy enough with one another to attempt to produce an heir, as awkward and uninspiring as the task would likely be. However, at the moment, he needed only to concern himself with attaining a wife by the end of his thirtieth year. And so Henry had, many months later, sent the proposal to Rose. Everything hinged on her answer.

"Will you be going out, my lord?" Stevens asked,

interrupting his thoughts. His eyes glanced up the open shaft of the stairwell in silent question about what to do with the women who had just recently been escorted to Henry's bedchamber.

He could not face them again. Not today. Perhaps not ever. There were plenty of other women he could call for... though if he was to be married soon, maintaining that sort of colorful company would be disrespectful to his wife.

"Yes," Henry answered his butler. "I'm going to Devon Place."

"Should I call for your carriage?"

"No," he answered quickly, the muscles in his legs aching at the thought of being confined to a boxed-in conveyance. "I'll walk."

Henry paused in the foyer, knowing his staff could be trusted with the utmost discretion. After all, they'd witnessed far worse debauchery in the residence over the past few years after his return from the Peninsula. The presence of two light-skirts wouldn't make Marbury or Stevens or any of them bat an eye. Hell, it was far tamer than the intimate gathering he'd had a few weeks ago that had lasted three full days. "Have Billings take the women in my bedchamber back to their place of employment in the east end."

"Of course, my lord."

He took up his coat and hat, permitted Stevens to tighten up his loose cravat, and stepped outside. Leicester Square was still a month away from greening, and so it appeared brown and dull as he walked south, toward Irving Street. His mother's home was along the Pall Mall, giving him a good ten minutes at his breakneck pace to clear his head and get his pulse back under control.

His mother would not press about the necessary marriage, he knew. She only wanted to wish him a happy birthday and had probably had Mrs. Baskings prepare the special French chocolate truffles she always did on this day. He'd stay for truffles and tea and then be on his way to the Palace of Westminster, where there was an expected address from members of Parliament. Losing himself in his political duties would be a fine way to pass the day and forget Camilla and Mary, who would be returned to The Cock and the Crown and tell all who listened how Earl Langlevit had panicked and run.

Bloody hell.

He increased his pace and tried to focus on the paving stones before him. The street was busy, the chilled morning air having warmed enough to invite the stench of refuse. He felt the press of people as they passed him on the right and veered around his left, heading in the opposite direction.

A sudden *crack* from behind took his breath away and made his legs freeze. *Just a driver leading a horse with his whip*, his rational voice told him. But then a creature rushed toward his ankles, yapping sharply, and it was all Henry could do not to kick at the animal in response, every nerve within him firing in violent bursts. His fingers curled into rigid fists at his sides as his muscles tensed, ready to attack. To defend. To fight.

A dog, the voice said. *Just a dog.*

His internal voice was soft, though, dampened by the thunderous rushing of blood in his ears. Henry darted around the animal and its mistress, who had scooped it up and tried to apologize. Nodding brusquely, he hurried on, his ears still ringing, his clothing heavy and suddenly too constricting. Underneath, his skin grew sticky and hot, then cold and clammy, and just when he thought he might never take another deep breath of air again, his eyes tripped on the familiar front steps of his mother's house, Devon Place.

He stormed up them and let himself inside without bothering to knock. The cool air in his mother's house hit him, and he sucked in a breath. Then another and a third, and he hated himself more with every one. The mere crack of a whip and the annoying bark of a dog had made him nearly lose his wits, bringing back nightmarish memories he fought to keep dead and buried. Bracing against the door, Henry closed his eyes and breathed deeply, just as a physician had instructed him to do after he'd been injured on the Peninsula.

Meditation, as the physician termed it, had helped Henry breathe through the pain of his wounded back and shoulders, and it had helped calm him after his last—and final—mission into France. A disastrous mission that he didn't wish to think about ever again. Instead, he pictured the green fields and hills of Hartstone in Essex. The deep, cool paths through the woods there and the sound of the gurgling Brecken Kill running through it. Mentally, he ran the deadly obstacle course he'd built deep in the woods of his estate, feeling the strain ebb from his body with each turn in his mind's eye—through the icy river, down the rocky hillside, across the gorge, back into the forest. After several breaths, his heartbeat slowed and calmed.

"Lord Langlevit?"

Henry opened his eyes and saw his mother's butler, Andrews, approaching him, a frown upon his face. "My apologies that I was not present to see you in."

"Not at all, Andrews," he said, whisking off his hat and allowing his mother's faithful servant to help him from his coat, as well.

"Her ladyship is waiting for you in the front parlor," Andrews said and then led Henry down the short hallway off the foyer. He heard her voice through the calming pulse in his ears.

Andrews announced him seconds before Henry stepped inside his mother's favorite day room. The light-blue walls were a soothing color, and his eyes went instantly to them, skipping over his mother's figure in one chair and a second figure on a sofa. The blue paint reminded him of the open sky over one of Hartstone's fields.

"Langlevit?"

His mother's voice crept into the imagined sky.

"Henry."

He finally let go of the image and met his mother's concerned gaze. Sense rushed back into him, and he remembered they were not alone. He stood taller and looked at his mother's guest.

A woman with dark, upswept hair, soft curls at her temples. A pair of unforgettable deep-blue eyes, nearly violet, stared at him, wide and alarmed. The apples of her cheeks were pink, her lips parted in surprise. And when Henry's mind slammed back into gear, he realized whom he was staring at.

"Darling," his mother said. "You remember Princess Irina, don't you?"

Chapter Three

At the appearance of the tall man in the doorway, Irina's pulse slowed and galloped in intermittent fits and starts. Her arms felt like rubber as she placed the teacup delicately onto its matching china saucer. She'd known she would see him at some point during the season, but not today. Not so suddenly. Not when she wasn't *prepared*.

All her carefully rehearsed imaginings flew out the window as she studied the earl and frowned inwardly. He did not seem the same as she'd remembered. Certainly, on the surface he was as handsome as ever, accounting for the rapid rise and fall of her chest, but something was different. Something wasn't *right*.

Two years ago in St. Petersburg, he'd been cold and aloof, but now he seemed as if he was holding himself together by the grace of one fragile thread. Harrowed or haunted by something. Lines of tension notched his wide brow, and his shoulders were rigid, as though bearing the weight of the world and more.

His eyes, warm amber she knew from memory, but now

dark with shadows, settled on her. There was recognition there, along with something fiercer, something that made an icy tremor race across her spine. Lana had confided, in secret, the earl's clandestine activities as an officer of the king, and Irina had heard even quieter talk about the unyielding core that had kept him alive on the Peninsula and inspired his promotion to Field Marshal. She saw it then in his eyes—a look that would make grown men quake—but Irina did not drop her gaze like a terrified mouse. Instead, she held his stare until he drew a measured breath and turned to the countess.

The tension slipped from his face and body as he crossed the room toward Lady Langlevit, his lips curving into a familiar smile. A shallow dimple appeared in his right cheek. Despite his earlier rigidity, the sight of it made Irina's bones turn to water. A handful of years ago, she'd been the recipient of those tender smiles, usually only reserved for his mother, and then her, whenever he'd visited the estate in Cumbria. In her childish infatuation, she'd craved them like a flower craves sunlight.

"Mother," he said and then aimed a short bow in Irina's direction. The smile shifted into something a bit lazier, the dimple disappearing, and Irina couldn't help but mourn its loss. Then again, she was a grown woman now, not a child. He obviously did not view her as anything more than an acquaintance. "Your Highness. You've grown."

"Lord Langlevit," she murmured, proud that her voice didn't sound like an indelicate croak. "That is the usual side effect of time passing, I hear."

One of his pale brown eyebrows arched, his smile widening at her glib response. There was no dimple in sight, though. A fake smile, then.

"So I see," he replied, taking the armchair opposite them.

"Would you like some tea, dear?" the countess asked.

Langlevit shook his head. "Something stronger, I think. It

is my birthday, after all." He signaled to the hovering footman who brought him a snifter of what looked like whiskey.

The earl had always favored whisky when he'd visit the estate, Marsden Hall, in Cumbria. He would sip it slowly, as if just having a glass in his hand was enough. The whiskey was likely from his own distillery in Dumfries, Scotland. Irina longed for a glass to fortify herself, as well, but she sipped her tea instead, peering at him over the cup's gilded rim. In other company, she might have been bold enough to ask for a few drops in her tea, but it would be unseemly in the countess's presence.

"Happy birthday, my lord," Irina said, surprised that she had forgotten what day it was. All those years ago, when she and the countess had been secluded in Cumbria, the earl had not been present for his birthday. But on March the twenty-first, she and Lady Langlevit had enjoyed a selection of divine French truffles in his honor. Irina had never tasted anything so decadent and wonderful as those chocolate morsels, and when the countess had explained that they were "Henry's favorite," she had decided that they would be hers, as well.

He nodded at her now, a tight incline of his head, his back and shoulders so straight they looked painful. It was all the acknowledgment he gave for her birthday wishes. His eyes did not even settle on her for more than a heartbeat. Irina felt a sinking sensation in her chest, quickly followed by a rising fire. Had he always been such a horse's ass?

"Oh, Andrews," Lady Langlevit called out to the butler, "would you please fetch the box from the mantel that was delivered earlier? And there is also a sheaf of papers in the study under the—" She paused abruptly and stood. Langlevit leaped to his feet, nearly spilling the contents of his glass over the pale blue-and-gold Aubusson carpet. "Sit, my darling," the countess said, patting his arm on her way past. "Never mind, Andrews, I'll see to the papers. I'll just be a moment, my dears."

Irina set her cup down again and folded her hands in her lap. Without the countess's gentle presence, the tension in the room became nearly solid. The earl studied her with a hooded gaze, the long fingers of one hand drumming against his knee. Irina could feel the leashed energy vibrating off him. With his tousled, dark-blond hair and Cimmerian gaze, he had the air of a captive lion more than that of a man. He did not want to be here. She saw it in every tap of his finger. Well, he was not the only one. He sipped his whiskey, and she followed the movement, wishing once more for a drink of her own. She'd become used to the relaxed rules of society in Paris, where women were not restricted to sherry and wine.

Something flared in his eyes for a moment, and then he extended the glass to her. "Would you like a taste?"

The question threw her years into the past. Like his rare tender smiles, he'd offered occasional sips of his family whiskey to her on return from his visits to the distillery in Dumfries. A taste here and there, explaining how it was made and aged, walking her through the complicated process and the uses of different grains and barrels. She used to love listening to him talk about a subject he obviously had a passion for, and it was, she supposed, the reason she'd developed a liking for whiskey in the first place. Or why whenever she drank it, she thought of him.

Glancing at the silent footman who hadn't blinked an eye at the earl's highly improper question, Irina leaned forward, taking the snifter. She breathed in the rich aromas of oak and vanilla. Henry slouched back in his chair, crossing his legs and watching her with a slightly bored expression. His aloofness chafed at her. Had she not changed enough in appearance to warrant some sort of response from him? Something more than a mundane, "You've grown?" Of course, she had not expected him to lose his mind or dissolve into absurd compliments, but did she truly not look any different to him than she had when she was fourteen? She would not stand for his cool reserve. Not this time.

Keeping her eyes deliberately on his, Irina turned the glass to where the outline of his lips remained on the rim and brought it slowly to her mouth. She pressed her tongue lightly against the edge as she sipped the smoky liquid. She heard his indrawn breath, saw his throat bob from the corner of her eye, but did not release him from her stare until she'd placed the glass on the table between them.

Irina licked her lips and savored the mellow bite, enjoying the lingering finish of the fine whiskey. Her blood boiled from the phantom imprint of his mouth more than the taste of the liquor, but she'd accomplished what she'd set out to do. Henry's eyes were narrowed on her, his nostrils flaring. She'd bet anything he wasn't thinking of her as some naive child now.

"Far better than I remembered," she said softly.

The earl half rose out of his chair, a muscle beating along his jaw, his eyes focused on her mouth. At that precise moment, however, Lady Langlevit swept back into the room. Irina let out a breath, uncertain what he'd been about to do. Her heart was racing at a fair clip, though, as if he had become that lion again, and she had become prey.

If the rumors about Langlevit were to be believed, he was no gentleman. At least, not anymore. Deep down, she knew she was playing a dangerous game. Though she was not ignorant of what happened between men and women, and she had flirted with the opposite sex in abundance, she had never been so forward in an attempted seduction. The word made her cheeks warm. She had not meant for it to be *that*. She had only wanted to shake that cool, unflappable exterior.

Refusing to feel one ounce of shame for her scandalous behavior, she watched as the countess shuffled a large stack of documents, which she placed on the cushion beside her as she sat. Langlevit took one look at them and also resumed his seat, his mouth tightening.

"When did you arrive in London?" the earl asked Irina, his cool tone at odds with the storm brewing in those tawny eyes.

"Two weeks past."

"Staying with Lord and Lady Northridge, I presume?"

The countess was quick to answer. "I'm glad you brought that up, dear. You see, Lady Northridge had planned to host Irina for this season, only she's had another horrible scare. Upon orders from Dr. Hargrove, she has returned to Essex for the duration of her confinement." With a pained sigh, she placed a hand to her breast. "After the last loss, it is best for her to rest as much as possible."

"I'm sorry to hear it," Langlevit murmured.

"The loss of a child is tragic, indeed." Lady Langlevit patted his hand where it lay on the arm of his chair. "My Henry was the fourth in a long line of similar tragedy. I would wish such torture on no one." The countess took a long sip of her tea and addressed her son. "As a result, I've offered to host Irina while I am in London. I'm in need of the company, and she is in need of a suitable chaperone."

The earl's entire body stilled. "Here?"

"Why not? I have more than enough room in this drafty old residence," Lady Langlevit replied. She sent a warm, reassuring smile in Irina's direction. The countess's elegantly appointed house was far from *drafty*. "It will do us both good." She eyed her son. "It would do you good to show your face in polite society, as well. Perhaps you can endeavor to act as Irina's escort to a few functions."

"I'm certain Her Highness will have more than enough suitors breaking down the door, as she did in Paris," he said, his snifter paused at his lips. "I wouldn't want to besmirch her reputation with attention such as mine."

Irina stiffened, and Lady Langlevit stared at her son with an expression of mild disgust. "Really, Henry, what has come over you?"

"I certainly would not wish to inconvenience anyone," Irina said, "much less take the esteemed Lord Langlevit away from his important *affairs*."

She met his stare, arching an eyebrow to make sure her emphasis on the last word hadn't been lost. She and everyone in London knew exactly what, and whom, he did with his time. His eyes remained fathomless for an eternal moment before an impassive look descended on the rest of that austere face. It rankled her to no end that he could dismiss her so easily, but two could play at this game. She hiked her chin and fought the slow bloom of embarrassment rising in her cheeks.

With a deepening frown that swung uneasily between the two of them, the countess signaled to Andrews to bring in the small velvet box she'd sent him for, which the butler placed on the small table between them. "In any case, before your mood sours further and ruins our lovely afternoon, this was your father's, handed down to each heir on their thirtieth birthday. I wish he could have been here to present it to you himself. He would have been proud of you, I think."

Irina's ears caught on that last "I think," and from the answering tightening of the earl's jaw, so had he. It appeared his renown of late as an unrepentant rake was even known to the countess herself. What had happened in the past five years to change him so? He'd been nothing but a dutiful son and an esteemed peer of the realm with an unimpeachable reputation. Over the past few years, the whisperings of his declining morals had grown loud enough to be heard on different continents.

The countess's voice softened as she reached forward to stroke his sleeve. "Happy birthday, my darling."

Irina took in a clipped breath as Langlevit opened the box to reveal a magnificent ruby ring with his family's crest. If she had remembered, she could have brought a gift, but then again, she no longer had any idea what his likes and dislikes were.

"And now that we have dispensed with that," Lady Langlevit continued, reaching for the pile of papers at her left. "It's high time you married."

Irina choked on her next breath of air. *Married?*

The earl's cold gaze flicked to her for a moment. "We do not need to discuss this here."

"I'm afraid we must," the countess said, causing the muscle in her son's cheek to make an appearance once more. "Each time I have sent word to your residence, you have been busy. You know the stipulation, Henry. You must marry, or the title and estates will revert to the Crown. As of today, the clock is ticking."

"The clock has been ticking for many years," he muttered.

Lady Langlevit ignored him. "And you have left things to the last minute. Now, these are the settlement documents your father was required to present to the House of Lords when we married, proving he had indeed met the stipulation King Charles—"

Irina stood while the earl's mouth thinned to a slash. She cleared her throat, drawing his harsh glance. "Lord Langlevit is right. This is a private matter," she said standing. "I will excuse myself."

"Please, that is not necessary," Lady Langlevit began as her son also abruptly stood. His knee caught the end of the tea tray and disrupted a teacup from its saucer. Black tea spilled across the tabletop, dripping onto the priceless carpet as the servants rushed forward to mop up the mess.

"No, please, do stay. I insist. This is now your home, after all," he growled, his teeth gritted as he stared at the mess and tried to right the teacup. A footman intervened to take over the task, and the two of them wound up fumbling the teacup straight onto the carpet.

Langlevit growled again, and Irina heard him swear beneath his breath. He closed his eyes, nostrils flaring. "I should leave," he said and, with his face still a mask of fury, strode from the room.

. . .

Henry paced in his study, forcing himself to pore over the account ledgers of his various estates. Numbers always helped to clear his head. Usually, they did. But not today. Not after what had happened hours ago at Devon Place.

He'd half wished upon his return that Mary and Camilla had still been there, but Billings had already seen them back. He'd briefly considered saddling his horse and finding them again at The Cock and the Crown to rid himself of the nervous energy that had built up like an angry squall within him, but for the first time in weeks, he'd resigned himself to his study for an evening of numbers and solitude.

A useless prospect, it seemed. Even the numbers weren't helping.

Nor was the copious amount of whiskey he'd consumed.

Henry could only think of *her*.

Irina Volkonsky had become even more beautiful than when he'd seen her last in St. Petersburg, as if the promise of womanhood had been fulfilled several times over. Her curves were fuller, her features less sharp. Her eyes now carried secrets, as did that seductive mouth. When she'd deliberately turned the snifter and pressed her lips to the place he'd drunk from last, tantalizing him with that whiskey-dampened mouth, it had taken all of his control not to toss that bloody tea tray aside and settle her into his lap.

If his mother hadn't entered at that moment, he likely would have. He'd given free rein to his baser instincts for so long that he had no inclination to curb them. If a woman offered a sampling of her charms, he would take it. It was that simple. He did not refuse pleasure in any form, and he had not been mistaken in what Princess Irina was offering.

But she was still his mother's ward.

He had been her protector five years ago for the better part of a year.

She was a *child*.

Henry swallowed hard, remembering the provocative swirl of her tongue against the snifter and the purposeful gaze that had held his. No, she was no child, that much was clear. He drew a cleansing breath. But she *was* young, and there was a reason he preferred the company of courtesans to young ladies: the exchange of coin kept things simple. Those women also weren't afraid of him...of his basest desires or of the outlet he needed. They accepted that once the act had concluded, there would be no intimacy.

It was Henry's hard-and-fast rule when it came to women, and it was not one that the princess would understand...not one that *any* gently bred lady would understand. Because at the heart of it, he was a monster. A madman who needed to be alone. So regardless of his blasted attraction to Irina, he would keep his distance. For her sake. And his.

"Focus," he hissed to himself. The princess was off-limits, and that was that.

Henry forced himself to stare at the intricate columns of numbers, totaling the expenses and profits of each estate. Many showed past-due dates. He'd shirked his duties for too long, it seemed. A reluctant grin tugged on his mouth as he recalled the disdain with which Irina had said she wouldn't want to tear him from his affairs. Her insult had been clear. Though her appearance had changed, inside she had retained the quick wit and sense of humor she'd had as a girl. He suspected the streak of stubbornness was still there, as well. Along with her insatiable curiosity. He remembered how easily she'd soaked up details about his distillery. Unlike most people whose eyes would glaze over, or who would pretend to care only to impress him, she had shown genuine interest. The intelligence in those violet eyes had not disappeared with time, either.

And the princess obviously had developed a fondness for whiskey. He recalled how she had rolled the liquid on her tongue, exploring and separating the flavors. He'd wanted her whiskey-spiced tongue in his mouth. He still did. With a soft growl, Henry tried futilely to push the thought from his mind.

A soft rap on the door drew him from his lustful thoughts. "What is it, Stevens? I said I did not wish to be disturbed."

"My apologies, my lord," Stevens said, opening the study door. "Lady La Valse is here and insists on seeing you at once."

He almost gave the command to send the lady on her way, but hesitated at the last moment. Françoise La Valse and he shared an understanding. Perhaps she was a blessing in disguise. A widowed viscountess with wealth of her own and a voluptuous body that was built for passion, they served as each other's companions whenever either of them were in London.

She, like him, had no interest in anything beyond the pursuit of pleasure, and that suited him fine. Though he knew it aggrieved his mother when he accompanied Françoise openly to the theater or the opera, Henry did not give a hoot for the thoughts of the *ton*. Neither did Françoise, for that matter. The fickle *ton* would tolerate both of them because of their wealth and titles. Henry glanced at the open books on his desk. The numbers would still be there tomorrow. And right now, his body needed a lot more than any whiskey could possibly assuage.

"Show her in," he said with a curt nod.

It was the right decision, he decided, as Françoise closed the heavy door behind her and discarded the floor-length fur she'd been wearing. She was naked beneath it. Seeing his look, she laughed low in her throat and unpinned her auburn hair from its combs. "Stevens was rather miffed when I insisted he not take my coat. That would have caused quite a scene in the foyer, don't you think?"

"I'm sure," Henry said, amused. "Give me a second to clear my desk."

Françoise walked forward to perch a rounded hip on the edge of the mahogany desk, entirely comfortable with her nudity. She studied the documents nearest her—the marriage settlement papers his mother had presented that afternoon at Devon Place and sent over to his house that evening. "I see you're still stuck with this ridiculous obligation."

"It's impossible to circumvent," he said. "I must marry by the end of this year or forfeit it all."

"If you do take a wife, I hope it will not affect our arrangement." She trailed a finger lazily down his shirtfront. "I'd hate to have to find a replacement."

Henry said nothing. He did not want to reassure her when he knew it would be a lie. If Rose accepted his proposal, he would be far more discreet in his choice of a mistress. He would be no freely philandering jackass, humiliating his wife among her peers with a lover so well known as Lady La Valse. No, if Rose agreed, his ongoing affair with Françoise would be over.

Shifting provocatively on the desk, the lady in question hooked a leg around his thigh and tugged on his cravat. "I've become quite fond of you." Her hand drifted to the front of his trousers. "Or parts of you, at least."

Henry drew in a breath as her hands stroked him. He cleared all the papers to the floor and ensconced himself between Françoise's willing legs. He'd look at the numbers, and the bloody settlement papers, later. Right now, he only wanted to sink himself so deeply into a fog of pleasure that he wouldn't have to think. And Françoise was nothing if not an enthusiastic participant.

The Earl of Langlevit fully intended to exorcise all thoughts of Princess Irina Volkonsky from his head, and as Françoise began to open the fall of his trousers, then tug at his shirt, his intentions succeeded. She pulled his shirt up, intending to push it over his head and toss it to the floor. Henry grasped her hands to still them.

She gave a light laugh. "Oh, my shy earl. What are you hiding under there? Why must you always remain clothed?"

Françoise knew. She had to. There was not one person in his circle of peers who did not know of his injuries sustained on the Peninsula. The munitions bunker that had exploded, killing several of his men. Burning them alive. With his own injuries, Henry had only been able to carry out one boy, the youngest of his regiment. It had slowed his escape from the bunker, but he could not have left the boy to be devoured by flames. The scars from those burns stretched over the breadth of Henry's back and shoulders, and for many years had pained him. A deep, reaching pain that had made standing and sitting, and even lying down, difficult.

"I like to be ready for any unwanted intrusions," he said to Françoise, the lie weak.

She shook her head and relented, her hands returning to the buttons on his trousers. "Should Stevens walk in while you are pounding into me, I shall not allow you to stop. Let him watch," Françoise said, her teeth nipping the lobe of his ear.

Her bold words hardened him as she finished her task and reached inside. But even as he took what she'd come here to offer, losing himself in the rhythmic thrusts and building pressure of the act, then the rushing break of release, he did not think of the gorgeous woman perched so lasciviously on his desk.

As he withdrew and buttoned his trousers once again, then draped the long fur coat back over Françoise's shoulders, it was not the widow's naughty words that kept him aroused. It was Irina's mouth, and the deliberate way she'd caressed that glass with her tongue and lips.

Had she meant to seduce him, or just tease him? And how many other men had the princess seduced in such a way? Henry gritted his teeth as Françoise closed the coat tightly around her and touched her hair, as if to make sure it had been well re-secured with its pins and combs.

She stopped to stare at him. "My, you look positively unsatisfied. Perhaps I should stay the night?"

Henry shook his head, an immediate reflex that would have come across as insulting to any other woman offering her company. Thankfully, Lady La Valse did not suffer a sensitive ego. Henry might take women to his bed at all hours of the day, but at night, he slept alone. Always alone. The probability of a visiting night terror, the ones that so often stalked him as he slept, was too high. They gripped him in his sleep more forcibly than when he was awake, it seemed, and Henry would rise from the terrifying stupors drenched in sweat, his sheets a tangled mass, the air around him snowing feathers from the pillows he'd torn to shreds with his own possessed hands.

Once, following his return from the Continent, he'd allowed a passing fancy to sleep beside him after their encounter was finished. Her terrified screams had snapped Henry from his hellish nightmare, only to find that he'd shoved her from the bed. Though she was more frightened than hurt, Henry knew it could have been far worse had she tried to awaken him. She would have suffered the same fate as countless pillows.

He had not made the same mistake again, nor would he

ever.

Françoise eyed him skeptically now, but before she could say anything, Henry continued, "I'm only bothered by this marriage business, that is all."

She rose to the tips of her lady's boots and kissed his cheek. "I understand. I don't care for the institution myself and can't tell you how lucky I am to be done with it. I'd feel guilty saying such, but I do believe my husband, God rest his soul, was relieved to be done with it, as well."

Henry huffed a laugh. Françoise's husband, the late Viscount La Valse, had been a stunted old knave. The marriage had solely been a profitable one for both him and Françoise, the latter of whom had reportedly thrown an intimate party at her home the day after the viscount's death.

"I'll see myself out. Good night, my favorite earl," she said as she made her way toward the study door.

He watched her go, slightly relieved to be alone again. At least now some of the well of restlessness inside of him had been drained. He would miss Françoise's easy humor. When he married and broke things off with her, she would not be sad. She had other earls and marquesses and dukes at her beck and call, and probably a whole brigade of the demimonde and gentry.

Henry left the desk and the scattering of papers upon the floor and walked toward the windows overlooking the gardens. It was late, the moon full and bright. He was not tired in the least and knew he would remain awake a few more hours, or even well past the first light of dawn, his lust unslaked, his mind prowling the undignified response he'd felt for Irina that morning in his mother's day room.

The numbers. He would have to attempt the ledgers again. Perhaps more whiskey.

He turned around and got to work.

Chapter Four

Hadley Gardens had changed drastically since the last time Irina had set foot inside its splendid walls. No longer the gilded interior it had once been for the previous duke, Her Grace, the Duchess of Bradburne, had completely redesigned the interior into shades of mint green, robin's-egg blue, and buttercup yellow. Only the ballroom remained as sumptuous and ornate as Irina remembered it, though for some reason it did appear a bit smaller and far more crowded than she'd last seen it, during one of the balls she and Lana had attended together just before her marriage to Lord Northridge.

At fourteen, Irina should not have been able to attend any society functions at all, but Lana had not possessed the heart to say no, and Her Grace had explicitly requested Irina's presence. In truth, Irina thought Lana had allowed her to tag along in society simply because she did not want to be parted from her, even for a few hours. After spending nearly eight months apart in England as they hid from their duplicitous uncle and his vicious cohort, Baron Zakorov, both Lana and Irina had clung to one another for weeks once they had reunited.

Irina, however, had soon returned to St. Petersburg and their limited family there, while Lana had remained in England, traveling only time and again to Volkonsky Palace. Lana had offered to let Irina live with them, but even at that young age, she had known married couples needed their space. And Irina had wanted to return home and be among familiar people and sights and sounds.

Besides, the Earl of Langlevit was often in St. Petersburg. He had been their father's friend and confidant, and had been in the city when she and Lana needed him most, for their quick, midnight escape. It was not as if she wouldn't see him again.

Or so she had thought.

"There you are!" A vibrant voice rising above the din inside Hadley Gardens' ballroom broke Irina from her reverie. She spun around to find a familiar face grinning widely, lips parted in astonishment. Lady Lyon, the countess she had met in Paris last year, embraced Irina openly, rather than bow and smile as most ladies would have done.

"Gwen," Irina said, breathless from the firm squeeze of her hug. "I did not realize you'd be here. How wonderful to see you again. As you can see, I followed your strict order and came straight to London."

The countess laughed loudly enough to draw glances of concern from those nearby.

"It is the opening ball of the season, my darling, I would not miss it! The sheer number of hopeful debutantes and randy bachelors promises fine entertainment for one evening," she said then leaning closer, whispered, "Look there. Next to Lady Rochester. Lady Eugenia Fairbanks. It's her *third* season, you know."

Irina eyed the pretty young woman, who was standing next to a potted shrub decorated with what appeared to be elegantly folded paper birds. Lady Eugenia stood primly to the side of the dance floor, a cup of punch in hand, watching the merriment with slightly desperate interest.

"It is my third season as well," Irina replied, expecting Gwen to gasp and apologize. But she did not.

"Yes, I know. And just like Lady Eugenia, it is an absolute travesty. You are much too beautiful to have not stolen the heart of a deserving beau." Gwen did not lower her voice as she went on. "I understand high standards, of course, but I really do think you should endeavor to settle on a husband this season. A fourth season would simply be pathetic."

Irina's lips parted with surprise, a smile of amusement tugging at the corner of her mouth. "My goodness, you say what you mean, don't you?"

"And not a beat of hesitation!" Gwen replied merrily. "That is why I like you, Princess. You can handle the truth."

"Indeed, she can," came a lazy male voice from behind them.

"This is Lord Remi," Irina said without having to turn and see him. "I brought him with me from Paris."

He slid in between her and Gwen, the countess eyeing him appreciatively. Irina didn't know the particulars of her marriage to Lord Lyon, but she didn't peg Gwen as the monogamous sort.

"Yes, rather like a cherished pet," he said, sipping his champagne.

Irina nudged him with her elbow. "I don't keep pets. I keep friends. This is Lady Lyon."

"I remember you," Max said with a gracious bow over Gwen's proffered hand. "Such beauty does not slip easily from my memory."

"And as your friend, I must tell you that is a terrible line," Irina said, fighting a roll of her eyes. Gwen only laughed heartily again.

"Terrible, yes, but effective. Lord Remi, tell me you agree that Lady Irina must choose a beau by the close of the season."

He murmured his agreement, and the two of them fell in easily, exchanging deft comments and replies regarding Irina's failed seasons. She let the words slide off, uninjured by them. She liked Max and Gwen, and while she let them have their fun, she didn't join in. The fact was, she had arrived at the Bradburne Ball with the Lady Langlevit more than an hour ago, and so far, not one gentleman in attendance had approached her for a dance. Her reputation for turning men down had made its way through the evening's guests, it seemed. Why bother to ask a known iceberg for a dance when there were so many other warm and willing ladies in attendance? *Iceberg.* She was not cold. Just…selective.

She had peered through the crowds, attempting to convince herself that she was only assessing the invited guests. But twice now her eyes had landed upon the back of a tall, straight-backed man with sandy brown hair and broad shoulders, causing her pulse to skip. Until the man in question turned, revealing an unfamiliar face.

He was not here. He would not be coming.

It had been over a week since that awful episode in the countess's day room. A week since she'd so bawdily sipped from his snifter. Every time she thought of it, she cringed. Had she appeared silly instead of sexy? Had Langlevit gone home, amused by her inexperienced demonstration?

Every time she doubted herself, however, she recalled his expression as he'd half stood from the chair. She still could not determine if it had been a look of barely contained anger or lust, or perhaps even disgust. She simply didn't know. She didn't know *him*. Not anymore. Perhaps she never truly had.

"Ah, look. She is pining away for a dance partner. It is the only excuse for not listening to us, I think," Max said, pushing into her thoughts by placing his empty glass on a passing tray and touching the small of her back.

"Come, Your Highness, allow me," he said, guiding her away from Gwen, who twitched her fingers in a playful wave—whether it was meant for Irina or Max, Irina did not know.

"Oh, bother," she sighed. "Now that you've asked me to dance I suppose there will be a tide of men lapping at my ankles, insisting they have their chance."

She smiled at her own sarcasm, hoping Max wouldn't see through it. But, truly, she didn't want to dance with a pool of men who would likely nip at her toes with their own. So long ago, at the Duke and Duchess of Bradburne's wedding ball at Worthington Abbey, her first dance of the evening had been with the Earl of Langlevit. He had not wanted to be there. She was certain he did not enjoy crowds, and it was most likely why he was not in attendance at this ball tonight. She remembered the easy glide of their feet and the firm, protective press of his large hand against her waist as he had led her through a quadrille.

"Oh, there will be. Leave it to me. I meant what I said last year about you becoming the excitement of the season," Max replied.

She glanced up at him as they waltzed among the other couples. "You really haven't given up on that betting scheme of yours?"

"Forgotten it? My dear princess, it is already in the works."

She tripped on a step. Max righted her and corrected their turn.

"What does that mean?" she asked.

He winked down at her. "Your friend Lady Lyon is correct. This season needs a spectacle, and you will be its star."

Irina frowned. She hadn't heard Gwen say the season needed a spectacle. Then again, she had been drifting off in thought while Gwen and Max had twittered back and forth.

She might have missed it.

"Why me? Why not some other wallflower?" she asked, feeling a strange pulse of worry. Men would be wagering bets. On her. For her *hand*.

"Because you are young and beautiful and exotic and rich, and"—he spun her around, lifting her feet from the floor and eliciting a gasp of surprise from a nearby couple—"because I am surely going to need the entertainment. My goodness, London is a box. No beauty. No air. Just these closed-up ballrooms and crowded assembly rooms and smoky parlors."

She sighed again. "Paris suits you better."

He shrugged. "It would be a bore without you."

Irina continued to dance, resisting the urge to kiss his cheek for the compliment. Perhaps in Paris it would have gone unnoticed, but not here, and she did not want to dish any embarrassment or scandal upon her sister or her current chaperone. Irina adored Countess Langlevit and for a long while, especially during those months in Cumbria, had considered her family.

As Max turned her again, this time more properly, she caught a blurred image of another tall, straight-backed man with broad shoulders and hair the color of beach sand. Immediately, she wondered how she could have possibly mistaken the other two men earlier in the evening for Lord Langlevit. He stood near the base of the grand entrance staircase in conversation with the Duke of Bradburne. This time, her pulse did not skip. It throbbed. Painfully.

He was beautiful. As Max turned her again, she noticed not only the evening kit the earl wore, though perfect, of course. What she noticed first and foremost was his presence. He wasn't the tallest man in the crowd, nor the largest or most muscular. It was the intensity of him that radiated outward, invisible but so very *there*. How could any woman not notice it? It went deeper than his handsome looks and impressive figure. It was as if his very body, even when he was just standing there murmuring with His Grace, Lady Bradburne's husband, sent out continuous waves of energy.

"You are clutching at me as if you're about to fall over," Max said, and Irina realized how tightly her hands had clenched around his arm and hand.

"Sorry, I…" but her mind refused to provide a creative excuse. Max followed her gaze and cleared his throat.

"Ah. The elusive Langlevit."

"He is not elusive," she whispered, uncertain why she was arguing with him. "I simply did not expect to see him here, that is all."

The countess had mentioned that she'd told him about the ball, but that she didn't think he would attend. *He never does*, Lady Langlevit had added with a sigh and a shake of her head.

"You want to dance with him," Max said with a perceptive wink.

"Hush. No, I do not," she replied, glancing around to make sure no one had heard him.

But it wasn't true. Had Henry made eye contact with her and approached, asking for a dance, she would have said yes without a moment's pause, even after his chilly reception last week. However, just as the waltz was ending and Max was escorting her from the dance floor, Irina saw a woman step up beside the earl. She was tall and lithe, beautiful the way hothouse flowers were…unnaturally pretty, but pretty all the same. She whispered something to Henry and his mouth quirked into a wicked smile.

"Your earl is keeping the right kind of company in my estimation," Max said as they reached a server. He took a glass of punch for her.

"You know her?"

"Viscountess La Valse," he said. "Widowed now, but she

was married to a transplanted Frenchman who won a title for services rendered to the Crown. She has quite the reputation for...*play*, I suppose you could call it."

Irina's grip on her glass tightened. She was one of Henry's mistresses, then. It shouldn't have bothered her, especially knowing what Henry had become. This woman had shared Henry's bed and knew him in ways Irina didn't. In ways, for years now, Irina had contemplated, and yes, dreamed about.

"I think I need some air," she said softly, but as Max released her arm, another young man materialized in front of her.

"Your Highness," he said, bowing so quickly Irina did not even have the chance to see his face. When he straightened again, she thought he appeared slightly familiar, though she did not recall his name or when she had met him before.

"Forgive my rudeness, but we were introduced many years ago, at His Grace's marriage ball. We danced a set." After an awkward moment of silence, Max smiling on as if vastly amused, the young man continued. "Allow me to introduce myself again. Lord Bainley, at your service."

He took another bow, this one briefer. He had dark, curly hair and a face that was not quite pudgy, but also not entirely healthy. His smile was a bit crooked, as if he had a secret to tell her. It was, she considered, a smile Max would often wear.

"It's a pleasure to meet you again, my lord," she said, hoping he would go away. But instead he gestured toward the dance floor.

"Might I accompany you for this next dance?"

Irina held her breath and listened to the musicians. Blast. They had started playing music for a cotillion.

"Of course," she said, knowing there could be no other acceptable reply.

As she handed off her punch to Max, he whispered, "Lapping at your ankles..."

She glared at him before taking Lord Bainley's arm and joining the other dancers on the floor. It was difficult to concentrate through the dance steps, though she did try. Her eyes kept wanting to drift toward the grand staircase and see if Henry was still standing with the viscountess. She was proud that she did not give in to the urge, though, and instead grinned at her dance partner whenever they were brought face-to-face during the dance. By the end of it her cheeks were aching.

"A breath of air?" Lord Bainley asked, glancing at her. "You look piqued."

Just frustrated, she thought to herself, but nodded in answer after seeing no sign of Max. The balcony was by no means a private area. Guests stood in scattered groups and servers brought around trays of punch and champagne and wine. Irina accepted a glass of wine from a footman and took a long sip.

"I must say it was my greatest pleasure to see you here tonight," Lord Bainley said, deftly steering her to a quieter area of the balcony, his body blocking the partial view of the other guests. "What brings you to London?"

"My sister," she murmured, closing her eyes and letting the cool night air fan her flushed cheeks. She opened them again, though, as she felt Lord Bainley's hand at the small of her back, once again shepherding her along the terrace. Something about the young man rankled, and the intense way he was staring at her made her uncomfortable. He had a face like a ferret, she thought, pinched and calculating. She realized the noise had lessened and that the thicket of people had filtered back into the ballroom for the next set. The balcony was far less crowded than it had been moments before, and suddenly, Irina found herself caged between a trellis and a determined Lord Bainley. She recognized that look.

Oh no.

Without warning, he plucked the wineglass from her fingers and placed it on a nearby ledge. "Your Highness," he began, drawing her hand toward his mouth and closing the gap between them.

"How…how is it that you have not yet married, Lord Bainley?" she hedged, calculating her odds of escape without making a scene. Irina wanted to slap the grin off his face, but pushed a patient smile to her lips instead and took a small step to the left.

He mirrored the movement, a smile playing about his lips. "Perhaps I have not yet found the right woman."

"I expect you have so many to choose from."

"And what if I've narrowed my choice?" he asked.

Sidestepping to the right, she encountered the cold stone of the balcony pressed against her right hip. Bainley moved closer, and her odds of escape diminished further. Worse yet, they seemed to be completely alone in an odd sort of alcove. It was made for this, she supposed, clandestine embraces. Would that it were the earl instead of the odious young man now breathing heavily across her knuckles and making her skin crawl in the process.

"Lord Bainley, I'd like to go back inside."

"Why? We both know why you wanted to come out here." His tone was suggestive, the lascivious look on his face even more so.

"I assure you I am not interested in whatever you have to offer."

His mouth curled, his fingers tightening on hers. "Is that so?"

Irina's entire body tensed. She'd dealt with overeager suitors before, but something glittered dangerously in Bainley's eyes, something she instinctively recognized as a pernicious will. Her uncle had been a man of similar temperament, one who was accustomed to taking what he wanted no matter the cost. Men such as these would not be deterred.

Not without force.

Irina reached into her reticule at the same time that his head descended toward hers, only to halt an inch away as the lethal tip of the diminutive folding knife she'd extracted pressed purposefully into the side of his breastbone.

"Are you mad?" he asked, his eyes goggling between the knife and her face.

"Mad enough, it seems," she said quietly. "Now please, Lord Bainley, do us both a favor and go back inside, or I assure you, the outcome will not be a pleasant one."

After a fraught moment, he stepped back out of reach, a sneer on his face. "You really are a frigid bitch, aren't you?"

"I've been called many things, but at least I'm not a man who forces himself on unwilling women."

"You'll regret this." He turned on his heel and stormed off.

With a relieved groan, Irina leaned heavily against the railing and tucked the steel blade into its mother-of-pearl handle. She had just threatened a peer with bodily harm. Though she doubted a weasel like Bainley would spread that bit of gossip about; his pride would never recover from being cowed by a woman. Irina didn't doubt, however, that he would do his best to shame or discredit her. Men like Bainley were nothing if not predictable.

She stared at the knife in her palm. The tiny contraption had belonged to her father—a clever combination of a penknife and a fruit knife. It gave Irina comfort to have it close by, and she'd taught herself to use it over the years. She never wanted to be in a situation as she had been when she'd been taken unawares by her uncle's men. Frightened and defenseless. And so, necessity had dictated she learn to protect herself from evil men like Zakorov and lesser ones like Bainley.

"I couldn't have handled that better myself." A shadow emerged from a darker corner of the terrace. She gripped the blade's handle but relaxed as Langlevit came into view. Irina didn't move when he came to stand beside her. Curiously, she didn't feel the same leashed energy she'd felt earlier. He seemed calmer, less agitated. Or maybe she'd been imagining she'd sensed anything at all. She had no intuition when it came to this man.

"Come to rescue a damsel in distress?" she asked lightly.

He pursed his lips. "Alas, this particular damsel did not need my gallant assistance. She seemed to be doing quite capably on her own." He reached out a hand toward the knife gripped in hers. "May I?"

Grudgingly, Irina handed him the penknife. "It was my father's."

"Do you carry this with you at all times?"

"Yes."

"Why?"

She exhaled slowly and met his stare with guarded care. "For protection."

Irina expected him to reply that she was being nonsensical or that it was ridiculous for a woman to have such a weapon on her person, but instead the earl nodded. He was well aware of what she and Lana had been through. He and Lord Northridge—Lana's husband—had been the ones to rescue them from her uncle's clutches and foil his murder plot. Irina had held the earl in profound esteem ever since.

Henry leaned his arms against the baluster, and even in the dim lighting, she could see the dark superfine pulling taut over the sleek muscle beneath. His long fingers traced the jeweled detail of the intricately carved hilt. Though he appeared to be relaxed, Irina could feel the readiness in him…that instinctive constant awareness of his surroundings and those around him. It was something she understood, something she also felt. Henry ran his thumb gently over the penknife's razor-honed edge.

"Sharp and beautiful," he said with an unfathomable look, handing it back to her. "Do you know how to use it?"

"Of course," she answered, tucking the sheathed blade back into her reticule. "I'm skilled with many weapons. Knives, bows, pistols, swords—I've mastered them all."

An amused eyebrow lifted in her direction, a reluctant twitch tugging the corners of his lips as he chuckled softly. "I wish I could say I am surprised, but I am not. You always did have a singular mindset once you set your sights on something. I still rue the day I taught you to play chess. It took all of three lessons for you to become the master and me the pupil." He laughed again and angled his face toward hers, the glow of the light from the ballroom reflecting in his eyes and making her heart thud painfully against her ribs. "So exactly how good is your skill with the bow?" he asked. "I seem to recall you mentioning it was your least favorite."

"I was fourteen, and my skill was lacking then." It was the first bit of the old Henry she'd seen in him, and the small glimpse gave her hope. Hope that the man she'd revered for so long was still in there somewhere. Irina smiled at him, wanting desperately to prolong the moment…to give freedom to the feelings blooming in her chest. After all, she wasn't fourteen anymore, and he was here just as she'd always envisioned in her imaginings. She would seize the moment. Her pulse hummed beneath her skin as she edged toward him, the narrow sliver of light between them disappearing. "I'm more than willing to offer a demonstration the next time we are in Essex, my lord."

"Essex," he murmured, distracted by the press of her gloved arm against his. Frictional heat seeped through the layers of cloth between them, and it singed. Simmered. *Burned.*

Langlevit's eyes clung to hers as his chin tilted toward her. Irina had never felt more aware of anything or anyone than she was right at that moment. The air was combustible, and still he held her stare with that relentless lion's gaze. He felt the rawness of the connection between them, too, she was certain of it. Hovering closer, their breath met and mingled, ready to ignite as if she were flint and he tinder. Irina could almost taste the whiskey lingering on his tongue, and she sighed deep in her throat. He was so close that she could reach forward and touch her lips to his if she wanted. Her center went liquid at the thought.

The warmth spread to her chest, pooling low in her belly, between her hips, making her feel like everything within was molten. Irina's breath shortened, and she licked her dry lips. The earl's eyes followed the movement. Desire darkened them, and a telltale muscle flexed in his cheek as his gaze shifted into something feral. It should have made her want to flee. Instead it made her want to throw herself forward and demand to be claimed.

Twisting slightly, Irina reached up to stroke his jaw, feeling the scrape of stubble as his skin there leaped reflexively at her touch. "Henry—"

He froze, his eyes boring into hers, and then pushed off the rail as if it were made of flame instead of stone. Shutters descended over his eyes within seconds, the leaping muscle in his cheek going unnaturally still. It was as if a light had been extinguished inside of him. Irina was shocked by the swift and brutal transformation.

"I won't be in Essex for quite some time," he said in a clipped, polite voice.

"What's wrong?" she asked, frowning and advancing toward him. "You felt something between us, I know you did."

"I'm not debauched enough to take advantage of a naive debutante."

Naive? She was *not* that. And she was not blind, either. Twice now he'd devoured her with his eyes. He'd responded to her suggestive sip of his whiskey glass last week the same way he'd responded to her closeness just now. It was dangerous, the way he'd looked at her. It was anything but gentle—or *gentlemanly*. Why wouldn't he admit that she affected him?

With a frustrated breath, she pushed up onto her toes and pressed her mouth to his. Heat licked across her skin at the feel of his smooth male lips, and thunder rushed in her ears for an infinitesimal moment. But then firm hands pushed down on her shoulders, separating them.

The earl's countenance was unmoved, his eyes like chips of golden quartz. "You have proven my point," he said softly. "Allow me to escort you back inside, Your Highness."

Heat flooded her whole body, rushing from her cheeks to her neck and back, then coursing along her arms. Even her scalp burned. Suffocating in humiliation, Irina swallowed past the aching lump in her throat and nodded mutely. *Oh dear God.* What had she done? She'd made a complete cake of herself, that's what. All because she'd thought...she'd been *certain* that he felt something, too.

The earl could have been a wooden soldier for the silent and brisk half dozen steps he took before depositing her back to where Lady Langlevit was sitting. After a short, polite bow, he walked away without a backward glance. It was at that moment Irina realized she'd been fooling herself by holding on to such desperate, ridiculous childhood fantasies. The Earl of Langlevit was not the same man she'd remembered...the same man she'd held in such high esteem...the man she'd adored.

No, there was nothing left of the Henry she'd known.

She'd been in love with a ghost.

Chapter Five

Henry had never been so affected by a virginal kiss in his life.

Days later, despite seeing her at two other crushes and keeping his distance, it still haunted his every waking moment. *She* haunted him. Nights were the worst, when that slight peck morphed into something far more carnal. He was sinking to new lows, his fevered imaginings conjuring up images of Irina, naked, with those endlessly long legs of hers wrapped around him. Twice now he'd woken up on the brink of spending himself like some adolescent, untried buck.

"Preoccupied, Langlevit?" Lord Northridge commented from the opposite end of the table with a laugh. "That's another loss for you. Either I'm on a lucky streak or you've lost your ability to bluff."

"North," Henry said, emerging from the fog that had been consuming him. "I didn't see you sit down. When did you arrive?"

"Three hands ago."

The men around them chuckled. Henry hadn't been paying attention, instead using the game as a means to pass the time and not think about anything. Especially her. He'd failed at the latter, obviously, if he'd lost three rounds without knowing. "How is Lady Northridge?" Henry frowned. "Surprised to see you here. I'd heard she'd returned to Essex."

"She has, and she is as well as can be expected, thank you for asking," North said. "I'm here on official business."

His frown deepened. "Is there a meeting at the House of Lords?"

North shook his head. "It seems my son forgot his favorite toy at Bishop House, which of course warranted my immediate return. Nothing like a half day of hard riding for no purpose at all."

Despite his disparaging tone, Henry couldn't help noticing the man's doting expression. It was clear he thought the world of his son and his family. It wasn't long ago when Henry had wanted to skewer Northridge for taking advantage of Princess Svetlanka, who had been hiding from her uncle by posing as a lady's maid in Northridge's household. But in the end, it had turned out to be a love match. Henry was happy for Lana. She deserved happiness after what she'd endured.

So did Irina.

Henry was well aware that this was her third season. She should have been whisked off the marriage mart within weeks. Hell, even days. Like her sister, the young princess was beautiful, wealthy, and titled. A prize amongst the *ton* and Russian royalty. Certainly, she was also stubborn and opinionated, but that wouldn't stop any man from wanting her.

After some quiet investigation last week, Henry had been stunned to find out how many gentlemen had offered for her. The number had surprised him, as had her flimsy reasons for rejecting them all. As such, she'd acquired uncharitable nicknames like Ice Queen, Iceberg, and Lady Frost.

He'd wanted to laugh. Irina was the furthest thing from

frosty. Passion had fairly crackled off her on that balcony. Her bold boast offering to demonstrate her skill in Essex had nearly made him press her into the shadows of that alcove at Hadley Gardens. Hearing the word "sex" uttered from those luscious lips, even as part of the word "Essex" had nearly unmanned him. It was only by sheer force of will that he'd been able to resist the inexperienced graze of her mouth on his. No, icy was the last word he'd use to describe her. Irina Volkonsky was pure, uninhibited flame. Fiery and dangerous.

"Good man!" someone shouted nearby, making both Henry and North glance up from their cards. Lord Bainley strutted into view, looking like an effervescent peacock, and was surrounded by a group of young men thumping him enthusiastically on the back.

"Well done!" another said.

Henry's eyes narrowed with distaste on the man. He'd been about to throw him over the balcony by the scruff of his neck when Irina had produced that knife of her father's. Still, the sight of him made Henry wish to tenderize that pompous face with his bare fist. His jaw clenched as the men drew closer.

"What's this commotion?" Sir Kelton, one of the men at Henry's table, asked.

"Bainley has won the first bet of the season!"

Henry wasn't interested in hearing about the latest wager written in White's infamous betting book. Despite the frequent bets placed on horse races or prize fighting or who would outlive whom, gossip and scandal tended to fuel most of them, especially as the season wore on, with wagers being placed on which gentlemen would win a lady's hand or steal a kiss. Henry's mouth tightened as Bainley and the other men, chattering like a gaggle of hens, moved toward the hazard room.

"One hundred guineas…with the princess!"

Henry stiffened in his seat and turned. "Princess?" he

repeated.

"Princess Irina Volkonsky, of course," one of the young fobs answered over his shoulder.

Sir Kelton laughed loudly, his jowls shaking. "Nearly every wager of late has her name beside it. Races, kisses, dances, favors, proposals, who will bed her, who will wed her. If I were younger in years, I'd have half a mind to give these dandies a run for their money," he said. "Egad, Langlevit, isn't she the same chit staying with your mother?"

North speared him with a steely glance.

"That *chit* is my sister-in-law," North said softly. "Guard your words carefully, Sir Kelton."

The man cleared his throat and took a healthy interest in his hand of cards.

"What was the wager for?" Henry asked, his muscles tensing.

"A stroll on the balcony," Bainley said, puffing his chest and sneering. "It would have been five hundred guineas more had the lady not been as arctic as a winter storm. The rumors about her are all true. I shudder to think who will win the wager to bed the Ice Queen. It would freeze a man's co—"

"Enough." Henry rose out of his chair, his fury barely contained. The rest of Bainley's words stuck in his throat, and as he sidled away, his Adam's apple bobbed nervously.

Henry signaled for a footman to bring him the book. He skimmed the list and sure enough, it was as Sir Kelton had said. Wager upon wager, all with Irina's name. Gentlemen betting others for dances claimed, suitors turned down, rides in Hyde Park. And those smaller bets did not include the larger pot as to whom she would accept in marriage. The fortunes being wagered were already staggering. With the exception of his, almost every eligible bachelor's name was in there.

"She's causing quite a stir, is she not?" a man said beside him.

Henry looked up to see Lord Remi, a baron he'd been introduced to at the Duke of Bradburne's opening ball. Lady Lyon had announced him as a distant cousin and childhood friend of the princesses.

"I'd say it is a little more than a stir, Lord Remi," he said in greeting, his finger sliding down the list.

"There are even a few married names," Remi said with a laugh. "Though it does not surprise me. She left Paris in a shambles last season and a trail of broken hearts behind her."

"But not yours?"

"Good God, no!" Remi laughed. "I have no wish for a marriage noose around my neck, not even from one as enticing as she. Honestly, Lord Langlevit, have you *met* Princess Irina? Trust me, as much as I adore her, I'd rather take my chances jumping naked into St. Petersburg's River Neva in the middle of winter." He shook his head. "Being married to her would be like trying to bottle a thunderstorm."

A glorious challenge, Henry thought. "I see your point."

Henry's eyes fell on a particularly lecherous wager that made him want to hurl the book across the room and squeeze the throat of the gentleman who had written it. Agitated, he made note of the man's name and slammed the book shut, giving it back to the footman. Bets like these stirred up a frenzy, causing men to behave in appalling ways. He'd witnessed it firsthand with Bainley and Irina on the balcony. And from the looks of the betting book, it would only get worse. She would be besieged.

His fingers clenched to fists at his sides, nervous energy whittling through him at the thought of her in any kind of danger. If he remained in here, he knew things would worsen quickly. Signaling to the factotum for his coach, he eyed the young man beside him. Remi seemed like a good sort, if a bit high in the instep for his liking. "You are her friend," Henry said in a gravelly tone. "She cannot know about these bets."

She had a temper, Henry knew, and after that kiss on the balcony, he was now well acquainted with how impulsive she was. There was no true need to inform her of these bets, risk a scene, and insult her. Not when he, and perhaps Remi, could watch out for her.

"I'm sure you can see how things could get out of hand," he said to Remi. "If you truly are on her side, I'd advise you to stay close to her to deter some of the more overzealous competitors."

"Irina can handle herself," the young baron replied with a circumspect look at him.

Henry nodded, remembering her boasting and her grim confidence on the balcony. "I'm sure she can. However"— his eyes flicked to Bainley, who was still in the throes of congratulating himself—"I would not wish her to be hurt if word gets out of the nature of these wagers."

"Of course," Remi agreed, lifting his glass to his lips, his eyes settling on Henry. "It's good to know we both have her best interests at heart."

Years of service to the War Office and the Prince Regent had taught Henry to express caution when it came to trusting acquaintances, let alone strangers. Though he could not yet trust Lord Remi—not without first thoroughly investigating his background—he also did not believe the man was lying. Remi did not want to marry Irina, of that Henry was certain.

He stood and with a nod to Northridge and the others at the table, including Irina's friend, took his leave. He wanted nothing more than to return home to Leicester Square and remove his starched cravat, but it was not possible. His mother was hosting a dinner at Devon Place and Henry was required to attend.

Being an only child exacerbated the feelings of guilt his mother plied him with when asking him to attend such social functions. Having a brother or sister who could ease the weight of his absence would have been welcome. Had he an elder brother to take the title of earl, he would also not have to be the one to heed the rules of the inheritance. *Not* being Earl of Langlevit had its appeal. Though Henry wasn't quite sure what he would do otherwise. Perhaps go north, to Cumbria. Disappear into the countryside and run the distillery. Drown himself in Scotch whiskey, milkmaids, grass, and fresh air.

The coach took but a few minutes to reach his mother's house, and once Andrews had shown him in, stripped him of his coat and hat and gloves, and led him to the receiving room, the longing for such a simple, satisfying life had sprouted like a seed inside his stomach. It made him ache. It made him feel the press of the dinner guests more acutely and the air thicker than it truly was.

He'd gone to White's in full dress in preparation for the dinner, and yet he still felt out of place among the other men here. Henry was experiencing the strangest feeling that he was nothing more than a wild animal stuffed into a fine suit, attempting to look and act human, when a high, alarmed voice cut through the chatter from the other side of the receiving room.

"To Essex already? But what about her season?"

He found the woman who'd spoken, Countess Vandermere, on a sofa, seated next to his mother and Lady Dinsmore. Henry was vaguely acquainted with her daughter, Lady Cordelia. Countess Vandermere had a shocked expression upon her face.

"I could not keep her from her sister's side even should I wish to," Henry's mother replied. He declined a passing tray of wine and went to the sideboard to pour himself a whiskey, one ear turned toward the conversation.

"Lady Northridge's letter was not urgent, but it worries Her Highness. And it has been so long since they have seen one another," Lady Dinsmore added.

They were speaking of Irina. Henry's eyes traveled the length of the chamber, searching for her, but without success. She was going to Essex? His body seemed to deflate, that awkward sensation of being a beast inside a suit relinquishing a bit. The farther away from that damned betting book at White's, the better.

"What is this?" Henry asked as he approached the women, a sip of whiskey already coursing down his throat and inflaming his chest. It felt good. Centering.

His mother met him with a wide, pleased grin. "Langlevit, I'm so happy you've come. I wanted to tell you in person, rather than send word. Princess Irina and I are departing for Essex tomorrow, first thing."

"My daughter-in-law wrote that she isn't feeling well. A little scare, that is all," Lady Dinsmore said with a slight wave of her hand, though she could not erase the crease of worry upon her brow. "However, Princess Irina insists upon going."

"It truly is a shame," Countess Vandermere said with an overly dramatic sigh. "The princess cannot afford to miss a fortnight of the season. It is her *third*, after all."

Henry did not miss the slight flare of his mother's nostrils at Countess Vandermere's barb, despite her own daughter's spinster status. He had heard whispered rumors that Lady Cordelia's unmarried state was quite by the young lady's own choice and not for lack of offers.

"A fortnight away from London will hardly diminish Princess Irina's prospects," Lady Langlevit replied tightly.

If Henry had any say in the matter, he'd suggest Irina's stay in Essex extend to a month. Perhaps even the remainder of the spring months. Anything to keep her out of the paths of those idiotic men placing equally idiotic wagers.

"I shall accompany you," Henry said. The draw of the countryside was too much to resist, especially right then, clustered together with a dozen or more other people in the receiving room.

"Oh, but that isn't necessary," his mother said. He shook his head.

"I have some visits of my own I need to see to," he said, and at her curious stare, he propped one eyebrow. She answered it with a nod, their silent exchange finished.

It was one visit, really. Rose's reply to his written proposal had arrived at Leicester Square the day before. It had been unfailingly polite, expressing surprise and gratitude, and quite unfortunately, a request to allow her time to consider the proposition. He shouldn't have been surprised. Rose had never been the sort to jump into anything without first analyzing all avenues of possibility.

"I will ride alongside your carriage," he said, already growing impatient for the departure.

"You are coming with us?"

Henry turned. His gaze landed first upon Irina's clear, dark-blue eyes, then her dusky-pink lips, and finally upon the crimson dress she wore. There his eyes stayed, a beat too long, though plenty long enough for him to experience a twin surge of annoyance and lust. The dress was little more than a silk sheath hugging her body's svelte curves, curves he felt entirely wrong to be noticing. The short sleeves sat off her shoulders, and while there were probably a number of women in attendance with the same style sleeves, certainly none of their shoulders were as naked as Irina's. He pictured his fingers touching the velvet skin there, then his lips.

Henry swallowed another mouthful of whiskey to try and burn away the desire.

"I hope you are not opposed to the idea," he managed to say, and in his attempt to avoid looking at her indecently bare shoulders, his eyes tripped to where the bodice of her dress gathered at her breasts in silky ripples. Breasts that mounded into two sumptuous rises that made his groin abominably tight.

"Of course not, Lord Langlevit," she answered, her voice light and with a matching smile. Addressing him so formally only served to remind him of how informal she'd been on that balcony when she'd touched his arm and called him Henry.

Thankfully, dinner was announced, and before he could offer to escort Irina into the dining room, Lord Dinsmore swept in and offered his arm. Henry extended his arm to his mother, who accepted with an indulgent grin.

"I hope you are not fibbing about needing to pay visits in Essex," she whispered as they walked.

"One visit, to be exact," he replied.

"To someone I know?"

Henry exhaled, wondering for the hundredth time if he should tell her about his proposal. He'd wanted to wait until he had a solid answer from Rose.

"Yes," he said. "And without specifics…it involves the marriage stipulation on the inheritance."

He felt her pull on his arm, and then her body sagged against his. Henry stopped and braced her, to keep her from slipping down to the floor. "Mother? What is it? Is something the matter?"

She righted herself almost immediately, shaking her head and pressing a hand to her cheek. "Oh, I'm sorry. Just a little dizziness. How embarrassing. Please, it's nothing."

She wasn't only speaking to Henry, but to all behind them, who had stopped short in alarm as well.

"Are you certain?" Henry asked, inspecting his mother's color. Her cheeks were not flushed, but drawn, as if she'd been about to faint.

"I must have stood up too quickly from the sofa," she said, again tugging his arm and indicating that they should carry on toward the dining room.

He relented, his grip tighter on her arm until he delivered

her to her chair at the head of the table. Henry took his own seat at the opposite head of the table, his eyes shifting from his mother to Irina, seated just two chairs down from his on the right.

Her head was turned to the man at her right, and by the man's smug grin, she was unleashing her illuminating smile upon him. The smile that brightened her eyes and crinkled the bridge of her pert little nose. The smile that showed one slightly turned incisor. A charming imperfection in an otherwise perfect countenance.

The soup course was delivered, and Irina had still not ceased conversing with her neighbor. They chattered like magpies, their heads bending toward one another. Marginally, yes, but noticeable. At least it was to Henry.

As he glanced around the table after their soup bowls were cleared away and the main course was presented, he saw that the other guests, each one conversing with their own neighbors, seemed unaware that Irina and the fop beside her were so openly flirting. *Gibbons.* That was his name. Sir Lawrence Gibbons.

Henry picked at his beef tenderloin, his gaze catching on his mother's. She frowned at him and then flared her eyes a bit, as if to tell him to stop glowering. He felt the heavy expression on his face then and tried to lift it.

Irina laughed at something Gibbons said, and the prick of annoyance returned, as sharp as that little penknife she kept in her reticule. Gibbons was a good-looking man, only a handful of years older than Irina. Henry thought back to the betting book and the columns of names he'd seen. Had Gibbons been among them? He couldn't recall. As a baronet and landed gentry, rather than a peer, a princess would indeed be a fine catch. His blood simmered anew.

"Princess Irina." Henry heard his own voice cut down the table, slicing into the buzz of conversation. Mouths closed and eyes turned toward him, including those that had, thus far, not glanced his way. This was his punishment, he realized. He'd rebuffed her kiss on the balcony, and now she was attempting to ignore his presence.

"How are you enjoying the London season so far?" he asked. It was a bland question, one that would not elicit anything more than a bland answer, but at least it had worked to sever her conversation with Gibbons.

"I'm finding that I like London," she said, pausing briefly to glance at Gibbons, "very much indeed."

The bastard accepted the compliment with a lecherous smile. Henry throttled his fork.

"Do you not wish to return home to St. Petersburg? You've been away for years now," Henry continued, wishing he could pick her up and carry her aboard a ship heading back to Russia right then and there.

She glanced at him coolly before again looking to the man at her right. "Not yet, my lord. I am rather taken with your city."

What was the chit doing? She would make a spectacle of herself if she kept addressing Gibbons so openly, a man she had just met this evening, most likely when they sat down to the dinner table.

"Well, in that case, Your Highness, you really must not stay in Essex for too long," Lady Vandermere put in. "It is such a pity that you must go so early in the season."

Why the woman was so distraught over Irina's plans to leave, Henry could not fathom. She did not have a son in want for a wife. Perhaps a nephew? Or, more likely, she was just a busybody matchmaker living vicariously through the young debutantes every season, especially as her own daughter remained woefully unattached.

"I enjoy London," Irina replied. "However, even when I return from Essex, I do not intend to parade myself around with the sole hope of procuring a husband the way I might a side of beef."

She gave a little laugh, though it was the only sound in the marked fall of silence. Even Lady Vandermere did not seem to know what to say. Henry watched Irina's smile fall off and her eyes round a bit as she realized that what she'd meant in good humor had not been received as such.

"I only mean to say that marriage should not be treated as if it were a commodity," she said with a shrug, in an attempt to explain herself.

It only served to stiffen the backs of nearly every guest around the table.

"Marriage *is* a commodity, Your Highness," Henry said, sitting forward and setting his fork down for good. "For those of our set, people must make connections that benefit not only our own positions but those of the tenant farmers who work our lands."

Irina lifted her chin, as if in preparation of battle. Henry braced himself.

"I understand how your system works here in England—"

"Then you should understand that a loss of income or a poor match resulting in a lack of funds could devastate hundreds of families we are charged to protect and cultivate. I would have thought a young woman of your position would have learned that by now."

The last cutting remarks had slipped out, born of pent-up anger and her flirtation with Gibbons, nothing more. He regretted the words the moment they were said, especially when the apples of Irina's cheeks grew splotchy and the tips of her ears went red. He might have thought she was merely furious if not for the sheen of tears causing her eyes to glisten.

Oh hell.

"Thank you for that illuminating lesson, Lord Langlevit," she said, her voice barely audible. She placed the napkin that had been in her lap upon the table, and a footman rushed forward to pull out her chair. "If you will excuse me, I am not feeling entirely well."

The men around the table all shot to their feet, though none faster than Henry. He threw down his napkin, too, but as Irina whisked out of the dining room, her chin held just as high as before, he remained where he was. To rush out after her would have caused a display much larger than the one that had just passed.

He took his seat again and avoided his mother's glare, spearing him from the opposite end of the table. He didn't need to meet it to be able to feel it. The next few courses dragged by, held back, it seemed, by the mundane conversation that slowly filled the awkwardness of the princess's departure and Henry's poor temper with her.

She hadn't meant anything by it, and yet he'd bit into her as if she'd disparaged the entirety of the English Crown. Because she'd been ignoring him. Flirting with another man.

Henry stood up the very moment the last guest finished their lingonberry torte and suggested the men retire to the billiards room. As they filed down the corridor to the gaming room, Henry did not intend to stay for more than one round. It was excruciating to carry out and he played badly, but once he excused himself and slipped out of the room, he felt a rush of warm anticipation loosen the muscles in his legs and back. He had to see her. Knew she would be furious and he'd have to apologize, but...he had to speak to her.

If she was not with the other women in the salon, he had a sneaking suspicion where he would be able to find her.

As he descended into the kitchens, footmen and kitchen maids bowed and bobbed, the maids gasping in surprise to find him trespassing in their realm. He did not often do so. But he'd remembered something from the time Irina had been staying at his Cumbria estate, when she'd been disappointed that a bundle of her sister's letters had been nearly ruined in a drenching rain on their way up from Essex. Two had been destroyed, the ink having run into illegible blurs, and the other two were only partly intact. Irina had gone into the kitchens and convinced the cook with her tears to let her sit down there and eat an entire lemon curd pie. Henry had found her hours later, asleep on a bench, crumbs still on her cheek.

"Her Highness is in there, my lord," a young kitchen maid whispered as she dropped into an untrained curtsy and pointed toward an arched doorway.

He nodded his thanks and entered.

She was seated on the table, which was set in the middle of the pantry, with her back to the door. Irina's legs swung forward and back lazily, and in the light of the room's simple, four-arm chandelier, he noticed she'd toed off her slippers. Henry heard the clinking of a spoon against a glass dish.

"How are the truffles?" he asked, and Irina jumped, twisting around to see him and receiving a glob of chocolate on her upper lip for it.

She set the plate and spoon down and wiped at her lip, turning away from him. Not fast enough, though. He'd seen the red rims of her eyes.

Damn it all to hell. She'd been crying.

"Irina," he started to say, stepping into the room and closing the door behind him. The last thing he needed were servants peering in and listening around the corner. The wood of the door was a heavy slab and would muffle their voices well. Especially handy for when she shouted at him, which she was certainly going to do.

"Don't," she said, getting down from the table and gathering the hem of her dress so she could slip back into her shoes. "Please, just leave me alone."

"I can't. I need to apologize for how I acted."

"Apologies won't change anything. They are useless. Just

like my being here," she said and once slippered again, started for the door.

He was blocking her path and did not move.

"They aren't useless, not when a person means them. And I do. I shouldn't have spoken to you like—"

"Like I was a brainless ninny. How could you humiliate me that way?" Irina's eyes flashed, and Henry suffered a cramp in his chest. He hadn't wanted to humiliate her, and yet...he had.

"I meant it as humor," she went on. "But I should have known better with all of you sitting there in your starched cravats, perched upon your high morals, blinded by your own importance—"

"Irina."

"I don't belong here; you've made that perfectly clear, Lord Langlevit. I don't know London. I don't know anything I thought I did—"

"Irina." He took a step closer, trying to meet her fevered eyes, but they seemed to be pinned somewhere around his chest.

"You think I'm a fool, but I am no such thing."

Every word out of her mouth was a fist closing tighter around his heart. "I do not think that."

"I won't pretend to be someone I'm not. I'll say what I please and...and..."

And for the moment it appeared she had run out of steam.

Henry lifted his hand and touched one of her bare shoulders, his palm resting gently on her velvety skin. A hot sweep of blood coursed through his veins.

"I like that you say what you please," he said, attempting to give her shoulder a reassuring squeeze. However, when it came time to pull his hand away, he couldn't. Instead, his fingers trailed down her arm, lightly brushing the underside of her wrist.

"You weren't pleased tonight," she replied, her voice catching.

His other hand rose to her other shoulder, but instead of trailing down her arm again, Henry's fingers drifted to her neck. Her skin was as soft and smooth as the silk of her dress.

"I am," he murmured, his mind wandering as his eyes and fingers did, as well. He cupped her cheek. She was warm and so beautiful, and those cheeks were now flushed with passion from shouting instead of embarrassment.

"You're pleased?" she asked, her eyes finally rising from where they'd been staring at his chest.

All Henry could see were her lips, forming that word. *Pleased.* Pleasure. He wanted it. Craved it. And before he could stop to think, he took it. Henry crushed his mouth to hers. The moment his lips made contact, the tight coil that had been twisting and twisting inside of him all evening snapped free. He surged forward, pressing her against the table. Irina's lips parted on a soft sound of surprise, and without hesitation, Henry's tongue delved past them. Instead of shyly retreating, she met him with equal fervor, matching his intensity beat for beat.

Passion.

She was brimming with it, her own tongue trying desperately to mimic and twine around his, her small hands wrapping around his neck, her fingers spearing into his hair and anchoring him closer. He needed no further invitation. The determined press of her warm, wet mouth consumed his every thought and made him senseless. Heedless of anything but satisfaction.

Lost to a wild swell of lust, Henry swept his hands down her ribs and over her hips, and with a fast jerk, lifted her from the floor. He set her on the edge of the table, his mouth ravaging hers, relishing the sinful remnants of chocolate on her lips and her heated breath. Kissing Irina was like nothing he'd ever experienced. It was like racing through a summer thunderstorm—exhilarating and alarming in equal measure—and despite knowing the obvious danger, he only craved more. Henry felt as if he were falling into something warm and soft, and he wanted only to breathe her in, taste her, pleasure her with the same sweet torture barreling through him.

As he parted her thighs and shifted forward to place himself right at the crux of her, Irina's answering moan made that snapped coil even looser. He pulled away from her mouth and nuzzled her neck, his tongue and teeth and lips skimming feverishly over her skin.

"Henry," Irina sighed, her fingers pushing at the collar of his dinner jacket.

The sound of his name on her lips made him want to claim them again. Henry couldn't decide which he liked more—the velvety soft skin of her throat or the chocolate glazed decadence of her lips.

Cupping her chin in his hands, he ran his thumb over her plump bottom lip and kissed her again. Gently this time. Sipping from her mouth and slowing his pace to something more tender, as she deserved. But Irina wanted no part of it. She tugged on his lapels and scraped his lip with her teeth. Her eyes met his, and desire shot through him in scalding bursts when she openly sought his mouth with hers. Matching his hunger equally, her uninhibited silken tongue stroked over his as if she, too, could not get enough of him. There were no walls, no pretenses in her desire. She met him with more honesty than any other woman ever had. He liked it. Far more than he should.

Reason lifted the fog of his ardor. Despite her natural passion, Irina was an innocent, and he...was not. Pulling back with a groan of misery, Henry took a grating breath and composed himself. "Irina—"

She placed a finger on his lips, her blue eyes like bruised

indigo. "If you plan to tell me this is wrong, then stop right now."

He swallowed hard and disengaged from the cradle of her thighs along with the heated brand of her finger. His entire body felt the loss of how perfectly she fit against him. Stepping back toward the archway, Henry steeled himself, reaching inward for the rigid indifference that had always fortified him. He'd never needed it more than he did right now with this slip of a girl who made him want impossible things. Things he'd stopped expecting years ago. Things men like him did not merit.

"Please don't leave like this." Her voice was quiet.

"I have to," he bit out without looking at her as he reached the door. "I am not the man for you, Irina."

"Why?"

He hesitated for a moment and then nodded. She deserved an honest answer. "Because I cannot give you what you want…what you need."

Her voice lowered, something indefinable threading between the words. "And what do you think that is, my lord?"

"You want what every debutante wants—courtship, devotion, happiness," Henry said. "And I am incapable of any of those things. Trust me when I say that I would only break you."

Chapter Six

The spring flowers in Hyde Park were beginning to emerge, their bright colors offsetting the richer chartreuse of the underlying grass. It had rained the night before, and their petals were still dewy and glistening. Even the Serpentine gleamed, the early morning sun dappling its surface with playful shimmers. The hour was early, not yet noon, so the park was not crowded with the beau monde dressed to the nines and showing off their equipages. Most of the *ton* would be out in the late afternoon.

Normally, people-watching was one of Irina's favorite things to do, but today she preferred to escape it. Her mind was tortured with other things as she rode along in Max's phaeton. Thoroughly indecent things. Like the way Lord Langlevit had claimed her mouth the evening before. Her lips still tingled. She hadn't simply been kissed—she'd been *branded*.

Irina had been kissed before, but none of them had ever been like Henry's kiss. Their lips and teeth and tongues had ground together in an embrace that had been violent, carnal, and intoxicatingly arousing. She'd found herself responding to it, wanting to devour him as he'd been devouring her. If he hadn't left when he did, she would have stripped bare and abandoned herself to ruination. Even now, warmth saturated her, pooling between her thighs and making her skin feel shivery-hot. Her breathing wizened to short pants just from the memory of the bloody thing. Irina's fingers curled into the folds of her riding habit, and she squeezed her legs together.

"Have you been listening to a word I've been saying?" Max asked with a laugh. "Honestly, what has gotten into you today? You've been distracted ever since we left Devon Place. What is it? A delectable new suitor you haven't told me about?" He eyed her, arching an amused eyebrow as he scanned her flushed cheeks. "Oh, do tell, you naughty minx. I should have known you were hiding something from me."

Irina's startled glance met his. Max was too perceptive for his own good, and his guess was far too close to the truth. Not that Langlevit was a suitor. In fact, he'd declared himself the exact opposite.

"I'm sorry, I was thinking about Lana," she fabricated wildly and then stifled the indelicate chortle that welled in her throat. The image in her head had most definitely not been that of her sister—not unless she'd turned into a handsome, if impossible to understand, earl. "And my return to Essex. What were you saying?"

His eye roll was worthy of an ovation. "You don't get to escape that easily, little liar, but I was asking how well you liked my new phaeton."

"I like it very much," she said. In other circumstances, riding on the high perch of Max's fabulous new carriage would be thrilling, but once more, it paled in comparison to her private thoughts.

"The horses are new, as well," he said with a wink. "Got them at auction."

She frowned at her friend. "Didn't you recently purchase a pair of Hanoverians? And I seem to remember hearing something of a new curricle, as well."

Max shot her an irrepressible grin. "Well, I can't have matching horses without a splendid carriage behind them, can I? This one was worth it, trust me. And I may as well spend my father's money if I'm not going to inherit it. I'm lucky my mother sends me any at all."

"Reckless spending isn't the way to get back into his good graces, especially if he discovers your mother is secretly funneling you funds."

Max laughed. "It will be a cold day in hell before the staunch and closed-minded Count Remisov welcomes this prodigal stray back into the fold."

Irina narrowed her gaze on him, not missing the pained look that was quickly concealed behind his usual smirk. She linked her arm into the crook of his. "It's been years. I can't imagine that he won't welcome you home. Maybe we should both go back after this season."

She'd made this same proposal a few times before, but he'd always put her off. He didn't wish to speak of it, not even to her. It had to be painful, whatever it was.

"I only look forward, my young princess, never backward. St. Petersburg is part of the past, and there it shall remain. And my dear father can go flog himself."

"Don't you miss them? Your family?" she asked as he steered the conveyance toward Rotten Row where a scattered few other vehicles and riders congregated. She didn't miss that he had neatly sidestepped her question. His estrangement had much to do with his choice of lifestyle, she knew, but blood was blood. She'd give her own life for the opportunity to see either of her parents again. But then, Count Remisov wasn't exactly the forgiving sort. He'd always been a cold sort of man, and he and Max had never seen eye to eye, not even when she and Max were children. The count didn't like being embarrassed by his son's proclivities, and when the sixteen-year-old Max had disappeared with a well-known Russian prince for a week, he had disowned his only son. It was why Max had moved to Moscow and then Paris.

"You're my family," Max said with a bright smile and leaned close to whisper in her ear. "Now come, let's talk about something less depressing, shall we? Tell me of your new secret lover."

"Max," she gasped, swatting at him. "You are abominable."

"Stop trying to elude me, my sweet. I know when you're hiding something. A stolen kiss, perhaps?"

Irina bit her lip hard to stop from blushing. "No."

"I will torture you until the end of eternity," he said teasingly. "And it can't be worse than the scandalous embrace Deroche claimed he got off you last season."

Her mouth fell open into a soundless *O*. "You are a shameless rogue to sink to encouraging such gossip."

"I cannot control what people choose to confide," he said with a dramatic hand to the chest. "Out with it, darling."

"Oh, very well, if you won't be deterred. It was only a kiss." She wouldn't give him a name, she decided, or details, but it wouldn't hurt to speak about it. To diffuse the memory of it a bit. "One of the gentlemen from dinner last evening. It was…nice." She almost choked on the feeble word.

Max squinted at her, and then his eyes lit up. "Gibbons! I knew you would fancy him." He pursed his lips. "He's not much of a catch, but is endowed where it counts. Or so I've heard."

"Oh, stop!" Clapping her hands over her ears, Irina laughed at his expression and shook her head. "My poor delicate sensibilities."

He snorted. "You forget I've seen you well in your cups, *Princess*, and your mouth is as bawdy as a sailor pulling into port." He surveyed her and nodded approvingly. "This should move things along nicely."

"What do you mean? What things?"

"The wagers," he explained. "They are heating up at White's."

"How is it that you've gotten access there?" she asked, frowning. "It's members only."

"I have ways and means, little one."

It did not surprise her. Well-accustomed to Max finagling his way to the most exclusive establishments across the Continent, Irina didn't want to know what those ways and means were. He was attractive, wealthy, and had the right pedigree. His glib tongue seemed to do the rest quite easily, especially when it came to rich and connected patrons. "Who have you charmed this time?"

Max offered her a sage look. "A gentleman never kisses and tells."

"Good thing you are no gentleman," she shot back, shaking her head. "Tell me more about the wagers, then, if you're going to be so close-lipped about your diversions after interrogating me about mine."

"Let's be honest, sweet, your diversions are far tamer than my own, most of which are not meant for such tender, *delicate sensibilities*." He winked at her, avoiding a second irritated swat of her hand. "As far as the wagers, Bainley claimed the first. A stroll on the balcony at the Bradburne Ball."

She scowled, recalling the odious man. "Would that there'd been a bet for him to return with a blood-spotted shirt. He's a despicable pig. Go on."

"Lord Marlowe earned five hundred for a dance at the Huntington Ball."

"Five hundred pounds?" she repeated, her eyes goggling. "For a *dance*?"

"A second dance," Max corrected, tapping his forefinger

against his chin. "Lord Crawley bet and won a thousand for a ride with you in Hyde Park."

Irina's jaw dropped again. She'd only ridden with Lord Crawley, a viscount who'd been an absolute gentleman, barely one afternoon prior. "Are you quite serious? A thousand pounds?"

"They're mad for you, as we predicted, and these men have nothing better to do than compete to see who has the fattest purse. And by purse, I mean manhood."

She swallowed her shocked giggle. "It's barbaric."

"It's men." His mouth quirked into a crooked smile, and he maneuvered the phaeton off to the side. "I've even lined my pockets at your expense." Turning to her, he patted his waistcoat. "Won a hundred quid on how long it would take for Lord Everton to be shocked by your controversial opinions."

Lord Everton had been one of the most aggressive in his pursuit since her arrival in London. Nothing was wrong with the man except that he was as stodgy as day-old pudding. Irina wasn't surprised that anything she had said had shocked him.

"Apparently," Max was saying, "your ideas on comparing women to breeding mares struck a particularly responsive chord in poor Lord Everton. His family owns a stud farm, you know."

Irina clamped her lips together to stop from bursting out laughing and then gave in to the inclination. "Now that's certainly worth a hundred pounds!"

Her unbridled laughter drew the attention of several people around them, including one who was riding hell-bent in their direction, his face blacker than the beast beneath him. The amusement died a swift death on her lips as Lord Langlevit pulled alongside the carriage. Her heart, however, surged to life in her breast, pounding against her ribs in a violent staccato. Never had a man had such a visceral effect on her. If she weren't sitting, she was sure that her legs would not be able to support her.

"Lord Remi," the earl said in greeting with a brisk nod and a shallow bow in her direction. "Your Highness."

His deep voice sent shaky bolts of pure heat spiraling through her.

"Lord Langlevit," Irina murmured, her fingers once more seeking the folds of her riding habit for courage or strength—she did not know which.

She was transparent as wet muslin to Max, and fearing he would notice the effect Henry had on her, Irina kept her face averted from him and forced a fixed smile to her lips. But she could not keep her lowered gaze from returning to Henry's face and roving greedily over his proud chin and stern mouth…the very mouth that had taken hers with such delicious ferocity. She wanted to feel those commanding lips on hers again. As if he could read her scandalous thoughts, Henry's eyes met hers for a charged instant, leaving her incapable of breathing before they broke away. Beads of sweat broke out on the nape of her neck as the fire within leaped to uncontrollable heights. He was not immune, either, she noticed. The knuckles of his fingers on the reins had gone white.

"Langlevit," Max said jovially. "Lovely day for a ride, is it not?"

"I fear I won't see much of it as I am departing for Essex within the hour," he said. "Lady Irina is supposed to be riding with my mother. I've come to fetch her."

"You did not have to put yourself out, my lord," she responded lightly despite her wildly scattering pulse. "I am well aware of the hour and had planned to return shortly."

"It was not out of my way."

"Heavens, Langlevit," a breathless female voice called out, and a stunning woman on a prancing white mare approached. Viscountess La Valse. Of course, Henry was not alone, nor was it, as he'd said, out of his way. He had been here already. *With his lover.* "You took off so suddenly, I had a devil of a time following you." Laughing, she cleared her throat and threw a meaningful glance at the earl to perform the introductions.

"Princess Irina, this is Lady La Valse, a friend," he said with a slightly sardonic look. "Lady La Valse, may I present Princess Irina Volkonsky."

Irina noticed he said nothing after her name, and though small, the slight gutted her. Perhaps she should be grateful that he hadn't called her his ward. Gritting her teeth, she lifted her chin and smiled graciously. "A pleasure, Lady La Valse."

"Likewise, Your Highness." She turned to Max. "And of course, Lord Remi, we need no introduction, not after our last adventure." Irina's gaze shot to Max. His mouth twitched in an unapologetic smile. Clearly, Lady La Valse was also part of his kissing and not telling repertoire. He truly was a shocking reprobate.

Max tipped his hat toward her. "Since we are being abandoned by these two, I suggest you allow me to accompany you to the opera tonight."

"Wonderful idea," she agreed and tugged on the reins, whirling her horse about with practiced ease. "Enjoy Essex, Your Highness."

"Thank you."

"We leave within the hour," Henry told Irina curtly as he made to follow the lady.

That was it? *We leave within the hour?* She stared after him with an urge to fling her ankle boot at his arrogant head. How dare he parade his lover about without a thought for her feelings? Or maybe he'd intended to do so all along. Irina was so angry she would put a hole in the fabric of her habit if she continued wringing her hands. Aware of the sudden silence and the fact that they weren't yet moving, she looked up, only to meet Max's thoughtful stare.

His eyebrow vaulted irritatingly. "So, Gibbons, eh?"

"Sod off, Max."

Her friend took her hands gently, ignoring her unladylike retort. "He's not good for you, Irina. The earl."

"I don't know what you're talking about."

"It's written all over you." His voice remained soft and quiet. "A fool could see it." Irina exhaled as Max continued, his fingers stroking hers compassionately. "I know you were close once, and I know what he's done for you and your sister, but you should know that he's not a man given to emotion or mercy."

"And how did you come by this sudden knowledge?" she hissed. "Let me guess, from your new friend, Lady La Valse?"

He squeezed her fingers, leaning close in earnest. "Please don't be angry with me. You know she's a means to an end. A diversion, nothing more. And she's been a veritable fountain of information about most of the *ton*, including Lord Langlevit. The stories I've heard about him paint a ruthless picture. She revealed he's never quite recovered after what happened in France."

"What happened in France?"

Max stared at her for a long while before responding. "I don't know how much of this is true, but apparently, Langlevit disappeared into France a few years ago. He was gone for eight months, unaccounted for. Lady La Valse has reason to believe he was taken prisoner during that time." He paused, and lowering his voice, added, "And that he suffered torture at the hands of King George's enemies."

Irina stared at him, unblinking. Max's words horrified her.

"Lady La Valse is sure of this?" she whispered.

"She has friends in high places. Places like the War Office," he replied, still hushed. "She knows enough. Whatever happened to him during those months he was missing affected him greatly. Lady La Valse says he's closed himself off. That he'll never open his heart to anyone."

Taken prisoner. Tortured. Henry had been *broken*. Last night he said he would break *her* if he stayed.

Irina's heart trembled within her chest as she realized he'd likely only said that to protect her from him, as if his brokenness were somehow catching. But what he didn't realize was that she was damaged, too. After what she'd endured at the tender age of fourteen at the hands of her kidnappers—being snatched and trussed like an animal—she had wounds and scars of her own, ones fissured so deeply that no one, not even her own sister, knew they existed. Irina understood what it felt like to feel deficient and hollow, as if gaps in her soul were missing.

"He wasn't always like that," she said softly, more to herself than anyone.

With one last empathetic squeeze, Max released her shoulders and resumed his grip on the reins. "Stay away from him, love. He's heartless, and a man with no heart has nothing to offer. Come, we'll have a quick turn, and I'll see you back to Devon Place."

Irina nodded dully. Max was wrong. Henry did have a heart. It was fractured and beaten and hidden deep, but it was there. She'd felt it thudding against hers when he'd kissed her. She saw it in the tender way he looked at his mother. She'd seen it on the balcony at Hadley Gardens—the barest glimpse of the old Henry wrapped up within its confines like the tiniest ray of light. Her throat felt tight.

The earl wasn't heartless.

But maybe what Lady La Valse had told Max was true. Perhaps Henry would never open his heart to anyone again.

Chapter Seven

The moment he entered the outskirts of London, Henry's mood lifted. He took deeper breaths and marveled at the simple satisfaction of filling his lungs with what actually felt like air and not smog.

The city's chimney stacks pumping out coal smoke over the winter months had thickened the air to a toxic brume in some places, but he knew the real reason he breathed easier now that he was departing. With the congested press of the city behind him, Henry no longer felt penned in. Even riding in a near-empty Hyde Park that morning, with lawns, ponds, trees, and gravel footpaths stretching for miles, Henry had felt the constant need to check over his shoulder, to know who was behind him, how far away, and how fast they were riding.

An instinctive and constant awareness was the one thing that had kept him alive all these years. Although, it made what should have been a leisurely ride into a mission to keep a safe distance from any approaching riders. He had not even liked to have Françoise on his horse's heels.

Why the horse and rider currently trotting just behind him

on the post road north did not make him feel like a trapped animal, Henry was not certain. For years, ever since he'd set foot back on English soil, bruised and broken, he'd avoided having people walk or ride closely behind him whenever possible.

Something about Irina made things different.

He sat straight in his saddle, hands light on the reins, and listened to the steady clicking of her mount's hooves. His mother's barouche rolled along just ahead, trunks and boxes and valises lashed to the roof. Another, smaller carriage had set out earlier that morning carrying more luggage, a few maids, and Henry's own valet.

However, Irina had appeared in the foyer of the Devon Place wearing naught but a pair of tall boots, riding breeches, a feminine waistcoat, and a long, swan-tailed riding coat. He'd had the instant thought that the odd ensemble suited her willowy frame to perfection. Then again, she could have made a burlap sack look fashionable.

"Does your backside ache yet?" he asked her now.

"It is not gentlemanly to inquire about the state of a woman's backside, my lord," came Irina's tart reply.

He twisted around to meet her eyes. They flitted away from him, pretending to be interested in the trees off the side of the road.

"You should be inside the carriage," he said.

"As you've already stated numerous times."

He faced forward again with a sigh. "It is a six-hour ride."

"As you've *also* already stated. Lord Langlevit, please, I prefer to ride in the open, aching backside or not, rather than to be closed up inside that box for hours on end."

Something in her voice made him glance back again. Her expression had hardened, and the space between her full, dark-brown brows was pinched, as if the mere idea was disagreeable. His eyes narrowed. It was a curious look, one that drew his attention. It wavered between fear, revulsion, and reluctance.

"That *box* is a conveyance suitable for a king," he said, watching for her answering expression. Her lips thinned but not in annoyance. She was agitated. Truly bothered, it seemed, at the thought of riding in the carriage. Henry had been trained to read the truth behind even the faintest of facial expressions. The twitch of a nose, the shifting of eyes. Licking lips, blinking too rapidly. They were all tells.

"It is a beautiful conveyance, but I...simply don't care for long carriage rides."

Irina continued to gaze into the trees.

"That's the second thing we have in common," he said, succeeding in drawing her attention back to him.

"What is the first?" she asked.

"Resorting to chocolate when upset."

Her lips twitched, a warm blush rising into her cheeks. "Chocolate solves everything."

So far, neither of them had spoken about what had happened in the pantry the evening before, though every time he let his eyes rest on her, he felt warm and slightly panicked. How could he have given in to his base desires? *He'd* kissed her. *He'd* acted first. Rejecting her kiss on the balcony at Hadley Gardens had sapped him of his willpower, it seemed. Of all moral decency.

Because there was nothing remotely moral or decent in the way he wanted Princess Irina Volkonsky.

He'd gone to Françoise after leaving Devon Place. He wasn't proud of slaking his lust with what most people would consider a high-ranking courtesan, but it had served to remind him what *he* was, and what he could never be, especially for a woman as young and untouched as Irina.

She was wild, yes, and passionate, but the frantic, needful press of her mouth, the unskilled but torturously perfect fumbling of her hands as she'd tried to push past the barrier of their clothing, had assured him of her innocence. Henry might have considered taking any other woman's virtue if offered to him so willingly—but this was *Irina*. A changed and grown and beautifully surprising Irina, but Irina just the same.

"Do you like to go fast?" she asked, and Henry realized he was still staring at her, the awkward twist of his back beginning to ache near the ruined skin and muscle of his shoulder blades.

"Excuse me?" he asked, his mind leaping into dangerous territory.

"Upon a horse," she clarified, her pinched brows smoothing out with humor. "Do you like to race?"

He cleared his throat and faced forward. "Not upon a horse."

"Then how?" she asked, trotting forward and entering his line of vision.

"On foot," he replied, fighting the urge to look at her. Instead, he scanned the tree line to the left and right of the road. An old habit he couldn't seem to break.

"You race on foot? Against whom?" She sounded a cross between amused and confused. He didn't blame her. Earls did not usually participate in foot races.

"Against myself," he replied, his attention catching on a strange darkness within the tree line to the right. He watched it another moment before realizing it was a large boulder shrouded in shade. Relaxing slightly, he spared a glimpse to the woman riding beside him. She arched a questioning eyebrow, her violet eyes alight with curiosity.

"I have a course at Hartstone," he went on, his longing for the three-mile obstacle course he'd lain out and built over the last handful of years growing.

"A path?" she asked.

"A challenging path," he replied, smiling inwardly.

Rock walls, pole bridges, rope swings, and netted canopies strung between treetops were only a few of the dangerous obstacles he'd implemented. Running the course, always aiming to improve his time, helped him focus. It was a different kind of physical exertion that released his pent-up tension, and oddly enough, it was better than anything Françoise or any girl from The Cock and the Crown could manage.

"What's it like?" Irina asked, and from the inflection of her voice he could tell she was truly interested.

That was another thing that hadn't changed over the years—that insatiable curiosity and bright intelligence of hers. Whenever he had visited the estate in Cumbria, Irina had always asked insightful questions about his travels with genuine enthusiasm. He supposed it was why he'd always enjoyed conversing with her, and perhaps that was why he felt so at ease with her now. There were no games, no artifice, no trickery. Henry exhaled, his eyes scanning the area once more. It'd been so long since he had trusted anyone, especially a woman.

"It's fashioned after a military training area," he said. "With walls and hurdles and ditches. I like to exert myself," he added with a tight shrug.

"Ah," she sighed. "Now I see."

"See what?"

Her teasing smile caught him by surprise. "How you stay so physically fit if indeed you do eat your sorrows as you've confessed to doing."

To his even greater surprise, Henry found himself smiling and bantering back. "And what is your secret, then?"

"Why dancing, of course." She flung her head back, staring to the sky. "And riding. Though neither of those sound as exciting as this course of yours. Will you show it to me?"

He was about to say yes when reason latched onto the heels of his impulse.

"Perhaps," he replied stiffly. Taking a woman on the course would be dangerous. He could not be responsible for broken bones or anyone's death. Before his best friend, John's, passing two years prior, he'd broken his arm on the first half mile of the course, narrowly missing breaking his neck instead. No, it would not be a place for anyone bar him, especially not any gently bred young woman, not even one as adventurous as the lady beside him.

Irina stayed quiet a moment, and when she spoke again, her tone had turned playful. "Do you see the curve in the road ahead? If I beat you to it, you will agree to show me the course."

Henry couldn't help smiling at her tenacity. And her competitive spirit. The curve was a good four hundred yards or more in the distance, the canopy overhead tangled with what appeared to be bare tree branches.

"And if you lose?" Henry asked, eyeing her sideways.

"Name the forfeit," she said, meeting his glance and raising one brow in challenge.

He shifted in his saddle, trying not to sink to new depths while imagining all manner of things he might take from her. Her offering was innocent, but his thoughts were decidedly not.

"You'll show me your skill with a sword," he said, recalling her offer on the balcony moments before she'd kissed him. "Do you require a head start, my lady?"

Her full lips broke into a wide grin. It tugged at him, hard. Henry's mouth was still slowly forming his return grin when Irina slapped her reins and took off in a lurch. "Head starts are for amateurs!"

Henry's reflexes sprang into gear, and he dug his heels in, urging his mount forward. He shot past the barouche, the shades of which were drawn, his mother hopefully ignorant to their race, and quickly caught up with Irina's horse. She was laughing, and when she saw him, gave a little squeal of delight before speeding up. She had skill on her side and the youth and speed of one of the finest riding horses from his stables, but he had the steady grace and strength of his trusted six-year-old Arabian—and an objective. He wanted to see her swinging a sword, and he most certainly did not want to share his dangerous obstacle course with her. Knowing her propensity for danger, she'd likely try to run it.

"I cannot wait to see your secret course," she shouted breathlessly to him, leaning low over her mount's neck, her thighs gripping the saddle.

He was distracted for an instant at the sight of her trim legs encased in those buckskin breeches as she rose in the stirrups, catching a healthy eyeful of the shapely backside he'd worried over earlier. *Lucky horse,* he thought and felt an immediate stirring of lust in his groin. Henry shook his head, uttering a growl of laughter. He'd lose the race *and* his dignity if he lost his concentration because of an ill-timed erection. Still, the sight of her braced on that horse was nothing short of spectacular.

His horse nosed past hers, the curve in the road fast approaching as their mounts rode hard toward it. Irina's hat remained pinned to her head, though from the corner of his eye, he saw her hair streaming behind her in long, undulating waves. He'd lost his own hat somewhere, though he was certain Billings, his carriage driver, would stop to retrieve it.

Movement along the branches that crisscrossed above the curve in the road drew Henry's eyes away from Irina's flowing hair. Blurred streaks of reddish gray fur were scurrying along the branches—a pair of squirrels. They screeched violently in their mating chase, causing the bare, withered-looking branches to sway. A third squirrel dropped from a higher branch, landing upon the other two.

Henry heard the deep crack of wood above the panting

horses and their pounding hooves. Somehow, it was louder than Irina's laughter and the slap of her swallowtail riding coat in the wind. Time slowed as he saw the squirrels scattering fast, leaping upon a safe branch as the one they'd been on began to fall. The branch itself, so much larger now that he really saw it, seemed to fall at an impossibly slow speed. Henry's eyes and mind quickly worked in tandem to calculate where he and Irina would be when the thick tree limb landed in the middle of the road.

The answer slammed into him: *they would be directly below it.*

"Stop!" he shouted, but knew the rushing wind coursing past her ears had muffled his shout.

There wasn't time to reach for her reins and pull her to a stop. He pushed his mount forward just enough to come alongside hers as they crested the bend. And then he threw himself to the side, falling off his horse and into Irina's. She screamed as he hooked her with his arm and pulled her from her saddle. He fell, back first, toward the hard-packed road and braced himself for the collision, cradling Irina best he could with his arms and chest. They hit, the ground pummeling the air from Henry's lungs.

His head knocked off the dirt, and his ears started to ring. The world went dark and silent. The pain lancing through Henry's back and ribs, along his arms and legs, cut through the high-pitched bells in his ears and became a horrendous cry of anguish.

The screaming continued, the caterwauling unbearable. Mean laughter, men shouting in his ear. Words he didn't understand, and some he did. Threats he knew would be fulfilled. A gunshot. A bullet striking the cold, damp stone wall Henry was chained to. A piece of rock exploding and burrowing into his cheek. He couldn't move. His hands were chained, his bare feet in pure agony from where they were weighted down in a bucket of ice and freezing water.

The images rushed at him, piling on top of him, drowning him. He'd never get away. He'd die here. He'd die a prisoner.

"Henry?"

A voice reached for him in the dark, dank cell where he lay, caught in the monstrous pit of his memories.

"Henry, open your eyes. It's me."

The voice grew louder, and he grasped for it. He heaved for air, and the rotten stink of excrement and blood was becoming the sweet scent of tea roses.

"*Please*, Henry, look at me."

He cracked open his eyelids to blaring sunshine and a pained, beautiful face hovering above his. Silence thundered in his ears. *Was he dead?* An angel such as she did not belong in his world. Such beauty would not suffer to be surrounded by such filth. Henry struggled to breathe as reality returned in fractured swatches, dissolving the nightmare that had gripped him. His angel remained, staring at him, her hat gone, and he remembered who she was. Where he was. The road. A tree branch falling. "Irina."

"Oh thank God," she gasped, her hands cradling his cheeks.

"Branch," he ground out, the back of his head blaring with pain. Like waking after one of the night terrors he used to have almost every night, the memories of that foul French prison cell throbbed with stark clarity. His stomach was tight, his heart racing.

"I know, I saw it just as you dove for me," she said, her thumbs still gently caressing his cheeks and jaw. "You saved my head, but I'm worried about yours. You took the brunt of the fall."

"I'm fine," he said, trying to sit up. Irina leaned on his chest and pushed him back down onto the ground.

"You are not," she insisted. "You were shouting. You

were in pain."

"I'm in pain now, with those pointy elbows of yours in my ribs," he grumbled. She ignored him.

"What happened? Henry?"

His name like that, so soft and concerned on her lips, with her hands stroking his jaw…a wall fissured inside of him.

"A memory," he whispered, closing his eyes again. "Nothing more."

One of her thumbs swept closer to his lower lip. "A memory of what happened to you in France?" she asked with caution.

He stiffened under her hands. "What do you know of that?"

He did not discuss it. With anyone. The only people who knew about his time as a prisoner were his mother, Rose, War Office officials, and the Prince Regent himself. He was certain of rumors and whispers, too, but nothing true or substantial.

"Only that it haunts you," she answered. Irina's thumb touched the curve of his bottom lip. Her eyes bored into his, the balm of her compassion like a salve on his ragged emotions. Inexplicably, his breathing slowed and calmed.

His heart, too, had lessened its gallop, and the pulsing images of the prison had slipped into the closed-up room in his mind where he preferred they stay. Usually they persisted for hours, and he was forced to run or call for a woman to distract him. But they were gone now, swept away by only the gentle press of Irina's fingers and her sweet concern.

Irina levered her hands to her side and adjusted her position over him so that her breasts lay flat against his chest instead of her elbows. Her dark curls spilled over her shoulders, and Henry had the indescribable urge to bury his face in them. She was staring at him now, a look of unhidden yearning in those magnetic eyes, and the space between them shifted into something charged.

Her chest rose and fell above his in shallow pants. With a soft inhalation, Irina drew a bare fingertip across the parted seam of his lips. The dull throb in his skull was replaced by a throb in another region of his body. She'd removed her riding gloves, he realized, and he could taste the salt on her skin. Henry wanted to suck that teasing finger into his mouth and then replace it with her tongue. Hell, he wanted her to straddle where he ached, right here in the middle of the post road, and grind herself against him, finding her pleasure even through the friction of their breeches. He wanted it with a kind of need he hadn't felt in a long time.

Reason returned with the sound of the carriage nearing the blind curve of the bend.

"I should attempt to get up before my mother sees us and has heart failure," he said softly, and with a groan of effort, pushed her body gently from his ribs and sat up.

Irina kneeled beside him, dirt smudging her breeches and riding coat. She tried to secure the tangled mess of her hair, and Henry wanted to tell her to leave it. She looked like a beautiful and wild forest sprite. He said nothing, however, watching as she pinned the heavy mass in place. He had no claim on her hair…or any part of her, for that matter.

A few paces away, a massive branch lay in the center of the road. It had splintered in places, the wood having been old and dry. Just beyond that, their horses waited, luckily also unharmed.

"Thank you," Irina said as the loud rattling of carriage tack came up behind them. Billings wouldn't have seen what had happened even from his driver's perch given the sharp curve, which meant the countess would also be none the wiser. Henry was grateful for small mercies. He did not want her unduly worried, and apart from a bruised shoulder and head, he was fine. He got to his feet, his back smarting with pain from the fall and extended his hand to help Irina stand, as well. "For saving my life. Again," she finished.

Henry held onto her fingers, reveling in the difference in size from his own. His hand dwarfed hers, and he was struck with the urge to do it all again. To protect and to keep her safe. He didn't make a reply but released her hand as the door to the barouche opened and his mother called out.

"What in the name of the king is going on out here? Henry? Irina, dear, are you injured?"

"No," they both replied quickly, to set his mother at ease. They grinned at one another, though only briefly.

"A fallen branch," Henry explained, choosing to leave out the rest as Billings hopped down to help clear it from the road.

"Thank goodness," she replied, a bit too dryly. "What a mess that branch made. We are lucky it did not fall right on top of us. Come now, we should be off."

Henry went for the horses. "Will you ride in the barouche now?" he asked Irina. She took her horse's reins and climbed into the saddle. He shook his head and grimaced at the spear of pain. "Fine. Have it your way, princess. But no more racing."

After a few minutes, she turned to him with an impish look. "I have it on good authority that I was in the lead when that branch fell."

"Whose authority?"

"Mine, of course," she quipped. "Which means I won."

Henry favored her with a benevolent nod. "Since I do not wish to call your honor into question, I shall offer a tie. Otherwise I will be forced to call you out at dawn, and I hope to keep my present body intact given your boasts of your consummate skill." He shot her an arch stare. "Which by the way still needs to be demonstrated."

"A tie?" Irina snorted. "That means no one wins."

"Or it means we both win."

Her animated eyes met his, and once more Henry fought the stirrings of lust. There was another, far more pleasurable race he envisioned in which they would both be victors. Irina, riding him as she had the horse, with nothing but abandon and enthusiasm spurring her on. The tantalizing mental image of Irina caught in the throes of passion atop his body nearly unseated him. Henry growled low in his throat and adjusted his suddenly uncomfortable position on the horse. If he wasn't careful, the rest of this journey would be the bloody death of him.

He cleared his too-tight throat. "Why did you learn to fight?"

"I wanted to be able to defend myself," she replied after a prolonged moment, her humor fading rapidly. Henry almost regretted the question and the swift change in her demeanor, but his interest was piqued. Irina carried her father's penknife on her person at all times for protection, she'd told him. Did she truly believe she was in any danger? Henry frowned. Her vicious uncle, tried and convicted of treason against the Russian Tsar and the murder of her parents, and summarily executed, could not hurt her.

"For what reason?" Henry probed gently.

The muscles in her throat worked compulsively as if it were a fight to expel the answer. "After what happened, I don't ever wish to feel defenseless again. If I'd known what I do now, those men who kidnapped me would be dead." She grew quiet. "I was the reason my sister nearly died. Because I was weak." Her voice broke on the last word, her fists tightening on the reins. Frustrated anger streaked across her face. She'd confided something she hadn't meant to say.

"You're not weak."

"I'm not now."

Irina's stare was fierce, her gaze probing his as if daring him to contradict her. In delayed understanding, Henry realized that her past, much like his, tormented her daily. He understood the sway of those inner demons more than she knew, the ones she tried to keep tightly reined, and the residual fears that plagued her. Her uncle could no longer hurt her, but she'd done all she could to ensure that no one else would. Pity and admiration for her courage surged in equal measure in his chest.

"I can see that," he said softly.

Her eyes flashed. "Don't you dare feel sorry for me," she whispered, her voice shaking with suppressed fury, which seemed to be directed more at herself than at him. A mask of shadows descended across her face as she slowed her mount and stopped. She would not look at him. "I think I will ride with the countess for a spell after all if that suits you, Lord Langlevit."

Henry bowed and signaled to Billings. "Of course."

His frown was thoughtful as they resumed their pace once she was ensconced in the carriage. Though clearly Irina loathed it, she preferred the confines to whatever she'd seen in his face or heard in his voice after her whispered confession.

It was yet another thing they shared in common—she didn't like being vulnerable.

Chapter Eight

Stanton Park, Lord and Lady Northridge's Essex home, was somehow more stunning than the last time Irina had visited years before. Though Lord Northridge's family estate, Ferndale, had its considerable charm, there was something about the lushly tended gardens here that reminded Irina of the ones at Volkonsky Palace. Irina eyed the carpet of vibrant blooms that graced the massive courtyard from the window of Lana's upstairs nursery. Most of the similarities, she knew, were due to her sister's specifications.

Watching the delicate swatches of flowers, Irina felt a pang of nostalgia for her home. As much as she loved seeing Lana and playing with her nieces and nephew, there was something about London that didn't sit right. It carried a thread of ugliness that lingered beneath all the brightness, like a tiny piece of lint caught in her eye. Some days, she felt like she never should have come back. There was nothing truly of interest to her here.

Except for Henry.

And the way he looked at her when he thought she wasn't

looking…as if she were something he could never dream of having. Irina knew she'd been infatuated with a phantom from the past, but now, the more she got to know him, the more she craved him. Something in his spirit called to hers, an instinctive feeling that he needed her as much as she needed him. Irina wanted to peel back all his layers, break down all the walls he'd surrounded himself with, and unveil the real Henry hidden behind it all. Hell would freeze over before that happened, she thought with a sigh.

"Is there something in the courtyard that deserves such a scowl?" Lana asked, sipping her chamomile tea.

Irina looked away from the windowpane and pushed a smile to her face. "I'm not scowling, merely thinking."

Lana motioned for the nursemaid to collect Oliver and Kate from the nursery floor where they were nearly falling asleep. "It's long past the time for their nap. You've quite worn them out from your games earlier."

"Where is Sofia?" Irina asked as the nursemaid shuttled the two from the room. She hadn't seen her eldest, seven-year-old niece all morning. "Still with her tutors?"

"Still terrorizing her tutors, you mean," her sister said with a laugh. "She's exactly like her father. Same devilish charm and love of pranks. We've been through two governesses already. She simply refuses to do as she's told, arguing her position with logic better suited to a thirteen-year-old."

Irina lifted an eyebrow. "That she gets from you. She only mimics what she sees." She bent to press a kiss on Lana's head before resuming her seat in the sofa opposite. "And you shouldn't worry too much about that, anyway. She'll be a strong woman, like her mother." Her eyes narrowed on Lana's drawn face. Motherhood had been kind to her, but her normally glowing complexion was pale. "How are you feeling this morning?"

"Mostly tired. The nausea is unbearable. I don't recall

it ever being this bad with Oliver or Kate. Dr. Hargrove has prescribed lots of rest and chamomile tea to settle my stomach."

"It will pass soon," Irina said. "Especially now that I am here to distract you."

"Speaking of distraction, what's this I hear of your antics in London with Max? I know you care for him, but he's a terrible influence on you," Lana said, making Irina frown. "And I also heard that you've already turned down suitor after suitor. Are you intending for this to be a scandalous repeat of last season in Paris?"

The last thing Irina wished to discuss was her friendship with Max and her prospects in London, or worse, have her sister find out about the dratted bets. Lana would not be accepting or forgiving if she knew what Irina had been up to. She gritted her teeth. "It's only been two offers, and I barely recall the gentlemen's names. Anyhow, I don't wish to marry. And, well, Max is Max."

"Max is a scoundrel. If he weren't our relative, you would require multiple chaperones to be in his company. Don't think I'm not aware of the scrapes you've gotten into because of him. And I'm certain I don't have to remind you that this is your third season, Irina. You need to settle down."

"But why?" She glared at her sister and then gentled her expression. "I'm not like you. I'm not perfect and beautiful and poised with lords falling at my feet and spouting sonnets."

"I'll have you know I did not fall," a laughing voice said from the entryway.

"North!" Irina exclaimed, standing to embrace her brother-in-law. Her ill humor dissolved within seconds. She was more than grateful for his timely interruption.

Lord Northridge moved toward where his wife sat, his eyes glinting with mischief. "If I recall correctly, she fell at *my* feet, begging for me to marry—" A swat from Lana cut off his teasing as he bent to kiss her. "Hello, my love."

Something in Irina's heart tugged at the obvious connection between them. She would never have what they did, no matter how many offers she received. Love like theirs was rare, and she envied them that. She was just about to tell them so when a tempest swirled into the nursery and flung itself into Irina's lap.

"Aunt Irina! You must save me from the dragon!" Sofia screamed theatrically, her blond curls a rumpled mess.

Irina stifled a grin and hugged her favorite niece. "Dragon?"

"The governess dragon of deathly horror."

"Come now, she can't be that bad," Irina said. "The governesses your mama and I had were the real monsters. They would threaten to cook our bones and boil our flesh if we did not do our lessons."

Sofia giggled loudly. "Fibber!"

"Your Aunt Irina is right," Lana said. "There's actually a part of her left ear missing from such a punishment."

"Mama," Sofia said with an eye roll and launched herself toward her mother. Lord Northridge stopped her just in time, tossing his daughter over his shoulder.

"Careful, sweetheart, we have to be gentle with your mother," he said before turning to Lana to stroke her cheek. "You should get some rest, darling, and we should be going," he continued, tickling Sofia and striding from the room. "Or you will be late for your riding lesson."

"You should come see my new pony, Aunt Irina," Sofia said upside down.

"I will. Have a good lesson. Perhaps we shall have a race later this afternoon, what do you say to that?" The girl's eyes lit up as she nodded emphatically, and Irina couldn't help smiling.

"You're good with children," her sister commented as

they left. "You should think about having some of your own."

"I am content with yours, thank you."

"Irina—"

She stood, raising a hand and strode back to the window. "I don't want to fight with you about this, Lana. The truth is I have no interest in marrying anyone. And, yes, I do intend for London to be a repeat of Paris: diverting and fun. I won't be anyone's trophy."

"Is it because of Lord Langlevit?"

Irina's breath halted painfully in her lungs. She turned to face her sister, composing her face into a mask of indifference. "What do you mean?"

"You've carried a tendre for him for five years," Lana said quietly. "Ever since you were fourteen. I suspect you still carry it, which is why no one else can measure up."

A hundred reasons, excuses, words popped into Irina's brain. Her sister had always been able to see right through her. She settled for four hard ones. "You mean my infatuation."

"That doesn't mean your feelings weren't real." Her sister rose unsteadily and met her at the window as Irina's fingers wound into the folds of her skirts. "Certain events draw people close, tying them together in inexplicable ways. It's not surprising that you…cared for Henry."

"Hopelessly unrequited, as it were."

"Be that as it may," Lana said. "Henry is not the same man you knew, and I know you can see that for yourself. He has changed."

"Because of France," Irina whispered.

Lana nodded. "He's never confided in me, but yes, Lady Langlevit has suggested that what happened to him is beyond understanding. I fear much of him was lost there." She pulled Irina close. "I don't want you to lose your heart to him and have it broken. You cannot save him, no matter how much you may wish to." Her voice wavered. "Trust me, Henry does not want to be saved."

"How do you know?"

"Because he told me so." In the same breath, Lana's body swayed slightly against hers and Irina wrapped her arms around her.

"What's wrong? Are you well?"

"Yes, I am." Lana gave a reassuring, albeit wan, smile. "Can you ring for my maid? I may need to lie down after all."

Once her sister was ensconced in her room and Irina was convinced it was only fatigue, she made her way downstairs. She did not wish to remain indoors. The walls of the manor felt like they were closing in upon her. Her body felt restless and on edge. She needed a ride. Or a run.

Despite Lana's cautionary statements, Irina wanted to see Henry.

Decide for herself that he was a lost cause.

Save her heart, if she could.

With a firm nod, Irina strode to the foyer and instructed Morley, the butler, that she was in need of a horse. Returning to her chamber, she dressed in one of the special riding habits she'd had designed in Paris, ones that allowed her to ride astride. She loathed riding sidesaddle. The earl hadn't seemed too shocked by her unexpected attire the day before, and she was now in the country with everyone of importance still in London.

As a lady, she had no business riding unchaperoned and uninvited to the earl's residence, but perhaps, if necessary, she could simply say she'd come to visit Lady Langlevit, who still resided in a collection of rooms at Hartstone.

Hartstone was not far, and she made the trip in under thirty minutes. Her heart racing, she knocked at the door, which was opened by Henry and the countess's ancient butler, who'd been with them in Cumbria, as well. Carlton's face cracked a doting smile as he ushered her into the foyer and bowed low. "Princess Volkonsky."

"You look well, Carlton," she said with a smile. "Is Lady Langlevit at home?"

"She is not, Your Highness."

"And his lordship?"

"You have just missed him. He's taking a tour of the north end of the estate." He peered at her. "Shall I leave any message?"

"No, thank you, Carlton. It was impulsive of me to arrive unannounced. Actually, please do convey my thanks to Lady Langlevit for allowing me to accompany her yesterday. I shall see myself out. Good day."

"And to you, Your Highness."

Outside, she saddled the horse and made to return to Stanton Park. She paused at the end of the long drive and studied the north end of the estate over her shoulder. If Henry had only just left, she would be able to catch up to him. *You are behaving scandalously*, her inner voice warned, but Irina paid it no notice.

Her inner voice sounded too much like Lana.

Turning her mount about and consulting the rising sun's position, she headed north. She had no idea where she was going, but she followed what looked like a well-used bridle path.

"This was a silly idea," she said to herself after a quarter of an hour had passed with no sign of anyone, much less the elusive Earl of Langlevit. The manicured grass of the landscaped gardens had turned into something wilder, and the surrounding wood had thickened considerably. Defeated, she was about to turn around when she heard a soft nicker. Following the sound, Irina found herself in a small clearing with a stable. She recognized Henry's favorite horse. Dismounting and latching hers to the fence post alongside it, she stroked its velvet nose. The horse's flanks were still warm, as if Henry had only just left.

"And where is that wandering master of yours?" she asked in a whisper.

Leaving the horse, Irina walked to the far side of the stable barn and her jaw dropped open in wonder. Henry hadn't been joking when he'd said that his course was fashioned after a military training area. Her eyes fairly goggled at the start of the path, which included some kind of woven rope ladder and a massive wooden wall pierced with studs.

She knew she should turn around and go back the way she'd come. But seeing the course was like a gauntlet being thrown. Irina grinned. There was no chance she was going home.

Adrenaline thumped in her chest as she bent to tighten her boots and then discarded the swallowtail coat. It would only get in the way. With a running leap, she threw herself onto the roped grid, hauling arm over arm as she grappled her way across some kind of mud pit. The studded wall was trickier. It was built for the span of a man, but with some creative maneuvering, she was able to get herself to the top. She rappelled deftly down the other side, feeling pleased with herself.

"That wasn't so bad," she said aloud, making for the next set.

Thirty minutes later, she was cursing, instead. Her lungs ached as if they were on fire. It had felt like she'd been climbing up for hours. She'd wrenched her ankle jumping from rock to rock, and was currently attempting to slide down a gravelly hill on her bottom. It was not pleasant. Or fun. Or fast.

If the earl had come this way, he was miles ahead of her by now. Dusting herself off, she navigated another rock wall and hopped across a series of carefully placed beams. Every muscle in her body burned, but even though it was difficult, Irina couldn't help feeling a fierce burst of pleasure beneath the ache. The exertion was exactly what she'd needed.

A flimsy slatted bridge hung across a narrow gorge and swung in the breeze. It was dizzying to look down, so she hastened across as quickly as she could. Every step made it sway precariously. Gulping, she flung herself the last four feet to the other side and collapsed onto the ground. She lay there, staring up at the bright blue sky. Lord help her, she wanted to laugh with pure exhilaration.

Pushing to her feet, she followed the rest of the winding path. It seemed easy, until it opened up to a precipice. She had indeed climbed upward, she realized. The winding path through the wood had led her up to where a narrow waterfall tumbled to a pool below. Looking over the edge, she could see the stable down in the distance. It felt like she was on top of the world.

"What the hell are you doing here?"

Her breath trickled to honey in her throat as she turned. The earl stood there, a bronzed god with wide sculpted shoulders and a magnificently bare chest that tapered to a trim waist. Good Lord, he was mesmerizing, like the nude statues she'd seen in sculpture gardens in France. She wanted to stare at him, devour his shirtless nudity to her fill, memorize every single stunning line of hard, muscled flesh so that she could analyze it later at her leisure.

Beads of sweat dampened the front of him, turning the waistband of his fitted tan breeches to the color of dark wet leather. Irina couldn't speak, much less catch a breath at the sight of the hard, defined ridges of his stomach. She dared not look lower. Dragging her burning gaze upward, her attention caught on several raised scars reaching from beneath his arms to the sides of his torso. Irina noticed other details, too, and what looked like bunched tissue at the tops of his shoulders. They did not detract from his beauty or strength, but something in her heart twinged all the same.

Seeing her stare, Henry backed away, keeping his front to her, and reached for his discarded shirt. Once reclothed, Henry strode back toward her. Swallowing hard, Irina's gaze lifted to his, and she nearly retreated right off the edge of the cliff. He was furious, his anger fairly snapping off him as his eyes roved her from head to toe.

He clenched his jaw. "Why are you here?"

She blinked, her mouth opening and closing. "I…had to give you a message from your mother."

"My mother?" he said, staring at her blankly. "You followed me here?"

"Yes." Her excuse rang emptily in her own ears as she floundered in the lie, and then gave up. "I needed to find you," she admitted.

"You fool," he growled. "Don't you know you could have been killed?"

"Killed? It is hardly a deadly course," she replied, lifting her chin in the face of his fury. "How do you get down?"

"You jump."

"Oh." She looked down and grinned. "Scary. I can see—"

Her words cut from her lips as a piece of the cliff crumbled from beneath her sole and she lost her balance. Strong fingers curled round her wrist, hauling her body back to safety and slamming her into the solid, immovable column of his body. Every tingling inch of her was plastered to every inch of him. Henry's eyes glittered into hers, their breaths coming in short pants as she clutched at his arms, one hand lifting to thread into the hair at her nape. With an animalistic growl, he bent his head.

Irina met him in the middle.

Henry claimed her mouth as if he owned it with hot, savage fervor. She welcomed it, savoring the arousing taste of sweat and whiskey. Heat shot through her in lightning bursts, pulsating in the area between her hips—hips that were currently glued to his, like every other shamelessly willing part of her. Henry nibbled across her lips, tearing away to nudge wet bites and scrapes along her throat, only to return to ravage her mouth, his tongue teasing hers with silky nudges and velvet licks that made her insides dissolve to water.

Sweet Lord, the man knew how to kiss.

Running her hands up and down his arms, Irina dragged his head closer, luring his tongue back into her mouth and circling hers around it with a purr of pure feminine satisfaction. The mix of lust and adrenaline shooting through her veins was like nothing she'd ever felt. The tips of her breasts ached, pressed against him as they were, and she had the indecent desire to drag them across the sprinkling of bronze hair on his chest that she'd glimpsed during her earlier inspection.

Slipping her fingers beneath his untucked shirt, she reached upward to find puckered skin.

Henry froze.

He dragged his lips away with a strangled groan. "Enough."

. . .

Struggling to catch his breath and his sanity, Henry wanted to wring her lovely neck as much as he wanted to continue plundering her sultry, decadent mouth. Christ. What had he been thinking? That was just it. He *hadn't* thought. All of his discipline, his willpower, had disappeared. He'd only reacted...as he always seemed to do when it came to Irina. More so here in these woods, where he always gave in to his intuition and base instinct. If she hadn't touched his back and jolted him out of the moment, he might still have been lost to the fog of lust blanketing them.

Henry couldn't believe she had followed him, but he had to admit it wasn't surprising. Irina was fearless.

And bold.

And too bloody tempting.

Standing before him, she was a mess and covered in dirt, but the sight of her made his blood heat. That glorious hair of hers tumbled in silken waves down her back, making him want to sink his fingers into it once more. Henry wanted to rip the sodden, muddy waistcoat from her body, run his palms over her bare torso and around her trim bottom, still clad in those indecent breeches. He wanted to peel them from her, to kiss every inch of velvety skin, tease her with his hands and lips and tongue. Right here on the ground. She would let him, he knew, because she wanted it, too. No woman had ever met his need the way she had, the force of her desire matching his, beat for beat.

But defiling Princess Irina was not an option.

It hadn't been before, and now that Rose had replied to his proposal, just that morning, with her conditional acceptance, it most assuredly was not.

Clenching his teeth, Henry backed away from the magnetic lure of her. No matter how many times he told himself to stay away, he could never do it. No woman had ever affected him the way she had, driving him half delirious with lust. Even now, his body craved to return to hers, to feel its long warm length plied against his...her breasts crushed to his chest, her thighs wedged against him. One kiss and he was as hard as the rock beneath his feet. Henry stalked to the far side of the space, attempting to get his rampaging desire under control. He'd meant what he'd said about not being the right man for her.

He could never be a true husband.

Rose was different. She had consented to be married to him in name only, as a friend and nothing more. One of the conditions of her acceptance was the maintenance of separate residences, which suited him well. Per her letter, she neither wanted nor required his love or his fidelity. She already had a son, which boded well for begetting him an heir. And once that was complete, their entire marriage would be a matter of public record to satisfy the ludicrous Langlevit codicil. Rose no more wished to share his bed than he wished to share hers, and both of them would be all the more content for it.

Henry could not see Irina being so accepting of such a situation—separate homes, separate beds, separate lives. Nor would she deserve that. She deserved a real marriage with a devoted spouse…nights spent in her husband's arms without the fear of being harmed in her sleep by a raging man possessed by unshakable demons. She deserved everything he was incapable of offering, and more.

He cleared his throat. "Irina, this cannot happen again."

"Marry me."

His heart stopped. "What?" he bit out.

She drew a controlled breath. "Your mother told me about the stipulation in the letters patent of your title during the carriage ride to Essex. You could marry me."

"She should not have burdened you with that."

Irina stepped closer, seemingly confident in herself and what she was saying. "It is no burden. Marry me, Henry, and save your title."

"I cannot."

"Why?"

Here it was. He could end it once and for all. Henry knew how she felt about him, the infatuation she'd borne for so many years. He cared for her, too, but they both knew he was no longer the man she'd known…the man she held in such high esteem. He'd made that more than clear. Henry steeled himself for the stroke he was about to deliver. It was for her own good. And his.

"Because what I feel for you is not as remarkable as what you are clearly imagining it to be."

She laughed in disbelief, but not before he saw the flash of surprise in her eyes. "Not remarkable?" she repeated, her voice rising in octave as her gaze slid low. "Not to be vulgar, but I am not so naive as to believe that the way we've kissed is *un*remarkable."

"Not to be vulgar," he mocked her. "But you *are* naive if you believe this isn't a typical male response. Or perhaps you have not been kissed very much. Trust me, it could be any other female standing there and my reaction would be the same."

Henry braced himself against the shocked hurt brimming in her eyes. Regardless of her bravado, he could not fall prey to her tender feelings. He had to end the cycle, and for that, he needed to be brutal. *Ruthless.*

He waved a careless arm. "You could just as easily be Lady La Valse, or a courtesan from a gaming hell. It's all the same to me. I am a red-blooded man, and it only takes a beautiful, willing woman, after all, which is what you are, but nothing more than that. Do not deceive yourself otherwise."

Irina sucked in a gasp and bit her lip, but Henry forged on even as his heart shriveled in his chest at his horrible, unforgivable words. "And as much as I appreciate your kind offer, Your Highness, I am already betrothed to someone else."

"You are a bastard," she whispered.

"I told you as much."

"I wish I'd never met you." Her eyes were bright with the sheen of tears. "The old Henry would despise you. He'd be ashamed of who you have become."

With that, she turned and jumped from the cliff's edge. Henry darted forward, what was left of his heart throbbing in panic at the splash below. But she surfaced without so much as a shout. He stood there, watching her as she swam the length of the pool to where her horse was waiting. Irina did not look back, not once, before saddling her horse and riding away, out of his life. He'd done it, pushed her away. He should be happy, and yet it felt like everything around him had turned to gray, as if the world had suddenly been deprived of all its color. That was his world—one that was gray and dark and angry. Just because an angel had appeared for a moment and driven the shadows away didn't mean he deserved any of it.

Irina was right about one thing though—he'd never despised himself more than he did at that moment.

Chapter Nine

In the two weeks Irina had been away from London, the city had shaken off its winter shell and cloaked itself in a bright yellow-green shawl of tree buds and new grass. It had disappointed her, coming back to town and finding it all awash with spring. She'd looked forward to the dusty, crowded, and pale city as she'd left it. After suffering the last fortnight in the lush countryside, drowning in lovely breezes, fresh air, and birdsong, she'd only wanted to return to London and ensconce herself in surroundings that matched the state of her heart.

But London was all too bright and healthy, and as she'd ridden back into town the same way she'd left it, traveling alongside Lady Langlevit's barouche, she'd seen far too many people out and about with smiles upon their faces.

Henry had not been with them on their ride south from Essex. He'd left Hartstone only a few days after Irina had made, quite possibly, the biggest mistake of her life by setting out on that damned course of his. Not one hour of one day had passed since that she did not spend torturing herself over what she'd done or what she'd said.

What she'd asked.

Good Lord, she'd *proposed*. She'd asked the Earl of Langlevit to *marry* her.

The humiliation of his cruel rejection still made her ill to her stomach. Irina placed a hand to her waist and closed her eyes, shutting out her reflection in the vanity mirror. She was seated before it, her maid, Jane, putting the finishing touches on her hair.

"Your Highness?" the young girl squeaked, her voice so like a small mouse's it made the hairs on the back of Irina's neck stand on end. "Are you not well?"

She shook her head and opened her eyes again, the surge of unpleasantness receding. Though not very far.

"It's just a spell," she replied, forcing her voice to push through the lump in her throat. The one that had been sitting there ever since that afternoon at Hartstone, growing larger by the day.

"The traveling must have made me ill," she added, deciding to blame her weakness on the six-hour journey she and Lady Langlevit had taken that very morning. They had left before dawn in order to arrive back at Devon Place before the ball that evening.

The invitation to the Earl of Langlevit and Lady Carmichael's engagement gala had arrived at Hartstone less than a week ago, and from that moment forward, Lady Langlevit had been planning their return to London…and Irina had been vacillating between desolation and fury.

She hadn't wanted to return to London at all, and she certainly did not want to go to the ball at Leicester Square in less than an hour. But with Lady Langlevit as her chaperone, there was no choice in the matter. She would go. She would congratulate the earl and his chosen bride, and she would hopefully get through it all without a single tear. Without a single bitter word spoken from her tongue.

He did not want her. He could never love her. He'd made that blisteringly clear, and Irina would not disgrace herself any further.

"You look beautiful, Your Highness," Jane said as Irina got to her feet. The dress was a heavy affair, with layers of dark purple satin and lace designed to bring out the violet in Irina's eyes. The bodice was not as low or revealing as the others in her wardrobe, and the waistline was also obscured by a scalloped, beaded sash.

"I look like I am attending a funeral service," Irina murmured in response. Jane twittered uncomfortably, as if she didn't know how to respond without agreeing and insulting her.

Indeed, she felt like she was going to a funeral. In a way, she supposed she was.

A knock landed upon her door, and Jane went to open it. Irina expected it to be Lady Langlevit, come to fetch her, but instead, it was a footman. Andrews had sent him. There was a visitor here for Irina.

"Lord Remi," Jane said in a conspiratorial whisper as she quickly straightened the beaded sash. Dots of color on the maid's cheeks spoke to her admiration for Max.

Irina smiled. "He is a scoundrel, you know," she told her, taking up her gloves and moving for the door.

"Oh yes, I know," she replied softly, the shine of excitement in her eyes surprising Irina immensely. Perhaps this mousy maid was not as meek as her voice led her to appear.

With a laugh, and a most welcome bob of her spirits, Irina descended into the foyer. Max waited in front of the enormous gilt mirror hanging upon one of the walls, reflecting the stairwell and Max's impeccably dashing evening clothes. Irina shook her head.

"No wonder all the maids are mad about you," she said as she took the last step. Andrews rushed forward with her cape and helped settle it around her shoulders. Then with a bow, left them.

Max had his hands in his trouser pockets, his cravat in a loose knot that suggested a lady—or lord—had recently been playing with it in an attempt to reach his skin.

"What about the footmen?" he asked, and Irina shushed him with a wave of her hand.

"They are as well, I'm sure," she whispered. "What are you doing here? I don't recall asking you to escort Lady Langlevit and me to the ball."

They had exchanged at least a half dozen letters over the two weeks she'd been in Essex, and she'd told him everything about the disastrous afternoon in Henry's woods. She'd held nothing back, either. With Max, Irina knew she could be honest with all her flaws and mistakes and injury, and he would not judge her.

"I invited myself. After your last letters, I decided you might have a need for me tonight."

"Oh, Max," she said, crossing to him. He took his hands from his pockets and wrapped her into an embrace. "It's going to be awful." Her words were muffled by his crisp and spotless jacket.

"Come now, you are going to be far too busy to be mulling over that idiot."

"He is not an idiot," she said, pulling away from Max before her hair was ruined. She didn't know why she defended Henry. It was instinctual, perhaps.

"Whether he is or isn't, you're going to be the object of attention tonight, not him and his nobody bride-to-be."

She rearranged her cape and looked away from him. "Oh, don't be cruel. She might be perfectly nice."

Irina didn't want her to be, though. She wanted this Lady Carmichael to be perfectly terrible so that she could properly hate her.

Max frowned. "I have no idea who she is."

"Why should you? She's from Essex, Lady Langlevit says."

"I like knowing things about people," he muttered. "Strangers are boring."

"You like gossip," she corrected with an arched brow, meant to chastise. However, Max merely shrugged his agreement.

"I will have some for you by the end of the evening, I promise," he said. But Irina didn't care for gossip about Henry's betrothed. She knew enough already. He'd chosen Lady Carmichael and rejected Irina, and that was more than enough knowledge to keep her in a constant state of misery.

"And what do you mean, I will be the object of attention tonight?"

With that, Max's frown over not having any good gossip on Lady Carmichael changed to an expression of mischief.

"Have you forgotten how popular you are now that men are wagering small fortunes on you?"

Irina felt a new sickness in her stomach that had nothing at all to do with Henry or his ice-cold heart. She had, in fact, forgotten all about that silly betting book at White's.

"They are calling this newest wager 'The Quest for the Queen.'"

She began to pace the foyer, her palms sweating in her gloves. She'd told Lana that she wouldn't be anyone's trophy, but that was exactly what she'd become. A bloody prize. "I am a princess, not a queen."

Max sighed. "Yes, but that doesn't have the alliteration, now does it?"

"What kind of wager is it?"

"The big one, darling. Each gentleman nominates himself as your future husband, and the winner will take all." He grinned wickedly at her. "I have half a mind to enter and marry you myself. Think of it, we could go to Italy or Greece with our winnings."

"Lord Remi," Lady Langlevit said as she descended the stairs, Andrews at her side. He held his arm at a stiff right angle in order to allow Henry's mother to lean on him for support. She reached the bottom step breathless, her eyes blinking in what appeared to be fatigue.

"My lady," Max said, dipping into a low—almost unnecessarily so—bow. "I've come to escort you and Her Highness to Leicester Square, if you are not averse to the idea."

She laughed, though to Irina it most certainly sounded strained.

"Are you feeling well enough to attend?" she asked, touching Lady Langlevit's arm as she waited for her cape.

"Of course, of course," she said with a dismissive wave of her hand. "It is my son's engagement ball. I would not miss it for anything."

Irina couldn't argue with that. She knew the countess loved her son, and being an only child, Henry was all she had. She had been waiting a long time for him to marry and give her grandchildren.

At that thought, Irina felt the color in her cheeks drain. The stone in her throat tumbled and grew. Henry would have children with Lady Carmichael. He'd make love to her and stand by her as she increased, much the way Gray stood by Lana, admiring her so openly. So completely. Irina knew that Henry thought himself incapable of love, but he *would* love… for his children, and for the right woman. The knot in her throat throbbed.

"The carriage awaits," Andrews announced.

The drive to Henry's home was too brief. Before she could extinguish visions of him holding a swaddled infant in his arms, gazing lovingly into its little face, and then shifting that adoring gaze to his wife, a faceless woman in Irina's mind, they had arrived and the threat of uncontrollable despair loomed ever closer.

It was, she realized, the first time she'd ever been to his home on Leicester Square. Four stories of rusty brick facade with cream molding and trim, large windows on every floor, except for the attics where the roof scrolled down over smaller windows that belonged, no doubt, to the servants he employed. It was a grand home, and one glance was all it took for Irina to receive the impression of stoic, everlasting importance the architects had most likely intended generations ago.

Two liveried footmen stood at the front door, guttering torches hanging from sconces and warming her face as she approached. Her nerves were a bundle in her chest and stomach, and blast it, her palms were still damp. She required a drink, and the moment her cape had been shed and they had been escorted into the ballroom on the second floor, she whisked a tall flute of champagne from a passing tray.

"I thought you hated champagne," Max said, still at her side. Lady Langlevit had been surrounded by guests longing to congratulate her as soon as they had entered the ballroom.

"I would drink ale from a barrel if I had to, Max. I have to get through this evening."

He touched the base of the glass and stopped her from downing the contents. "Just stay sober, my darling."

She glared at him, but decided to heed his advice. And when Gwen found them a few minutes later, already giggling with a nearly empty glass of champagne in her hand, Irina was glad she had. The last thing she needed to do was drink too much and lose control of her senses.

Gwen peered over the crush of people, presumably to get a look at the lady herself. "I hear she is unrivaled," she whispered in a not-so-soft way. "Closing in on thirty years, but like her name, she is the perfect English rose."

Lady Carmichael was a widow, Irina knew. The countess had explained about Henry's best childhood friend, Sir Carmichael, and how the man had died a few years ago unexpectedly while on a foxhunt. His horse had slipped on a particularly rocky outcropping, and Sir John had fallen to his death. They'd had one son. Perhaps Lady Carmichael would be the one to finally calm Henry's demons. Irina had only seemed to incite them.

"Darling Irina," Gwen said loudly, drawing her from her thoughts. "May I present Lord Loftham and His Grace, the Duke of Moveton. Both have been pestering me for an introduction." She indicated the two gentlemen behind her. "You'd think they expect you to disappear at the stroke of midnight the way they've been hovering."

Irina knew well the reason they, in addition to the handful of unfamiliar gentlemen who had avidly noted her arrival, sought to meet her. She blinked, but nodded gracefully as they each took her hand. "A pleasure," she murmured and then practically shoved Max in front of her. "Are you acquainted with Lord Remi?"

The rest of the introductions and pleasantries faded into background noise as Irina sensed rather than saw Henry's approach. It was odd how aware she was of him, but then again, it had always been that way. She'd always known the minute he arrived at Marsden Hall in Cumbria as if they'd been somehow tethered to each other. She drew in a harassed breath, her fingers tightening on her fan as they stopped to greet the two gentlemen she'd just met.

Irina wished to press backward, against the wall. Into the wallpaper, even. But she could not avoid the crescendo of voices that heralded the couple's arrival. And so she stood, her back ramrod straight, and looked Lord Langlevit and Lady Carmichael straight in the eye to offer her congratulations. Though Henry was unsmiling and his face unreadable, the force of his presence was magnetic. And Gwen was right—Lady Carmichael was as she expected. Beautiful and poised. Perfect in every way.

As greetings were made and felicitations exchanged, Irina heard none of it, even though she smiled and nodded at all the right places. When they moved past to greet the other arrivals, she felt Henry's gaze linger on her for a prolonged moment, but Irina refused to acknowledge it. Instead, she laughed brightly at something Gwen said, her body aching slightly as he drew away.

Good. That's over and done with, she told herself firmly, draining the contents of her champagne glass. Ignoring Lords Loftham and Moveton who kept darting hopeful glances in her direction, she linked her hand into Max's and smiled brightly. "Shall we dance?"

"But of course," he replied with a jaunty wink. "I am at my lady's disposal."

Irina smirked at her friend, her sadness fading. "Is that the line that usually works for you?"

"No, darling, I usually add 'in the bedchamber' at the end. Never fails."

She chucked him in the arm. "You are incorrigible."

As they strolled toward the ballroom, stopping to greet people they knew, several other young gentlemen surrounded them, each vying for a space on her dance card. Irina knew her catapulting popularity was only because of the wagers, but she vowed to make the most of the rest of the season. She would wear the mask and play the part of the lofty, untouchable princess, and then she would return to St. Petersburg to nurse her wounds in private. But first, she would laugh and flirt, and teach these unprincipled, betting gentlemen a lesson.

In hindsight, Max's idea was brilliant.

Grinning, she tugged on Max's sleeve and drew him off to the side. "How much is the pot for this Quest for the Queen up to?"

He eyed her. "Nearly forty thousand pounds."

She stifled a gasp. It was an absurd amount of money. Why, men of solid fortune lived on a fraction of that sum for an entire year. Forty thousand pounds would afford a man a lavish lifestyle for a decade. And the pot was not even yet at its peak.

"How does it work exactly?" she asked, her mind beginning to spin in a new direction.

"A gentleman nominates himself as a contender and places his wager of two thousand pounds. If he wins your hand, he wins the entire pot." Max lifted an amused eyebrow. "The two bucks falling at your feet a moment ago, Moveton and Loftham, are the latest entrants."

Two thousand pounds, just for the chance to win her hand. She laughed softly. No. For the chance to win an unrivaled fortune. Irina herself truly had nothing to do with it. No man who entered the competition had done so because they cared for her.

"What is so amusing?" Max asked.

"I will not accept any of them. They must know this," she said.

There was but one man she wanted to kneel before her, a proposal spilling from his lips. But that proposal, those words she yearned for with a physical ache, had been said to another.

"Why should they know?" Max replied. "Look around us. Every young woman in this room is on the hunt for a husband. The men of this society expect nothing less from a woman." He lowered his lips closer to her ear so that he could whisper. "They are arrogant enough to believe *they* are *your* prize, Irina."

She wanted to laugh at the idea, but couldn't muster the energy. He was right. The self-important men of the *ton* were perfectly content treating marriage as if it were a game to be won. The thought of them cheering for the victor made her cringe. Irina glanced at Max. He'd joked about entering the pot earlier and dashing off to Italy or Greece with the winnings.

"Put your name in," she said.

Max pulled back and stared at her. "What?"

"There is no one for me," she went on. *Not anymore.* "And there is a fortune to be had."

He stiffened under her hands. "What makes you think I need money?"

Irina shook her head, flustered, and hoping she hadn't insulted him. "Of course I didn't mean you need the money, Max. When we win, we'll donate it to one of the Duke of Bradburne's children's hospitals."

His shoulders softened as he visibly relaxed. "My darling princess, winning involves more than just a betrothal announcement that we can break at a later date. It means taking real vows."

She stumbled on the next step as a stab of panic hit her in the chest. Marriage vows with Max. Well. She didn't love him the way she'd thought she loved Henry, and she certainly didn't have the same attraction to him. He was a friend. The very best of friends. And though he was technically a cousin, they were removed enough to be legally married without contest. As Max righted her step and they continued to dance, Irina realized she would much rather be married to her friend, someone she trusted and liked and could laugh with, than a man who was only out for money and bragging rights.

"It wouldn't have to be a *true* marriage," she whispered, widening her eyes to make her point without blatantly stating that they would not have to share a marriage bed.

Max peered at her. "You are serious."

"You were the one who suggested it in Lady Langlevit's foyer," she whispered again, suddenly feeling the urge to flee.

The last time she'd proposed, it had been to Henry, and he'd roundly rejected her. My God. If Max rejected her, too, Irina would not be able to staunch the sobs that waited just behind her mask of indifference.

"I did," he said, gliding smoothly as they danced. Thank heavens one of them was paying attention to their feet. "As a lark."

She felt the floor beginning to soften, and all she wanted was for it to open and swallow her whole. He was going to say no, tell her it was a terrible idea. And maybe it was. But the more she thought about it, the more she wanted it. If she were married, there would be no more need for her to present herself on the marriage mart. People would finally stop gossiping and leave her alone. She could return to St. Petersburg and live the life she knew and felt comfortable with.

She could go home and never have to see Henry again.

"However," Max went on, and when she looked up to him again, saw his lips pursed. He was thinking. "The idea has merit. Let's be honest: I would disappoint any young woman who entered a marriage to me who did not know of my… preferences. You know who I am, and you've always accepted me."

She waited on tenterhooks, the ballroom around her spinning.

"I daresay we'll be friends forever. Why not attach ourselves officially? I won't stop you from falling in love whenever you find a handsome beau, and you won't stop me. We could live separately and happily so. It's done often enough." A playful smile broke out on his lips.

"So you'll do it?" she said, so relieved she felt sick to her stomach.

His smile darkened. "I only wish you'd had this clever idea before I bought those Hanoverians and the curricle. I'm afraid for the moment, I'm rather short of the two thousand pounds it would take to enter the pot."

She wanted to jump and embrace him, she was so happy. Why hadn't she thought of such a brilliant scheme earlier? "I'll give to you," she said breathlessly.

"If that is what you wish," he said, his brows pulling together. Perhaps out of injured pride. As far as Irina knew, his mother afforded him a secret allowance twice a year, but clearly he had spent too much too fast.

"It is," she said, squeezing his shoulder.

His smile returned. "Then we are in this together." Max's grin widened to something wolfish as he lifted her by the waist and spun her in an elegant circle. "Shall we stir up the competition then? Give London a show to end all shows before we waltz into the sunset?"

Irina stared at her friend, her pulse hammering. She had nothing to lose. It would be the best thing for them both. "That sounds like a marvelous idea."

Chapter Ten

The Kensington ball was always one of the top crushes of the season, and it was the sole reason that Henry held up yet another marble pillar in yet another crowded ballroom.

He tugged at his expertly tied—and tight as a garrote—cravat and took a long draught of his whiskey. He would give anything to be at Hartstone in quiet and privacy, running his course and his demons into the ground, instead of here, surrounded by people he hardly knew and making small conversation about nothing of consequence. But receiving a thousand and one invitations was part and parcel of an earl announcing a betrothal agreement during the height of the season. And he owed it to Rose to do it right.

Henry watched as she danced with Stephen Kensington, Earl of Thorndale, their host and his longtime friend. Rose was exquisite, there was no denying it. Her peach-tinted complexion set off her blond hair and blue eyes to perfection, and her slender form was full and curved in all the right places. She had a reserved sort of grace that came across as both admirable and unattainable. While Henry could appreciate her beauty as he would a fine piece of art, there was something missing.

Of their own volition, his eyes flicked to the laughing sprite dancing in the arms of Lord Remi, and his fingers clenched involuntarily around his snifter. He'd have expected the sight of Irina to become easier the more they saw of each other, but the invisible fist punch to the gut was always the same: swift and brutal.

Irina and Remi made a striking couple, his fairness complementing her dark beauty. Clearly, they had dressed to suit, she in a vibrant emerald green gown and he in a matching-hued waistcoat. Henry couldn't curb the scowl that rose to his face. From what he had heard and seen, they had been taking London by storm the past three weeks. The two of them had become the light of the season and *ton* favorites, their popular presence coveted at every ball and every social event.

As a result, it was no surprise that the betting book at White's had also gained notoriety with gentlemen placing wagers for winners as they would a horse race. It made Henry sick to his stomach, but it had taken on a frenzied life of its own. Every possible thing was accorded a price—a smile, a dance, a laugh. He could no more stop it than he could an approaching storm. It would have to run its course. Something else would take their collective fancy. Eventually.

Henry could not fault them for their fascination with the princess. Irina lived with such vivacity and passion, and her beauty was only enhanced by her animation…the *joie de vivre* she possessed. Even while dancing, her hands did not stop moving, her eyes sparkling. It was the same abandon with which she did everything else. Kissing, for example. Henry scowled into his drink.

"Is the whiskey not up to your standard, Langlevit?" a man on the other side of the pillar drawled. "I fear Thorn may take offense at your glower."

The Duke of Bradburne smirked, and Henry cursed how easily the object of his thoughts affected him. "Thorn is busy enough with my fiancée, and the whiskey is above measure, Hawk." Though Lord Bradburne had inherited a dukedom and his father's title, he was still known to his friends by a shortened name derived from one of his lesser titles, the Marquess of Hawksfield.

"Congratulations, by the way," Hawk said, lifting his own glass. "We have not seen each other since your announcement. My wife has taken it upon herself to retire to Worthington Abbey every other fortnight to check on Lady Northridge. Our daughters seem to favor the country more to town, as well."

Henry lifted his glass, accepting the toast. It was on the tip of his tongue to make a remark about Irina being as solicitous with Lana, but he wisely kept his mouth shut. Hawk was not an unintelligent man. "How are your children?" he asked instead, opting for the safer turn in conversation.

"Much like my duchess—the girls are intent on putting as many gray hairs on my head as possible." The duke smiled. "Though they are not nearly as mischievous as their little brother. How is Lady Langlevit? I heard she wasn't feeling well as of late."

Henry had known the whispers would quickly blanket London, but he still felt an edge of discomfort hearing it from his friend's lips.

"My mother is as well as can be expected, thank you for asking. She needs peace and quiet, and most of all, rest," Henry replied, a pang in his chest at the thought of her.

Ever since she'd seemed to stumble at the dinner she'd hosted early in the season, Henry had noticed more instances of her fatigue and loss of balance. He'd called for their family physician, who had delivered a mixed diagnosis: Lady Langlevit was indeed declining, however she was still strong of spirit, and Dr. Hargrove had stressed that her will would carry her for quite some time. Henry certainly hoped so.

While she had fully intended to remain in London, his mother had returned to Hartstone soon after his engagement ball.

"We wish her a quick recovery," Hawk said. "Please give her our regards."

"Thank you, I will."

Henry studied the man who had always been more of an observer than an active participant of the *ton* until his duchess had stepped into his life. Until recently, he and the duke had never been more than acquaintances, though he'd once considered making an offer to Hawk's half sister, Eloise, to fulfill the terms of his inheritance. She'd been caught and killed in the crossfire of the notorious Masked Marauder who had terrorized London five years before. Disfigured by burns to her face from a childhood fire, Henry had felt sorry for her, having been on the receiving end of a fire himself. A marriage to Eloise would have been a kindness, he knew, but beyond that, it would have been a means to an end.

"Lady Bradburne looks well," Henry said, watching as the duchess danced beside Rose in a rousing Scotch reel that had them both breathlessly laughing. He couldn't help noticing that Irina was now dancing with Lord Northridge, and inexplicably, the gathering tension left his limbs in a slow trickle. "I take it family life agrees with you despite the threat of gray hairs."

"It does," Hawk agreed. "As you will find, as well. Lady Carmichael is lovely."

Henry nodded brusquely. "We've known each other a long time."

He knew he should say more. Compliment her in some way. Something that pointed to why he and Rose would be happy together. But he could land upon nothing.

"Speaking of brides," Hawk filled in when Henry remained silent, "it looks like your old ward will have no shortage of suitors, either. Though I do hope she chooses one better than my whelp of a brother-in-law making a fool of himself in that set."

Once upon a time, the rivalry between Lord Northridge and the duke had been no secret, but now Hawk was only joking. Lady Bradburne's brother, Lord Northridge, was an excellent father and husband, and Henry knew that Hawk trusted North implicitly. Henry also knew from speaking with Lana that she was deliriously happy. "Princess Irina has certainly blossomed into a beauty," Hawk continued.

Henry felt his scowl return. He was well aware of how beautiful she had become. "She is on the verge of making a spectacle of herself."

"I take it you've heard about the wagers?" Hawk asked. "I've no taste for such bets myself, but the princess has become quite the prize."

Henry's lips thinned. "Quite so."

Hawk's gaze centered on where Irina was dancing with his brother-in-law. "She appears to be enjoying the attention. North reports that ever since she accepted the offer to stay with Lady Dinsmore, the invitations have been appearing at Bishop House en masse. Apparently, she declines more than she accepts, and yet she is still out almost every night."

Irina could not have stayed at Devon Place alone, without a chaperone, and so when Lady Langlevit had returned to Essex for rest, Lady Bradburne's mother had happily stepped in and offered to host the princess. Henry respected Lord and Lady Dinsmore, but he was not at all pleased with the rest of the situation.

"She should be in Essex with her sister instead of cavorting about here with that cousin of hers," Henry snapped, unable to help himself.

"Cousin?"

"Lord Remi. By marriage, twice removed." *So not really a cousin at all*, he added sourly in his own head. "That peacock assured me earlier this spring that he had Irina's best interests at heart. Now, however, it seems he has no care for her reputation. And it appears neither does she."

"Perhaps Princess Irina only wants for a strong husband to take her in hand."

"Oh, is that what you did, Your Grace?" a laughing voice said as the duchess approached, her eyes glinting with humor. "Took me in hand?"

The duke gazed down at his wife. "Firmly, as it were."

"I'll remember that," Lady Bradburne teased and turned to Henry. "You are not dancing, Lord Langlevit?"

Henry tapped his leg where a bullet had torn through years before on the Peninsula. "I fear my body can only handle a few dances a time, Your Grace, and I would not want to deprive anyone of a more capable partner."

"I am so sorry," she said, an immediate look of regret on her face.

"Don't be, it was a long time ago," Henry reassured her. "I much prefer the slower dances to the faster ones anyway. Gives a man a chance to get to know a lady."

"A novel idea." Hawk's lips curved into a knowing grin, and he bowed to his wife, lifting her hand to his lips. "Your Grace, shall we get to know each other a little? I believe I hear the start of a waltz."

Lady Bradburne hesitated, frowning slightly. "Lord Langlevit, do you mind?"

Henry was on the verge of sending them on their way with a laugh, when a huffing Lord Northridge approached them with Irina in tow. "Langlevit can take a turn with my young sister-in-law," North said, his face red from exertion. "She has worn me out and is in dire need of a better partner for the next set."

Henry's breath caught as her bright eyes met his and slid away, as if he merited nothing more than a glance. "I am sure Her Highness has more than enough partners to choose from."

Lady Bradburne laughed. "Come now, my lord, don't ignore a damsel left in distress by my brother's lack of skill on the ballroom floor."

"Not lack of skill, dear sister," North said, leaning weakly against the column. "Lack of breath. Scotch reels are my nemesis." His eyes narrowed on her. "I'm amazed you are still standing, given your lungs."

Lady Bradburne's childhood breathing affliction did not make itself known as much as it had in the past, but Henry often saw both North and Hawk watching her closely, especially when she danced.

"It's called pacing," the duchess said dryly, glowering at him before smiling sweetly in her husband's and Henry's direction. "I see your Lady Carmichael already has a partner. Shall we, my lords?"

Irina's chin jutted, something indescribable flashing across her transparent face. "I do not wish to put his lordship out, and I see Lord Remi over by—"

Henry took her by the elbow and steered her to the ballroom floor, clipping the words from her lips as the strains of the waltz began. "No, this dance is mine."

He'd be damned if he was going to allow her to dance a fourth time with that man.

Irina's eyes widened at his gravelly tone, but she allowed him to escort her without protest. Sliding one hand around the ruched emerald material at her slim waist, Henry drew her close. He felt Irina's intake of breath through the layer of silk. His palm warmed to her skin, and as the faint waft of lavender drifted into his nostrils, all the other dancers around them fell away. Henry noted once more how tall she was and how perfectly they fit together for a dance like the waltz. She had fit into him equally well in Essex on his waterfall cliff. The recollection made the muscles low in his abdomen tense.

"How are you?" he said.

Her violet eyes met his with a searching look. "Well, my lord. Yourself?"

"Well, thank you." He cleared his throat. "You look like you've been enjoying the dancing."

Irina chuckled, drawing his attention to the slender column of her throat. He instantly pictured himself pressing his lips there. "I've worn through two pairs of slippers," she replied.

"Are you not tired?"

"Dancing is my means of release," she said simply.

She did not have to explain. Henry knew exactly what she meant. He flattened the palm of his hand, brushing his thumb against the smooth material and skimming the sides of her ribs as they took the first turns.

Dimly, he focused on the steps, surprised that for once his leg did not pain him. Dancing with Irina was much like everything else—an unexpected revelation, and for once, he found himself enjoying it. They moved as if they were one, in perfect accord, though she was not laughing or smiling as she had been with her other dance partners. His gaze dropped to her mouth and climbed to her eyes. They had not left his, and the limpid look in them nearly made him sink to his knees.

"Are your accommodations suitable at Bishop House?"

A blank look flicked across her eyes before she answered. "More than suitable."

"Lady Langlevit misses you." He'd missed her, too, he realized with a start. Devon Place had seemed brighter somehow, more alive while she was in it. Much like any other place graced with her presence.

"As I miss her," Irina said. "Have you heard from her? How is she feeling?"

"Better lately, but still in need of rest." Henry cracked a smile. "She never was too fond of listening to orders from doctors. I've hired a private nurse to remain with her for the time being."

"I shall visit when I am next in Essex," she murmured.

"She would like that very much."

The rest of the dance drifted into silence. Odd that their conversation would be stilted and awkward, but not their silence. It was unlike anything Henry had ever encountered. He struggled to categorize it into words, but it was as if the space between their bodies began humming in tune, and while they danced, their pulses seemed to align. Henry could feel the strong beat of hers beneath his hand, pushing against his skin up into his veins.

Irina's eyes widened as if she could feel the force of it, too. The connection that bloomed between them was more powerful than any words, and it was with regret that he released her as the last bars of music faded.

"Thank you for the dance, my lord."

"It was my pleasure."

Henry watched as Irina was whisked away for the next set and preceded to hold up his usual pillar once more. The others had not yet returned, and for the moment, he was content to relive the last quarter of an hour at his leisure. The following set began, and partners shifted once more. He nodded to Rose who was accompanying Lady Bradburne to the retiring room. He was glad that she was enjoying herself, despite her protests that she much preferred country living to the fast pace of London. It would be a good match, then, he thought as he noticed something out of the corner of his eye.

Irina. She had just darted behind a large potted plant and slipped from the ballroom, unaccompanied by her usual entourage. Henry frowned and followed. With the number of bets placed on her, she would not find herself alone for long. The balcony was set kitty-corner to the larger outdoor terrace, he noticed, and accessible only by the narrow doors she'd just exited. To his surprise she stood there, both hands on the stone railing and her head turned to the moonlit sky. Her face was pale and drawn. The vibrancy she'd shown in the ballroom had been replaced by a heavy expression. Tension weighted down her shoulders as she rolled them and pinched the bridge of her nose with her fingers. Suddenly, he wanted nothing more than to draw her into his arms and soothe whatever ache was plaguing her away.

Henry plucked two glasses of whiskey off a nearby footman's tray and closed the paned French doors behind him. "Escaping?" he asked, making her jump and whirl around.

"Oh, it's you."

"Who did you expect it to be?"

She shook her head and shrugged, not even attempting to put up a mask. "I don't know. Max, perhaps."

"Here," he said, handing her the snifter. Hesitating for the briefest of moments, she took it and sipped. "It's not as good as mine, but will do the trick," he told her, watching as some color returned to her cheeks after another sip. "Better?"

"Yes, thank you." Irina turned toward him, but kept her distance. "Now that we are in private and not on a crowded ballroom floor, may I once again offer my congratulations on your engagement? Your fiancée seems truly lovely." She eyed him, drawing the snifter to her lips as if considering her words. "She's obviously much better suited for the role of countess than Lady La Valse or a courtesan from some obscure gaming hell."

Henry drew a harsh breath, feeling the weight of his words from the waterfall hanging between them. He could never take them back. "Irina, I am not sorry for what I said, but I am sorry for hurting you. You must see that I want only what's best for you."

"Stop! You are no longer my warden, and as such you no longer have any right to impose what you think is best for me," she replied, her bitter tone searing him with unexpected power. "Besides, your idea of what is in my best interests is the very opposite of my own."

"Does yours include making a fool of yourself with Lord Remi?"

"At least I'm not a coward," she shot back, her eyes flashing fire as she approached him. "And leave Max out of it."

"What do you mean by that?"

Irina's eyes narrowed to slits. "He's honest about who he is. You hide behind so many walls that no one even knows who you are, least of all yourself."

"You are calling me a coward," he said softly, the blow striking deep between his ribs. She'd reached into his chest and stilled his heart with those words.

She walked past him, toward the doors where she paused, her hand resting on the handle. "I am finally seeing you as you are. Perhaps it is time you did, as well. Thank you for the drink, Lord Langlevit."

He stood unmoving on the balcony as she left. She thought him a coward. It was a word that had floated around his mind for many years but had never, ever, come close to being attached to his name. In the army, cowards ran. They abandoned their men and sought safety for themselves. They broke under the hands of their enemy torturers. Henry was not a coward. He had not run. He had not broken, even when the pain had been blinding, his death all but certain.

"I am not a coward," he whispered to himself on the balcony.

The doors opened, and a couple drew short when they

saw him, standing alone. Henry nodded to them and slipped past, re-entering the ballroom.

Irina was nowhere in sight, but he'd had enough of the evening. He could not stomach another dance or another inane conversation about his marriage plans with anyone. Locating Rose where she stood conversing with the Duke and Duchess of Bradburne and the Earl and Countess of Thorndale, he signaled the butler to retrieve their cloaks and call for their coach while they said their good-byes.

In the carriage, he remained preoccupied until Rose gently touched his shoulder. "Something troubles you?"

Henry pushed a smile to his lips. "I am tired, that is all."

"It is more than that," she said. "We've known each other forever, Henry, and you could never lie to me. It is about the princess, isn't it?"

Hellfire. He just wanted the evening to end.

"No."

Rose squeezed his arm. "Your mouth says no, but your eyes say something else. I saw the two of you dancing. You were staring at each other as if there was no one else in the entire room."

"I—"

She raised a hand. "No, let me finish. I am not angry, Henry. Far from it." She smiled, and he knew she was being honest. "It was the same way I used to stare at John when we danced, as if no one else mattered in the world but us."

"You're imagining things, Rose," Henry said, a surge of pain stabbing through him. "You saw two people who can't even begin to share something as rare as you did with John." His voice broke. "He deserves to still be here with you."

"He is," she said, patting her chest. "In here. In my heart."

"I should have been the one to die that day, not him. He was a good man."

"So are you," Rose said fervently. "And you deserve to be

happy. You deserve to have the chance to find someone who loves you, even if, like John, it's only for a little while."

Henry dropped his head into the cradle of his hands, his eyes gritty. "She loves a man who no longer exists. A hero on a pedestal. I'm not that man."

"Why not?" Rose countered.

"Because he's gone," he whispered. "Gone to a place no one can ever find him."

Coward.

A coward who has run.

She leaned in to hear his barely audible words. "Why, Henry?"

"Love is a weakness, Rose. I learned that well when they had me," he said, surprised he was speaking of it with her, and yet, unable to stop. Maybe it was because of Irina's earlier words. A justification, perhaps, even though he knew no absolution would come from it.

"I never told you or John, but my captors brought in a young girl, a servant from the tavern where I'd been staying. They tortured her…right in front of me. They believed I'd break, that I'd give up the names of my allies, and so they broke her fingers. Her hands. Her knees. They bruised her face and split her lip. They…"

Henry's stomach turned, the familiar sweat of panic and powerlessness threatening to suffocate him.

"Oh, Henry," Rose whispered.

"Do not feel pity for me," he bit out. "I did not know her. She was just a girl. I did not even know her name, and that is the only reason I did not break. If I had known her, if I'd known her name…if I had *cared*—" He swallowed hard. "I would have broken. I would have given them whatever information they wanted."

He closed his eyes, still able to hear her screams echoing down the long corridor to his prison cell.

"They stripped away any capacity for love I might have had that day, though perhaps I never had it in me to begin with. Perhaps there was ever only brutality."

Henry stared at his palms, clenching and unclenching his fingers, his mind going dark with the memories that haunted him. Even Rose didn't know what he was capable of…what he was *still* capable of when his nightmares took him back to dark, harrowing places. No, it was safer for everyone for him to be alone.

Rose stayed quiet. Appalled, perhaps. What did it matter?

"You are kind, Rose, but I am ruined in more ways than one," he murmured, touching his leg, the old wound stiff and aching. Along his back, the old burn scars, reopened by the lashes of a whip in France during his imprisonment, itched as if alive.

"Some say that about me because I am a widow," she responded.

He was glad she hadn't tried to argue with him again. "Then perhaps," he said with a weak, forced grin, "the two of us make sense together."

Companionship. Convenience. Safety. That is what this marriage would be. She nodded, but said nothing more.

It would have to be enough.

Chapter Eleven

Irina was relieved she'd brought her own mount to the house party at Peteridge. The Duke of Hastings's country seat was a short jaunt from London, and though Lord and Lady Dinsmore had balked at her insistence that she ride there on horseback rather than inside their carriage with them, they had, in the end, relented.

It had been well over a week since the Kensington ball. Since Irina had called Henry a coward and stormed from the balcony. She'd tried to focus on anything other than the startled hurt she'd seen in his eyes, as if she had thrust a blade into his heart, but it had proven difficult.

True to her word, Irina had arranged for two thousand pounds to be delivered to Max in as discreet a way as possible, and had then reserved all her focus on waiting for news that he had officially entered the pot. When it had come, she had felt an initial rush of relief, quickly followed by one of nausea.

She was going to marry Max.

It didn't seem real, but…it would be. She'd get used to the notion, she was certain, and they would both be better off together than they had been before—alone. They were a good team, Irina knew. Everything would be fine.

Packing for Lord Marston, the Duke of Hasting's house party had thankfully consumed the last handful of days, and now that she was there, she could focus her attention on the diverting events the duke had planned, like the archery contest.

Lord Marston's stables were not lacking in the least, but when he had announced an archery competition to be held on a course designed for a horse and rider, she was happy she would not have to compete on an unfamiliar mount.

The fact that Jules belonged to Henry only rankled a little.

The fact that Henry himself and his gorgeous bride-to-be were also in attendance at the duke's annual midseason house party had rankled quite a bit more.

Though if she was being truthful, Irina was starting to like Lady Carmichael. She hadn't expected to, and she didn't want to, but when they'd been paired off for a game of shuttlecock on the first day of the house party, she'd found herself enjoying the older woman's company. Lady Carmichael was fresh and direct, but not in as ostentatious a way as say, Gwen. What was more, she did seem to care very much for Henry. In fact, she reminded Irina much of her own sister, Lana. She'd even stood up to an inquisition from Gwen, which was a feat in itself.

How long had she known the earl? *Since childhood.*

For how long had she been a widow? *Two years.*

Did she know that her betrothed was once the Prince Regent's secret spy? *You can't possibly expect me to dignify that with an answer, Lady Lyon.*

The response had won Irina over, especially because Gwen had been fishing for gossip. But it was mostly the fact that Lady Carmichael seemed devoted to Henry...which Irina knew he needed, and despite her hurtful words about his apparent cowardice when it came to her, she only wanted for his happiness.

"You care for him, don't you?" Irina had asked her over afternoon tea.

"Very much."

"He deserves to be happy," she'd said softly.

Lady Carmichael had stared at her with an odd, assessing expression. "Yes, he does."

Irina adjusted her seat on her horse, pushing the conversation with Lady Carmichael from her mind as the man ahead of her forged forward for his turn at the archery contest. The bustle of her riding habit was ridiculously intrusive. It weighed heavy behind her, as did the pleated tweed skirts of her habit that obscured the pair of buckskin trousers underneath. There were only two other ladies participating in the contest, though they were sticking with tradition and riding sidesaddle, as good and proper ladies did. Irina, however, intended to win the contest, and so riding astride was the only fathomable option.

Beside her, several more contestants waited for their chance. Targets had been set up along a ribboned-in course lain out in the open field before them, and the rider to complete the circuit with not only the fastest time, but also the most accurate shots at the targets, would be the victor.

Lord Beechum was currently taking the course with all the focus of a drunken butterfly. He swerved along, readying his bow and arrow with such slow precision that he was not bothering to see to his mount's direction.

"I've seen grass grow faster than this," Max muttered. He stood beside Irina's horse, his hands on the traces in an attempt to help calm and steady the animal as they waited. She was up next.

"It isn't as if we have anything better to do," she replied. The rest of the women were currently taking tea and painting portraits in the garden. She suspected that was where both Lady Carmichael and Gwen were. Irina turned in her saddle, and far across the grounds, near a pond, stood a grouping of men holding long-barreled rifles. They were waiting for the archery contest to conclude before lining up to shoot at their own targets, set up on haystacks across the pond. Henry was among them.

And he was looking at her.

Their eyes met, clashing with a jolt Irina felt in her spine.

She turned away first.

"Finally," Max sighed as Lord Beechum let his last arrow loose, the arrowhead striking the outermost rings on the target.

Max snorted.

"Be polite," Irina chastised, trying not to laugh as well.

Laughter behind them at the pond drew her attention, and again she glanced toward the men. Henry was no longer watching her, so she allowed herself a moment to look her fill. He was the only one not holding a shotgun, and as he swung up onto his mount—a borrowed gray, she noted—she realized he wasn't going to participate. Lord Thorndale was there, however, and the two of them seemed to be in conversation.

She still couldn't believe she'd called the earl a coward. Every time she thought of it, she wished for the chance to take it back. He was a war hero. He wasn't a coward, not truly, and yet...he was running. For whatever reason, he was running from her.

"Darling, have you fallen asleep up there waiting for Lord Beechum to complete the course?" Max said, tugging on her skirt. She blinked and looked toward the starting line. The others were waiting for her to begin.

"I'll be but a minute," she said confidently, turning the reins and trotting forward.

She had her bow in hand and a sheath filled with six

arrows slung over her horse's neck, the cardinal fletching feathers waiting for her to grasp as she rode the course.

"Your Highness," one of the footmen said, his eyes on a pocket watch. He raised a small tea towel, and when the second hand clicked at the top of the watch, he brought the linen down.

She took off, racing along the course entrance while pulling the first of her arrows from the sheath. Holding the reins while taking the shot would be impossible, so she clenched her legs, pressing her knees into her mount's sides to stay straight in the saddle as she nocked her arrow.

Irina let it fly, rushing past the first target before she had the chance to see it bury into the bullseye. She just trusted that it had, and taking the reins again, steered for the turn in the course and the second haystack target. Without slowing, and rising slightly in the saddle, Irina released her second arrow to hit the target dead center amidst wild cheering before racing for the third.

A gunshot cracked through the air, and she faltered, her concentration ripped away. Irina twisted in her saddle, slowing her pace and no doubt seriously damaging her time. But when she saw a horse and rider barreling in the opposite direction, around the pond and toward a stone wall, she brought her mount to a complete stop.

The group of men near the pond were shouting at the one who'd fired the shot; the man holding the smoking shotgun wore a look of surprise and chagrin, and Irina knew right away it had gone off unexpectedly.

Her heart spluttered as she looked to the horse and rider again, riding wildly toward the stone wall. It was the borrowed gray. It was *Henry*. And something was wrong. He wasn't sitting right in the saddle, but bouncing around, as if he had lost control. He seemed to be hunched over, too, his head turned down.

Good Lord. Had he been *shot*?

Irina dropped her bow and tugged the reins, redirecting Jules until his nose was pointed toward the periphery of the ribboned-off course. She gave him a firm nudge with her heel and he was off, rushing toward the hip-high ribbon. With a cry of alarm from the crowd looking on, Jules jumped the ribbon and bolted away from the archery course. She thought she heard Max calling after her to stop, but she could only concentrate on Henry's slumped back. She swallowed a scream when his gray hurdled over the stone wall far ahead, and his figure swayed perilously to the side, as if he might fall off. But he stayed seated, his horse continuing to flee.

The men near the pond shouted after her as she raced past, Lord Thorndale roaring instead to a footman for him to bring his bloody horse at once. None of them had mounts at the ready, but they all seemed to know what Irina did: that the Earl of Langlevit was in trouble.

The wind took her hat as she passed the small pond, and as she leaned over Jules's neck, her backside out of the saddle, her grip loose on the reins so Jules would only go faster, she felt as if she were flying. And yet, not fast enough.

She jumped the stone wall, and as she came down into the green grass on the other side, spotted Henry and his mount at the bottom of the hill below. The gray seemed to have slowed, thank heavens, but it was still cantering toward an outcropping of elm trees.

"My lord!" she shouted, swallowing air and knowing her voice could not possibly have reached him.

However, the gray seemed to have heard it. It slowed further and with agitated shakes of its head and mane, came to a prancing halt just before the trees.

Henry remained in the saddle, his head bent forward, his body stiff and hunched as he rocked forward and back. Jules descended the hill, and she reined him in, coming to a stop just beside the gray.

"Henry?" she said. He didn't appear to be injured, or shot, but he was muttering to himself, his lips moving over words she couldn't make out.

Irina recalled the stupor he'd been in on the road to Essex, after the tree branch had fallen. Lying there in the road, his eyes closed, it had been like watching someone unable to wake up from a nightmare. The crack of the gun had likely startled his horse, but it might have done something worse to him. Unlike the last time he'd gone into shock, his eyes were open now. Whatever he was seeing, she guessed, it was not their current surroundings.

"It's Irina, Henry. I'm right here," she said, reaching over to touch his arm. Her hand settling upon the rigid muscle of his bicep. "Look at me, Henry. You're in a field. You're home, in England. You're safe."

She felt silly, talking to him this way, keeping her voice purposefully calm when her heart was thrashing madly in her chest. But she knew that whatever he was seeing right now was painful and frightening. She needed to bring him back.

A sound from the top of the hill where the stone wall was caught her attention. She turned and saw Lord Thorndale and two other men had acquired their mounts and were approaching.

"Henry, *please*," she said, turning back to him. He would be humiliated if his peers found him this way. "People are coming. Wake up!"

He stared blankly ahead, his brows furrowed. At least he was still upright in his saddle. Irina grasped his mount's reins and tugged them, leading the gray beside her as she turned to face the riders, one of which was Lord Marston, the Duke of Hastings.

"Langlevit, what the devil?" Marston asked.

"Is he shot?" Lord Thorndale asked, his eyes roaming

over Henry with concern.

"No," Irina answered. "He might have…hit his head."

"Upon what?" Thorndale asked, his keen eyes coming to rest on her.

"I'm…not sure, however, he's just told me his temple is paining him. Lord Marston, does that path over there lead back to the main house?"

Irina pointed toward a trail through the field, cutting up the opposite side of the hill and into the trees.

"Why yes, but, Langlevit, you're sure you're not shot? I'm going to thrash young Bucksley with that blasted shotgun of his. I don't know what he was thinking, walking around with it primed like that. He could have killed someone!"

"Oh yes, yes, he's perfectly fine, aren't you, Lord Langlevit?" she asked, quickly leading the gray toward the path and continuing her babbling to try to cover for the fact that Henry was completely unresponsive.

"Just a headache, isn't that right? I'll go with him to the house, and you men can return to your competition. Tell everyone all is well! Good afternoon!" she called, before kicking Jules into a trot and praying Henry did not slide off his saddle, straight into the grass. It was absurd, and she knew Thorndale at least had not bought one bit of her blabbering, but for the moment, they were alone again.

"Henry, you must say something," she said, quickly leading him out of the field and into the tree line. Once they were in, obscured by the thick elm trunks and canopy of leaves, she let the muscles in her back go slack. "I cannot return you to the house like this."

She slowed their mounts and turned to him again. Removing her glove, she reached across the divide and cupped his cheek, recalling the way she'd done so that day on the post road. When he did not respond as he had then, Irina felt a flutter of panic.

"What can I do?" she asked, suddenly worried that he might be stuck like this forever.

Irina brushed her thumb along his skin, tracing his lower lip. He'd stopped his incoherent murmuring, at least. She released his cheek and took up his hand, resting limp on his thigh, though his fingertips were pressed hard into his leg. She softened each finger and held his hand, bringing it to her lips.

Irina removed his glove and kissed the ridge of his knuckles, her heart aching. "Tell me what to do."

She stroked his hand, tracing the tracks of his veins with her fingertips and brushing her lips against his skin in their wake. It was like he was a statue, made of human flesh and bone, but inhabited by nothing. His complete lack of response and catatonic state frightened her.

His demons, the ones she knew tortured him, were much like hers—dormant most of the time, but when they struck, they came with a vengeance. She had never fully recovered from being kidnapped by her uncle's men. Though it took years before she was able to sleep comfortably, night terrors still came once in a while, their grip inescapable. Much like the state Henry was in right now.

"I'm here, Henry," she whispered, brushing the heart of his palm with her thumb. "Find your way back to me. I'm not going anywhere. Listen to my voice, please."

Irina kept distractedly stroking his hand with her fingertips, and after a while realized she'd been drawing her initials and then his, over and over, but the motion was calming. It helped her to focus on something even as she continued to repeat her whispered pleas for him to hear her voice. It seemed like hours had passed before she finally felt his fingers flex against hers.

"Irina." His voice was a dry croak.

She looked up at him, wanting to sob in relief. "What happened? Are you hurt?"

Henry licked his lips and blinked, as if trying to get his bearings. "I'm...there was a gunshot. After...what are we doing here?" he asked, glancing at the woods around them and blinking in apparent confusion.

He didn't remember any of it?

"Where did you go?" she asked, frowning slightly. "France again?"

Henry rubbed the back of his neck and rolled his shoulders, his lips pressed tight. Not looking at her. His body had gone rigid again, but this time it was discomfort and not some repressed memory that held him in bondage. Taking the reins of his mount, he fiddled with them a bit, as if trying to decide whether or not to trust her. She waited in silence.

"Yes," he whispered finally.

"What do you see there?"

Irina was certain he would not reply this time. But he surprised her. "Someone I cannot help. A young girl who suffered because of me. Because I would not give in to save her." His voice grew quiet and Irina sat still, knowing if she moved or uttered one word, he would stop. "In my mind, I hear her screaming. Begging for mercy and never receiving it. What she endured was worse than hell, and I was the one to condemn her there. Sometimes, in my memory, the girl has other faces...faces of those I— " He cut off then, his breathing ragged, his fingers convulsing on the reins. A muscle throbbed in his neck as he visibly struggled to compose himself.

"I am sorry," Irina said gently, knowing he might pull away, but needing to comfort him nonetheless. "There is nothing I can say that will lessen the pain you both endured, but horrible things happen in times of war. You must know that it's not your fault."

A flare of self-disgust lit his eyes. "I know that. Logically, I know." His expression shifted to frustration as his posture loosened a little. His stare dipped thoughtfully to their joined hands, but he made no move to pull away. "It's just…some part of me won't accept it. A part of me forgets."

Irina couldn't begin to imagine what he'd seen or the pain and suffering he'd borne. Nor could she imagine what it had taken to remain silent under the brunt of such barbaric torture. The poor girl's suffering wasn't on him; it was on *them*. His vile captors. But Irina also understood the power of guilt all too well. There was precious little she could say that would absolve him of his demons. Instead, she defied all modesty and pretense, and pushing the leather strap of the rein out of the way, threaded her gloveless fingers between his. Sensation flooded her at the meeting of their hands, making it difficult to draw in air as his eyes met hers. The skin of his bare palm sliding against hers was warm and rough. He needed comfort and she would offer it, without giving a damn to who might see and judge her scandalous behavior. Irina simply did not care. And neither did he. Henry's thumb grazed over the back of hers, brushing back and forth in a caress so tender it took her breath away.

"Come," she whispered after a while, breaking the spell and retrieving her glove. She handed him his. "We should return to the house before Lord Thorndale sends out a search party, and I wouldn't want to cause any gossip to endanger Lady Carmichael's reputation." His eyes shot to hers in surprise, but Irina meant it. Though she didn't care a whit for the *ton's* views of her, she didn't want her actions to have any impact on Rose.

Oddly, Henry's expression lightened. "Thank you," he said.

Nodding, Irina turned her horse to travel along the path and forced a careless shrug despite the considerable lump forming in her throat. "Think nothing of it. Though you might need to convince Lords Thorndale and Marston that you hit your head upon something to make yourself so…

uncommunicative when they saw you."

He trotted alongside her. "Saw me?"

"They followed when your horse bolted. I covered for you."

Henry's gray caught up to Jules, bringing her knee and his into contact. "It seems I am once more in your debt."

"You owe me nothing, my lord." And it was true. There was nothing she wanted from him. Nothing she could now have from him without hurting another. She sucked air past the growing brick in her throat. "It is the least I could do in return for everything you've ever done for Lana and me."

They rode onward, both of them quiet. Both of them, Irina suspected, suppressing words that could never be spoken.

Chapter Twelve

It wasn't Hartstone, but Henry was glad to be back at his London residence just the same.

The day before, he had given his regrets to the Duke of Hastings and taken his leave from Peteridge in order to travel back to London early. He had not been able to endure a moment longer of the concerned and pitying glances sent his way. Inside, he knew he was being overly sensitive. Only a handful of people had actually seen his horse bolt, and that was exactly how Lord Thorndale had framed the tale…that the *stallion* had reared up at the unexpected discharge of the gun, not that the Earl of Langlevit had lost his mind like a demented, pathetic fool, tortured by faceless ghosts no one else could see.

Somehow, Henry had convinced Rose to stay and return with Irina on the following day. He needed time alone to compose himself, he'd told her. Rose hadn't needed much explanation—she was more than familiar with the devils that haunted him. But she'd seemed reticent to let him depart alone. Irina, too. They would both be headed back soon—Rose to her late husband's London residence, which she still kept, and Irina to Bishop House with Lord and Lady Dinsmore.

An ache opened up in his chest at the thought of the princess. Besides the little he'd told Rose, he'd never spoken of the Parisian servant girl to anyone, nor his detestable apathy toward her. But he'd somehow confided in Irina. His heart clenched at the return of the visceral memory.

He'd watched as they'd tortured her. It had been surprisingly easy to cut off every emotion trying to claw its way into his heart as they had broken her, bit by agonizing bit. He'd viewed the horror as if he'd been a great distance from it, instead of sitting chained within the same cell. Reciting the Latin alphabet in his head and then memorized passages from Plato and Aristotle, Shakespeare and *The Iliad*, had helped to keep that distance. It had been the only way he'd been able to cope. And it had worked.

However, he'd never been able to close that distance, not even after he'd escaped and come home and found himself among people he did not have to protect himself from. It was as if a permanent chasm had opened up inside of him that day, a chasm that had helped him stay true to his duty, stay silent and removed.

The chasm made him forget how to feel, how to care. How to love. He'd become cold and inhuman just so he could survive. And yet that had been the day everything within him died.

Until Irina.

She made him feel things that had long been dead and buried. It was as if she already understood, as if she could see to the heart of him—to all the dark, terrible secrets buried inside—and none of it mattered.

"Damnation," he muttered, pressing the heels of his palms against the mantel in his study. He wanted to remain invulnerable and emotionless. Keep the past where it belonged. Yet one gentle touch of her fingers, one whisper of her voice, and the emotions he'd held at a safe distance for so long flared closer. He wanted to lay himself bare. Confess all his sins and secrets. Find forgiveness in her. Lose himself in the bliss of her body. Find mercy in the warmth of her smile.

"This is absurd," he bit out aloud. "Get a hold of yourself."

"You called, my lord?" Stevens asked from the doorway.

Henry frowned and was about to dismiss the butler with a curt nod, but he paused, his fingers gripping the ledge. He was not a man given to drinking to excess, but suddenly he had the notion that a good glass or two was in order. "Fetch me a cask from the cellar of my single malt. The last batch from Dumfries."

"Of course, my lord."

When Stevens returned as requested, Henry nodded his thanks and poured himself a liberal serving. "See that I am not disturbed, unless it is an emergency."

"Yes, my lord."

Henry settled himself in his armchair and consumed the entire glass in a single swallow. The liquor burned a hot path to his belly. He groaned and tossed back a second. Breathing heavily, he poured himself another, swirling the amber liquid in the crystal snifter and catching wafts of its peaty, rich notes. He should have chosen something other than this if drowning his demons in spirits was what he truly sought. Consuming it in so uncouth a manner was sacrilege to such a carefully crafted malt, aged for twenty-five years before being uncorked. Taking another swallow, this time slower in order to savor its taste, Henry closed his eyes and let the warming liquid flow over his tongue. It was complex and beautiful and lush.

Much like Irina.

She would appreciate this vintage, he thought. He'd never met anyone who loved the taste of whiskey as much as he did. Henry smiled. Yet another of the things they had in common.

The list was getting longer. With a sigh, he stared into the fireplace, watching the flames leap and dance, his mind again consumed with thoughts of her.

Once more, she'd been the one to draw him back from the abyss. And both times, he'd managed to calm himself in minutes instead of hours. Henry had no illusions that that miracle was because of Irina. He trusted her, he realized with a start. And trust was not something he gave lightly.

If she knew the truth of everything he'd done, she would not be as enamored of him as she had been in the past. Would she hold him in such high favor if she knew he'd cowered like a dog as his captors had taken turns shooting at him in the prison courtyard, a bag placed over his head for sport? That he'd lost his bowels when one bullet grazed his scalp and another nicked his ear? Ever since, the sound of a gunshot was enough to drive him to madness. It did not matter where he was, the sound dragged him back into that courtyard, those cracking shots coming his way through clouds of gunpowder smoke, any one of them a promise of death. No matter what Henry did, he would never escape his past.

The servant girl's death, as painful as it had been, had not been drawn out for weeks. Unlike his torture…beaten to within an inch of his life and then nursed back to health for months on end. An unending cycle of pain and horror and misery.

Henry drained the contents of his glass and clumsily refilled another, his hands shaking.

What would his innocent, beautiful princess think if she saw his back and knew that he'd been whipped like an animal? The scars there were testament to his powerlessness and his eternal shame.

She wouldn't have him.

No one should have him. No one deserved someone that was broken beyond repair. Destroyed beyond redemption.

A soft knock drew his attention. "My lord?"

Henry scowled, tearing his cravat loose with an angry tug. "Stevens," he barked. "I said I did not wish to be disturbed."

"My apologies, my lord," Stevens said, cracking the door open. "But it's Lord Thorndale, and he is most insistent on an audience."

"Send him away."

"Too late," a voice said as a large shape vaguely resembling Thorndale pushed his way into the room and closed the door behind him. "What kind of man only shares his best whiskey with himself?"

Henry's scowl descended into a ferocious glower. "One who values his solitude."

Removing his coat as if he meant to settle in for the afternoon, Thorndale laughed in his face and poured himself a glass, refilling Henry's at the same time. "Drowning your sorrows?"

"Call it whatever you like," Henry said. His eyes narrowed on the man who had boldly ensconced himself in the armchair on the opposite side of the fireplace—uninvited—with a drink in hand. He stared at Henry with an inscrutable expression. "And don't mind me, help yourself," Henry added sourly.

"Won't mind if I do." Thorndale took a delicate sip and sighed his appreciation as he sampled another. "Now, *this* was worth returning to dreary old London for."

"You left early," Henry said, an edge of accusation on his tone, even though he himself had done as much.

"A few of us decided to depart after breakfast instead of this afternoon, including Her Highness with the Earl and Countess of Dinsmore. We took the liberty of seeing Lady Carmichael home."

"Thank you," Henry murmured.

"My wife and I have an engagement this evening, but I thought it best to stop by." Thorn peered at him. "Suffice it to say that a little bird was worried about your possible concussion."

"I did not injure my head," he snapped, something shifting inside him at the thought of Irina's concern.

"I rather thought so," Thorn said over the rim of his glass, one booted foot propped up against his knee. "So, are you going to tell me what happened, or do I have to pry it out of you?"

It was on the tip of Henry's tongue to tell the earl to go tup himself, but he stalled, staring at the whiskey in his snifter instead. He eyed the man opposite. "You know what happened. My horse startled and bolted."

"We both know you are a far better horseman than that, Langlevit." Thorndale paused. "When we came upon you, you were unresponsive, wouldn't say a peep. If it weren't for the chit babbling on to conceal your state of confusion, both of us would have been hard-pressed to explain to Hastings why you refused to offer so much as a word."

Henry stared into his drink as if the answers he sought were in its depths. He didn't speak for a long time, but when he did it was with a question, not an explanation as the earl expected. "When we served on the Peninsula under Wellington, you had to do things, terrible things, correct?"

"We both did."

"Do you think about the ones who died? Are you ever haunted by their faces?"

Thorndale inhaled sharply. "Every day."

Henry sighed, his head drooping. When he spoke, his voice was barely audible. If anyone could understand, he knew it would be Thorndale. "I thought I could do it, remain detached, not feel a thing. That's how officers like us do what we do, isn't it? But it's impossible. Sometimes, I feel the memories clawing at my skin. Lately, it seems that anything can trigger them." He chanced looking up at Thorn. "Like a snapping branch or a fool's gunshot."

Thorndale sat forward in his chair, his brow furrowing. "Nostalgia?" Henry frowned as the earl went on to explain. "Indifference brought on by the toll of war. Homesickness, it's called." He shook his head thoughtfully. "I should have guessed that was it."

"How could I be homesick? I *am* home."

"You're still suffering from the symptoms, however. Perhaps they are related." The earl nodded more firmly. "Christine's father was acquainted with the Austrian physician who coined the term." Thorndale hesitated before going on. "Much like what you've experienced, though not as brutally, I suffered from night terrors for years. My father-in-law suspected that nostalgia was the root cause."

"What can I do?" Henry murmured, raising his snifter. "Besides drink myself into oblivion."

"Talk."

Henry looked up at him. "Is that what you did?"

"Yes," he replied. "With Christine. For so long, I was haunted by demons of my own making. I didn't think I deserved to be happy, and then I met her. She refused to let me push her away, even though I tried. I did not want to sully her with my sins."

Henry swallowed hard, his despair pushing to the surface. The man had uncovered the truth of it in one breath. "She did not...hate you for what you've done?"

"No, on the contrary," Thorndale said gently. "Perhaps your Lady Carmichael will do the same for you."

Henry's eyes flicked to the earl. He hadn't been thinking about Rose at all. He'd been thinking of Irina...of the way he had been able to talk with her. He recalled her gentle words in the hidden glade after his unexpected confession. There had been no incrimination in her gaze, no judgment in her voice. She'd only listened, sweetly saying he owed her nothing. And for the briefest of moments, Henry had felt an odd peace in the center of his soul.

"Perhaps," he said eventually.

Thorndale finished his drink and declined the offer for another. "As much as I'd like to sit and drink this fine whiskey for the rest of the afternoon, I must be off or Christine will have my head." With an apologetic smile, he shrugged into his coat and approached Henry. "There is another reason I am here."

Henry gave a short bark of laughter. "Besides seeing about my concussion?"

"I took a turn at White's for luncheon," he went on. "In fact, that was where I'd expected to find you."

"I contemplated it," Henry said. "And?"

The earl drew a breath, an uncomfortable look crossing his face, and suddenly Henry knew exactly why he'd taken it upon himself to visit. He could feel every muscle in his body bunching in irritation.

Thorndale cleared his throat. "Speaking of the young lady who so eloquently saved your arse, I'm certain you already know of the wagers being placed."

"I know of them," Henry ground out.

"There's a new wager that has recently been penned in that is of a particularly indelicate nature, and one that I fear may affect the young lady's reputation."

Henry stiffened. "What is it?"

"The first man to steal a kiss—witnessed, willingly surrendered, and not on the cheek—will win the staggering sum of five thousand pounds."

Willingly surrendered? The whiskey sloshed in Henry's glass as he lurched up out of his chair. "This is beyond madness," he growled. "I'd like to set that bloody wager log on fire."

"I am of a similar mind."

"Who made the wager?" Henry asked, already imagining the satisfying feel of his hands around the odious man's throat, whoever he was. These men had no honor. Irina wasn't some trifling thing to be won. She was an aristocrat for God's sake, and this kind of betting could put not just her reputation at risk, but her personal safety, as well. He would not stand for it.

"That's just it," Thorndale hedged. "It is the real reason I decided to seek you out. The wager was written in by one Lord Remi whom I believe is the princess's friend. It struck me as odd that he would be the one to encourage such behavior."

Friend? Henry thought viciously. The crystal glass shattered in his hand. He watched dully as blood welled from a narrow cut.

"Bloody hell, Langlevit," Thorndale swore, tossing him a cloth napkin from the mantel. "You'll give yourself a nasty bout of sepsis if you don't take care of that."

Henry wrapped the cloth around his hand but ignored the throbbing wound. "It's of no import. When was the wager penned?"

"This morning."

Henry's lips thinned with ill-concealed fury. Max Remi was no friend of Irina's. He was an opportunist and one out for his own gain with no thought for Irina's wellbeing. When he saw the cur, he fully intended to put the bastard into the ground. But first he needed to put an end to Irina's antics once and for all. She would go to Essex for her own safety, and that would be the end of it.

"Stevens," he barked and tore from the room on the heels of Thorndale. "Ready my horse and send a footman ahead with my card to Lord Dinsmore." He nodded to his friend who exited to his own waiting coach. "Thank you, Thorn."

"Go easy on her," Thorndale said with a tight smile. "It's not her fault."

Henry jaw clenched. Though she could not know about the wagers, he felt inexplicably angry with her for being so damned appealing in the first place. He'd watched her for weeks, laughing and flirting and scandalously encouraging the entire male set.

"Of course I will," Henry bit out. He would never hurt her, but he fully expected to give her ears a blistering about her choice of companions and knowingly endangering herself at every turn.

After Thorndale took his leave, Henry rode like the hounds were after him, his brain agitated with the incendiary combination of drink and emotion. His injured palm stung, but the pain only served to spur him on. By the time he arrived at Bishop House and was escorted into the foyer, he was enumerating all the ways he'd drag Irina bodily back to Essex.

"Lord Langlevit," Lord Dinsmore boomed, striding to the salon where he waited. To his credit, he passed a blind eye over Henry's hastily re-knotted cravat and his excessively rumpled appearance. "What a surprise. I just this moment received your card. Is something amiss?"

"No," Henry said. "I've come to speak to Her Highness. It is a matter of some importance."

He shook his head. "I am sorry, but she decided to continue on to Essex. It seems she wished to visit my daughter-in-law and the countess. She left some hours ago."

"Essex?" Henry echoed. "Does she travel with Lady Dinsmore?"

Dinsmore shook his head. "Lady Dinsmore required a rest from the carriage up from Peteridge, though we'll set out in a few days ourselves. I do envy Lady Irina's wherewithal, riding up north six hours upon horseback!"

He gave a little hop on his heels as if to punctuate his awe.

"She is riding *alone*?" Henry asked in a deadly voice.

"Of course not!" Lord Dinsmore laughed and clapped him on the shoulder. "She's in the capable hands of that cousin of hers, Lord Remi. No need to worry; he'll see that she arrives safely."

Chapter Thirteen

The journey to Essex had been hellishly long, and after a long, warm bath, all Irina wanted to do was sleep. Her backside was still sore from the ride. She did not know what had possessed her to continue on, but she had not wanted to remain in London. She didn't want to see the inside of another ball or entertain the flirtations of some gentleman who was only out to win a few guineas. Irina corrected herself—far more than a few guineas. She had learned that some of the bets were astronomical. The bloody wagers were starting to take a harsh toll on her emotions.

And then there was Max.

Soon to be her betrothed.

The thought bothered her more than it should. Somewhere and somehow, something had shifted imperceptibly within her. It wasn't that she did not love Max—she adored him— but the idea of becoming his *wife* made her feel strangely sad. Perhaps it had to do with what had happened in Peteridge with Henry. Irina had thought she had done an adequate job of distancing herself from him over the past few weeks, but all it took was one unguarded moment, and she was right back where she'd started. Half in love with a man who didn't believe in love.

Irina inhaled deeply. When he'd spoken of that young girl, she'd seen a side to him she had never imagined. The raw ache in his voice had been unbearable. A man who felt nothing would not have spoken as he had...would not have felt regret or sadness as keenly as he did. She adjusted her earlier statement. It wasn't that he didn't believe in love, he simply guarded against it. Henry had blocked himself from all feeling, and from any of the vulnerability it could bring. She understood it because she had done the same over the past five years, holding everyone at arm's length.

Except with Henry, it seemed.

"Sixpence for your thoughts?" Max asked from where he sat beside her in Stanton Park's exquisitely landscaped rose garden. After her bath, she'd felt too restless to be cooped up inside and had suggested a stroll with Max. The children had all gone on a jaunt to the village with their father, leaving Lana to rest. "You seem quite preoccupied."

"I am exhausted."

"No surprise there. Riding several hours on horseback is apt to do that. And on the heels of such heroic actions, too. You really shouldn't be so gallant next time," he quipped with a mocking smile. "Everyone was talking about your daring rescue of Lord Langlevit's runaway horse." He eyed her, arching an eyebrow. "Though you never did quite tell me the whole story."

Irina shrugged and kept her face blank. "There's nothing to tell. I managed to stop his horse. That is all."

"It's surprising that Langlevit would lose such control," he said.

"The stallion was young and untried. It could have happened to anyone."

"True." Max shot her a sidelong glance as if he could see right through her lies. He usually did. She smiled brightly at him. "However, you took quite a long time to return," he added. His insouciance irritated her more than the question.

"What is the problem?" she asked, her smile whittling to a glare. "It seems that you are insinuating that something untoward happened between the earl and me."

"Did it?"

"No!" She sighed. "It took some time to find and calm the horse, that is all."

He reached out an arm to her. "Don't be upset with me, I'm just worried about you where he's concerned. I don't like the way he looks at you, the way he's always watching you, especially when he should be concerned with his own fiancée."

"Max!"

"Well, it's true," he said. "When you started the archery contest, Langlevit couldn't take his eyes off you. No wonder he lost control of his horse if his attention was attached elsewhere."

Irina pursed her lips, ignoring the quiet rush of delight his words ignited, and rolled her eyes at her friend. "I certainly didn't take you for the jealous type," she said dryly.

"I'm not."

"Then what is this truly about?"

"I think he's dangerous," Max began. "Françoise—"

She poked him and feigned a shocked look. "You're on a first name basis with Lady La Valse? That's a new development." Irina shook her head. "You must take every confidence she shares with a grain of salt. Lord Langlevit hasn't been seen with her for weeks. He's no longer interested in her charms, it seems, and so it's no secret that she's upset. After all, hell hath no fury…"

Max's gaze hinged to hers. "Like a woman scorned?"

"Exactly."

"You sound strangely pleased."

"I'm simply stating the truth." Irina stood, irritated with the turn of the conversation. She couldn't give one whit about the Earl of Langlevit's bedtime partners, though the thought of the voluptuous Lady La Valse in a fit of rejected pique did give her some satisfaction. "If you're going to be a squawking mother hen all day, I'd rather spend time in Breckenham with the children."

"No, no, stay," Max said. "I promise to behave. It's dreadfully dull here without your company, and I fear I'll go mad if you leave me to my own devices."

Irina laughed at his theatrical expression and waved her arm. "How could you find any of this dull? No smog, no smoke, just blue skies and nature's own beauty." Irina raised her arms to the sky and twirled. "Smell that clean country air. It's a gift."

"I'd much prefer a new pair of shoes," Max grumbled. "There's far too much mud in nature if you ask me."

"Come now, poppet, it's not all that bad."

Scowling at her veiled sarcasm, he chucked the head of a rose at her. "I think I will see myself in for a rest, after all. Do we have anything diverting planned for later?" he asked hopefully. "Croquet? Shuttlecock? You know I love anything with that word in it."

Irina squealed, covering her ears and glancing around. If anyone heard, they would be appalled. "You are shameless."

"And yet you love me."

"You are lucky that I do, and yes, there is a dinner planned at Worthington Abbey," she replied, her lips twitching. "With the Duke and Duchess of Bradburne and some prodigious fellow named Max Remi who has apparently lain all of London at his feet. It should make for scintillating company indeed."

He stroked his chin and pulled his face into a leer.

"*Prodigious*. So, the country folk have heard of my... substantial endowment."

"Honestly, is that all you think about?" she asked with a mortified giggle.

"What else is there in life other than the pursuit of carnal pleasure?"

Blushing fiercely, Irina shook her head at him in consternation. He was such a scoundrel. As her humor subsided, she grew pensive. "Max, can I ask you a question?"

"Anything, my dear."

"Do you ever imagine that one day you'll fall in love?"

Something dark flashed across his face before it was quickly erased. He twittered under his breath. "What have I always told you? Love is for fools and old men, and luckily, I am neither."

"I'm being serious."

"As am I," he said. "Love is an illusion, a beautiful one while it lasts, but such intrigues always come to an end, and what awaits at that juncture is not enjoyable in the least. At least, not in my experience, which is why I keep all my options open. Carnal pursuits and all that." He waggled his eyebrows. "I've decided that the children's governess is quite attractive."

"Profligate!"

"*Prodigious* profligate," he said, grinning.

"You are far too jaded for your years."

Max nodded with a sage look. "There is that, too. Ah, here comes your lovely sister back from her walk to join us." He bowed as Lana approached and took his leave, winking wickedly at Irina. "I'll leave you two to catch up while I suss out the kitchen girls."

"Behave," Irina said.

Lana looked fetching in a bright yellow muslin dress and far less pale than she had the last time Irina had been at Stanton Park. Irina kissed her on the cheek, and they linked arms. "I'll walk you back to the house. You look well rested."

"My darling husband has been an exacting nursemaid of late."

"Gray is wonderful, and you know it." Irina defended him with a loyal smile. "How is the babe?"

"Well, I hope." Lana smoothed her hands over her barely noticeable bump, warmth glinting in her green eyes. "How was London?"

"Fast." Sighing, Irina leaned her head against her sister's shoulder as they strolled along the curved flagstone pathways. "Although I did enjoy the weekend at the Duke of Hastings's estate. I spent some time there with Lady Carmichael."

Lana's eyes flicked to hers. "And?"

"She's lovely," she said. "You would like her. She reminds me of you in some ways."

"I'm glad." Lana interlaced her fingers with hers and squeezed. "Though I'm also sorry. I know how you felt about him. It can't be easy seeing him promised to someone else."

"I just want him to be happy."

"As do we all," her sister murmured.

They walked in silence for a while, each occupied by their own thoughts. It was the first time that Irina felt she could breathe and just be herself without the pressures placed upon her by her position. Yet for some reason, her blood burned restlessly in her veins. Despite her fatigue, nervous energy looped in coils within her. By the time they reached the entrance to the manor, her fretfulness had only grown. There was only one place she could go...only one place she *wanted* to go. She seized upon the course at Hartstone. Henry would still be in London, and no one would be the wiser.

"I'm going for a ride," she announced to Lana as her sister walked inside. "I'm not quite ready to retire."

Lana sighed in envy. "I do miss riding so."

"My dear brother-in-law would murder me if I even let

you look at a horse," Irina said. "No, my sweet sister, you need to rest, but I will be sure to enjoy the ride for both of us."

Running to her bedchamber, anticipation building like a tide in the pit of her stomach, Irina changed quickly into her favorite breeches, ones that laced at the front, and shrugged into the matching riding coat. She was almost breathless by the time she raced back downstairs.

"Where are you going?" Max asked curiously from where he stood near the kitchens, finishing off a fruit tart that he must have gotten off one of the kitchen girls he'd managed to charm.

"Nowhere in particular," she said as casually as she could manage. The last thing she wanted was Max on her heels, asking questions that she wasn't prepared to answer, least of all why she felt so compelled to run Lord Langlevit's course. It was a poor substitute for what she really wanted: to see him.

Bother!

"I'm of half a mind to accompany you," Max said, licking the crumbs off his fingers.

"There'll be lots of mud," she teased with a grin. "Don't worry, I won't be long. In the meantime, try not to deflower anyone."

"I shall make no such promises."

Hoping that Max wouldn't take it into his head to follow her out of pure perversity, Irina hurried to the stables and chose the first available horse on hand, a sleek brown mare, and waited impatiently while the stableboy saddled her. She spurred the horse into a gallop, her pent-up frustration only leaving her body when she saw the turrets of Hartstone come into view. She did not go up the winding driveway but galloped past, into the woods instead. The clearing with the barn was easy to find, but Irina decided to tie her horse in a thicket a little farther along in case any employees from Hartstone *had* noticed her arrival.

All of her worries seemed to melt away the minute she walked back to the makeshift stable, the sounds of the nearby waterfall muffling her footsteps. Taking her time, she explored the unlocked barn, noticing that it wasn't a stable at all, but a self-sufficient cottage of sorts. There was a well-made bed in one corner and a table with a stove on top of it. An armchair sat in one corner with a stack of books arranged on a nearby shelf. There was no food in sight, but she didn't expect there to be with Henry being in Town. Feeling as if she were intruding, Irina slipped from the barn and decided to wander down to the pool before attempting the course.

Whereupon she froze in shocked wonder.

A man stood beneath the waterfall. Not just any man. *Henry.*

Irina's breath deserted her body in a wild exit. What was he doing here? He was supposed to be in London. She blinked, wondering if she'd somehow managed to conjure him with her thoughts, but when she opened her eyes, he was still there. Like some kind of mythological river god, he stood with his back toward her, which was mostly obscured by the bubbling flow of water cascading onto his wide shoulders and streaming toward his narrow, muscular hips. The paleness of his lean and scandalously bare posterior in contrast to the rest of him drew her attention, and she flushed deeply. It was suddenly difficult to draw in air. The water blocked enough of him from view, but exposed tantalizing glimpses of bronzed limbs that made her knees feel like rubber.

Sweet Lord, he was naked as the day he was born, and she couldn't stop staring.

If he turned around, he would see her standing there. And that was something she could not risk. With reluctance, Irina forced her feet to twist and move back in the direction she'd come, but halted once more as a voice filtered through the trees near the path leading to the barn.

"Irina?"

She recognized that voice. *Max.*

She didn't dare turn around to see if Henry had heard, but remained frozen like a trapped fox in the hunt as Max called out again. That conniving, sneaky rogue had followed her after all. Irina swallowed her irritation as real fear rose in its wake. If Max caught her with Henry—a naked Henry at that—especially after his earlier misgivings, all hell would break loose.

She would have to deter him and somehow explain her presence here on someone else's private property, along with the nature of the secret course belonging to the Earl of Langlevit, no less. Gritting her teeth, Irina made to move toward him when a large wet hand reached around to cover her mouth. It startled a surprised, though muffled, squeak from her.

"Shhh," Henry whispered into her ear, drawing her out of sight behind a large oak tree just as Max appeared on his horse at the top of the path. "Be still."

Sandwiched between the large tree and the equally large man at her back, Irina obeyed, her heart thumping in her chest as Max frowned, his eyes canvassing the area. He took in the start of Henry's course before his curious gaze moved back to the waterfall. Irritation surged once more at the fact that he had followed her. Trembling with suppressed fury, her fingers gripped the rough bark of the oak. Max stood there for some time and called her name again. To her horror, he dismounted and started walking down the path. It wouldn't take much for them to be discovered.

Irina stiffened, and Henry's thumb stroked across her chin in a quiet attempt to calm her rattled nerves. Her breathing eased somewhat as Max halted a stone's throw away, his eyes studying the waterfall and then the pool. Irina noted sourly that he didn't seem to mind the mud too much. What a little liar! With a shake of his head, Max headed back toward his horse, and within moments, was gone. Neither she nor Henry moved for a long minute, in case Max decided to circle back.

A slight cramp in her leg made her wriggle, and she heard Henry's sharp inhalation as her hips rocked into his. She was getting quite adept at freezing mid-motion, but this time, everything *inside* her body went feral even as she went completely still. Her blood simmered like a wild thing, her heartbeat trebled its pace, and her breath rattled in her lungs.

She was alone.

Pressed against a tree.

With a naked man glued to her back.

Henry's hand released her chin and dropped to rest across her collarbone, his fingers stroking lazily across her throat. Without a word, he drew her against him. Irina sucked in a soft gasp, realizing the dampness from his nude body had seeped into her own clothing. He was so warm she'd noticed none of it. Her breath came in shallow agonizing pants as his hand wandered down the front of her, skimming over her breasts to her stomach and back up. He still hadn't said a word, even though she was quite sure that Max had gone.

Mesmerized by the sensual stroking of his fingers along each of her ribs that left rivers of warmth in their wake, Irina remained silent. After a moment, she felt his warm breath on her neck and then his lips, planting sweet touches along the crest of her nape. Climbing up the sensitive column of her neck, he sucked her earlobe into his mouth. She nearly collapsed. Heat shivered through her in molten waves while his mouth continued to explore her skin and his hand drifted upward.

Cupping her jaw, Henry tilted her chin up and took her lips in so gentle a kiss that it made her want to swoon with the tenderness of it. He teased the seam of her lips with his tongue before delving inside to stroke against hers. The kiss turned carnal, and he groaned low in his throat. Arching her neck, Irina attempted to twist her body around, but he kept her firmly still, with her back to him.

Henry was hard everywhere. She squirmed against his uncompromising frame, and he laughed quietly, one of his hands falling to her hip. "Stop moving, sweet," he whispered, his tongue shifting to trace the outline of her ear, making her daft. "Or you'll unman me."

Freezing once more, she felt heat rush into her body at the insistent prod of him against the seat of her breeches. She'd forgotten he was naked. And that was his...*oh God*. Irina sucked in a shuddering breath. She was innocent, but she was not naive. Max had never been scandalous enough to deluge her with details of what happened between lovers, but she'd heard enough salacious talk to discern what the bulge pressing into the base of her spine meant. The hot, hard length of him made her blood thicken to molasses in her veins and her toes curl in her riding boots.

Her thighs went weak. Good heavens, there was nothing soft about him. Henry's hands roved over her body restlessly as his mouth claimed hers once more. Lost in sensation, she opened for him, relishing his taste and the seductive feel of his tongue rubbing against hers. Once more, she made to turn in his arms, but he held her still. "No, I like you like this." His voice was like rough velvet across her rapidly fraying nerves.

Irina gasped as his hand slipped inside the neckline of her coat and under the cotton chemise within. He rolled an aching nipple between his fingers and then shifted his attention to the other breast. Sharp bolts of liquid fire shot from their tips to the center of her hips, making her moan his name into his mouth.

"Henry, please," she said, not knowing what she was asking for.

But he seemed to, and obliged with a muffled growl as

he nipped and suckled at her throat. His hand slid down the front of the coat, undoing her buttons as he went, until it gaped open. Both his hands reached beneath her chemise to cup and knead her breasts as she lolled back against him in senseless abandon, lost to the storm he was inciting inside her. With deft fingers, he skimmed down her torso, his warm hands exploring the waistband of her breeches.

"Laces," she murmured as his fingers fumbled in search of a clasp. *Good Lord.* She couldn't believe she'd just instructed him on how to loosen her clothing. But if his touch felt anything like it had when he'd undone her coat, she wasn't about to complain.

The laces unsnapped loop by loop, each flick of the leather cord making her pulse leap in reckless anticipation, until she felt the waistband loosen and Henry's large hand inch its way downward past her silk drawers. Irina held her breath as he pressed his palm against the very core of her. Moaning, she writhed against his hand, wanting him to touch her more but unable to articulate exactly what it was she wanted. Everything ached at the point where his palm met her body.

"God, Irina, you're so warm," he whispered into her ear. One teasing finger slid past the slit in her drawers, threading through the soft curls there. Irina arched back against him in bewilderment. "Relax," he coaxed, scraping his teeth along her neck. "Let me touch you."

Words failed her as his fingers began to stroke through her sleek, damp center, causing white-hot sensations to streak through her limbs and into her belly.

"Oh—*oh.*"

Suddenly, Irina couldn't focus a single coherent thought in her head—her brain had become as utterly pliant and useless as her body was in his hands. Those clever, devious hands that were doing things that could not be decent. A decadent shiver took her unawares, and she gasped. She didn't *want* decent.

"You feel like silk," he murmured, trailing scorching kisses along her jaw. "Hot, wet silk."

His words seduced almost as much as his fingers did. Irina's mouth fell open on a shattered exhale as pressure began to build with each glide of his finger against her. She moaned in deliciously shocked surprise as Henry strummed her body like a virtuoso. He plucked and stroked and circled her flesh, making her mad with desire, while his mouth continued its lush sampling of her sensitive nape.

Irina knew she should have been frightened. She was alone in the woods with a man…his hands caressing places that had never been touched. But she also knew Henry would never hurt her. Alone with him at last, she wasn't afraid. She wasn't wary. She felt bold, wanton. Like a free-spirited Greek nymph.

Pleasure built in lavish surges within her as his fingers and mouth coaxed unbelievable sensations from deep inside. He groaned when she arched backward and tilted her neck, a sigh rising in her throat. Was he enjoying this as much as she was? Was she wrong to crave his touch so shamelessly?

Whimpering softly, Irina tipped her chin up and sought his lips. His tongue mimicked the motion of his wicked fingers below. Pleasure ebbed and flowed in surges as her hips rocked against his hand.

"Henry—"

"It's yours, just reach for it," he told her and took her lips again, his clever fingers quickening their pace.

Her thoughts turned to nonsense. With a soft cry, she felt her body tightening until she could hardly bear it, and then she shuddered against him as violent waves of pleasure rocked through her. When the inner storm finally subsided, her brain felt numb and her sated body boneless.

Never had Irina felt anything so stirring…so soul

shattering.

So unbelievably *wicked*.

Weak-kneed, she sagged backward into the spooning arch of his body. Supporting her weight, Henry removed his hand from the damp crux of her, still cupping her intimately as she collapsed against him, her breath coming in short, strained pants. She wanted to laugh at the shocking pleasure of it. She wanted to weep with how tender he'd been.

Neither of them spoke as Henry finally turned her to face him, his patient fingers re-lacing her breeches and buttoning her coat. Irina felt herself coloring fiercely. Only now she truly understood the meaning of carnal pleasure. She had just been the willing recipient of it.

Embarrassment filled her in a blazing rush at how wanton and pliable she'd been in Henry's arms. She had let him touch the most intimate part of her, and worst of all, she'd enjoyed every blissful minute of it. Irina dared a look up at Henry through her lashes and felt the warm satiety depart her body. This time a whole other unpleasant emotion gripped Irina, something that matched the brooding, furious expression on Henry's face. Confusion swiftly followed, and once more, she became fixed in place. He stared at her as if she'd grown a pair of horns, when he'd been the one to incite the devil in the first place.

She'd done nothing wrong. Had she?

Chapter Fourteen

Henry stepped back from her, his bare feet treading upon his clothes, which he'd dropped to the ground seconds before grabbing her from behind and pressing her against the rough bark of the tree. That had been his first mistake—putting his hands on her at all. His second had been in not sending her home the minute Remi left. His third...well, the state of his engorged body was proof enough of that.

As if in response to his thoughts, Irina's eyes dropped to his naked front, and the stain of color on her cheeks intensified. Her eyes rounded in shock as her mouth, those perfect lips he'd been plundering seconds before, parted in unconcealed astonishment at the unobstructed—and unabashed—view of him. Henry crouched and took up his trousers, pulling them on with angry tugs as she spun away, averting her hot stare. He suppressed the sudden, demented urge to drag her to the forest floor and bury his rigid arousal in her warm, willing body. The cling of her dewy skin on his fingers had been drugging, her moans and whimpers even more so.

"You are intent on ruination," he muttered, buttoning

the fall quickly over his straining anatomy, gooseflesh rising on his arms and stomach despite the heat of exasperation simmering just beneath his skin.

"I—I only wanted to run the course again, and I thought you were still in London," she said, turning slightly to see him.

His shirt was damp, the linen sticking to his wet arms as he dressed. Noticing her perusal, Henry's jaw clenched. She'd been at the pool, he knew, watching him. His ravaged back must have been on full, grisly display then. Had she felt horror? Revulsion? Or worse…pity?

"Did you tell Lord Remi about this place?" Henry asked, finishing with his shirt and grabbing his stockings and Hessians. "Did you intend to meet him here for a rendezvous, believing I was still in town?"

"Of course not," she answered, and from the insulted tone of her voice, he believed her. "He followed without my knowledge. How dare you suggest I intended for a tryst."

Henry stepped toward her, water dripping from his hair and soaking his collar. "Intended or not, you received one just the same."

He stormed past her, toward the path that led to the small cabin in the clearing, unable to hold her livid glare. He'd lost control the moment he'd tucked her against that tree, his dripping wet body plastering the back of her shirt and trousers. Even as Remi had called for her, his eyes searching the thick wood for any movement, Henry had felt the weightlessness of abandon lifting him. Dressed as she was, the full curve of her backside on such luscious display, he had wanted only to sink into her.

He heard Irina following him now along the path, her feet breaking small sticks as she rushed to keep up.

"Why are you acting as if I am the one who has done something wrong?" she asked.

Henry faltered in step. She had done nothing—*nothing*—

wrong. He was the one who couldn't seem to stop making these mistakes, even though in the moment, they felt the furthest thing from wrong. He'd been standing under that waterfall, fantasizing an erotic scenario, one in which Irina joined him, stripping herself slowly before wading into the pool to meet him. He'd been at full mast even before he'd seen her.

Henry had been yanked from his fantasy by the sound of a male voice calling Irina's name. And when he'd turned, Henry had seen her figure standing stock-still on the brink of discovery. He'd stared at her for a half second before swimming toward shore, irrationally concerned—and elated—that somehow his thoughts had summoned her.

"You should not have come here," he replied, wishing to hell she had stayed away.

"So why did you just… What was that back there, then? Punishment?"

He strode into the clearing, relieved to see Lord Remi had not hung about, waiting for Irina to return to her horse.

Henry turned to her, his gaze snapping to hers. "Did it feel like punishment to you, Princess?"

She drew back, those violet eyes of hers going heavy with the memory of what had just transpired between them. A furious blush rose, warming her neck and suffusing her cheeks. God, he'd wanted to strip her bare and take her right then and there. Had she been wearing a skirt, easily tossed up over her hips, instead of those damned breeches, he was not quite certain he wouldn't have. He'd reached into her instead, touching and stroking her, until she cried out, his name upon her lips.

Without waiting for an answer, Henry turned away, toward his horse, hoping to shield from her the renewed ridge of his erection.

"We cannot be found here," he said, thinking only of the possible firestorm of scandal that would smudge her reputation. But when she spoke he grew disappointed in himself yet again.

"No. I imagine Lady Carmichael would not like to hear such gossip."

He had not thought of Rose. Not once.

"That is a business arrangement. In name only. Rose is aware of what that entails." Henry drew a calming breath. "If you'll meet me back at Hartstone— " he started to say, but Irina went to her mount and began untying the mare from the post.

"I cannot stay," she said, unable to look at him.

"We need to talk," he replied, thinking of the betting book at White's and the reason he'd come to Essex in the first place.

"There is nothing to say. Nothing that will change anything. Leave me be," she said, setting her booted foot in a stirrup and hoisting herself into the saddle. "I must find Max before he alerts Lana or Gray that I've gone missing in the Earl of Langlevit's woods."

"It is Remi we must talk about." He was trying to think of a way to tell her what he knew without mentioning the bets. Or perhaps he *should* mention them. If she knew the truth about why men kept falling at her feet, making fools of themselves, perhaps she'd be more cautious at society events. Not that the bets were the reason he seemed to keep making a fool of himself. He wished it were as simple as money.

Irina gritted her teeth and gathered the reins. "Why must I say this yet again? Max is my *friend*."

Henry took her mount's bridle and stopped her from riding away. "That is what he would have you believe. I have it on good authority, however, that he has other designs upon you."

"Whose good authority is this?"

"That does not matter."

"It does if you expect me to listen."

He groaned. There was something off about Lord Remi, and Henry needed her to listen. Needed her to believe him. There could be no skirting around the issue any longer.

"There are wagers being placed at White's," he said. "They involve you."

He'd expected a scathing glare or an immediate refusal, but instead Irina broke into a slow smile. And then she laughed.

"What do you find so humorous?" he asked, still holding tight to her bridle.

It was as if she'd found his revelation lacking in some way.

Her laughter calmed. "Nothing, nothing at all. I'm only curious…*Max* hasn't wagered anything…has he?"

Henry curled his fingers tighter around the leather bridle. "You don't seem surprised in the least to hear that men have been betting on your favors."

Because she isn't, he realized. The hellion. She'd *known.*

Irina shifted uneasily in her saddle, the mare trying to prance away from Henry. The animal likely sensed his simmering anger.

"Oh, stop. The wagers are innocent enough. A stroll in Hyde Park. The first dance at a ball. Why, I think the most scandalous wager I've heard of yet involved touching a palm to my lower back while guiding me to the dance floor."

Again, she laughed. Henry released the bridle and instantly wished for the neck of that bet's winner to strangle.

"Oh, trust me, Princess, there are wagers in that book that are far from innocent, and your dear friend Max is encouraging them. As are you."

"He is only having a bit of fun—"

"Yes, at your expense and at your peril."

"Peril!" she scoffed. "I'm hardly in danger!"

"Yes, peril. As the book is at White's and women are not permitted, I am certain you have not seen the current list of wagers. *I* have, however."

Irina's mare, restless, trotted in a tight circle. "I do not believe it. Max would never play with my safety. What sort of peril?"

He wanted to drag her out of her saddle and shake sense into her.

"A kiss," Henry replied. "And not a chaste peck upon the lips."

Her brows pinched in confusion. At least she was not dismissing it with another lighthearted chuckle. She appeared to be mulling it over at first, but then, with a shrug, said, "It seems you've won that bet."

"I don't want to win any ridiculous bets," he bit out, his frustration boiling over.

"What *do* you want then?" she shouted, her horse's legs shifting forward and back in response to her agitation. "One moment you're professing that you feel nothing for me and that you never will, and the next you…you're touching me in ways no man ever has. You're either lying to me about how you feel or you're lying to yourself, and I don't know which one makes me more furious!"

The mare whinnied and spun, nearly breaking free of his grip, but Irina managed to hold her in check. Henry had lied, yes. He'd lied to them both. And he was as tired of it as she.

"You desire the truth? The truth is uncomplicated. I want you. I want you in ways that would shock you, ways you cannot begin to imagine." He stepped forward, the grass against his bare feet somehow urging him onward with the truth. "The things I want to do to you, Irina, they are…base. Far too sordid for even that damned book at White's."

Going still, she stared down at him with an unreadable expression, even the mare quieting beneath her. "So it is only lust? You wish to bed me."

"Yes, it is lust. Yes, I want to bed you," he answered without a moment's hesitation. God, *yes*. But it was also more. He wanted to be in her presence. He wanted her to look at him and smile and laugh at the things he said. He wanted to hear her voice whenever one of his memories paralyzed him.

He wanted to keep her far away from the arrogant pricks in London making wagers on her as if she were a racehorse. They knew nothing of her, or of the real prize she offered.

How in hell was he supposed to say these things without laying himself bare?

Or perhaps that is exactly what he needed to do.

"Irina—"

"You've made yourself clear," she said, blinking rapidly. "I will not lie and say your...attentions have made me feel nothing."

Good. It would have been an obvious lie. Her response had been more magnificent, more honest, than any woman he'd ever encountered before.

"However, you've made your promise to Lady Carmichael, and regardless of the nature of your agreement, I will not help you treat her with such disregard." Irina spoke with a lofty air, as if she were addressing a royal assembly instead of the man whose naked body had just been pressed against her, whose hands had pleasured her, coaxing her to blissful release.

"Do not kiss me again," she added. "It will only serve to further lower my opinion of you. And of myself. Good afternoon, Lord Langlevit."

And with that, she dug her heels into her mount and shot across the clearing, kicking up clods of dirt and grass in her wake. He watched her disappear into the trees, along an overgrown path that would lead back toward the lane instead of Hartstone.

Henry's opinion of himself had already been as low as he'd imagined it could sink, and it had been a long time since it had bothered him. Since he'd felt a scorching disgust for what he'd let himself become.

But with that cold and brutal set down, Irina had swiftly reminded him.

. . .

Irina was so furious and so intent on escaping both the man she'd left behind as well as the bright prick of her conscience, she didn't realize she'd ridden clear past Stanton Park. She and the mare came to a lathered stop in a meadow she did not recognize.

"Sorry, Primrose," she murmured to the horse as she dismounted, stroking her damp flanks. "We'll walk back, shall we?"

Her body ached. Her heart, even more so.

Henry *wanted* her.

Of course, he did. Irina had seen the evidence of that clearly. Heat swamped her as the memory of the glimpse she'd caught made her breath hitch. In Paris, she'd seen enough nude sculptures to know what the male form looked like, but none of them had prepared her for the staggering and unapologetically erect eyeful of him she'd gotten.

He wanted her in ways she could not begin to imagine.

Irina's core went liquid. She'd be lying if she said she didn't want him as well. In her bed. On the floor of that clearing. Anywhere. She craved his hands on her as they had been, and hers on his glorious body, exploring her fill. She wanted to give him the same incandescent pleasure he'd given her.

"Deep breaths," she told herself, coloring at her wanton, indecent thoughts. Irina drew a restorative breath as she approached the drive for her sister's estate. One of the stableboys — Percival, or Percy, he was called — rushed up the lane to take the horse. "Give her a good rubdown and some extra mash, Percy," Irina said to him. "She deserves it."

"Fer sure, Your Highness."

The boy led the mare away, and Irina straightened her hair on her walk to the manor, hoping to God she didn't look like some light-skirt who had just been ravished by a devilishly charming highwayman. It wasn't far from the truth. Langlevit may not have been a highwayman, but he was every bit as much a rogue. A handsome, seductive rogue who had made her completely forget herself.

Intent on ruination, he'd accused.

Little did he know that at the sight of him in that waterfall, she'd been *desperate* for it. She flushed at the memory. Irina's lips burned. The space between her legs tingled. Though frustrated afterward, Henry hadn't seemed displeased while he'd been kissing her. He'd been…tender. For a moment while he'd been touching her, it had felt much like him needing *her*. And when she'd found her release, he'd held her close.

Right before pushing her away.

Irina sighed. The man was impossible to fathom. Hot one minute, cold the next. As arctic as a winter storm. She huffed a laugh. He deserved some of her old nicknames more than she did. Despite what he'd confessed about his platonic arrangement with Rose, in a few short months, he would be a married man. And if everything went to plan, she would be married, also.

To Max.

"Where have you been?" her sister shrieked as she entered the foyer, already dressed in a lovely light blue gown and looking frazzled. "Rolling around in a barn? Hurry, we're going to be late."

"Late?"

"Dinner with Lord and Lady Bradburne."

Irina groaned. She'd completely forgotten. The last thing she wanted was to go anywhere and have to be social, but she'd promised her sister, and Max couldn't very well go alone. With his cutting sense of humor, he'd likely end up offending someone.

Frowning as she went directly to her chamber, she recalled what the earl had told her about the latest wager and felt instantly irritated. Though why she was annoyed Max was participating baffled her. She was the one who had encouraged him to do so. Max was simply playing the part of a gentleman in her thrall. He was a performer at heart, after all. Still, it rankled slightly that he would pen in a wager for such a scandalous bet.

A kiss, of all things. And apparently not a chaste one, either. What had Max been thinking when he'd made the wager? Had he entered it, too? She had no intention of kissing him in public. Or kissing him at all. Something like that could indeed lead to her ruination, though one could argue she'd already been well and truly ruined in that clearing. Her body shivered in vivid response at the memory of the earl's stroking touch, and she willed herself to forget it. It had been a mistake.

Oddly disgruntled, she washed in the slipper bath while her lady's maid readied her gown for dinner at Worthington Abbey. For the evening, she had chosen a pale lavender silk Parisian concoction with a high waist and long sleeves. The modest bust line only served to accentuate the stunning feature of the dress—a rather shocking expanse of her back. A special corset had been cleverly designed to accommodate the scandalously low rise. The gown was one of Irina's favorites, and why she felt the need to wear it, she had no idea. Perhaps because she knew she could never wear it in London, not after Henry's warning. It was far too daring, and as much as she had scoffed at the idea of being in peril, she *had* noticed an increased level of intensity on the heels of those damned wagers. Not that she'd ever admit that to anyone.

Particularly Henry.

"A loose knot will do," Irina told Jane as the maid finished combing her hair. "Quickly, and use those matching combs." It only took five minutes for Jane to complete the task, and Irina thought she'd done a perfectly acceptable job. Her dark hair was secured at the crown, with a few tendrils pulled loose at her ears.

"Don't you look beautiful," a sardonic voice said from the doorway. Max stood there, dressed in showy evening clothes and looking quite dashingly handsome.

From the coy looks she kept darting in his direction, Jane obviously thought so, too. Max winked at her and nodded toward the door. The maid scurried from the room as Irina rose, attempting to clasp a diamond bracelet to her wrist. She vaulted an eyebrow. "Do you wish to incite my sister's wrath and cause a scandal?"

"Then you will be forced to marry me." His smile was lazy as he approached. "Allow me."

She frowned at him as he reached for the bracelet. "I'm already marrying you, remember?"

"Yes, I can tell you are eagerly awaiting my proposal," he said as he deftly fastened the clasp. He kept a firm hold on her wrist. "Where were you this afternoon?" The sour waft of wine drifted toward her.

"I told you I went for a ride." She narrowed her eyes at him, noticing the high color of his cheeks and his bright eyes. "Are you foxed?"

Max ignored her question and instead brought her fingers to his lips. "I followed you to Langlevit's estate. Hartstone, is it not? But somehow, I managed to lose you."

"I may have ridden through his estate, what of it?" She wrenched her hand from his. "And why would you follow me in the first place?"

"You seemed agitated," he replied mildly. "I was worried."

"Max, I am a grown woman."

"Who seems intent on putting her reputation at risk by riding on strangers' properties alone and unchaperoned."

She shot him a glare. Max was the last person who would give a hoot about reputations, hers included. Otherwise he never would have written in that damned wager. Scowling, she swallowed the accusation on the tip of her tongue. Seeing how he was her sole source of information on the White's wager log, Max would know instantly that she'd heard it from someone else, and she wasn't prepared to have that conversation.

"The Earl of Langlevit is no stranger, and anyway, he is in London."

Max looked at her strangely for a moment before shaking his head. "Langlevit is here in Essex. Lord Northridge has just told me that he will be in attendance at dinner tonight."

"Is that so?" Irina's throat grew constricted at the announcement, but she forced her face to remain composed, knowing Max's perceptive gaze had not slipped from hers.

Taking hold of her nerveless fingers, Max squeezed gently. "Irina, if Langlevit gets wind of what we are planning, it will all be for naught." He softened his voice. "I'm not blind. I know you care for him, but he has chosen another. You need to let him go. Deep down, I know you know this. In a few months, we will be done with this dreary old place and back in Europe where we belong, with nothing but pleasure awaiting us. Will that be so bad?"

Irina said nothing. She didn't know when it had happened, but she didn't think England was so dreary anymore. At least not this part of it, and even London was a bit beautiful and stately in certain areas. Her grand scheme to return to St. Petersburg after bringing London to its knees had somehow lost its luster, too. Irina felt lost. She cared for a man who wanted her body but could never return her affection. She craved a storybook ending that was out of reach. She had never been one for fairy tales, but for once, her heart pined for the impossible.

But Max was right. Perhaps there were no happy endings to be had.

"You're right," Irina agreed softly. "It wouldn't be so bad."

Chapter Fifteen

Course after succulent course was served in the lavish dining room at Worthington Abbey, but Irina tasted none of it. Her mouth was dry, her hands clammy. When they were not busy at the task of moving food around on her plate, she kept them fisted on her lap, working the delicate folds of her dress. The low undertones of conversation hummed about her, but she heard none of that, either. Her entire attention was focused on *not* noticing the man seated across from her.

But he was all she'd noticed since the minute she'd arrived.

Stealing a glance at him, she thought the Earl of Langlevit looked a far cry from the man in the middle of the woods earlier that afternoon, though he was no less attractive. He was devastatingly so. His tailored evening clothes did little to detract from the pure male presence of him, and his volatile energy remained leashed beneath the surface of his now polished and poised exterior. Irina wondered how she'd never noticed that about him. Though relaxed and laughing at something the duchess had said, he was still all coiled, bunched, and bracing intensity.

"Are you not hungry?" Lana whispered from her left. "You've barely touched your food."

"No," she said. "It's delicious. I'm distracted, that's all."

"Distracted, Your Highness?" Max said loudly, making her want to kick him underneath the table as all eyes centered on her. "Is it a diverting distraction?"

"Quite boring, in fact," she said, glowering at him. "A needlepoint project."

Max grinned. "Needlepoint is my absolute favorite thing in the world. Please, do share."

Irina nearly rolled her eyes. Max full well knew she had no inkling of anything remotely related to needlepoint. She opened her mouth to bluff her way out, but her rescue came from another direction.

"It is my understanding that Princess Irina prefers the sword to the needle," Henry said, his eyes settling on her.

"That is true," she said after an awkward beat of silence, though she could not discern whether his tone was disparaging or complimentary. "I'm afraid I'm not adept in most ladies' pursuits, and Lord Langlevit is right—I do seem to take an exceptional aversion to needles of all sort."

To her surprise, the duke erupted in laughter at the other end of the table. "You find yourself in good company then, Princess, for my wife cannot sew a stitch to save her life."

"Yes, my dear, I leave the knitting and mending to you," the duchess replied, not at all perturbed by the duke's teasing, and winked at Irina. "His Grace admittedly has far better needlework than I. It's no secret that I much prefer fencing to crocheting, though I have found that knitting needles make excellent darts in a pinch. I keep a pair in my reticule for that very purpose."

The duke lifted his glass with a laugh, eyeing his wife. "To the women who fence and do not knit, and to us unfortunate men who adore them."

"Here, here," everyone said, laughing.

Irina grinned and sipped her wine. No wonder her sister had become so close to the duchess over the last handful of years. She was lovely, and her rakish sense of humor was much like her brother, North's. For the first time all evening, she found herself relaxing slightly.

Lana shook her head. "I, for one, do not agree. I do love a good cross-stitch. Though I also adore fencing. Arguments can be made for both."

"A toast to my radiant wife," North crowed. "Ever the diplomatic peacemaker." He paused, reconsidering his toast for a moment, and frowned. "Unless she is cross. Especially while pregnant. Then everyone should run for their lives."

Lana laughed and lifted her water goblet. "I make no apologies."

"Nor should you," he agreed and rolled his eyes at the last moment, making Lana throw her napkin at him.

Laughter broke out once more while the last course was cleared and the dessert course brought in. "It's your favorite," the duchess announced to Irina from down the table as the footman placed a selection of delicate French chocolate truffles in front of her. "Lana told me that you have a weakness for chocolate."

"Ever since she was fourteen," Lord Langlevit agreed. Irina's eyes shot to his and fell away just as quickly. She needed to remain impervious. "I saw her eat an entire dozen once."

"Irina," Lana admonished though her eyes were twinkling. "Such habits are meant to be kept *secret*."

"I never was much good at those," Irina said and took a delicate bite of one of the morsels. She nearly swooned in her seat at the decadent taste of the rich ganache melting on her tongue.

Max lounged back in his chair. "Oh, I beg to differ, my

dear. You are truly wonderful at keeping secrets." He smirked in a suggestive manner, drawing everyone's notice, including Lord Langlevit's. Irina didn't understand if he was deliberately being perverse by baiting Henry or whether he simply wanted to torture her. "Especially ones of importance," he added, ignoring her glare.

What was he playing at, the wretch? He downed his wine, and Irina watched as his glass was refilled by the hovering footman. Max had been in his cups when he'd visited her chamber, and he'd already had a few glasses of wine at dinner.

"Lord Remi." She placed her fork down.

"Oh, please, my lady, I would never divulge anything that would impeach that perfect reputation of yours."

"But have you *done* anything to threaten it, Remi?" The silky question came from Lord Langlevit, and immediately, the tension at the table thickened.

"Whatever do you mean?" Max tossed back airily.

Henry crossed his arms across his chest. "I heard you took her to a gentleman's gaming club in Paris."

North gave a bark of laughter that he quickly muffled, and Lana practically choked on her water. Dimly, Irina recalled Lana mentioning something about their stay at a bawdy gaming hall. Apparently, she and Lord Northridge had been caught at an infamous one themselves in London's North End after their carriage had hit a log en route to town. Irina's eyes narrowed as something jogged her memory. Come to think of it, said hall was the same one Langlevit had mentioned—the Cock and the something or other.

"The club was my idea," Irina announced in a sudden fit of contrariness. "I wanted to go."

"You invite scandal and ruin upon her," Henry said in a low, controlled voice, ignoring the fact that she had spoken and keeping his eyes centered on Max.

"At least I'd be willing to propose marriage," Max

countered, eliciting gasps from Lady Bradburne and Lana. "If it did come to that. Ruin, I mean. But sadly, Princess Irina is far too straitlaced to be seduced by any gentleman."

Except for the man directly opposite, Irina thought.

"I am in no danger of being ruined," she muttered. It was hardly appropriate dinner conversation.

Feeling Henry's eyes drift to her, Irina squirmed inwardly and kept her own gaze focused on her plate, for fear of how transparent she would become if she so much as looked at him.

"I beg to argue," the earl said. "Take the recent wagers at White's for example."

"Wagers?" both Lady Bradburne and Lana asked in unison, their interest roused while Irina's heart sank. Though the wager book at White's was also not appropriate dinner conversation, no one in attendance here seemed to give two figs for propriety. Both North and Bradburne treated their wives with far more freedom than did most other gentlemen of their set. Not that either Lana or the duchess would have it any other way, Irina suspected.

"Explain yourself, Lord Langlevit," Lana said tightly.

Irina's eyes rose to clash with Henry's amber ones. Would he expose the fact that she knew about them? Encouraged them, even? Would he be so cruel? Her sister would be mortified and utterly furious. Lana and North, as her guardians, had the power to confine her to Stanton Park. And though Irina would rebel against being kept prisoner, she also did not wish to compromise her sister's health by any means. Her fate, as it were, rested in Lord Langlevit's hands. Her heart hammered in her chest, and she waited with bated breath.

"For Lady Irina's favors," Henry said. "A dance, a stroll, a kiss, a ride…" He trailed off and paused, those glittering eyes delving into hers, and Irina jutted her chin. She couldn't control her violent flush at the silent confrontation. The innuendo on the word *ride* was subtle but clear. Everyone else at the table missed the inflection, though, except Max. He had gone rigid in the seat beside her.

"Well, this conversation has quickly gone to hell," Lord Northridge commented in the widening silence and drained his wineglass. This time, though, no one laughed.

"This is atrocious, an absolute travesty," Lana said with an affronted expression, her gaze sliding to Irina. "She is not some ridiculous prize."

"The Prize of London, to be exact," Max drawled in a tone that made Irina again want to kick him.

"Unacceptable." Lady Bradburne scowled and nodded her agreement with her sister-in-law. "And it is truly disgusting the way you gentlemen wager every little thing."

"Not all gentlemen, dear," the duke said gently.

"It's harmless, I expect," Irina said with a laugh, keeping her voice light to dissipate the burgeoning tension and the look of murderous disgust on Lana's face. "I don't mind if the gentlemen at the club have a bit of fun. Being known as the Prize of London is far better than being known as an Ice Princess, I suppose. It will pass in time once some other fascination takes their interest."

"You must put a stop to this, Archer," Lady Bradburne said to her husband.

"I wish I could, my love, but the wager books are untouchable."

Irina cleared her throat. "It truly does not bother me, Your Grace," she said to the duchess, smiling brightly, and patting Max's arm beside her. "And I have Lord Remi to protect me from any overeager suitors."

Henry snorted, his eyes like ice chips. "It is not some unknown and overeager suitor that worries me."

"Do you have something to say, Langlevit?" Max asked

with an indolent grin.

His response was deadly low. "Should I?"

Irina's entire body went taut. She was sure Max was not aware how much danger of bodily harm he was in. Even she could sense the precarious shift in the air as Henry tensed across the table, his large body flexing like a jungle cat about to pounce on its prey. But Max only waved an idle arm, as if intent on provoking the beast. "It may come as a surprise to you, but Princess Irina does not do anything she doesn't want to do," he replied, unfazed, his expression cool. "And do not forget, Langlevit, you are no longer her guardian."

"Max," Irina hissed in warning, even as Henry's back went straight in his chair. The younger man was veering into dangerous territory by suggesting her honor had been compromised in any way, especially with her sister, her husband, and the powerful Duke and Duchess of Bradburne looking on with unsmiling interest. "Please, that is enough."

Max took her hand from her lap, and raising it to his lips, kissed her knuckles. "Apologies, Your Highness," he murmured. "I truly did not mean to cause offense or discomfort."

Irina did not fall for the act one bit. He did not mean his apology at all if the unrepentant look in his eyes was any signal, and he was only kissing her bloody hand to inflame the earl. Max *never* apologized, not even when he was in the wrong. Irina spared Henry a glance and hurriedly retracted her arm. A lethal glint shone in his eyes, as if Henry also suspected the apology was false. Irina was certain he was on the verge of leaping across the table to throttle her unsuspecting friend with his bare hands. She had to do something, and quickly.

Swallowing hard, she stood, a nearby footman rushing forward to hold her chair back. Four more chairs shifted backward as the men stood to their feet, and she smiled despite her grimly throbbing heart. "Gentlemen, please, let's not ruin what has thus far been a lovely evening. I'm sure a game of billiards would be in order, and a glass of sherry for us ladies."

Her sister also rose, her wan face catching Irina's eye. "I'm afraid I must make my regrets," Lana said, quick to shoot a reassuring smile to those around her. "I do admit to feeling a bit overwhelmed." She glanced at Irina. "Lord Northridge will see me home if you wish to stay. And Godfrey can return for you once he has seen us back to Stanton Park."

"No," Irina said. "I should accompany you."

"It's not necessary. I assure you that I'm only tired. I am a dreadful bore, I know. You should stay and enjoy the rest of your evening."

Irina said nothing, but if things continued on the path they'd been on with Max and the earl, the evening was sure to keep heading south. But she nodded and made certain Lana was safely ensconced in the carriage before going back inside. Irina had a sinking feeling that Lana would not forget about the wagers, which meant for a lecture or worse on the morrow. North hadn't been far off when he'd said that the better choice was to run when Lana was angry. Her temper could be formidable when provoked.

To Irina's surprise, when she returned, the drawing room and the salon were both empty. "Where has everyone gone?" she asked Heed, the Duke of Bradburne's longtime butler.

"Her Grace offers her sincerest apologies, but she has been summoned to the nursery," he said.

"Oh, is everything well?"

"Yes, Your Highness. Master Brandon is recovering from a cough," Heed explained. Irina recalled hearing of Lady Bradburne's lung ailments when she was a child, and she hoped it was nothing of the same. "Lord Langlevit and Lord Remi are in the billiards room," Heed said.

The two of them alone in a room? That was not wise.

"I suppose I should find Max and take our leave, as well," Irina murmured half to herself. She did not want to impose upon their hosts if they had a sick child on hand, and it wouldn't be long before Godfrey returned. "Where is the billiards room?"

"This way, Your Highness."

Irina followed Heed in silence, her feet making no sound on the thick carpets. The doors to the billiards room were open, but she heard no voices. Thanking Heed, she wandered in. The room was empty, thankfully not occupied by two men engaged in fisticuffs. She almost sighed with relief.

Irina ran her hands across the gorgeous red felt of the billiards table and rolled one of the white balls sitting in a felted box along its length. Max had taught her the game when they were in Paris, and she found that she'd enjoyed the play and its structured mathematical nature. Irina looked around. Where was that scoundrel anyway? She intended to give him a good piece of her mind on the way back to Stanton Park.

She placed the valuable pure ivory ball back into its box and nearly leaped a foot into the air as a lean shadow uncurled itself from a darkened corner of the room. "Are you going to play or just roll the balls around?" Henry asked, approaching with a drink in hand.

Irina's breath caught as she scanned the room for any other hidden bodies. They were alone. Well, not truly alone. A footman stood just beyond the door, which remained open. Henry prowled closer, and she had the sudden urge to back away. Not because she was afraid of him...Irina was more afraid of herself. She always seemed to lose every shred of sense and dignity wherever he was concerned, and she'd meant what she'd said earlier. Ignoring her scattered pulse, she straightened her spine. "I was looking for Max."

"He disappeared. Perhaps he decided to take some air."

Irina frowned at him, her reply sour. "You both needed some air."

Henry didn't respond, only stood staring at her with that unfathomable look of his. He sipped his whiskey.

"Would you like to play?" she asked, gesturing to the table after a few moments of awkward silence.

"No."

Of course not. And why would he? She'd given him the direct cut, asking him to keep his distance and not to kiss her again. He was simply playing by her rules, it seemed.

"All right, then," she replied, tapping another ball before starting away from the table. "I'll leave you be."

She'd barely turned her back when he said, "The cracking noise. It's not ideal."

Irina stopped and turned back to him, her heart tripping as a rush of pity filled her. He would not appreciate the sentiment, however, so she only smiled and nodded.

"However," he went on, placing his drink upon the mantel with a smirk. "If you were to crack the balls softly…"

Irina couldn't stop the answering grin that surged to her lips. "I am certain I could be gentle with them."

She was rewarded with a short bark of laughter. "Gentle? I fear that any man who allows his…balls near you will find themselves in the gravest of danger."

"My lord!" Her jaw went loose, and she stared at him, her laughter bubbling up. Henry's light humor reminded her of easier times…of happier times. Though she didn't quite trust herself with him, it was worth the few seconds of actually hearing him laugh. It was something he no longer did often, she knew. "Though you're probably right."

Henry vaulted an eyebrow in challenge. "Come now then, Princess," he said, grabbing hold of a nearby playing stick. "Let's see this skill of yours."

• • •

Henry braced himself for the first scattering of the three billiard balls over the felt. He'd allowed Irina the first move, and to his relief, she was indeed gentle as she sent the ivory cue ball marked with a black dot forward. The muted crack still held enough power to send the red ball landing straight into a side pocket.

"Well done," he murmured as he lined his cue up. "Two points."

"I'd like to claim that it was intentional, but alas, it was mere luck," she replied.

"Never divulge your strategy," he said, standing tall again and eyeing her from across the table. She was gorgeous in that gown, the back dipping so low Henry could see the soft, delicate skin of the small of her back; the curve of her spine and the play of slim muscles as she walked.

"In billiards or in general?" she asked.

Henry watched her eyes settle on the table. He took his shot with his plain white ball, striking hers before sinking the red ball into a corner pocket in a clever combination shot. "A cannon. Well played," she complimented.

"Thank you. In general," he replied. "And when luck strikes, never claim it as such."

Her lips pressed into a concentrated grin, and she took her turn. The cue ball knocked into his white ball, which rolled into a pocket and disappeared from view.

"*That* was not luck," she said, making a small and playful curtsy.

Henry felt the tension that had built between them at dinner beginning to dissolve. She'd commanded him earlier to keep his distance, and he had absolutely no intention of doing otherwise. He'd said his piece—or almost all of it— about what it was he wanted, but she hadn't given him the opportunity to explain all. That he wanted to take more than just carnal pleasure in her. That it was her company he sought and enjoyed. Moments like the one unfolding right now.

"Are you going to take your turn?" she asked, and Henry realized he was standing still, staring at her.

He was slow to move, something inside of him molten and heavy. Irina started forward, concern lancing through what had been a cheerful expression.

"Was it the noise? Did I crack the balls too loudly?"

Henry tried to stifle his laugh, but it threatened to become a snort, and he let it loose. "No, no. Though, I must say, Princess, I don't believe I could ever grow tired of hearing that word on your lips."

Immediately, a lewd image of Irina sprang to his mind, and he decided perhaps mentions of lips and balls should not be made so close together. She must have connected the words as well for her cheeks went a lovely shade of pink.

"Take your turn, my lord, and tell me—how did you know I visited a gaming hell in Paris?"

He walked around the table, closer to where Irina stood, to align his cue stick. He concentrated on the shot and took it before answering her question, earning himself another two points.

"I have contacts in Paris still. People who owe me favors." Henry leaned against the table. "I asked them to deliver information on Lord Remi."

"You're spying on him?" He noticed there was more curiosity in her expression than anger.

"I am simply gathering information," he replied. That it had reinvigorated him, he did not mention. "In case he does decide to offer for you, I need to be certain he's not after your dowry. I made a promise to your father, after all, to see you and your sister safe, and that includes pursuit from fortune hunters."

"Max has enough money of his own." Her cheeks tinting, Irina hiked her chin. "You behaved abominably with him tonight."

"I wanted to behave worse," Henry said, smiling to try and erase the pinch of a frown between her eyebrows.

It worked. Irina sighed. "He is only goading you on."

"He is pushing too far."

She fixed him with a withering stare. "And you never have?"

Henry held her challenging gaze. "I don't push where I am not wanted."

She had no response to that, though he could see in the trip of emotion on her face that she was searching for one. Something witty or clever, perhaps.

Henry took a step closer, keeping her command not to kiss her again in the very forefront of his mind. "Lord Remi was right regarding one thing, however," he said softly. "I am no longer your guardian."

No more than a foot of space separated them, he realized, as the warmed scent of her wafted toward him. He'd gotten drunk on the smell of her skin in the woods. Henry couldn't help but think of her as she'd been against that tree, only this time, he wanted her facing him…her dress hitched around her waist, those silken hips of hers on luscious, decadent display.

Unable to help himself, he reached out, the tips of his fingers brushed hers, resting on the raised bank of the billiards table. Irina held her mace stick in her other hand as tightly as she would a weapon and closed her eyes as if to brace against his light touch. Her chest rose and fell in a sharp, erratic motion, but she did not move away.

"You can do as you want," he went on, his fingers traveling over hers, skimming over her satin-encased knuckles and up her wrist.

The feel of her skin was addictive—one forbidden touch

was not enough. But Henry held himself well in check, staying firm to her request not to kiss her. Those lips. Knowing how soft and malleable and yielding they were did not make his task of holding back any easier. He knew all too well where a kiss between them would lead…to the fruition of his lewd fantasies.

A glimpse of her bare shoulders and back caught his eye in the gilded floor-length mirror, and an urge to trace his lips along the long, elegant rise of her spine overcame him. The near constant ache in his groin throbbed. Henry spared a glance to the open doorway, the arm of the footman just visible.

"Tell me, what is it that you want, Irina?" he asked softly, edging so close he could feel the heat rising from her body.

Irina parted her lashes to look up at him, the jeweled deep-blue depths of her eyes searching his. Desire swam in them, but something else did, too. Something that gave him pause. With a long inhalation, as if to fortify herself, she stepped away out of his reach to the other side of the billiards table.

"I can't do this."

"Do what?"

Irina looked sapped of all strength. As if it had taken all her willpower to step away from him. He, too, felt the loss of her keenly.

With a sigh of frustration, she shook her head and gestured between their bodies. *"This."* Her voice lowered, a blush filling her cheeks. "What happened at the waterfall. We both know it cannot happen again." She smiled brightly at him, though the heaviness remained in her eyes. "You did say no to my very unconventional proposal. Perhaps I thought obtaining a 'yes' was going to be as easy as the very first time I asked you to dance on the way to the duke's wedding ball so many years ago."

"Irina—"

"No, wait. This must be said." She paused, staring out to the candlelit gardens beyond the panes, as if to gather her thoughts. "I do not want us to fight or argue with each other. I wish for us to start over with a clean slate. As friends."

"Friends," he echoed.

"I know what you said at the waterfall, about what it is you want." Her blush intensified as she drew a ragged breath, her free hand fluttering to grasp her middle. "But you've also made it clear that there can be no future between us, and I don't want to lose you. As a friend." Irina stalled, going quiet for a long moment as if pondering her thoughts. "You asked me what I want. Well, I want something more for you, Henry. I want you to find love." Her throat bobbed. "And you have a chance at that with Lady Carmichael. She loves you very much, you must know that."

The statement left him slightly stunned. "Love?"

"Yes, love. She could make you happy."

Henry understood her words but still somehow *didn't*. She wanted him to be happy?

"I am happy," he said, frowning.

"You're confusing pleasure with happiness," she said, setting down her playing stick on the felt and moving toward the large windows lining the opposite wall.

Pleasure *is* happiness, he wanted to tell her, but the air had cooled between them, and Henry knew the moment was gone. *As it should be.*

He watched her at the windows, her face in thoughtful profile. She did not turn back toward him.

"I will leave you be," he said after a while, repeating the same words she had said to him when he'd first refused to play billiards and she had turned to go. He'd jumped at the chance to keep her in the room. With him. He paused a moment, waiting for her to do the same now. When she remained at the windows, looking into the darkness, Henry nodded to himself in understanding. She wanted him to go.

He left the room, closing the door behind him. The footman who had been standing just outside the door, he noticed, had gone. Henry turned right and started down the long corridor in the direction of Worthington Abbey's grand foyer. The walls were a rich and glossy mahogany with carved stone pillars arching overhead. It reminded Henry of a church, and as he passed underneath each one, he felt the increasing urge to apologize.

Irina wanted him to love and to be happy, and she'd turned away from him as if weighted down with sadness. As if she knew he would not be able to find those two things with her. *You are marrying Rose and should find them with her,* he told himself as he turned a corner and saw the foyer ahead. Strangely enough, it was Irina's voice he heard in his head saying this. And it was his own voice that responded with: *no, I won't.*

He did love Rose. He adored her, but it was as a brother. He would enjoy her companionship. They would be friends as they had always been. They shared a love for John and memories of him, but they would not share romantic love themselves.

Rose knew it, too. And like Irina, she'd urged Henry to search out happiness.

He stopped walking and stood still within the quiet corridor. The manor was so big and vast, he could not hear anything through the walls or ceilings surrounding him. Somewhere in the upper floors, Hawk and Lady Bradburne were tending to their children. Perhaps getting ready for bed themselves. Hawk adored his wife. Henry saw it in every gesture the man made when she was present. He'd change from surly and serious to teasing and relaxed. He'd become *happy*.

And that was what Irina wanted for him. More than pleasure, more than self-serving lust, she wanted him to be able to sit back and simply be *content*.

Henry turned around, and without thinking of doing anything more than thanking Irina and telling her he understood what she'd meant to say, started back for the billiards room. He'd been inside Worthington Abbey in the past, but the foyer was so grand, it was often the focal point of every ball. He'd never been in the deeper reaches of the castle before this evening. The mahogany corridor with its stone arches stretched onward and onward, until far, far down there was what appeared to be an arched window of stained glass. There were doors on both sides of the corridor, all matching flat panels of heavy wood. The billiards room was to the left, Henry knew that, at least. However, as he continued down the corridor, he wasn't certain which door it was exactly.

He stopped at one closed door, believing it was most likely the one, and grasped the knob. The moment he opened the door and stepped inside, he realized he'd been wrong. There was a little bit of light in the room, from a fire in a hearth, but there was no billiards table. And while there were large windows like the one Irina had been standing at, they were draped.

Henry was about to duck back out when a loud rustling sound stopped him. The room wasn't empty. Two figures were standing up from one enormous chair that had been pulled in front of the flames of the fireplace. That they were both men was the first shot of information through Henry's mind. That they were both hastily readjusting their clothing was the second.

And though the lighting was low, the shadows of the room heavy, Henry quickly discerned their identities.

"Lord Remi," he said, his eyes then cutting to the footman who had disappeared from the corridor outside the billiards room.

Irina's friend took a handful of steps away from the footman, who was fumbling with the front of his trousers.

"Langlevit," Remi said as he smoothed his cravat and then ran a palm through his hair. "Still skulking about, I see. I must say your timing is impeccable." His sarcasm was not lost on Henry.

The footman finished with his trousers and grabbed his livery jacket before rushing from the room, though not by Henry, still within the doorway. He took a back door, no doubt to a servant hallway.

"Henry?"

Irina's voice behind him startled him, and he turned quickly, knocking his elbow upon the doorjamb.

"What are you doing?" she asked, attempting to peer inside the room. He didn't know why he did it, but Henry quickly closed the door, shepherding Irina back into the corridor.

"Wrong room," he said, grasping for an excuse. His urge to apologize and thank her for her honesty had become tangled with preventing her from discovering Lord Remi, half undressed and caught in an obvious tryst, in the private home of her sister's in-laws, no less.

"I should not have left you alone in the billiards room," he said. "I came back to see you to the foyer and to your carriage."

Irina blinked a few times and frowned, as if she didn't believe him. Or perhaps she did and was disappointed.

As they walked to the front of the abbey in silence and then summoned their individual carriages, Henry wondered at Lord Remi's unabashed reaction to being discovered. He's a smug bastard, he thought. And good at covering the truth. The spy Henry had contacted in Paris to dig up information on Remi had written nothing about his preferences. Was it just men, then? Or women and men both?

His horse arrived first, and Henry bid Irina a distracted good evening before departing.

Lord Remi was becoming more of a nuisance and a mystery by the day. Henry needed better information, and he apparently couldn't rely on his known contacts.

He'd have to go digging himself.

Chapter Sixteen

A siren in lavender silk leaned against the billiards table, tempting him beyond reason. Irina's gaze hinged on Henry's as he approached. One shoulder of that beguilingly sinful dress had slipped, exposing her skin, and as he raked her over with his eyes, he noticed she wore no slippers. Something about her bare feet, those elegant, perfect toes buried in the plush carpet, drove an instant possessive need into him. A need to bare every inch of supple flesh to his greedy gaze. A need to take her. Claim her. To make her his and his alone. From the way his siren was looking at him, her lips parted and her eyes heavy with longing, he knew she would welcome it. She wanted him just as much as he did her.

Irina's nipples strained through the thin fabric of her dress, and Henry touched them, his thumbs rubbing rough circles as he kneaded her breasts. She threw her head back and moaned as he dragged the top of her bodice down. Her breasts came free, spilling into view, and then Henry's hands and mouth were on them. His tongue swirled the hard peak of one nipple while pinching the tip of the other, and Irina cried out his name.

He didn't care if anyone heard.

There were voices then, muffled and murmuring, but he could not stop. Let them watch. Henry felt himself bulging against the constraints of his trousers, so hard and swollen he could barely breathe. His desire was a wild, bucking thing, trapped and in anguish, thrashing for release.

He felt her hot breath against his ear as her hand grasped and stroked his length, only heightening the sweet torment. Henry lifted her upon the table and pushed her back until she was fully reclined on the red felt. Her dress was gone now, her naked form writhing beneath him, her legs parting in eager welcome. He climbed onto the table and kneed her thighs farther apart. He would not be gentle. He couldn't be. She screamed her pleasure as he drove into her, thrusting hard and deep and fast, again and again, marking her as his own as his seed rushed into her.

Henry moaned his satisfaction and opened his eyes. He was not atop the billiards table. He was not atop Irina.

He was alone. Staring at his bedchamber ceiling. In his bed. And his smalls were wet, plastered to his thighs. Henry swore under his breath as he realized it had been a dream. A blissfully erotic dream that had been so real, he'd spent himself in his sleep.

Hell.

He lay still for a few moments, his heart thundering back to its normal rhythm, and felt a rapid hollowing sensation in his chest. Not because he had only bedded Irina in a dream, but because she was not truly there, at his side. It had been years since he'd allowed a woman to spend the night through in his bed, what with the constant threat of his body becoming a weapon during one of his night terrors. But for the first time, Henry wondered what it might be like to wake to the sight of her. He pictured her sable hair spread out in waves across his pillows, her violet eyes sleepy in the early morning sunshine. She'd sleep in the nude, he imagined, his sheets a flimsy covering, barely veiling her nipples. He would greet them first, nipping them with his teeth through the linen and then pulling the sheet low to expose the rest of her, his mouth traveling down her bare stomach to the dark curls below.

Henry opened his eyes again and felt once more the sticky cling of his smalls. He could not lie in bed fantasizing about Irina all day, and he wanted to get up and cleaned before Marbury knocked upon the door and let himself in for Henry's morning ablutions.

He tore off his smalls, washed himself, and found a clean, ironed and starched pair in his dressing room moments before his valet arrived. Still grappling with the disturbing remnants of his dream and his surprisingly undisciplined climax, Henry dressed, and after, Marbury performed his usual morning shave and trimmed his hair. He frowned.

He hadn't been with anyone but Françoise since Hyde Park. Since the first time he had left for Essex…when Irina had raced him, and when she had coaxed him out of one of his episodes. That had been *weeks* ago. Sweet Christ, it was no wonder he'd spent himself.

Heading downstairs and walking past his own billiards room, Henry felt an immediate visceral twitch in his groin and suppressed a groan. He would be ruined for billiards forever. Tugging on his suddenly too-tight cravat, he headed for his study. Henry knew what would put Irina Volkonsky firmly out of his mind, and that was an in-depth and thorough analysis of his tenant ledgers. He was meeting Lord Northridge for a local horse auction at the breeder stables in the neighboring village of Horton, which gave him two uninterrupted hours.

Once ensconced behind his desk, however, Henry could not concentrate, though not for lack of trying. After an hour of staring at the same columns and raking through his hair a thousand times, he rose and called for Carlton.

"Where is the countess?"

"In the music room, my lord," Carlton answered.

Henry found his mother sitting at the pianoforte. He recognized the lilting strains of Haydn's sonata in E-flat major, her favorite of his musical compositions. The sound of it immediately drew him back to his childhood. Dismissing the waiting maids and without alerting her to his presence, he sat in the armchair directly behind her and closed his eyes. It was exactly what he needed. Though her health had been declining, her skill had not. Her fingers danced over the keys as she played the second movement, the melancholy notes delving into his soul.

When she finished, he gave her a standing ovation. "You continue to astound me with your talent, Mother dear."

She blushed from his praise. "Henry! I did not see you come in."

"Will you play another piece?" he asked.

"Which would you like?"

He swallowed. "Beethoven, number five, the adagio."

His mother slid him an arch glance, and he kept his face composed. It was arguably one of Beethoven's most romantic pieces. As she began the first few bars, he closed his eyes in bliss. The music flowed over him, doing what nothing else could. He'd first heard it in Vienna, amidst reports that the composer had written it hiding in his brother's home there while under attack from Napoleon. It astounded him that such beauty could be created in the midst of so much horror.

"Thank you," Henry said when she finished, standing and walking over to kiss her on the brow. "I'll leave you to it."

His mother cleared her throat and shifted on the bench to face him, reaching for his hands. "Henry, I'm glad you are here. I did want to speak with you about Lady Carmichael."

"Rose?" he asked, arching an eyebrow. "I thought you approved?"

"Of course I do. Her mother is my best friend, after all, and I know why you have chosen her," she said. "She will no doubt make an excellent wife. And dear William...I should be happy to have him as a grandson, and she will no doubt procure you an heir."

"Then what is your concern?"

"You do not love her." The brief, bold statement threw him. He blinked his surprise as she went on. "There is friendship between you, certainly, and caring, but beyond that there is no passion. No love." Lady Langlevit pressed his hands between hers, and Henry couldn't help noticing how like parchment her skin had become. He perched on the bench beside her.

"It is my duty to marry, not pursue such frivolous notions."

"There is more to life than duty, and it saddens me to think you view it as such." She lifted a veined palm to stroke his cheek. "Oh, my darling boy, you've seen so much pain. If only you could leave the past where it belongs and allow yourself the chance to truly live. Happiness is right in front of you—you only need to open your eyes and reach for it."

Henry stood stock-still. Had all the women in his life suddenly gone mad?

First Rose, then Irina, and now, his own mother.

"I *am* happy," he insisted, standing. Forcing a smile to his face and quelling his irritation, Henry kissed her hands and called for the maids waiting beyond the door. "Now you must excuse me, I have an engagement. I'll see you later. I will be dining at the residence tonight."

He felt her eyes on him as he left the room, but thankfully she did not press the issue.

"Carlton, have one of the stableboys ready my horse at once," he said to the butler, tugging on the riding gloves and jacket that Marbury had brought downstairs. "The black."

Carlton bowed. "Of course, my lord."

It wasn't long before North rode up the driveway, and

Henry joined him, pulling himself up onto the sleek, prancing four-year-old Orlov, a gift from the Russian tsar after Count Volkonsky's arrest. The stallion seemed restless, too, but Henry kept him under firm rein as they rode toward the lane. Cerus was temperamental at the best of times.

As the fresh country breeze hit his face, Henry felt his muscles relax. It was good to get out of the house. "How is Lady Northridge?" he asked. "Not too tired, I hope."

North shook his head, his big gray Andalusian easily keeping pace with Cerus, and grinned. "She is fine, but has yet to awaken."

"Last evening was entertaining," North commented a few moments later. "Remi was in fine form."

"If you call that form," Henry said, recalling the man's tryst with one of Hawk's servants with distaste. "How much do you know of him?"

"Not much, other than he was a childhood family friend of theirs. A distant cousin. Lana mentioned something about his father being particularly exacting when he was a young boy. He spent considerable time at Volkonsky Palace in his younger years before he ran away."

"Ran away?"

"To Moscow, I believe," North said, his brow crinkling as he tried to remember details.

Henry hesitated, wondering how to delicately ask the question about the man's proclivities, but in the end he didn't have to ask at all. North explained.

"Something about a flagrant affair with a well-known prince. Apparently Count Remisov did not approve of his son fraternizing with other men."

Henry frowned. "Remisov, did you say?"

"His family name. Maxim Remisov."

That might explain why Henry's colleagues hadn't been able to find any information on a Lord Max Remi from St.

Petersburg, despite what seemed like an obvious similarity in the names.

North continued. "He and Irina reconnected in Paris." He pursed his lips. "Irina is headstrong enough as it is without any of his encouragement. My wife is not happy with his influence."

Neither am I, Henry thought grimly. "I find him offensive," he said.

North nodded his agreement. "What's not to like? He's young, arrogant, and angry. Much like we were at his age."

"I suffered wounds from a hellish war. You had an illegitimate daughter. Exactly what does our entitled young lord have to be angry about?"

"Being disowned would be enough to make me damned angry."

Henry's brain came to a reeling stop and then churned back into motion. He chewed on that tidbit of information. Lord Remisov had been disowned? Had the young lord now latched on to a young and wealthy patron? That would be the obvious answer. But Irina had said that Max had wealth of his own. Henry trusted his instincts, but perhaps he was being too presumptuous because he simply disliked the man. He was well aware that his judgment became muddled when it came to Irina.

As the road widened they increased their pace, making further conversation impossible, and arrived in Horton in less than an hour. Henry wasn't particularly looking to add new stock to his stables, but he'd agreed to accompany North, who was interested in purchasing a mare or two. Dismounting, they tethered their mounts to a nearby fence post.

The bidding got underway after the men had had a chance to inspect the stock on display, as well as two pregnant mares due to foal with sires from an excellent pedigree. While North was busy, Henry ran his hands along the glossy reddish brown flanks of a young gelding as the horse nuzzled into his shoulder. He'd always loved the graceful, magnificent animals.

"You're a beauty, aren't you?" he whispered, stroking its nose. The thought that Irina would love the horse flicked into his brain. It would be a nice gesture.

In friendship.

Without thinking twice, he nodded to the nearby stableman. "Tell your master to have this one delivered to Hartstone."

"Yes, my lord."

"Easy!" The shouted command caught his attention. A large stallion was rearing upward in a nearby riding paddock. A gentleman with a crop held on to the reins as he brought the horse roughly under control. Henry flinched as the crop whistled across the beast's side. He had no love for the crop or for striking defenseless animals. The man struck the horse again, and Henry had the distinct desire to split the offending crop in two. As the horse made the turn, he recognized the rider with a sour start—the very object of his ill humor.

"I'll take both Arabians," Lord Remi announced loudly. "This one only needs some discipline."

Henry remained out of sight, unwilling to enter into any conversation with the young lord. He'd had enough of it the night before, and already, his first impulse was to put the odious man right on his arse. Henry's eyes narrowed at the two gorgeous steeds he had purchased. They would not be cheap, which confirmed what Irina had said: Remi did not seem to suffer from a lack of funds.

So, he was not a fortune hunter.

Shaking his head, Henry walked back to where North was concluding his dealings. Max Remi might be a pompous prick, but that did not mean he was deserving of mistrust. Henry was uncomfortably aware that what he was feeling might also be jealousy, and jealousy had a way of twisting even the most innocent of things.

. . .

Irina strolled beside Lady Langlevit's Bath chair as it was pushed along the brick path in Hartstone's lavish gardens. The countess was wrapped in a woolen blanket against the light evening chill of the air. Irina could not believe how quickly she'd gone from standing on her own to being pushed around in a chair meant for the invalid. She'd insisted on walking at the start of their excursion, with her maid and a footman following discreetly behind with the chair, and after a short time, she became out of breath.

"Sadly, I am not as young as I once was, my dear," she said apologetically to Irina as the maid settled her into the wheeled conveyance.

"You only need rest, my lady," Irina replied.

"How is Lady Northridge faring?" the countess asked.

"Well. She and the babe are both fine. Like you, she tries to do too much and ends up overexerting herself."

"The curse of the strong woman," Lady Langlevit said. "We refuse to accept help until it is thrust upon us." She slid Irina an assessing glance. "I suspect you are still much the same. That hasn't changed from when you were a girl."

Irina smiled. "I do like to do things on my own, but sometimes help is necessary."

"Yes, it is."

Irina had the sneaking suspicion she was no longer speaking of herself, but the moment passed as the countess stopped to smell some of the brilliant tea roses blooming in the rose garden. They were at the entrance to a massive hedged maze where a beautiful fountain with carved nymphs stood. A nostalgic smile graced Lady Langlevit's lips.

"When Henry was a boy he would hide for hours in there,

calling out for me to find him." She paused. "Have you been to the center?" Irina shook her head. Like riding in a carriage, enclosed spaces made her nervous.

She'd been walking along a garden path alone that day so many years ago when her uncle and Victor Zakorov's hired thug had grabbed her, clapping a hand over her mouth and running through the paths, forcing her into a nearby waiting carriage. Irina could not abide the twists and turns of garden paths or labyrinth-like mazes now. She preferred the open gardens where she could see her surroundings.

"There is a lovely greenhouse at its heart," Lady Langlevit was saying. "My Edward built it for me before Henry was born. It is sad to say that seeing it now pains me considerably."

"I am sorry."

"Do not be," the countess said, patting her arm. "It is a happy kind of sad. The memories will always be tucked away in my heart. He was the only man I ever loved, my Edward. Henry is very much like him."

"What was he like?" Irina asked.

"Edward?"

Irina flushed. "Henry. As a boy."

The countess motioned for Irina to sit on a nearby stone bench beside a fountain. "He was a mischievous lad. Clever, too. Always thinking up pranks. He and John would get into the most ridiculous scrapes, with poor little Rose looking on and trying her best to defend them from Edward's wrath." She laughed at a memory and pointed at a nearby towering tree. "They used to torture her dreadfully, sending her up into that oak once to save an invisible kitten while they made mewing noises from behind the fountain."

"Telling stories again?" a deep voice asked. It sent a throb through Irina's bones. Henry strode toward them, looking incredibly handsome. His bronzed cheeks were flushed with healthy color, and his sandy blond hair was windblown. "Your

Highness," he said with a short bow. "I hope you have been having a pleasant visit. I am sure my mother is glad for your company."

"Yes, thank you, my lord," Irina murmured.

"No stories, just the truth," Lady Langlevit said as he bent to kiss her head with a fond smile. Irina once more marveled at the obvious affection between them. "As naughty as Henry was, he was always the joy of my life."

Henry's mouth twisted into a smirk. "Turning me into a martyr already, Mother?" He glanced at Irina. "Don't believe a word she says. I was a handful."

"Did your auction go well, dear?" Lady Langlevit asked.

"I bought one horse, a gelding," he said, propping a booted foot to a second stone bench a few feet away from where they sat. His gaze moved back to Irina. "When it is delivered, perhaps you'd like to have a look at it."

Irina frowned. Why would he ask her to look at a horse? Unless it was intended for a female rider…for his fiancée, in fact. Suppressing the brisk twinge of an unsettling emotion, she nodded. "Of course."

"And perhaps you will honor me with another race?" he added in a teasing voice, and her eyes shot to his. "Since you were confident in your winning of the last, I deserve a chance to soothe my sore pride."

Once more, Irina inclined her head in gracious agreement. "As you wish."

Henry did not seem as broodingly preoccupied as he usually was and his lightness of spirit was surprising, but perhaps he was taking her request of friendship seriously. It chafed and mollified at the same time.

"You should show the princess the greenhouse one day, Henry," Lady Langlevit was saying. "She would love it."

"Perhaps," he said in a noncommittal tone. "How are you feeling, Mother? Better?"

"I am lovely, thank you." She smiled fondly at the two of them. "Being in the company of two of my favorite people is wonderful. But as much as I would love to tarry, I'm mortified to admit that the good country air has made me quite famished. Cook should have a lovely tea ready."

"Very well, then, shall we?" Henry stood, extending his arm to Irina as the footman turned Lady Langlevit's chair around. Irina accepted, ignoring the little jolt that raced up her gloved hand through the wool of his jacket. It was exceedingly odd how his touch, even through so many barriers of clothing, had such a visceral effect on her.

Henry slowed his step, Irina noticed, so that they walked a few paces behind his mother, out of hearing but still within sight. "Would you like to see the maze one day?" he asked.

"Not particularly," she replied softly. "While I love the idea of a whimsical greenhouse at its center, I fear it will be too constricting. I much prefer open spaces. The closed-in hedges would drive me mad."

Henry faltered in step, staring at her. "I completely agree."

"I suspect that is why I like your course so much," she ventured, hoping the friendly interlude between them would continue.

"It impressed me that you completed it," he said. "Without injury."

She laughed. "It wasn't easy in the least," Irina admitted. "But I found it exhilarating."

"I find it calming," he said as they entered the rose garden. "When my body is driven to the point of exhaustion, my mind seems to quiet."

Irina felt a surge of compassion. "Was it because of the war?"

"In part, and also what happened in the years afterward." He stumbled over the words, as if they were unfamiliar, or as though he'd never said them aloud before. Irina's fingers tightened compulsively on his arm, and he stared down at them, an inexpressible look on his face. "It helps to keep the horrors at bay."

"I am sorry."

"It's not your fault," he said with another of those indecipherable looks.

Nearing the stables, they walked on in silence as the green landscaped lawns of the manor came into view. A smile chased away the somberness on his face as he changed the subject. "How is your skill with a pistol?"

She glanced up at him. "Is there anything in particular you'd like shot?"

He laughed and shook his head. "I am only curious as to your prowess."

"You'll have to see to find out," she said, grateful for the shift in conversation.

"Better than your billiards skill?" he asked, and Irina couldn't help the wash of heat that swamped her cheeks. She had come dangerously close the evening before to throwing her body on said billiards table and offering herself to him for the taking.

She jutted her chin, unable to resist the twinkling challenge in his eyes. Irina had no idea why it was so difficult to refuse his every challenge. They were far too similar in their competitive natures. "What was it you said, my lord? Never divulge my strategy?"

Henry grinned at her, his golden eyes dancing as he stopped to remove a stone from the sole of his boot. Irina kept walking, clasping her hands behind her back. "There's a winner's board here at Hartstone," Henry said from his crouched position. "John and I remain the reigning champions at a hundred paces. Neither of us has ever been bested. Care to try your skill?"

"How old were you when it was made?" she asked over

her shoulder.

"Seventeen."

Irina grinned. "Then I accept your challenge."

They had almost caught up with Lady Langlevit when a screeching noise from the stables startled a brace of pheasants from a bush. They rushed skyward and flew directly into Irina's path. She flailed and stumbled backward, catching her heel on the edge of the stone path. Gasping for breath, Irina felt herself falling. This was not going to end well. Henry was too far away to be of any use, and there was nothing nearby she could grab ahold of to stabilize herself.

Preparing herself, the breath was knocked out of her as she collided with a strong male body instead of the unforgiving ground. Somehow he had managed to catch her, breaking her fall with his body. Irina didn't know that it had hurt any less. Like the flagstone at her feet, Henry was all hard, rigid planes.

Caught in his arms, she stared up at him, her breath sticking in her throat at the solid and warm feel of him. The heat of his body seared her, making her nerves tingle and burn. "How did you get over here so fast?" she gasped.

"I prefer foot racing to horse racing, remember?" he said, righting her to her feet. "Can you stand?"

"Yes," she murmured, still staring at him in wonder. "I've never seen anyone move so quickly."

"The course has helped me to hone my reflexes," Henry said.

Irina smoothed her dress as he deposited her to where the countess was waiting. She eyed the two of them, concern in her gaze. "Good heavens, Henry, you should investigate. That sounded rather ominous." She studied Irina. "Are you well, child? Good thing my boy is quick on his feet."

"I am quite well, thank you, my lady," Irina said. "And I am indeed grateful for Lord Langlevit's timely assistance. Such a fall would have been humiliating. And painful. Thank you, my lord."

Henry bowed, drawing her gloved knuckles to his lips. The moment drew out between them, and time seemed to slow to an interminable pace as he pressed his lips to the kidskin of her gloves.

"I am ever at your service," he murmured. "Your Highness."

Henry's eyes caught and held hers. The heat from his mouth scorched and branded, and when he kissed her hand, Irina felt the chaste touch to the tips of her toes, as if he had plundered the inside of her mouth instead. It was suddenly difficult for her to draw a single breath. She didn't know if she imagined him lingering over her hand or not, but he seemed reluctant to release her.

He did, however, and after bowing to his mother, strode away in the direction of the stables.

Chapter Seventeen

As Irina resettled into Bishop House on St. James's Square in London, she felt a strange restlessness. She was glad to be in London, oddly enough, though she also wanted to be in Essex, with her sister. Lana, however, had insisted upon her return to town. One cannot spend one's season in the country and expect to find a husband, Lana had said, before then launching into a strict lecture about not falling prey to any of the men placing wagers at White's.

Irina wished Henry had never breathed a word about the damned wagers but had covered her irritation and regret at Lana's well-meant lecture with a solemn vow to her sister to be sharp and cautious at every public function. She had promised Lana and Gray no less than four times that she would remain within Lady Dinsmore's view when at a ball, and under no circumstances would she take air on a balcony, or stand within any alcoves, or remove herself into the lesser populated rooms of the host's home.

There could be no telling which gentleman was out to win a wager and which one was a genuine admirer, so from this point onward, Lana had declared, she had to assume every gentleman was a schemer—and then wait and hope to be proven wrong.

Irina would not have much difficulty with that. If there was any man or woman in London who was *not* a schemer, she would have enjoyed meeting them. Even she was a schemer, really. She'd been a part of the whole wager business to begin with, and if that ever got out to Lana or Gray, or good heavens, to Henry, she would be mortified. Why had she even considered any of it in the first place? She'd been frustrated and bored and…well, if she were being honest, she'd wanted the attention. *Henry's* attention.

As she paced the upper floor of Bishop House, waiting for her maid to arrive and signal it was time for her to appear in the grand ballroom, she prayed there would be no wager business tonight. Lord and Lady Dinsmore were hosting a small soiree—small meaning no fewer than two hundred of London's finest—and she felt a swarm of nerves in her belly at the thought that there were men in attendance planning to corner her somewhere and steal a kiss.

And not a chaste one, came the echo of Henry's warning.

Her hands were fairly sweating within her silk gloves, an ivory white to match her gown, which was threaded throughout with small green flowers and vines. The needlework was simple and lovely, and she'd chosen the demure dress with the hopes that it would not garner her too much attention. Or lust.

Jane appeared at the end of the hallway, and from the small bob of her head, Irina knew it was time. Lady Dinsmore wished for her to make a grand entrance. The countess was thrilled to be hosting Irina while Lady Langlevit continued to rest at Hartstone and had decided to throw a ball in the princess's honor. Irina was certain she was not going to enjoy the attention, especially now knowing that there were crude wagers in that book at White's. Henry had only divulged the one about a kiss, but by the way he'd acted there were others. Others that were far more risqué.

She hadn't seen Henry since the day at Hartstone a week before when they'd strolled together on the lawns, and when he had caught her in that fall. His reflexes had been cat-like. Honed, he'd said, on his course in the woods, which had only reminded her of the afternoon she'd seen him in the waterfall, and then when he'd pressed her against the tree and done things to her that had given her a taste of bliss.

What would it be like to be able to have more than just that one taste? Though she'd tried not to think about Henry that evening, the next morning—and every day after that— she had failed. She'd found herself imagining scenarios in which she and Henry were together, at Hartstone and in London, in public and in private. She would be on his arm at every ball and dinner, and at home she would be his to ravish as he pleased. And for her to explore him, as well. After viewing him in his full glory, Irina couldn't help but long for the chance.

However, Henry was not hers to know. Not in that way.

He'd stayed in Essex with his mother, she was sure. And Lady Carmichael preferred the countryside to Town, too. Perhaps she would not see him again before his wedding. Something she was certain to be invited to. Unless she was already back in St. Petersburg by that time. One could only hope.

Bracing herself, Irina entered the sunken ballroom and descended the handful of marble steps, her eyes landing almost immediately upon a tall couple standing in the center of the ballroom. Why she saw them first among the scores of other guests that had turned to watch her entrance she could only put down to pure self-torture. It was Henry and Lady Carmichael. They were here after all. Her luck was already failing, it seemed.

They were a beautiful couple, both looking completely at ease and comfortable next to one another. Lady Carmichael, so graceful and amiable. Irina could see the gentle kindness in the smile she beamed at him right then. Henry would be happy with her. The thought both pierced her heart and buoyed it at the same time.

"Your Highness."

Max appeared before her within moments, blocking her view of the rest of the ballroom. He dropped into an exaggerated bow, and when she looked over his lowered back, she could no longer see Henry. Max rose to full height again, and she met his mischievous smirk.

"You have flour in your hair," she said in a low whisper, watching as he discreetly pushed a gloved hand over the strands at his temple, dislodging the white dust.

"Don't give me that look, Princess," he whispered back. "I was only passing time until your grand entrance."

Normally, Max's dalliances would amuse her, but for some reason, she felt mild annoyance instead. "Who was it this time? Another footman?"

"A lovely young scullery maid," he replied with an affronted look. "I'll have you know, there's more than enough of me to go around. I am not of a discriminating nature."

"Perhaps you should be," she muttered.

He shot her a dry look. "By contrast, you look utterly innocent in that dress," Max remarked, perusing her from head to toe and extending his elbow. She took it and allowed him to lead her toward the dance floor. "Are you quite certain it was not designed for a first communion?"

"What did you expect me to wear, a negligee?" she asked in a whisper while nodding demurely toward Lord and Lady Dinsmore, the latter of whom wore a resplendent gown and an even more resplendent look of pride. Irina could only smile—Lady Dinsmore might enjoy soaking up the attention from the *ton*, but she had been kind to Lana when she'd been employed as a maid within their household. For that, Irina would always be grateful.

"I expected something to whet appetites and increase interest, not dampen desires, my darling," Max replied, swiping a flute of champagne from a passing tray. He did not offer her a drink, and she was both glad and bothered by it.

"I do not aim to please men when selecting a dress, Lord Remi. I aim to please myself, and tonight, it pleases me to wear this gown."

He swallowed a gulp of champagne and slanted a look at her. "Touchy, are we? *Lord Remi.* My goodness, should I expect you to use my middle name next?"

Irina didn't bother to reply that she didn't even know his middle name. She had been surprised to see Henry among the guests at tonight's ball, pained yet resigned to see Lady Carmichael at his side, though it was what she wished for him, and annoyed when Max had immediately swooped in to claim her. She wasn't sure why it bothered her. It never had before. And tonight was the very sort of night she would usually most appreciate Max occupying her attention, especially when she was supposed to be social and greet everyone.

"Forgive me," she said, feeling at odds with herself. "I don't mean to be so waspish."

"No, no, let's use this mood of yours for good," he said, chucking her chin and downing the rest of his champagne. "I think tonight is the night, my darling."

She frowned up at him. "What do you mean?"

He leaned closer, and she could feel the heat of his body and the strong, biting cinnamon scent of his cologne. "The moment word hits that you might have chosen a suitor, the stakes will go through the bloody roof. No one wants to lose the pot, Irina. They'll be desperate to win your favor. It will be an absolute frenzy."

The twist in her stomach returned, and her hands felt clammy again. "Chosen a suitor? Oh, I don't know, Max, I'm starting to grow weary of all this betting nonsense." She speared him with an arch glance. "Lord Langlevit mentioned something about a wager that you penned. A kiss, and not a chaste one. Why on earth would you do such a thing?"

Something like annoyance flickered in his eyes before it vanished. "To fan the flames, of course. And why does it matter? I'll be the only one kissing you."

I don't want to kiss you.

Irina did not voice the thought, however. "I'm tired, Max, of all these bets and games and intrigues."

"*Tired?* Irina, we haven't even announced our betrothal yet," he whispered underneath the strains of the violin music.

Now her heart constricted, and the closely packed crowd suddenly seemed to push in toward her. She looked into both familiar and unfamiliar faces, wanting only to see one man. The one face that would set her at ease.

"I'm not even sure," she said, her breathing coming in short puffs, "about that."

His grip on her elbow tightened, and he steered her toward a pair of open French doors. "What do you mean, you're not sure? Irina, this was your idea."

She allowed him to lead her toward the doors, the need to breathe in cool, clean air, free from perfume and cologne and body heat undeniable.

"I know it was, Max, I *know*," she said, avoiding glances in her direction, people wanting to stop her to say hello and pay their respects, and countless other men seeking a smile or a dance, driven no doubt by wagers they had made. Irina felt sick to her stomach…sick of it all.

She'd been the one to suggest Max toss his name into the pot for the grand prize; it had been her scheme to marry, collect the winnings, donate them to the Bradburne Trust where it would be spread out to local hospices, and then retreat to St. Petersburg where they could live in privacy and in friendly separation—and away from Henry.

But now…perhaps she had been too hasty.

Irina went to the terrace edge and gripped the cool stone balustrade. She closed her eyes and leaned forward, sucking in air to clear her head.

"What has happened?" Max asked, his tone firmer than before. As if he were truly vexed.

"You don't want to marry me," she said, keeping her own voice low so no one below on the lawns, just beyond the terrace stairs, might overhear.

"Of course I do," he replied, taking her arm yet again and leading her toward the steps. "Come. I think we need a stroll to get your head on straight, my dear."

"I shouldn't, Max. Lana made me promise—"

"It is me, Irina. Your virtue is utterly safe."

"But if we're seen—"

"This is the problem," Max said, leading her down the steps and onto the grass. "What do you care if we are seen? Haven't we made this decision already? I'm going to propose. You're going to accept. We will be married. So if someone stumbles upon us in the shadows of this lawn, it won't matter in the least."

When he put it like that, no, it wouldn't matter. If she were going to accept his suit and go through with the marriage, the whole guest list could come upon them skulking about in the gardens and there wouldn't be a problem at all. And why shouldn't she marry Max? She couldn't have Henry, and he was the only other man she'd ever want as a husband. But was that a good enough reason? It was *marriage*. A lifetime of commitment, a forever choice. And she did not *have* to marry in order to go home and never see Lord Langlevit or his beautiful bride again.

She wasn't ready. Perhaps if she hadn't come upon Henry in that waterfall pool, or if he hadn't touched her and brought her to raptures, or if she had not then been able to play billiards with him and then walk with him so companionably at Hartstone, she might be ready to give up. To let go of any hope. Any dreams.

She knew he cared for her. He *had* to care for her, even if he did not want her for a wife, even if he'd already proposed and decided to stick by his proposal. Even knowing all of that, Irina could not let go.

"Max, I've made a mistake."

He stopped her just beyond the trellis arch, blooming with roses and ivy and blocking a clear view of the terrace.

"Don't do this," he said. "Don't give up your chance at happiness because you're still clinging to hope."

"Marrying you is not my only chance at happiness."

"And what of my chance?" Max released her and ran his fingers through his hair, clutching the blond strands at the crown of his head. "You have no idea what it is like, being rejected by your own kin. Your own father. To be sent away because you're an embarrassment. You have no idea what it's like to live on a clock, quickly winding down, knowing soon… you'll have nothing."

Irina tried to sharpen her eyes through the darkness, wanting to see his face. She only saw him release his hair, his arms falling at his sides.

"What do you mean, *soon you'll have nothing*?"

He exhaled long and loud, and she got the feeling he was about to part with a secret. "I was disowned, Irina. My title stripped away. My cousin will inherit everything, and when he does…I'll be cut off. My father made certain to tell me as much. Enjoy my sinning while I can, he advised. When he's dead, I'm on my own." In the shadows, she saw him hang his head. Irina's heart ached for him. She took his hands in hers.

"I didn't know," she whispered.

"Irina, if I don't have you…I thought that I would at least have you. That I wouldn't be left alone," he said. "In Paris, you accepted me for who I am. You've become my light in all of this."

She squeezed his hands, uncertain how to reply. She didn't know if his father was ailing or not, but soon Max would be cut off. If his cousin inherited everything, Max's mother would be cared for but not to such an extent that she could send him thousands of pounds every year. He didn't know how to work. He didn't know how to earn a living wage. What on earth would he do?

"I thought you would be my friend," he went on.

"Oh, Max, I am your friend," she said, feeling torn and frustrated. It made her stomach churn angrily. Had he only wanted her for her dowry? She shook her head. No, Max had been there for her, and the idea for him to put his hand in the marriage pot had been hers. She'd led them both here…she'd given him false hope.

"I thought you wanted this," Max whispered, and Irina could feel the gust of his breath against her cheek. She hadn't realized they'd come to be standing so close. "I thought you wanted me this way. You care for me, don't you?"

Irina closed her eyes, consumed with guilt. How could she not help him? How could she say no? She couldn't. Max was her friend, and he needed her. There was only one answer to give: "I do."

Chapter Eighteen

Henry came to an abrupt halt. Irina's voice had traveled through the darkened lawn, from the other side of the rose trellis. Beside him, Rose also pulled to a stop, a small gasp escaping her lips.

"I do," Irina repeated.

Henry had heard Lord Remi's words seconds before. *I thought you wanted me this way. You care for me, don't you?*

Irina could not possibly be accepting him. Had Remi lured her out here to propose? Or perhaps he wasn't proposing at all. Perhaps his aim had been to win the latest wager, one that would put Irina at risk. Thank God Henry had decided to quit Essex and return to London. He could not leave her alone for a minute without her walking straight into disaster.

"I know that it would be wonderful between us." This from Lord Remi. The bastard. "We're perfect for each other, and you know that. Let me show you."

Rose squeezed Henry's arm. "We must do something," she whispered. "The princess will ruin herself."

It was in the back of Henry's mind the moment he'd seen

Irina and Lord Remi darting onto the terrace. Why in hell did these bloody ballrooms have to have so many balconies and terraces anyway? They should be chained off during balls. Better yet, blown to rubble entirely.

He'd taken Rose's arm and asked her to go with him to the terrace once Irina had disappeared through the French doors. The press of the crowd was unsettling, yes, but more disturbing was Lord Remi's grip on her arm. Henry could not have left Rose standing there in the ballroom, either. She knew barely a soul. So, he'd led her outdoors and then, when the terrace had been empty, down the stairs to the lawns. Rose had said nothing all the while.

Except now.

"Henry," she whispered.

"Yes," he replied. Of course, he knew he must do something. What he wanted was to put his fist through Remi's teeth. He wanted to pick him up and hurl him as far from Irina as he could and then stand guard over her to prevent his returning. However, he knew both of those options were out of the realm of possibility. So instead, Henry stepped under the rose trellis and cleared his throat.

Irina whirled around, her figure a dark stamp against the night shadows in the garden's entrance. Lord Remi remained steady, not reacting visibly to the interruption at all.

"Hen—Lord Langlevit," Irina said, slipping up and nearly addressing him by his first name. She then saw Rose. "And Lady Carmichael."

"Your Highness," he said, attempting to keep his voice under control. It still sounded like grinding rocks. He clenched his fists. "I believe Lady Dinsmore is searching for you."

It was much more civil than the string of curses he wanted to sling at both Irina and Lord Remi. What the devil had she been thinking, accepting Remi's invitation to the gardens? Knowing the manner of wagers that were now on every bachelor's mind, how could she risk it?

"Yes, I am sure she is," Irina said, beginning to detach herself from Remi's side.

Lord Remi, however, was not so avid to leave the garden entrance. He stepped in front of Irina, blocking her from reaching Henry's side. "Lord Langlevit, I am afraid you have rather rudely interrupted what was going to be an important moment."

"Max, don't," Irina said sharply.

"You were saying quite the opposite a moment ago, my dear," he murmured.

A ferocious pulse quickened through Henry, the need to destroy coming back, untempered.

"Careful, Remisov," he growled.

There was a beat of silence, and then Lord Remi chuckled. "A name I've not heard in quite some time. You have been poking around, my lord. Turn up anything interesting yet?"

Henry took a step closer, his footfalls churning up the earthy scent of grass and night dew. "I'll show my cards in due time. Until then, I believe I will deliver Princess Irina to her chaperone."

"I told you, Langlevit—we were in the middle of something."

His control snapped and Henry strode forward, coming toe to toe with the young, arrogant lord. "And I am telling you that whatever it was, is over. Stand aside or, God help you, I will move you myself."

The poor lighting made it impossible to see into Lord Remi's eyes, but Henry held the man's pitch-black stare for a handful of moments, neither of them breathing as the air turned thick with threat.

"That is enough," Irina finally said, pushing past Remi and then farther, past Henry. At some point, Henry had released Rose's arm, and a back segment of his mind tickled and stung with the recollection that she was here, in the garden entrance with them. It was the only thing that kept him remotely tethered to rationality.

"I will see myself inside," Irina announced, and with a muttered apology to Rose, disappeared under the trellis and back toward the terrace steps.

Henry followed, wanting only to be certain she did in fact make it back inside the ballroom safely. He stood on the other side of the trellis, watching as she did.

"You have an appalling sense of timing," Lord Remi said lazily, and when Henry turned back to him, caught the tail end of an equally lazy—and sarcastic—bow. "Good evening," he said as he stood tall again, turned on one heel, and walked deeper into the garden.

Within seconds, he was out of sight.

The muscles along Henry's shoulders, bunched and tense for the last several minutes, did not relax at his departure, setting off a painful ache near his old wounds. Every inch of him remained on edge, ready for attack, and it was only the soft touch of Rose's fingers on his elbow that made him gather himself.

"Henry?"

"I'm fine," he said eventually, concentrating on the contours of her face and the shape of the arbor around them. Henry's breath calmed little by little as he forced his rigid muscles to loosen. Focusing on minute details helped, though bloodlust still simmered like molten lead in his veins. It would not have taken much provocation to rip the man limb from limb. In fact, it was surprising that Remisov had made it out of the arbor unharmed, but if he had laid one finger on Irina, the outcome would have been much different.

Henry frowned as if doubting his own view of Irina's reentry into the ballroom. "Did you see the princess go back inside?"

Rose nodded. "Yes, she entered the ballroom just before."

"You're certain?"

"Yes."

"And Remisov?"

"Not that I saw. He stalked off in the opposite direction. Perhaps he'll cool his heels a bit," Rose said, her brow creasing in worry as Henry rubbed his aching temples with the heels of his palms. "Perhaps we should also tarry a moment," she said, pointing to a nearby stone bench that offered an ample view of the terrace and the entire wing of the residence.

Henry drew a pained breath and nodded. Not that it would stop the reckless hellion from escaping via another exit, but it would set his mind at ease for the moment. At least while he composed himself enough to return to the ballroom.

"Good." She smiled and took the seat beside him. "You'd terrify the guests with that ferocious expression in your eyes alone."

Henry cringed. Rose was never one to mince words. "I'm sorry you had to see that."

"Please," she said gently, laying her fingers on his sleeve. "I've seen far worse, remember?"

Henry swallowed. It was true that both Rose and John had seen him at his very worst in the first few weeks after his return from France. They were the sole reason he'd managed to survive…and had been able to come back from the brink of what he'd endured. Henry had moved out of Hartstone for fear of unknowingly harming anyone and had stayed with them for some months until he'd started to feel less like an animal and more like a man. Until he was sure that his own mother would be safe in his presence. The obstacle course had been John's idea to keep the devils at bay. Holding his head in between his palms, Henry groaned. He could use a round or three on the course right about now.

"I wanted to kill him," he heard himself say after a while.

"You would not have."

Henry lifted a tortured gaze to hers. "I *could* have. Easily. It was only by a miracle that I did not." He sighed, returning his face to his hands. "I am a killer, after all."

"You're not that man anymore, Henry," Rose said. "And men are forced to become killers in times of war. You stopped now because it was the right thing to do."

He admired her unswerving loyalty, but no, Rose was wrong. It had nothing to do with doing the right thing or not. He had stopped because he had not wanted Irina to see the beast that lived deep inside of him, the one that had so nearly reared its vicious head. Deep down, it was the true reason he had asked Rose to marry him. She'd *seen* him. She *knew* him. If Irina ever caught a glimpse of the monster he worked so hard to keep buried, she would never be able to look at him the same way. That man had come dangerously close to making an appearance tonight.

Henry had never known anyone who could drag him to such uncontrolled extremes. One minute he wanted to kiss her, and the next he wanted to throttle her. The exacting self-control he held over himself seemed to fly out the window when she was near.

"She is a danger to herself," he growled.

Rose took a deep breath and squeezed his forearm where her fingers still rested. "I haven't seen you this angry over anything in a long while."

"If we hadn't come upon them, who knows what would have happened." He raked a furious hand through his hair. "She is my ward."

"She is far more than that," Rose replied quietly.

Henry's eyes met hers in the filtered moonlight as a host of emotions barreled into him. "She is a friend to my family."

"You're lying to yourself, Henry, and you know it." She looked him directly in the eye. "You are in love with her. And if John were here, he'd tell you the same."

Pain stabbed his heart. "If John were here, you'd be happily married while I would—"

"Have to find some other poor excuse for a wife," Rose finished with a bright smile. "And heaven knows if I would have been able to stand by and watch you marry Lady La Valse. Even if John were here, you'd still have to deal with the stipulation on your title, or give it up entirely."

"Sometimes I think that would be the better course," he said softly. "To walk away and disappear. I deserve to be alone."

"Stop being silly. That would destroy Lady Langlevit." Rose twisted on the bench, her hand angling toward his jaw. "I'll tell you what you deserve—you deserve to forgive yourself and allow yourself the chance to be loved." She cupped his chin, forcing him to face her. "That young lady loves you. And you are too intelligent not to recognize your own feelings when it comes to her, otherwise you would not have reacted as you have. You would not have dragged me out here the minute you saw her leave the ballroom on the arm of that young man."

"Remisov is a snake."

"This is not about him. It's about *her*."

Pushing her hands down, Henry stood and paced to the start of the arbor. "Of course I care for Irina. I always have. I probably always will. But she is a child who is infatuated."

"You keep saying that."

"What do you mean?"

"She is nineteen and of marriageable age," Rose said calmly, flicking an eyebrow upward at his tone. "She is a woman, even if you choose to convince yourself otherwise."

Visions of Irina clamped up against him: her lips glued to his, the soft feel of her warm, willing body in his arms as she'd been at the waterfall. They tortured him. He swallowed thickly, driving the stirring, all-too-seductive image from his brain.

"I want nothing more than for her to marry," he ground out.

"If she has to choose a husband, why should it not be you?"

He strode back toward her, his voice cool though his pulse leaped frantically at her suggestion. Because he could not be a proper husband. Because he could hurt her with his bare hands. Rose did not know the vile truth of what he was capable of—how close he had come to unknowingly harming the courtesan who had warmed his bed. If he hurt Irina while caught unawares in the savage throes of a nightmare, he would never forgive himself. Rose's condition of separate residences had been a godsend…for him and for her.

"Because I am engaged to you, Rose."

"A farce."

"What's to say that love won't come in time?" Henry asked, resuming his seat beside her. "Or passion."

"I do love you." She laughed at him. "But you're like a brother to me."

"And?"

"You know I don't fancy you that way," she said, traces of amusement still in her eyes. "Very well, I shall prove it to you. Kiss me."

His gaze narrowed on her. "Kiss you now?"

She nodded. He wasn't sure what her endgame was, but he leaned in all the same, and brushed his lips across hers. Henry lingered, counting the seconds in his head. "There," he murmured after five very appropriate seconds and pulled away. "Perfectly pleasant."

"Perfectly perfunctory, you mean," Rose said, laughing again. "That was appallingly similar to the one you gave me when we were twelve at the country fair. And honestly, I have no wish to ever repeat that again." She eyed him, tipping her head to the side. "Tell me the truth—did you feel anything?"

Henry wanted to be offended—his kisses had never been called appalling before—but he only laughed. "No," he admitted.

"Neither did I. Honestly, it was like kissing a stone statue." Henry gave a short bark of laughter at the revolted look of mock distaste on her face. "As the alchemists say, we have no chemistry, Lord Langlevit," Rose continued, "and though I will love you as a friend until the end of time, I have had my *grand amour*, and I am content to be a happy widow for the rest of my days and live contentedly with my son."

"What are you saying?"

She nodded firmly to herself. "I cannot in good conscience stand by and watch you throw away a chance at love because you're too blind and stubborn to see it. I refuse to let you use me as some kind of excuse. I cannot do this, Henry. I will not marry you."

Oddly, Henry did not feel anything at Rose's words. He felt no disappointment, only a strange sense of relief. He did not stop to analyze the odd response, however. "I understand."

"Do you?"

"It was too much to ask of you."

"I agreed because you are my friend, and I wanted to help you." Rose leaned in. "But you and I both know that I would make you a terrible wife. You need someone who can keep pace with you. I cannot climb a tree without getting stuck and needing to be rescued. I abhor sweat and dirt in any measure. I'd rather be indoors perfecting my cross-stitch than riding outdoors, or playing bridge instead of fencing. I would bore you to tears in a matter of months."

"You would not," he said loyally.

Frowning at him in silence, Rose pursed her lips. "What are you so afraid of, Henry?"

He did not reply for a long time, but when he did, his voice was quiet. Henry couldn't tell her the real truth, so he told a partial one. "That my heart is damaged beyond repair."

"We're all flawed in some way or another, you know. No one is perfect, and no one expects perfection, least of all, I suspect, Princess Irina." She stood and reached a hand out to him. "Promise me you'll at least try."

"I am not the man for her, Rose."

"I think you're wrong about that." She glared fiercely at him. "And if I see a betrothal announcement to Lady La Valse in the *Times*, it will be closely followed by an obituary because I will personally murder you."

Henry shook his head and bit back laughter. She was a good friend. Honest and blunt, and she was right: they would make a perfectly boring couple. Tepid at best.

"You're not to worry," he said, standing from the bench and extending his arm to her. "Lady La Valse has an aversion to marriage and monogamy—otherwise I would have asked her first off."

"Are you saying I'm second fiddle?" Rose swatted his arm, pretending to storm away. He caught her elbow, and she turned back to him, smiling.

"No, Rose, you are my rock," he said quietly. "And I am deeply grateful for your friendship."

Rose's eyes glinted with the sheen of tears. "As I am yours."

"Thank you," he said, all honesty now. "I'll take care of everything, Rose. The announcement, the gossip—"

"Oh, I'm not certain people care enough about me to gossip for more than one or two days. I'll return to Breckenham on the morrow, and all will be forgotten."

Henry suspected she was right about that, as well, but made no reply as they walked up the terrace steps and back into the ballroom.

They stood along the periphery of the dance floor, Henry's eyes in a frantic search for Irina. For a split second, his heart and stomach swapped places with the fear that she'd slipped out another exit and had returned to Remisov's side. She was undoubtedly irate that he'd followed her and challenged her friend yet again. *Friend.* Maxim Remisov was no such thing, and once more, Henry felt the pressure to prove it to her, and fast.

Her whimsical dress swirled into view, and he relaxed at the sight of her dancing with Lord Thorndale. Her gown was far less revealing than any other dress he'd seen her wear, but something about the sight of her in it made him think of a spring goddess. The only things missing were flower wreaths in her hair and bare feet. He could almost picture her racing across a meadow filled with spring flowers atop a wild horse with blooms bursting in her wake.

Hell, he was in danger of turning into a poet.

Rose was wrong. He wasn't in love with Irina, though he did feel something beyond friendship. It wasn't simply lust, and it wasn't love, but something indefinable caught in between. The problem was he didn't know if it would be enough. Women wanted love, and Henry didn't know if his damaged heart would ever be capable of that. Or his damaged mind. He still couldn't trust himself…not with her. If he did take her to wife and she fell asleep in his arms, she would not be safe.

"I'm going to see myself home," Rose said, beginning to pull away.

Henry did not allow her, however. "I will take you."

"No, you should stay," she said and lowered her voice. "At least until Lady Irina retires for the evening. I wouldn't put it past Lord Remi to return to finish what he started."

"Are you certain?"

"Of course."

After he'd made sure that Rose was tucked safely into his carriage and on her way home, Henry headed back into the ballroom. Nursing a glass of fine whiskey, he scanned the space, searching for Remisov's blond locks, but the man was nowhere to be seen. If he hadn't already left, he was likely cooling his heels in the arms of one of Dinsmore's servants.

Henry didn't tend to judge other men and their appetites, but something about Remisov's utter dissoluteness got under his skin. He was a man who used and discarded people as one would a soiled napkin. The thought of such a man kissing Irina, *touching* her, made Henry feel physically ill. He frowned. On the surface, Remisov was a handsome and charming young lord, but there was something that did not feel right. He was too smooth, too slick. And Henry trusted his instinct, even though it had grown rusty with disuse.

"I see you are holding up your usual pillar, Lord Langlevit."

The lilting voice made a jolt spark up his spine. He turned in slow motion to see Irina standing there, nursing a glass of champagne. She was unaccompanied by anyone, though he saw Lady Dinsmore hovering nearby. Henry almost rolled his eyes. North had once called her a marriage juggernaut, and it wasn't far from the truth. Celebrated for pulling off two brilliant matches for her children, Irina was obviously her next protégée. The thought brought an instant rush of irritation that he quickly stifled.

"I fear the entire room may collapse if I shirk my responsibilities," he said with a smile.

Irina's eyes brightened with humor at his quip. "Like Atlas, then? Holding up the sky?"

"You flatter me."

Irina hesitated for a moment before placing her full glass on a nearby stand and smiling dazzlingly at him. "Will you risk the fate of the ballroom for one dance, my lord?"

When put like that, Henry had little choice. He could for her. A hazy recollection of a doe-eyed young Irina arguing the merits of dancing decorum with her sister at Lord and Lady Bradburne's wedding ball flicked through his brain: *what if the gentleman I wish to dance with doesn't ask?* Laughingly, he'd replied then that it was a risk.

No more so than the one he was taking now.

Pushing off the pillar, he extended his arm. "It would be my pleasure."

Most things never fit together exactly in life, but Henry was astounded once more at how perfect Irina felt in his arms. Her height and lithe slenderness complemented his. She was strong, but still feminine.

Henry slid his palm across the ruched ivory chiffon along her back and felt her swift intake of breath. Every touch felt amplified, underscored by a subtle awareness that left his skin inflamed and tingling. Irina's muscles leaped beneath his fingertips as his palm shifted to the curve of her waist, his little finger flirting with the rise of her hip. He suppressed the instant urge to slide his hand downward to curve over her bottom and crush her hips to his.

They had danced the waltz before, but something seemed different between them this time. The space between them was charged as if a lightning bolt was suspended in the middle of their bodies. It was to be expected, of course, after the intimacy that had occurred between them. The human body had a tendency to remember things that incited pain or pleasure. Henry ached to give her that pleasure again, to see and feel her shuddering in his arms.

After they completed the first turn, she exhaled and lifted her gaze to his. "My lord, I wish to apologize for what happened in the arbor."

"You have nothing to apologize for."

Her eyes searched his. "You must have overheard…"

"That Lord Remi, or Remisov, or whatever his name is, intended to propose?" Henry said stiffly. "I'm not sure what I did hear, but surely you are not considering accepting him?"

"I've had no better offers." Irina studied the knot in his cravat. "Every man here is interested in a game…the thrill of the prize. At least I know that Max cares for me."

"Does he?"

Irina nodded. "Yes, I believe he does."

Henry's palm shifted at her waist, his fingers moving restlessly. He knew if he said the wrong thing that she would shut him out. Clearly, she was blind to her friend's faults. "And what if there are others who wish to make their interest known, but may be deterred by your obvious favor of Lord Remi?"

"Are there others?" Her voice was a whisper.

Henry made a split-second decision as they spun past one of the many open balcony doors. He'd wanted to eradicate them before, but now he was grateful for the escape and the privacy they offered. He intended to say his piece.

"What are you doing?" Irina asked, gasping as he drew her in the shadow of a lush treillage.

"What I've wanted to do since I saw you in this dress." Irina blinked in surprise as he plucked a fragrant purple blossom from the nearby vines and tucked it into her hair above her ear. "There, now you are truly the goddess of spring."

"You think me a goddess?" she asked, blushing.

Henry's fingers brushed the soft skin of her nape, his knuckles skimming across the modest bodice of her gown and down her arm. He lifted her hand to his mouth, his intended words slipping away. "I think you are more beautiful than any goddess."

Though her violet eyes held his gaze, he saw them begin to shutter. "You should not say such things. Lady Carmichael—"

"Has left," he said, with a rough breath. "She has broken

our betrothal."

"She has?" Henry heard the shock in her voice. "But… why?"

"Because it was a farce."

Irina bit her lips. "What about your title?"

"I don't give a damn about it." Henry drew a deep breath, his eyes flicking to a tall blond gentleman who had just appeared on the far side of the ballroom, his gaze searching the throng of dancers.

"You can't mean that. You don't plan to marry at all?"

"No," he said, distracted. "I don't know."

"You don't know," she repeated very slowly and very softly.

"Yes, you know it's complicated, Irina," he said, scrubbing a frustrated hand through his hair. Henry knew he did not have much time before Remi discovered them on the terrace, and all he could think of was warning Irina away. Save her from making a terrible mistake. "Irina, you cannot accept Remi."

"Why not?"

"He is not good for you," Henry said, noting the suddenly brittle tone of her voice and the pinched slant of her features. "He is not worthy of you."

Irina's reply was quiet, her gaze following his through the paned glass of the French doors. Her face hardened with understanding. "You are the last person to judge who is or isn't worthy." Her voice broke on the last word. "It's not that complicated, after all. You don't want me, but you don't want anyone else to have me, is that it?"

"No, Irina—"

"Just leave me be, Henry." She plucked the blossom from her hair and let it fall from her fingers as she pushed past him. "Forget me and go back to your life. Let me *go*."

As Irina left him to enter the ballroom and meet Remi,

one thing gripped him with a violent certainty: he could never let her go. He'd always thought himself incapable of love, but that did not mean he didn't have a desire to protect...to guard...to cherish...to make Irina smile and laugh...to give her pleasure in every form. His happiness began and ended with her.

On cue, Henry's demons churned within him, filling him with instant crippling doubt. If he laid himself bare, would Irina accept him as he was? If she truly saw him and knew everything of his deepest, darkest secrets, would she stay? Or would she flee like that courtesan had, looking at him in horror for the monster he was? His fears threatened to derail the fragile realization unfurling like a new bud finally given sunlight. Stopping to retrieve the fallen flower, Henry studied the bloom. In some unexpected way, Irina had found his cold, shriveled, broken heart and made it whole again.

Rose, it seemed, had been right after all.

Because somewhere, somehow he'd fallen in love with the stubborn, willful, outrageous little hellion. Henry laughed out loud, the knowledge knocking the wind out of him but making him feel as if he could indeed hold up the sky. It was time to do something that he hadn't done in a long time... fight for something he desperately wanted.

Win or lose, he had to try.

Chapter Nineteen

Lady Dinsmore had wanted Irina to remain at home the next morning, at least until after luncheon, in order to receive any callers, flowers, or notes from possible suitors. The ball had lasted until the small hours of the morning, though Irina had taken her leave close to midnight, after Max had left and then Henry immediately after. She'd danced with a handful of gentlemen, though when she'd settled into bed, her feet sore and her cheeks stiff from holding a false smile all evening, she hadn't been able to recall specifically whom.

By morning, she could barely remember anything from the evening before that did not consist of Henry or Max. Irina would never have been able to concentrate on politely receiving visitors, not when her mind and body felt torn in as many directions as it did. So, she had called for her maid earlier than expected, dressed, had breakfast sent up, and then departed before noon, before Lady Dinsmore had even emerged from her own bedroom.

Most of society would be out strolling in Hyde Park, Irina figured, so she had instructed her driver in another direction.

Yardley Botanical Gardens was in southwest London, along the banks of the Thames, and was a collection of glass greenhouses, a bowling green, and topiary gardens. As the driver set out for the gardens, Irina's maid squirmed on the backward facing bench, across from Irina.

"Oh, Your Highness," Jane said in her squeaky voice. "You don't really want to see the death flower, do you?"

She wore a serviceable black dress and bonnet, making her sudden look of pure revulsion even more pointed.

"Of course I do. I hear it is enormous and strange—did you know it doesn't have roots? It's a *parasite*, Jane."

"A what?"

"A living organism that survives on another organism. In this case, I've heard the *rafflesia patma* has bloomed out of a spongy old tree trunk."

Jane grimaced as the carriage rocked over the streets toward the southern edge of the city.

"I've heard it smells like a rotting corpse," Jane said. Her coloring, usually flush and healthy, had gone a bit yellow.

"I doubt it is as offensive as that," Irina replied, though she secretly hoped it was. In fact, she was counting on it being too odious for most ladies and gentlemen to visit. She knew there would be people there, coming only to view the rare flower and to be seen doing so, but she also knew there would have been far more people clucking and crooning around Hyde Park and Rotten Row.

When they arrived, however, Irina took one look into the lake of carriages, curricles, and broughams parked outside the botanical gardens and decided she might have been wrong. She considered leaving, but then thought of the *rafflesia patma* and realized she was actually excited to see it. Even smell it, oddly enough.

She and Jane got out of the carriage and, almost immediately, Irina was spotted.

"Princess!" cried a voice from near a long, sleek topless carriage. Lady Lyon hopped and waved to gain her attention, and Irina started for her. Gwen had a man with her, and by his paunch and glowering expression, Irina figured he was Lord Lyon. He looked just as pleased as Jane to be there.

The countess kissed Irina on both cheeks before glancing back at her husband.

"Darling, this is Princess Irina Volkonsky," Gwen said, to which Lord Lyon clicked his heels and bowed in a surprisingly fashionable manner. She'd expected a grumbled hello from his sour expression.

"Are you on your way in?" Irina asked.

"Oh yes! This is our second time coming. We were here last week. I cannot describe just how *awful* the stench was!"

"I could think of a few words to describe it," Lord Lyon said, his nostrils flaring.

From behind Irina, Jane made a soft mewling sound. She turned and saw her maid's coloring had drained some more.

"I'm afraid my companion rather fears the odor the flower is said to put off," she explained when Lady and Lord Lyon eyed Jane with concern.

"Oh, well she isn't the first one, I'm sure. Why, last week when we were here, Lady Rochester fainted! Keeled right over and bumped her head on the trunk the flower sprouted from!"

At this, Jane's eyes went wide with alarm. Irina had never seen a person's skin go green until that moment.

"Poor dear," Gwen said, her good humor ebbing. "Perhaps she should stay with the carriage? Irina, you could come with us."

The offer had much more appeal than the alternative. She'd have to drag Jane to the flower and then perhaps deal with fainting. Or worse.

"Thank you," Irina said with a nod to Jane, who scurried

happily back into the carriage.

Inside the main greenhouse, the cool spring morning became a humid summer day with voices rising up to the soaring glass ceilings and becoming strangely muffled. There was a sickly sweet odor that greeted their noses, too, and Irina figured it was the *rafflesia patma*, more easily remembered as the death flower.

Gwen was rambling excitedly about not just the flower the dozens of people were all here to view and smell, but of upcoming balls, parties that had passed, and whom had been seen with whom. Irina tried to keep up with the flow of gossip, but like the night before, when the memory of faces and names of the men she'd danced with had started to fade, so too did Gwen's voice.

Until the countess said one name that yanked Irina from the haze: "Lord Langlevit."

Irina stopped in the center of the greenhouse, where thick shrubs of bright pink bougainvillea were flowering, and looked at Gwen, who seemed to be looking at someone.

Irina followed her gaze and saw the last person she'd thought to see here. Henry was walking toward them, a small piece of paper in his hand. He stopped before them and tipped his head.

"Your Highness. Lord and Lady Lyon," he said, his eyes lingering on Irina an extra moment. "I am surprised at how many people I know wish to subject themselves to this particular fragrance."

The pungent odor had intensified since they'd first entered the greenhouse, and now, meeting with Henry when she had not wanted to at all, made Irina feel just as ill as Jane had claimed to be.

"And yet you have come, as well," Gwen put in.

He held up the scrap of paper in his hand, and Irina could see the etching of a flower with enormous petals and a black hole in the center of the cabbage leaf-like petals.

"My mother has an interest in such things. If she were in London, she would have come. I thought I would see it for her," he said, tucking the small sketch into his breast pocket.

It was kind of him, and Irina instantly wished he hadn't explained. It made it more difficult to remain angry with him.

"You are an artist, my lord?" Gwen asked because Irina's own tongue had suddenly become heavy as sand.

"Far from it," he replied. "I can copy a basic likeness, nothing more."

Lord Lyon took his handkerchief and put it to his nose. "My dear, I do not think I can get much closer than this again."

Gwen sighed with mock annoyance. "I think perhaps you should have stayed with the carriage, too. Come now," she said, taking her husband's arm. "We'll wait by the orchids while the princess has a look."

Irina wanted to insist that they both stay, but knew it was pointless. She would have had to face Henry at some point. Last night on the balcony, he'd yet again pulled her close then pushed her away. Why did he keep doing that? And worse yet, why did she keep allowing him to do it?

"Shall we?" Henry gestured toward the crowd of people surrounding what she knew must be the death flower.

"You needn't accompany me," she replied, walking forward and ignoring his arm, which he'd extended graciously. She didn't want to be gracious in return. She wanted to bite his head off and spit it out.

He made no sense, and when she was with him, she made no sense, either. Even here, in public, among scores of other people, Irina did not trust herself. When she was not with him, she seemed to spend every moment building a fortress around her heart. A fortress that fell, time and time again, whenever she was with him.

"I know," he replied, coming to walk beside her anyway. It

was abominable, the way his mere presence obliterated every ounce of her good sense. Because deep down, she was glad he had ignored her dismissal. It was sickening. *She* was sick. And it made her angry.

"I think it best if we stop seeing so much of one another," she murmured, aware her voice would carry easily.

They had stopped behind the crowd and were waiting for their turn to step forward.

"I don't want that," he replied, also softly.

She refused to look at him, and instead stared ahead at a trio of ladies in soft pastel-colored walking dresses.

"No, you wouldn't, would you? You want to kiss me. You want to bed me. But you don't want to marry me," she said, practically breathing the words to keep them from other ears. "For all your warnings against the gentlemen placing wagers and seeking my hand in marriage as a prize, you, my lord, are the most dangerous one of them all."

He angled himself toward her, and she could feel the heat of his body, even through the already humid air.

"Those men care nothing for you."

She blinked long and hard. There they were: words that burned yet soothed, prickling her skin and tormenting her with what they could mean…that *he* cared. But she would only be deluding herself—Henry had made his position more than clear. Multiple times.

"Max does," she said.

Henry huffed and crossed his arms. "Lord Remisov is exactly what my instincts told me he was: a fake."

Irina spun toward him and forgetting to whisper, said, "What do you mean by that?"

The ladies in pastel dresses turned to glance at her, but only for a moment, and Irina didn't recognize them anyway. Still, that did not mean they didn't recognize her.

"A letter from my contact in St. Petersburg arrived this

morning. It seems your dear Max stole quite a bit from his coffers of family heirlooms years back, before he was shipped off to Paris."

Irina frowned. Max had been "shipped off" when he'd been no more than fourteen or fifteen. He'd been bitter toward his father when she'd reconnected with him in Paris, so she could only imagine he'd have been furious and hurt when he'd first been sent away.

"That was years ago," she said. "If he did steal family heirlooms, I'm sure it was only in an attempt to strike back at his father for sending him away so heartlessly. It doesn't make him a *fake*."

To which Henry replied, "It makes him a thief."

"They would have been his items eventually," Irina said, even though she knew it wasn't quite true. Max had been stripped of his title. He never would have inherited the things he'd stolen. If he'd stolen anything at all! Henry's contact could have gotten his information wrong.

"He was disowned, Irina," he said just as the crowd in front of them drew apart and started away from the flower.

It came into full view then, a colossal flower that had emerged from a woody trunk on its side. Once the barrier the crowd had provided had disappeared, the stench seemed to reach out and curl around Irina and Henry. She covered her mouth and nose with her hand and stepped closer, her mind jumping between the oddly shaped flower and the words Henry had just said.

"What did you say?" she asked, still eyeing the five big pink petals, speckled with white, and the cavernous hole in the center. The whole thing was at least the size of a carriage wheel. And the stench…good heavens, it smelled like meat left out to fester in the sun. Carrion flies buzzed around the flower, darting into the hole and back up out of it.

"I said he was disowned," Henry answered.

"Yes, I know. He was stripped of his title. If you think his father's cruelty and closed-mindedness would be enough for me to judge him as a poor acquaintance, then I'm quite sure you know nothing at all about me."

Even with her gloved hand covering her nose and mouth, the rotting flesh stink seemed to be pumping into her, coating the back of her tongue. Jane had been the wisest one of the bunch, she realized, and quickly walked away.

Henry followed her.

"Leave me be," she hissed, walking faster toward an exit that led onto the lawns.

Henry stayed on her heels.

"Good heavens, what is it?" she asked, hurrying into the fresh air and relishing the loss of the humid stink that had been filling the greenhouse. "Is there some wager you've a wish to win? Perhaps some idiot has put up a thousand pounds to the man who is seen strolling with the Ice Princess near the death flower."

"I've already told you, I have no desire to win any bloody wagers," he replied, his words raspy as he kept her quick pace. The grass had been level, but had changed over to brick at the beginning of a path leading into a grove of trees, the limbs severely trimmed into near-perfect box shapes.

"Well, maybe you should, my lord. With the liberties you've taken, I'm certain you'd be up to your knees in winnings."

Henry caught the tips of her fingers and pulled her to a halt. "Is that what Remisov is up to?" His chest heaved for air, and Irina realized how fast she'd been walking. "Of course. Entering wagers, cozying up to you—"

"He is my friend. There is no need to cozy up," she said, her heart pounding as Henry closed in on the scheme she and Max had concocted. A scheme she had started to get cold feet over.

"If I were to go to White's and look in the betting book, what would I see, Irina? Lord Remisov's name written in for the grand prize? Has he put up his two thousand pounds yet?" He shook his head, laughing and yet not really looking amused at all. No. He looked utterly ferocious. "That is it, isn't it? He knows he's won you. He knows you'll marry him, and he'll rake in his insane amount of winnings and be able to return to St. Petersburg a wealthy man, with or without his damned title."

"You're wrong," she said, moving backward off the brick path and onto the grass, closer to the boxed edge of a low-branched tree. "He is already a wealthy man. Whatever winnings there are will go to the Bradburne Trust."

Henry followed her off the path, a growl low in his throat. "He has told you this?"

The pruned branch tugged her linen dress, and Irina wrenched her arm away, backing up some more.

"You think you know what he intends?" Henry asked. He continued to push her backward, toward another box-shaped hedge. An alcove had been cut into it, and as Irina staggered into its bracket shape, she realized the danger it posed.

"You think you know what any man intends?" he went on, stalking her backward some more until she'd hit the meticulously pruned wall of the thick hedge.

"I know Max will honor his promise," Irina said, the pulse in her throat jumping the closer he became. She'd seen him angry before. She'd seen him caught in the throes of a memory that would not loose him from its clutches. But she had never seen him look like this. Like a prowling beast who wanted satisfaction and would stop at nothing until he had it.

"He won't. He will take what he wants and be done with it." Henry cornered her then, blocking her view of the alcove entrance, of the boxed trees beyond the hedge hideaway. Irina swallowed a spike of dread. Worry shot through her chest, but another paralyzing sensation struck lower, too, as heat throbbed in her abdomen. Good Lord, the way he was looking at her made her feel feverish. Every inch of her hummed in his presence.

"Is that the sort of man you want?" he asked, lifting his hand and touching her side. He formed his palm to the shape of her hip and squeezed. Irina felt the immediate answering tug between her thighs.

"No," she said, but he only responded by raking his hand up the side of her dress, pressing into her ribs.

"Do you want a man who takes what he wants?" His thumb dragged boldly across the underside of her breast.

"Henry, please," she gasped. "This is—"

"This is a prize I want," he said hoarsely, and as his fingers curved up her breast, toward the bodice top, Irina knew he was already lost. So was she.

"How much do you think it is worth?" he asked, the question both crude and thrilling. And when he pulled the top of her bodice down, exposing her breast, Irina whimpered.

Henry pinched her nipple gently, and she arched her back, wanting to thrust her breast deeper into his hand. Henry lowered his head and took the hard peak into his mouth, suckling her, scraping his teeth against the sensitive tip until it hurt. She almost didn't feel the bunching up of her dress until Henry's palm was sliding up her thigh, rustling over the silk of her stockings and brushing the lace edges of her drawers.

"How much to touch you here?" he asked, his fingers instantly finding the slit in her drawers. Irina knew he was being purposefully lewd, but she didn't want him to stop. That was always the problem…once Henry was touching her, she *did* feel like a prize had been won. *Him.* His touch, his attention, the pleasure he was more than willing to give her.

His fingers skimmed her wet heat, but instead of pushing inside to touch her deeply as he had before, he paused.

"Ah, but that has already been won," he said. "A new wager, then. To up the stakes."

Henry gave her nipple one last nip and then lowered himself to one knee. He picked Irina's foot up from the grass and placed it on his thigh before tossing her skirt and petticoats up, exposing her stockinged legs and garters.

"Henry!" she gasped, her fevered eyes looking up to the alcove entrance. "What are you doing?"

His fingers kept the slit in her drawers open and cool air rushed against the most private part of her. His eyes took her in, and for the first time since this mad display in the hedge alcove had started, she saw him falter.

"I told you I wanted you in ways you could not fathom," he said, his breath gusting against her center.

"But if we are seen—"

"I know," he said, and then with a groan, he put his mouth to her core. Irina tensed and moaned her surprise as his tongue pushed inside. Henry licked her, scraping his teeth against the small nub at her entrance. Blood pounded through Irina's ears, her head spinning, her breath all but lost as he made love to her with his mouth. It was wrong. It was so wrong, but it was the most glorious sin she'd ever known.

"I thought I saw the princess come this way." A voice knifed through Irina's delirium.

Lady Lyon.

Henry released her and pushed her skirts back down before standing to full height again.

"Stay here. I'll lead them away," he whispered, and started to leave. She clutched at his arm, uncertain what she wanted to say, only knowing she didn't want him to leave.

"I will make it right," he said softly. His glittering amber eyes, still glazed with unsatisfied desire, searched hers. "You have my promise."

And then, before she could make any sort of reply, Henry

turned and left.

Her body was buzzing from his touch, from her own unsatisfied desire, when she heard his voice speaking to Gwen. Something about not being able to catch up with the princess. A maze farther ahead, near the bowling green. Perhaps they should all try there.

Irina realized her breast was still exposed and she quickly covered herself, straightening her dress and bodice, and touching the simple knot of hair at the base of her neck Jane had fixed earlier.

As soon as her knees would hold, Irina peeked around the corner of the hedge. There were a few ladies strolling in the distance, but neither of them were Gwen. Irina started back toward the greenhouse, trying not to rush and draw attention to herself, but also desperate to leave. Oh, good heavens, what had she just done? What had she allowed Henry to do?

She never would have imagined he'd drop to his knees, right there in the hedges, and kiss her...*there*, the very heart of her. Somehow, it seemed even more intimate than she imagined the act of lovemaking would be. Her chest felt hot, and the space between her thighs was still thrumming as she avoided entering the greenhouse and walked the periphery of it instead. There was a brick path leading to the front entrance, with topiary along the way, but the shrubs clipped into the shapes of horses, goats, elk, and fish could not distract her mind from reeling with questions.

What would happen now? He'd said he'd make it right... but what did that mean? *I will make it right. You have my promise.* His promise? He couldn't mean a promise to *do* right by her...could he? Because that would entail a proposal. A wedding. And he didn't wish to marry her or anyone.

Or had something changed?

Irina realized she was walking back toward the sea of conveyances and horses without so much as a good-bye to

Lord and Lady Lyon. It was abysmally rude, but she could not see Henry again. Not yet. Not without flushing the deepest shade of puce and giving everything away. Gwen would pounce on such a delicious morsel of gossip in a second.

"It appears the death flower has had its most distinguished visitor yet." Irina looked up at the sound of Max's voice. She saw him walking toward her, having just arrived, she assumed. And on his arm was Lady La Valse.

He grimaced. "It also appears the stench is just as awful as has been reported. You're running from the greenhouse in near tears."

Tears? Irina blinked and realized her lashes were indeed wet. She'd been on the verge of crying, it seemed, and she had not even known it.

"It is," she said.

Max and Lady La Valse stopped before her.

"Awful," Irina went on clumsily. "The stench."

Max peered down at her while Lady La Valse looked confused, as if Irina were speaking a foreign language. What the woman thought meant nothing to her, though. It bothered Irina just having to stand so close to this woman who had bedded Henry God knew how many times in the past.

"What is the matter?" Max asked, lifting her chin an inch so he could inspect her gaze. "Are you feeling ill?"

"I know I am going to be ill," Lady La Valse said, sounding bored. "I cannot believe I allowed you to bring me along. I swear I can smell rotting meat from here."

Her nose crinkled, and Irina wished it would stay that way permanently.

"No, I'm…I'm fine. I just need to leave," she replied, purposefully ignoring Lady La Valse.

"We'll walk you to your carriage," Max said, whereupon his companion sighed heavily.

"I want to get this viewing over with, Remi. I'll be inside," she said, and having noticed Irina's lack of greeting, returned it in kind. She sauntered away without a word to her.

"Come," Max said, and Irina fell into step beside him. "And tell me what is wrong. I know you, Irina. Something has happened."

She couldn't speak of it. Not to anyone, and especially not Max. He didn't like Henry, just as Henry didn't like him.

She recalled his accusation earlier, that Max had stolen from his father, but pushed it aside. There were more important things to discuss at that moment.

"Yes, something has," she said, taking a fortifying breath. It was time. She knew she had to break it to him and now before things got further out of control. "I'm calling it off. Our planned betrothal. It can't happen. You must withdraw your name from the wager book at White's."

She'd known it for a long time, perhaps even from the start. Something about the way Henry had said she had his promise to make it right…if that meant a proposal, Irina would accept it without hesitation. No, he may never love her, but he longed for her. That had been more than evident in the alcove, and every other time they'd been alone. Henry wanted her, and she wanted him. They got along well…more than well. They could enjoy one another's bodies, and company, and maybe one day Henry would come to realize he cared for her. It was a wishful thought, but Irina couldn't marry Max and live a lie. She'd regret it forever.

Max walked her silently the rest of the way to her carriage. Only when her driver jumped as he saw her unexpected approach did he speak.

"There is nothing I can say to sway you?"

He didn't sound angry or frustrated as he had before, but resigned.

"No," she answered.

Max opened the door for her, revealing a napping Jane

inside the carriage. "I thought this might be your decision."

Good. So, it hadn't come as a complete surprise, then. Irina let out a relieved breath and kissed Max's cheek. "Thank you for understanding."

He helped her into the carriage and smiled up at her. "Of course, my dove. All will be well, you'll see." He pursed his lips into his usual smirk, his eyebrow rising. "So is this remarkable death flower worth seeing or not?"

Irina smiled back at him, grateful for small mercies. "I suppose if you want the stench of putrefying fish singeing your nose hairs for the next week."

"That sounds lovely." Max grinned at her. "Though I can't imagine it's worse than the Boulevard de Rochechouart in the height of summer."

"Well, prepare yourself, my lord. I do look forward to comparing notes."

With a jaunty wink, Max shut the door, and the driver called to the horses. The carriage pulled away, and Irina's maid startled awake.

"Did you see it?" she asked groggily.

Irina nodded, but didn't feel like conversing. She leaned back against the squabs and looked out the window, the narrow streets of London filtering past. Irina drew a deep breath, chasing the last of the death flower's stink away.

Max was right—all would be well on the morrow.

Chapter Twenty

White's was teeming with activity, but Henry turned a deaf ear to it. He expected it had everything to do with that damned wager book, which had become the bane of his existence.

Now that he had admitted his feelings to himself where a certain princess was concerned, the copious lists of bets chafed more. The only way he could stop it would be to make an offer of marriage himself, and that he would not do without first speaking with Irina's guardians or his mother. He'd almost ridden straight to Essex after their brief interlude at the Botanical Gardens, and if it weren't for the fact that he'd had business to tend to with his solicitor regarding Rose, he would have.

Sipping his whiskey, he exhaled sharply at the memory of Irina and the bemused look of astonishment on her face when he'd hiked her skirts and settled himself between her thighs. Christ, he'd have given anything to lay her down on the grass and finish what he'd started. The taste of her had been scintillating, the sight of her lissome, slim legs even more so. He wanted to behold her in all her natural beauty without a stitch of clothing on…feast his eyes on her with no fear of interruption. Henry could have cheerfully murdered Lady Lyon right then, although her unknowing intrusion had likely been a blessing in disguise. If he and Irina had been discovered in such a scandalous position with his head buried between her thighs in a public garden, the gossip would have been unstoppable.

But good God, the risk had been worth it.

Henry shuffled his cards in restless agitation, his body twitching with immediate lust at the erotic recollection. If the mere thought of her brought him to such a state of readiness and a dream could make him expend himself, he couldn't begin to imagine what the actual act would bring. Henry smiled to himself as he enumerated all the ways in which he would give her pleasure. Irina would be an eager student. Though she'd been stunned at the intimacy at the waterfall and at Yardley, Henry knew that she would revel in learning everything he had to teach her about her body. And his. Irina took pleasure as he did, without shame or artifice—she luxuriated in it with abandon and enthusiasm.

Henry was looking forward to the task already.

"Smiling because you're fleecing them all, Langlevit?" the Duke of Bradburne asked as he sat across from him in one of the empty chairs with a knowing grin. "Or because you have other more pleasing affairs on your mind?"

"A bit of both," Henry replied lazily, glad for the table's low overhang as he placed his latest bet, carefully watching the faces of his two opponents—two young peacocks he barely knew. He'd chosen the outlying table for that very reason. Henry did not want to converse with anyone, he simply wanted for a quiet diversion.

Playing cards was only a means of passing the time until another of his horses was re-shod for the journey to Essex. His favorite and fastest horse had turned up a stone in his hoof, and Henry did not want to put him through the grueling pace of a trip to the country. And when he'd finished his business with his solicitor, he'd decided to take luncheon at the club and enjoy a few quiet hands of *vingt-et-un*.

He did not mind the duke joining him now, however. Too much of his own thoughts left him in an engorged state unfit for polite society. "How long are you back in town, Hawk?"

"For the week," he said.

"And Her Grace, is she with you?"

"No," Hawk said. "She is still in Essex with the children. Lady Northridge has been committed to bed rest for the remainder of her confinement, and my wife has taken it upon herself to see to her comfort."

Henry frowned. He'd received no such information as to Lana's worsening condition, and Irina would have said something or insisted on returning if she'd known.

"It is only a precaution," Hawk added, as if he could read the worry on his face. "Lady Northridge did not want to needlessly worry her sister."

After a few minutes of intense play, Henry decided to fold, awarding the winning hand to the duke, who grinned with satisfaction. The two other young gentlemen who had been sitting at the table groaned their disappointment and rose, deciding to try their luck elsewhere. Henry nodded to the dealer to continue, despite it being only Hawk and him remaining.

He glanced up at the duke who seemed intently focused on the new hand he'd been dealt. "Hawk, may I ask you a question?"

"Of course."

Henry cleared his throat, lowering his voice. He knew the dealer would be discreet, but he could not account for other more curious ears around them. "How did you know...that Lady Bradburne was the one? That it was a love match."

Hawk's stare met his, a slight crease puckering his brow. "That's a rather loaded question."

"Yes, I know." Henry shrugged in apology. "It is fine if you do not wish to answer."

"No, you just took me by surprise," Hawk said, taking a draught from the glass of whiskey at his side. "I suppose I always knew somewhere deep down that she was the one for me. She made me want to change, and no woman had ever done that before. I was quite set in my ways, as you know." A fond smile settled on his face. "Briannon was…is…a force of nature. She saved me from myself."

"So it was always love?"

"Not at the start," Hawk said grinning. "She nearly drove me to madness first. Still does, but I would not have it any other way. Briannon is strong of heart and mind, and she challenges me every single day to be a better man."

Henry smiled into his own drink. "So, what you're saying is that finding the right one makes you feel like ripping your hair out at the roots *and* inspires a deep desire to improve yourself?"

"Exactly." Hawk arched an eyebrow at his dry tone. "Although I don't recall Lady Carmichael being of a particularly vexing temperament. She seems rather even-keeled."

"I'm not referring to Rose," Henry confessed after a beat. "She decided we didn't suit, after all."

"I am sorry to hear it."

Henry shook his head. "Don't be. It was a farfetched scheme to solve a ridiculously inconvenient matter of a stipulation on my title."

"So of whom do you speak?" Hawk asked, humor alight in his eyes. "Or is the young lady's identity of a delicate nature?"

"Clearly not, especially if it has a wager against it," Henry muttered, his eyes darting a vicious glower to where even more young men had congregated since his last look around that bloody book.

"Ah, of course." Hawk nodded, following his stare. "Her Grace did remark that she thought there was something between the two of you at the dinner at Worthington Abbey. Women have a certain intuition with that sort of thing. Might I assume that an announcement is in the works?"

"One that can't come soon enough," Henry said with a nod. "I intend to speak with North and Lady Langlevit on my return to Essex this afternoon. Then I plan to chuck that wager book into the fire."

The duke barked a laugh and leaned in, raising his glass and keeping his voice low. "Then may I be the first to offer my unofficial congratulations to your forthcoming nuptials."

"Thank you, though the lady and her guardians still have to accept."

"Lord and Lady Northridge should find no fault with your offer," Hawk said. "I think Lady Northridge wants those wager sheets destroyed as much as you do. Things have gotten out of hand." He signaled the dealer for another card. "As far as your Princess Irina, if she's anything like Briannon, I can only wish you fortitude and forbearance, and an endless supply of patience."

The devoted look on Hawk's face was at odds with his words. It was clear that he adored his wife even if he claimed she did try his patience, and it was also clear that Hawk would not have it any other way. Henry thought of the warmth he'd noticed between them, much like the connection he'd seen between North and Lana. Both strong men, North and Hawk had chosen to wed equally strong women, and they seemed more content than they'd ever been.

As much as Henry joked about ripping his hair out, he knew he would not change one thing about Irina, either...not her spirit, her daring, or her spontaneous joie de vivre. He liked her cheeky humor and her intelligent, albeit argumentative, opinions. He especially liked that she did not conform to what society expected of a lady. No such debutante could have run his course and completed it, nor would she have expressed an unabashed desire to do it again.

No, he wanted her exactly as she was. Fearless and unapologetic.

Henry's eyes fell on a tall newcomer who joined the throng, and the noise rose rapidly upon his arrival. His fingers gripped the snifter as pieces of the conversation reached where they sat.

"We have a new winner!"

"Well done, mate!"

"It still needs to be verified."

"Christ," he muttered as Hawk shot him a sympathetic smile over the table. Henry nodded to the factotum to finalize his account. He'd had enough, and clearly, the raucous celebration of whatever new favor Lady Irina had given away was not about to conclude any time soon.

"Why, there's the man who can verify the wager was met," a familiar voice drawled, making the air in Henry's lungs compress into a tight aggravated space. "Sitting right over there. Lord Langlevit, in fact."

Henry's eyes narrowed on the approaching horde with Lord Remi at its center. "Verify what?" he growled.

"That Lord Remi escorted Lady Irina into the arbor at Lord and Lady Dinsmore's soiree," a young buck said in a bawdy tone, making Henry instantly want to knock the man's teeth into the back of his throat. "The winnings are one thousand pounds, but we must have proof. A witness must confirm the claim!"

A bloody fortune, Henry thought.

Henry had no intention of willingly besmirching Irina's reputation by confirming any such intimate tête-à-tête with

Remi in the garden. A muscle tensed in his jaw as he set down his cards and folded his murderous hands into his lap. A brawl in the middle of White's would not be a wise idea, though every nerve in him screamed for such satisfaction.

"I witnessed nothing of the sort," he said coolly.

Remi's stare never wavered from his, though a challenging smile played about his lips. "Is that so?" he said. "I seem to recall you finding us in a very compromising position when you announced that Lady Dinsmore was looking for her delectable young charge."

Henry's chair scraped back on the carpet, and the noise died down to hushed whispers. He rose, menace fairly rippling off of him. The duke stood as well, dispersing most of the closest spectators with a lethal glance. "I caution you, Lord Remi, to reconsider your words," Henry said in a deadly quiet voice. "The lady's honor is in question."

Remi laughed, unperturbed. "Alas, that was not the bet, otherwise it would be a compromising situation indeed, would it not, Lord Langlevit?" He waved a careless arm as if unconcerned for his own safety. "Luckily the wager was only for a private and delightfully chaste stroll with the lady in the arbor." He paused. "Which you can confirm, of course, upon your word as a gentleman."

Henry tensed, every muscle within him itching to lay the arrogant man flat on his dandified back.

"Never you mind," someone shouted from the rear of the gathering. "Lord Everton saw Lord Remi and Lady Irina enter the arbor from the balcony and can corroborate Lord Remi's claim. The wager is won."

The crowd dispersed, but Remi remained standing before Henry, triumph in his eyes for a long moment as tension spiked between the two men. He leaned in, his voice whisper soft. "You don't know her like I do."

"You disgrace her," Henry said through clamped teeth.

Remi smiled. "I've never done anything Her Highness did not want done."

"What do you mean by that?" Henry snapped, his self-control wavering as visions of Remi's neck in his hands made him see red.

"Like I said, Lord Langlevit, you will never know her like I do." His smirk widened. "Whose idea do you think all of this was?"

Henry faltered. Was Remi insinuating that Irina had *encouraged* the wagers? Advocated placement bets on his behalf? His brows slammed together. Never had Henry wanted to give in to his savage inclinations more than he did at that exact moment. His entire body shook as he willed himself under control, his fist clenching and unclenching at his side.

"Easy," Hawk cautioned from beside him.

"I'm fine," he ground out.

"I see you've taken my meaning," Remi said, "and if you don't believe me, ask her. I have nothing to hide, after all, and neither does she. I certainly did not intend to set my cap in a ring." The young man eyed him with a singular smile. "You are aware of my tastes, after all. I have nothing to gain."

"You have a fortune to gain."

"I have more than enough coin at my disposal, my lord."

"You were cut off from your family," Henry hissed. "You have no income."

"But I do have many, *many* friends." Remi bowed in a mocking pose before turning on his heel and striding away to collect his winnings.

Ah. He had sponsors. Much like a mistress, Remi was kept by his guarantors in lavish style in return for the favors he performed, Henry realized. Which was why he never seemed to want for money. Or company.

"I must take my leave," Henry bit out to Bradburne, and

he called for his carriage in the same breath. He would not be responsible for his actions if he remained in the room any longer.

The ride to his house was quick, and Henry hoped to God that his horse was ready. The sooner he could put an end to the betting, the better. Even if Irina had been a part of it at the beginning, he knew that she would not have encouraged it now. She was impulsive, certainly, but she was not foolish.

"Stevens," he barked with impatience as he strode through the entryway, noting the complete lack of noise. "Where the devil is everyone?"

Stevens rushed into the foyer, his normally stoic countenance ruffled. He held a folded piece of parchment on a silver tray. Henry's eyes narrowed on the note, and his first thought was that it was from Irina. "What is it?"

"It's from Dr. Hargrove, my lord," Stevens said. "It arrived not long ago by express delivery."

Henry snatched the letter. It was about his mother. She'd taken a turn for the worse, and Dr. Hargrove had instructed Henry to leave for Hartstone at once. The strength drained from his limbs, cold fingers taking hold of his heart. "Where's my horse?"

"Ready and waiting in the mews, my lord."

Henry did not want to waste a single minute changing into traveling clothes. He strode toward the back of the house and headed for the stables. The young stableboy had his mount saddled out in the front.

"Thank you," Henry said, hauling himself astride and turning the horse about.

As much as he wanted to race out of London, he kept the pace sedate as he rode along Cranbourn Street leading out of the mews, careful not to trample anyone walking underfoot. Turning onto a far less crowded street toward Charing Cross Road, he came upon a carriage standing clear in the middle of the road. Its owner, a richly dressed lady, seemed to be in dire need of assistance. She was waving madly at him as he approached and placed herself directly into his path.

Henry wanted to lead his horse around. He did not have the time to stop. He did not *want* to stop, but years of good breeding demanded he do so.

"Please, my lord," the lady begged. "Can you please help? Our carriage wheel broke, and I fear my daughter's leg is injured. She fell. She's only three."

Cursing beneath his breath, he alighted. "Where is she?"

"Inside, my lord. I am Lady Barnelby. Please, I beg you, help my poor Sadie."

As he approached the carriage, his irritation mounting by the second, Henry blinked, taking in the woman's tear-streaked face and her obvious distress. A thick strand of pearls lay at her throat, though her richly embroidered dress seemed threadbare upon closer scrutiny. His gaze dropped to her gloveless hands, noticing the brown sunspots discoloring her skin. They seemed odd and out of place. Other things like her pronunciation of "you" niggled at him.

The street suddenly seemed unnaturally quiet as they stopped at the entryway to the carriage, the door hanging open drunkenly on one hinge. There was no coachman in sight, either. Henry's entire body tensed as his brain analyzed the details he'd seen, putting them together and coming up with a tableau that did not make sense. Now he understood why the sunspots had bothered him and why she had an accent. They weren't out of place, but the gown and jewels were.

Because she was no lady.

She was a highwayman.

Instinct alerted him to the movement of a person inside the carriage far larger than that of a small child. Her accomplice, he presumed.

Henry reached into his own jacket pocket for his pistol

and gnashed his teeth. He had not bothered to change into his riding clothes. He had not even stopped to retrieve his bloody pistol for the six-hour ride to Essex.

He felt the cold butt of a gun poke into his ribs as the women in distress pressed close to whisper into his ear. "Inside we go, love. Careful, now."

Henry wasn't afraid. He could handle one woman and one gun. What he didn't know was how many accomplices lay in hiding, not counting the large one inside the carriage. His brain calculated the odds of escape and survival as she shoved him toward the side of the coach.

"I don't want to have to hurt you," he warned through his teeth.

"Do ye now?"

Henry lunged forward, knocking the gun out of her palm with one stroke and sending it skidding across the dusty road. He had seconds before the hulking person in the carriage came to her assistance. His pulse pounding in his brain, Henry kicked a leg out, catching her in the backs of hers. She went down like a sack of bricks. This was it. His opening to escape.

Out of the corner of his eye, he detected movement. Another assailant? No, it was someone on a horse that looked vaguely familiar. A boy. Squinting, he recognized one of his stableboys from the mews and the leather harness he carried. Along with his pistol. Stevens must have sent him to deliver it.

Henry hesitated, deliberating whether to run toward the boy or into one of the nearby houses for cover as he'd planned to do.

"Get 'im, Crow," the woman on the ground screamed.

Henry turned to run, but his hesitation cost him dearly as something unforgiving crunched into the side of his head. Pain flowered in angry waves behind his eyes, making him reel and sway. Dully, Henry looked around to see Crow the coachman, an ugly lumbering beast of a man, wielding a wooden log in hand. The log came toward him again, but Henry was far too disoriented to duck.

It caught him square in the skull.

The last thing he saw as his vision ebbed was the boy riding closer. Henry wanted to warn him to stay away, but no words came. And soon, his thoughts disappeared altogether.

Chapter Twenty-One

Even as a morning person, waking alert and ready without the hazy grog so many others complained about, Irina had always enjoyed a quiet breakfast, especially one after a brisk morning ride.

She preferred chocolate to tea, and would sip it slowly while reading through whatever material was available at the table. Countess Langlevit had always kept papers and journals and pamphlets in the breakfast room, and at Bishop House, Lord Dinsmore would part with his copy of the *Times* as soon as he was finished with it, though there were always little *tsks* of disapproval from Lady Dinsmore, should the countess be seated with them. Irina would claim to only be reading the gossip columns, but would happily peruse all the pages, sometimes reading whole articles, other times scanning them quickly.

The morning following her outing to Yardley Botanical Gardens, Irina sat at the breakfast table without her usual calm. Her short ride in Hyde Park had done nothing to temper her anxious spirits. She tapped her foot, the inked headlines made little sense, and she had drained her chocolate within minutes. She couldn't concentrate on anything it seemed, and the flutter of restless energy in her stomach and chest also made her limbs feel achy with idleness. It was as though her body knew she had to do something but her mind was at a complete loss as to what.

"My dear, are you quite well?" Lord Dinsmore asked from his chair at the head of the table. It wasn't a long and grand table like the one in the dining room, but a smaller, square table that seated no more than a half dozen people. They were the only two breaking their fast at the moment, though Lady Dinsmore would be arriving shortly, Irina imagined. She nearly wished the countess would arrive, if only to fill the silent room with her chatter.

"Oh yes, of course," she answered, knowing it was the only acceptable answer. The truth was certainly impossible. Admitting to the Earl of Dinsmore that she could not stop thinking about the salacious way Lord Langlevit had knelt before her in broad daylight, in a public space no less, and set his mouth to the most private part of her body would have given the man a case of apoplexy.

It had even been giving *her* heart stutters and random flashes of heat and longing. If only they hadn't been interrupted…if only he could have continued stroking her, caressing her with his tongue and teeth, making her feel equal parts goddess and sinner. It was deliciously wicked, the effect the man had on her.

A rash of warmth swept over her chest, and Irina forced her mind back to her plate and the half-consumed toast and marmalade. She wasn't hungry, though.

Braxton, the Dinsmore's butler, entered the breakfast room with his straight-backed, hiked-chin posture and a silver salver in his hand.

"Her Highness has a letter," he announced and bringing

the salver to Irina, bowed as she reached for it. He was, Irina noted with amusement, even more starched with her than he was with his employers. She smiled at his show of propriety as she slit the envelope. The stationery was of Lady Langlevit's pale-pink stock, and Irina was anxious to hear news of her health. Its downward turn over the last handful of weeks had been startling and concerning, and there was a small palpitation of fear as she unfolded the letter. However, as she noted Lady Langlevit's own scrawling script upon the paper, the tightness in her chest abated.

Dearest Irina,

Let me put your mind at ease by announcing that I am feeling leagues better than I have been of late. Truly, Doctor Hargrove has commented numerous times over our last few visits that I seem to be on the mend. He has even given me the nod to take a short holiday in Brighton with Lady Umbridge, which I will be departing for on the morrow.

Irina eyed the date at the top of the letter. It was dated from two days before, and so by now Lady Langlevit was already on her way to the southern coast. If she recalled correctly, Lady Umbridge was Lady Carmichael's mother, who lived in Breckenham. Two days ago, both the countess and Lady Umbridge would have still been in the dark about the dissolution of Henry and Rose's engagement. Perhaps it was for the best for now...they could take their holiday in Brighton still anticipating the joining of their families. If it made Lady Langlevit happy and helped to improve her health, more the better.

Irina finished reading and folded the letter again.

"Good news, I take it?" Lord Dinsmore said as he guided another kipper onto his fork. "You're smiling," he added.

She felt the grin upon her cheeks then. "Yes. The countess is feeling much better and is on her way to Brighton."

"Ah, yes! I have read that sea bathing is quite the restorative. The salt, they say, and the temperature of the water helps improve circulation." He took an excited breath and continued, "Did you know, there are bathing machines they draw right into the water at the coast? A covered cart really, and the ladies can bathe in complete privacy. I have thought about a trip myself…"

Irina listened politely as he expounded on the benefits of sea bathing, but her mind had already turned a corner ahead and was thinking how Henry must have received a similar letter this morning. He would be glad to hear that his mother was making strides in her health.

It would also make him happy if he knew that Irina had called all of the nonsense off with Max. The betting book at White's was too far out of her control to stop, but at least Henry would know that she would not be encouraging Max's suit or accepting any offer. And if he had meant what she'd thought he'd meant yesterday, about making things right, she had to make things right, too.

She had to tell him everything.

Irina stood abruptly from her seat, causing Lord Dinsmore to drop his fork and knife and push back his chair.

"If Lady Dinsmore asks, please let her know I've taken Jane and gone out for a drive."

Irina didn't want to lie and say she and her maid would be shopping or in the park, but she also couldn't part with the truth—that she was going to Leicester Square to once more throw herself at Henry's feet. He would be furious, she knew, but the moment the idea of telling him about her decision regarding Max had cropped up, the restless humming in her stomach and chest and limbs had silenced.

She would tell him that she wouldn't marry anyone she

didn't love.

And she still loved *him*.

Henry was the man she wanted, above all others. No, he wasn't perfect, and he wasn't the same man he'd been when she'd first fallen in love with him so many years ago. He had changed. He had become a darker version of that white knight she'd always envisioned him to be. But she still loved him. She always would.

Lord Dinsmore wished her a pleasant outing as she left the breakfast room and signaled a footman in the hallway to fetch Jane. The maid appeared in Irina's room a handful of minutes later, breathless.

"We're going out," Irina said, to which Jane's expression fell.

"Does my lady wish to see the death flower again?" she asked, likely remembering how Lady Lyon had been on her second visit the day before.

"I'd rather eat a slice of arsenic pie than smell that wretched parasitic flower again," Irina declared, working a gasp of laughter from her maid. "No, we're calling on Lord Langlevit."

The gasp from Jane this time was one of scandal. "But, Your Highness, shouldn't Lady Dinsmore accompany you for such a call?"

"Yes, she should," Irina replied, eyeing her figure in the vanity mirror. She had not yet changed into a day dress, wearing instead a forest-green tailored riding habit. Nothing overly lovely, but she wouldn't have been able to sit still another moment while Jane searched for a suitable gown.

"However, I am thoroughly tired of the rules I am supposed to play to," she said more to herself than her maid. She picked up her reticule and gloves. "I have something important to say to the earl, and it must be said between the two of us, alone." She glanced at Jane.

"Of course, Your Highness," she said with a reverent nod of her head.

They left Bishop House with Beckett at the reins of the carriage, who seemed to take the roads at much too slow a pace. Irina was certain it would have felt slow even had the carriage sprouted wings and flown to Leicester Square. She just wanted to see Henry and tell him everything, get it out into the open. And if he chose to walk away from her...well, then she would go. She would pack her things and return to St. Petersburg as soon as possible. It would be too much torture to be so close to him and not have him the way her heart desired.

There could be no more encounters like the one the afternoon before, unfinished and unfulfilled with no promises or real honesty attached.

Beckett pulled around Leicester Square and came to stop outside Henry's home. Once again, Irina peered up the stately facade in wonderment and hesitation. *Don't be a coward,* she told herself.

She and Jane descended onto the curb and approached the front door. Henry's butler, Stevens, answered it only moments after Irina's first knock.

"Your Highness," he said, immediately dipping into a bow and stepping aside. She entered the foyer, and this time, without the crush of guests, it felt cavernous.

He's not here. She wasn't certain how she knew it, but she did.

And then his butler spoke. "My apologies. His lordship is not at home at present."

Just because she had sensed as much didn't mean she wasn't disappointed. This had not been part of her plan.

"Do you know when he will return?" she asked, not wanting to leave her card, and not wanting to stay and wait, either.

Oh, why couldn't he be home?

"Not for some time, Your Highness. He has been called away to Hartstone."

Irina frowned. "Whatever for?"

"An urgent letter from Lady Langlevit's physician, Your Highness, alerting his lordship that her health had taken a turn for the worse. He thought it wise to leave for Essex immediately."

The words fell through her, tumbling and sliding, but not making an ounce of sense.

"But that's not possible," she said, her mind whirling back to the letter from Lady Langlevit. "The countess is feeling much better...she's on her way to Brighton as we speak. I've had a letter from her myself this morning, dated from only two days ago."

Henry's butler's brows pulled together into a frown that she imagined must have matched her own.

"That does seem at odds with what his lordship reported. He was quite upset and fairly rushed to leave London. I do not believe he even changed into riding clothes before setting out."

It made no sense. Why would Dr. Hargrove write to Henry with such news when the countess was doing well? Unless Lady Langlevit wasn't as well as she'd claimed to be in her letter. But then...lying about anything at all was so far from her usual behavior. No. She had never lied to Irina before, and would not do so, not even to protect Irina from the truth of her ill health. She certainly would not have involved Lady Umbridge in the lie, either. So, that meant that Dr. Hargrove had been the one to send false information. But why?

"When did Lord Langlevit leave?" she asked.

"Less than a quarter hour ago," he replied.

Something was wrong. Henry had been drawn away from London based on a lie, though he couldn't have gotten very far just yet. She might be able to catch up to him along the road. The restless feeling returned, and Irina felt an edge of nausea.

"Thank you, I'll see myself—"

A commotion of heavy footsteps, raised voices, and the slam of a door cut her off. A man rushed into the foyer, his livery marking him as a servant in the earl's household. He was tall—taller even than Henry—and perhaps that was why the boy he dragged along by the elbow appeared so small.

"Needham, what is—"

The servant cut Stevens off. "It is his lordship," he said, breathing hard. "Joseph says he is in trouble. We must call for the constable at once."

The young boy nodded, his eyes wide with alarm. Irina hurried forward. "What has happened?"

The boy licked his lips, and she saw how out of breath he was, as well. "I was sent off after 'is lordship, told to hurry and catch 'im afore he gone too far. He rode off without 'is pistol," the boy said, and Irina's heart stuttered. He was unarmed. In trouble and without a weapon to protect him.

"Yes, but Joseph, what did you see?" Stevens asked, his worry showing through as impatience. Irina felt it as well.

"Highwaymen, sir. A group of 'em. A lady, too. They knocked 'im clean unconscious!"

Behind her, Jane gave a little screech. Irina's throat felt swollen, unable to breathe.

"And then what?" she asked, needing more information almost as desperately as she needed air.

"I tried gettin' closer, but couldn't hear much," the boy answered. He dropped his eyes to the marble floor. "One saw me, so I rode off to get help. I couldn't've fought one of 'em, forget all four."

"A wise decision, Joseph," Stevens said, his eyes hardening. "Needham, send for the parish constable. Send another man to Bow Street."

"And another to His Grace, the Duke of Bradburne," Irina said, her heart thrashing unevenly in her chest. She turned to the stableboy, gentling her voice. "Joseph, you've been very brave. Can you tell me when you got closer, exactly what you heard?"

"They was whisperin' about gettin' his lor'ship into the hack. Sorry, mum, it was hard to make head o' tails of it." The boy shook his head, looking sick with guilt, and then hesitated as if deciding to tell her something. "The woman said sum'fing about a ship bein' turned over." He grew red with embarrassment, knowing how silly it would have sounded, and shrugged. "'Twas hard to hear."

Her mind racing, Irina tore through the facts, considering and discarding a hundred possibilities. They hadn't hurt Henry, which meant they'd intended to take him somewhere. If the boy had indeed heard the word ship, perhaps Henry's captors were heading for some kind of port. One with a turned-over vessel. Was a disabled ship their lair?

"Can you show me where you saw the earl last?"

Joseph nodded. "Yes, mum."

"We shall take my carriage, and you can hop up front with Beckett."

Wishing she were on a horse instead of in a coach, Irina gritted her teeth and fought the rising tide of fear that pooled in the pit of her belly as Joseph directed Beckett to the scene of the crime. What the boy had heard made no sense, but she knew that it had to mean *something*. The words could be jumbled, she just had to think it through.

The coach pulled to a stop, and Irina hopped out before Becket could dismount to assist. There was no carriage in sight, but the obvious signs of a scuffle in the drying mud drew her attention. Walking over to it, despite the protests from Jane and Beckett, she studied the damp ground, bending to study the carriage wheel marks and other wider imprints.

"What color was the carriage, Joseph?"

He bit his lip in concentration. "Brown, my lady, with green markings."

Something glinted in the sunlight near one of the wheel ruts, and Irina knelt to retrieve it. One of Henry's cufflinks. She recognized the etched family crest on its sterling-silver face. Clutching it in her palm, Irina felt sick. She tried to keep her mounting nausea at bay, but doubled over, a sob choking her throat. Henry had been *taken*. To a shipping port somewhere. Where a ship was turned over.

Suddenly, Irina stopped breathing.

"Joseph," she asked urgently, looking up over her shoulder. "Could the lady have meant a ship in *Dover*?"

"Mayhap," he said, though his eyes remained doubtful.

It wasn't much, Irina knew, but it was all she had. She wouldn't wait to let Bow Street determine whether she was right or not, and Stevens would make sure that Lord Bradburne had also been alerted. There was not a moment to waste as she calculated the time and distance in her head. They would have had a head start of thirty minutes in a carriage for the six-hour ride, if they were indeed heading to the Dover coast. The pace of a horse would triple that of a coach. With a fast mount, she could catch up to them quickly. But not alone. She needed help.

Rising, she hurried back to the carriage. "To Lord Remi's lodgings at the Clarendon Hotel," she said to Beckett. "And hurry."

To his credit, Beckett did not drive as sedately as he usually did, and they made it to the Clarendon in short order. Irina prayed that Max wasn't still abed, and drummed her fingers nervously on the seat as Becket disappeared inside. Within a few minutes, Max's blond head appeared. He did not seem to have been woken mid-sleep, but was fully dressed.

Despite her surprise to see him awake before noon, Irina breathed her relief, gesturing to him from the coach window. They would lose less time.

"What's the matter?" he asked, his brow pinching. "I couldn't understand a word your coachman was saying. Something about an abduction? Are you hurt?"

"Get in," she said.

"What has happened?"

"Those horses you purchased, the Arabians," she said urgently as he climbed in and sat next to a wide-eyed Jane. "Are they here in London?"

He frowned. "At the Gower mews, yes."

She nodded feverishly and instructed Beckett to drive there. "Good, good. I need your help. Something terrible has happened. Lord Langlevit has been taken by some highwaymen. I think they're headed for Dover. The stableboy overheard something about a ship."

Max reached out, his hands grasping her clammy, nervous ones. "Calm down, love. Start from the beginning and tell me what happened. I will help you, but you must try to relax."

Drawing a breath, Irina nodded and attempted to speak clearly and slowly. "The earl received a note that his mother was ill, so he left for Hartstone, whereupon he was attacked by highwaymen. Joseph, the stableboy, saw them overcome him. However, I received a letter from Lady Langlevit only this morning that she was in better health and about to take a trip to the coast."

"You think the two are connected?" Max asked. "The note he received and the abduction?"

"I don't know," Irina replied, her anxiety cresting. "But how could they not be? I fear the worst." Her voice dropped, her glance sliding to Jane who held her head in her hands. "That he has been taken by old enemies," she whispered. "Dover is the closest port to France, where he was held captive for so many months. He's in danger; I can feel it."

Max squeezed her hands, his face determined. "We'll find him, love, do not worry."

"Thank you," she said, breathing deeply for the first time in the last hour.

Max rapped on the carriage roof and helped Irina down from the coach. "Take Jane and the boy back," he said to Beckett. "I'll see to the lady."

Max eyed Irina as they headed toward the mews where he instructed the stable master to ready his horses at once, handing over a few discreet coins to hasten the process. As requested, the horses were ready within a few minutes.

"Are you certain this is what you want to do?" Max whispered. "It could be a foolhardy chase."

"Yes," she said in impatience, stepping on the footstool and pulling herself astride. "And I am well aware of that. You needn't go with me."

"And leave you to chase down a carriage on its way to Dover all by yourself? I think not." He pulled himself atop his stallion. "Though you'll likely be recognized leaving London," he said. "With me."

"Do I look like I give a bloody damn about my reputation?"

He grew quiet. "No."

Managing their pace while they rode through London made her worry spike, but once they rode past the narrower streets and got onto the Dover Road heading southeast, Irina shifted her weight and settled into the saddle, her thighs gripping the powerful beast's sides. For once she was grateful for Max's impulsive purchases. Arabians were built for speed and distance, though she didn't intend to run the horse into the ground. Her half-cocked plan was to intercept the carriage.

Kicking her heels, she did not have to signal to Max to follow when she sped forward. His pace matched hers as huge clumps of dirt spewed upward in their wake. Irina did not want to talk, even though their brutal pace would not have allowed it anyhow. She was driven by one need: to catch up to the brown carriage with the green markings as soon as possible. They rode hard for the first thirty minutes, stopping only briefly to water their horses before resuming their course.

"Irina," Max began, handing her a cup of water he'd gotten from the nearby inn as their horses grazed in an empty pasture. "You know I will do whatever makes you happy, but the chances of us finding Langlevit are — "

"Don't say it," she said through clenched teeth, sipping the water and returning it to him. "He came this way, I can feel it."

"You can feel it," he said again, staring at her.

"Don't ask me how I know," she said, tears stinging the backs of her eyes. Turning away, she leaned against her horse, resting her head against its neck and feeling her tears dampening its velvet hide. "I just do. Please, Max. I have to do something, otherwise I'll break apart."

He sighed. "You love him."

Her shoulders shook with the force of her sobs. "You know I do."

"And there's nothing I can say that will deter you from riding blindly toward Dover with only your heart guiding you, as misplaced as that feeling may be?" he asked.

"No." She raised her head to eye him over her shoulder, her eyes damp.

Max approached to gather her into his arms. "Then we'll find him, I promise."

"I'm so afraid."

"My daring little princess, afraid?" he teased, pushing her a few inches away to smile at her, his hands remaining on the upper part of her shoulders and lightly kneading her stiff arms. She sighed at the soothing ministrations.

"They're highwayman, Max. And armed. I couldn't bear it if anything happened to Henry, or to you."

"Then we shall have to take them by surprise." Max winked at her, his thumb rising to stroke a tear from her cheek before falling back to rub the length of her upper arms. "Where's my fearless little partner in crime? Together, I think we can foil four clumsy highwaymen. And one a woman. That alone increases our odds a thousandfold."

In sticky slow motion, Irina stiffened, her body going still under his hands. Perhaps she had heard wrong, but those four words thrummed to her pulse in a violent staccato: *and one a woman.*

She exhaled. "Max, I never told you that there was a woman."

At that moment, there was a shout and muffled laughter in the far corner of the inn's yard. Irina flicked her eyes in that direction and saw a carriage in the process of changing horses. Four lathered steeds were being led away while four fresh ones were being harnessed. The carriage, however, was what seized her attention. Brown. With green markings.

"Didn't you?" Max said casually. "Perhaps the boy mentioned it, then."

Irina's breath ground to a stop as she looked back to Max, meeting his eyes.

"Joseph wasn't in the carriage when we spoke," she said slowly. Something swam in the blue depths of his eyes... something that chilled her to the bone, even as panic made every muscle in her body bunch.

"For Christ's sake, Max, tell me it wasn't *you*," she whispered, denial surging through her in vivid bursts.

Without answering, Max's grip on her arms tightened like a noose, one palm sliding upward to cover her mouth. He moved like lightning to twist her back up against him and then pushed her against the body of the horse, limiting her movement while his other arm slid up to crook around the front of her neck. Slowly, he depressed the air from her throat even as her frantically churning brain strained to catch up.

"Max, what are you doing?" she gasped against his gloved hand, wriggling madly.

Deep-seated terrors rose up to torture her…memories of another man holding her down and forcing her into a carriage. Her demons cackled and crowed with glee as they rose from their cages. *Oh God, oh God, oh God…* Irina felt a dragging numbness take hold, and she fought against it with everything she could muster. She was no longer a terrified fourteen-year-old, and this wasn't a stranger. No, this was Max. Her friend.

"Max, please, I can't breathe."

"Don't struggle, love," he said against her ear. "It'll only make it worse."

It was all she wanted to do—rail and scream and fight—but as the air departed her wheezing body, she could only succumb…succumb to the man she had trusted for what seemed like forever.

Chapter Twenty-Two

The sloshing of water and the sick sensation of his stomach rolling side to side jarred Henry awake. He opened his eyes with effort, half afraid the giant called Crow would, once again, rap him on the skull and make him crash back into unconsciousness. It had happened twice before — or was it three times? He'd lost count since he'd been in that darkened carriage, jolting over endless rough roads. The moment he'd start to wake, Crow would hit him, and the blackness would swallow Henry. Each time, he'd hear a muffled scream, but he couldn't tell if it was real or in his head.

Only now, as he took in the sight of a ship's deck and felt the cool, salted air blowing into his face, did he begin to hope that he would be allowed to wake fully. It was dark, with guttering torches and oil lamps strung along the railings. Henry's skull throbbed, and he was thankful for the lack of bright sunlight. Blinking away the pain, Henry took in the details surrounding him. He was on a small boat, and noting the compact sails above, figured it to be a cutter. Some kind of packet ship meant for quick travel. He'd heard the word

Dover murmured once when he'd risen to consciousness, and knew they had to be in the Pas-de-Calais, heading toward France.

There were no other passengers save for him on the deck, and his captors were nowhere in sight, but Henry didn't doubt they wouldn't be too far away. His hands were bound behind his back, though the ropes were loose enough for him to possibly work his way out of. He tried, rubbing his wrists forward and back, pulling them apart and grimacing at the spikes of pain in his back and head, and now, wrists. The last time he'd been bound and gagged like this... He closed his eyes and breathed evenly. He could not slip back into that memory, not now. He needed his wits about him, and panic would only serve to turn them to mush.

"Git up," a voice growled from over his shoulder. Henry opened his eyes and felt the familiar coarse tug of Crow's hand. He gripped Henry's arm and yanked him to a standing position. "High tide and rough water tonight. Don't want you rolling overboard—just yet."

"What is it you people want?" Henry asked, the rag in his mouth smothering his words. His mouth was parched, and he realized he hadn't had a sip of water for hours on end.

"Shut it," Crow warned and with a violent nudge, pushed him toward the mouth of a companionway leading below.

Money. Revenge. Information. These were the only reasons people kidnapped in Henry's experience. As he stumbled down the narrow flight of wooden steps to below deck, his mind accelerated through every available possibility. Someone knew he'd been a spy for the crown. Someone wanted revenge or information, yet again, on other officers still in the field.

Every single thought, however, came to a roaring standstill when he saw the people in the space below deck. His eyes landed first on Irina, seated in a wooden chair. Her mouth had been gagged, her ankles bound, her wrists tucked behind her back. Beside her stood Lord Remisov, free as a bird and wearing a cocky and rather put-out expression. Crow kicked the back of Henry's knee, and he slammed onto the floor, his knees digging into the pitted boards. Irina's scream was muffled by her gag, but it was familiar…and he understood then that the scream he'd been hearing whenever Crow would knock him unconscious in the carriage had been hers.

Henry sprang back up to his feet and paid the price as his vision swam.

"I'd truly hoped to avoid all of this," Remisov said, though his voice was not its usual, easy cadence, light with sarcasm. It was heavy and acerbic, and it matched his disgruntled expression perfectly.

"Had you remained the beast you were, Langlevit, everything would have gone off without a hitch. Or if I had been able to keep the princess away from you," he said, shaking his head as he stroked Irina's tousled hair. She flinched, and Henry lunged forward. Crow's big hand clapped down onto his shoulder and hauled him back with an easy pull.

"It is always the bad ones that are irresistible, though, isn't that right, darling?" Remisov went on, his question directed at Irina. She glared at him, her eyes puffy from the tears she'd shed. What had the bastard done to her? Henry strained at the ropes at his wrists and gnashed his teeth against the sour-tasting rag in his mouth.

"You will come to see in time that I'm doing you a service, though of course, at this moment you cannot see it as such," he went on, still stroking Irina's hair, come loose from pins and combs here and there. "But he would only break your heart in the end, making all your time and care wasted on him pointless. I'm trying to save you, Irina. When we marry—"

Irina thrashed in her chair, the legs skittering over the floor, and she said something incomprehensible behind her gag.

"Yes, you will," Remisov said, also gathering she'd shouted an instant refusal. "We've already made our pact, and you know as well as I that it is the best decision for both of us. A marriage free from the regular ties that bind it, and the winnings...well, if you decide to give your part to the Bradburne Trust, that is your initiative. I will take my half and leave you be until you can forgive me for what I'm sure you think is a betrayal," he said with a gesture to their surroundings.

Henry marveled at how insane and delusional the man was. He had kidnapped an English peer and a Russian princess with plans to force Irina into marriage, and he didn't believe it was actually betrayal? Try as he might to convince Irina—and perhaps even himself—that this was an act of compassion and caring, Henry knew Remisov cared for only one thing: money. The fifty thousand pounds the marriage pot was currently worth, and then Irina's own inheritance, would set the conniving prick up for life.

Irina started to shout, all of her words muffled, but that didn't deter her. Remisov glanced to Crow.

"Have the tides cooperated? Are we far enough from port now?"

Crow must have nodded, for Remisov started to remove the gag from Irina's mouth.

"Say that again, darling. I might be able to understand you now. But I warn you—I have no patience for screaming outside of the bedchamber."

Once free to speak, Irina instantly turned to Henry. "Are you hurt? Your head—"

He shook his head tightly, receiving a shock of pain, but he was determined not to show it to her. He would be fine and would remain strong. For her. He'd get her out of this situation somehow. He only needed to stay calm and not allow the memories clawing at him to snag hold.

Irina, apparently convinced, whipped her head back to Remisov. "How could you, Max? I trusted you. That was the only reason I even considered marrying you! Our friendship! Not the money."

"Some of us don't have the luxury of not caring about the money, my dear princess," Remisov replied.

"You don't have to, either, not right away. Your father is in good health still, and that cousin of yours won't inherit for years and years. Your mother will continue to provide for you at least until—"

"There is no allowance, Irina!" Remisov shouted, and Henry saw Irina jump. "None. There hasn't been, not ever."

She blinked her surprise up at him. "But then, how have you…"

Irina stopped speaking as understanding dawned in her eyes. Henry knew she had pieced the answers together, just as he had. The expensive heirlooms Remisov had stolen before leaving St. Petersburg…they'd funded him for a time. Then favors to whomever paid for them. Men and women alike, it did not matter. Whoever would pay to "keep" him, be it for weeks or months.

"You should have told me," she whispered.

"And had you pity me? Endured having you give me money, like I was some pauper?"

"How would it have been any different than this? Any different than how you've been living all these years?"

"I've earned what I've received!" Remisov shouted, his collected calm shattering without warning. It alarmed Henry, who'd seen men snap before. Hell, he was one of them. There was a breaking point, and once passed, it was impossible to retreat.

"I've been surviving on my own for years, Irina. You have no idea the things I've had to do, so don't sit there and tell me you could have fixed it if only you'd known! It is my life, and you've made your promise to me to make it better. Now you wish to recant? Because you think yourself in *love*?" He sneered at the word, though Henry's chest throbbed with it. Love? Had Irina confided in Remisov that she loved Henry? Had she called the marriage scheme off? It must be. Why else would Remisov panic and stoop to this alternative?

"It was wrong of me to ever make that promise to you, I know that now," she answered, carefully choosing her words, Henry noted. She could see Remisov breaking as well. "But I will not marry you, Max. You cannot force me—"

"Oh yes, I can. And I will." He smiled coldly at her. "You've already given your pledge. Your *willing* pledge. Marriage was your suggestion, remember?" Remisov chuckled. "Though it was pathetically easy to put the idea in your head. You were so desperate for someone to marry you, after all." Irina's face paled as Remisov continued. "Ever the virgin wallflower. So many offers, except from the one you craved." His mocking eyes flicked to the earl. "Unfathomable that you would throw away your future for a man who will never love you."

Henry started to lunge forward again but stopped at the cool and insistent press of a blade at his throat. Irina gasped when she saw it. Crow placed a restraining hand on Henry's arm, just in case the blade he held to his jugular wasn't incentive enough.

"We are on our way to France, where we will wed," Remisov said. "Whether I deposit Lord Langlevit on the shores at Calais alive or dump his body into the Channel tonight depends entirely upon you."

Even in the dim lamplight, Henry could see Irina's color draining away. She stared at the man she'd trusted implicitly with an expression that was not quite fear and not quite disbelief. It was sadness, Henry thought, and disappointment.

"Even if I were to marry you, it would never last. I'll have it annulled the instant I am able. And besides, my sister retains control over my inheritance until I turn twenty-one. Once she hears about this, she will alter it so that you receive nothing."

"I don't need your inheritance, darling, not with over fifty thousand pounds at my fingertips. And I'm almost positive no court would grant an annulment when the bride is found to be with child," he said, and with a waggle of his brow, Remisov's meaning drove home. Irina gaped at him, and Henry pushed forward, against the resistance of the blade. A prick of pain at his throat, and Crow's fingers digging into his arm, slowed him.

Henry shouted through the gag, wanting only to launch into Remisov and rip him apart.

Irina shouted for Henry to stop. "Fine," she said quickly. "You get what you want, Max—I'll marry you. Just stop! Leave Henry alone!"

No. She would not. She would never marry that lowlife, scum-sucking leech. But Henry knew that if he kept struggling and fighting, driven only by hate and fear instead of reason and intelligence, he would get himself killed, and then she would be forced to marry him.

He stopped thrashing and shouting, and Crow tugged him to a corner where there was another chair. It was nailed to the floor, Henry saw, as he was thrown into it, his ankles tied to each front leg. Once they reached French soil, he would have to do something to put an end to this madness. There was time, though not much, to hatch a plan.

The clipper ship plunged toward Calais, ripping through the Channel at a speed that made Henry glad their chairs were nailed to the floor. Remisov had disappeared into another cabin belowdecks while Crow had been left to stand guard over Henry and Irina. The giant sat on the companionway steps, staring at the two of them in awkward silence. Though Irina's gag had been removed, Henry's had not, making any conversation impossible.

Soon after Remisov had left, Irina had mouthed "I'm so sorry" to Henry, who had quickly shaken his head. She could never have anticipated that he would take such extreme measures. He'd lied to her, leaving her completely in the dark about his financial straits. Henry wanted only to comfort her and let her know that he would take care of everything, but the gag stayed in his mouth, leaving him the next hour to peruse a possible course of action while watching Irina.

He took in every detail of her: her leather half-boot footwear was serviceable, and if she needed to run, the skirts of her riding habit were not so voluminous and cumbersome that they would hinder speed. A small drawstring pouch hung from one of her bound wrists, and it looked heavy enough to hold some coin, meaning she could support herself for a time if she got away alone.

Henry was surprised that Remisov's accomplices had not stripped her of the wrist purse and taken whatever they could. Which meant he'd likely instructed them to keep their hands off Irina and promised them a good amount of compensation for them not to try and take the minor amount in the pouch.

He hoped there was enough in that reticule to get her back on another packet—

The reticule. An image flashed in his memory of Irina on the balcony at Hadley Gardens, pressing the wicked point of a pen and fruit knife into Marcus Bainley's ribs. She'd claimed to keep the short, folded blade in her purse at all times.

God, he hoped she still had it.

Henry cleared his bone-dry throat and made some wretched sounds through his gag. His tongue was swollen and his head ached, so a sip of water was a necessary thing, but it wasn't his only objective right then.

"Please," Irina pleaded with Crow. "He's trying to say something."

"Nuffin' I want to hear," the man returned.

"He needs water," she went on, and he marveled at how she knew this. Then again, she was astute and clearly worried about him.

"Dead men don't need to drink," Crow replied, this time with a smirk in Henry's direction.

"Dead? Max said he wouldn't be harmed. I only agreed to the marriage because of it! If he's lying, I'll *never* agree—"

Crow stood up and cut her off. "All right, all right, just keep quiet."

He didn't want Remisov coming in and seeing that he'd upset Irina, most likely. Henry wanted to believe Crow had only been joking, but he couldn't quite shake the feeling that he'd slipped up and given something away.

He came to Henry's chair and took out the gag. His jaw ached, and he could barely move it to speak.

"Water," he said, and with a groan of utter annoyance, Crow went to a bucket and ladled up a spoonful.

"And...what about fruit?" he said, his tongue feeling board stiff and desperate for liquid. Both Crow and Irina stared at him, confused. "Do you have any fruit?" he asked again, looking directly at Irina with what he hoped was a barely discernable widening of his eyes.

If she could reach into her pouch and take her fruit knife, she could try to slice through the hemp rope at her wrists.

"Fruit?" Crow echoed, his face scrunching up in confusion. "I knocked you too hard, I fink. Like hell I'm gonna give you fruit, if'n I had it."

Irina was frowning at Henry, as well, her head shaking as if she also worried he'd been cracked over the skull too much.

"Or a *pen*?" he asked. Irina was cocking her head,

frowning still, when Crow came at him with the ladle of water.

"Shut it! A pen and fruit. What the bleeding hell is wrong wif ya?"

He poured the stale, slightly brackish water down Henry's throat, getting most of the water on his collar and shirtfront before stuffing the gag back into his mouth and knotting it tightly behind his head. Henry didn't care. Irina had stopped frowning and was now trying to school her expression of excitement. She'd caught on to his hints.

Crow went back to his post on the companionway steps and crossed his arms. He leaned his head back on an upper step and looked at the ceiling for a while. Then, even as the waves tossed the packet ship, he closed his eyes.

Irina instantly began to fumble behind the chair she'd been bound to, her fingers reaching and swishing around in a desperate attempt to open her drawstring purse and reach for her small folding blade. A few minutes later, she bit her lower lip and nodded, indicating she'd managed to get it. She then started to saw, the steady movements restricted and awkward, and by the expression on her face, tedious. They both watched Crow, anticipating his eyes to open on every violent plunge of the ship. She only got in a good five minutes of sawing the rope before the door into another cabin, the one Remisov had gone into, opened.

Irina went still, and Crow snapped to attention.

"We are pulling to port," Remisov said, passing Irina. Henry prayed she didn't still have the knife in her hand. He prayed even more that she did not try to stab Remisov with it as he passed by. The opportunity was not ideal, not yet.

"Durand should be waiting at the pier," Remisov said to Crow, passing Irina without noticing anything amiss. "Take our esteemed lordship above deck and send out the signal."

Durand? Henry tried to place the name, but his focus was still on Irina's hands. She didn't seem to still have the knife out, and he released a pent-up breath of relief.

"Remember your promise, Max," she hissed, her heavy gaze sliding to Remisov, who bent to replace the gag over her mouth. "If he's harmed, I'll fight you tooth and nail at every bloody turn."

Remisov's eyes glittered at her threat, but he nodded curtly, his lips a thin line. Henry knew he was a loose end. Whoever this Durand was, he would have been paid a handsome sum to get rid of Henry once Irina had done her part. Henry had seen enough deceptions to know Remisov's intent. His jaw tightened, but he kept his face calm. For Irina's sake.

With a rough shove, Crow obediently led him out of the cabin. Henry kept his eyes fixed on Irina, who had stopped talking and was instead staring at him when he walked past. There was so much in those violet eyes: dismay, fear, hope, trust. She believed in him. As she sat listening to Remisov and Crow muttering to one another in hushed tones, she looked at Henry as if she knew he would fix everything. That he would save them.

I will.

Even if it meant taking his last breath.

• • •

At their departure, Irina resumed sawing with a vengeance, the sound of loud voices filtering down through the open cabin door. It still seemed as if she were caught in some unending nightmare. *Max* had betrayed her. Max, whom she had trusted for years, had rendered her unconscious, shuttled her into a carriage, and gagged her like a trussed-up pig. Not to mention what he'd done to Henry. From what she'd been able to discern during Max's ranting, Max had delivered a forged letter from Dr. Hargrove, causing Henry to rush frantically from his home and onto a side road, where a band of criminals awaited him.

When she'd reached consciousness inside the carriage, the sight of a bruised and battered Henry had nearly killed her. And every time that huge beast of a man had hit him whenever he stirred, it'd been like a blow to her own skull.

But Henry was strong. He'd come through much worse.

That knowledge had been the only thing that had kept her from falling to pieces for every mile of that excruciating ride. Half asleep from exhaustion—she hadn't closed her eyes for one second in the carriage for the entire journey—she hadn't even thought about the tiny knife in her wrist purse until Henry had mentioned it. Not that she could have done anything in the confines of the coach with the female accomplice at her side, watching her every move.

Her fingers ached from the awkward motion of holding the knife, and the ropes burned into the tender skin at her wrist, but after a few minutes, she felt them fraying. Finally cutting free, she removed the filthy gag at her mouth and untied her legs. The cabin was empty, but Irina didn't know for how long, so she moved quickly, searching for a weapon or anything she could use. She kept up her search as she left the cabin, creeping up to the top deck. There, she saw a few boarding pikes secured in a becket near the mast. They were to deter pirates, she guessed, and she set her jaw grimly as she silently removed one from its mooring. A pike was as good as a sword.

Max's voice filtered back from the bow. "Quickly now, before we are spotted."

Staying out of sight, Irina peered over the side and noticed that they hadn't pulled into port but remained offshore. A tiny rowboat in the distance was leaving the pier. It was occupied by a handful of men and was headed toward them, fighting through the rough water of the harbor. The ship rocked wildly on the churning surface as the tide rolled in, but thankfully Irina had never been prone to motion sickness. Retaining her balance, she inched toward the bow where Henry was being held.

In addition to Henry, she counted four standing with Max, including the giant, Crow. The woman who had been in the carriage was nowhere in sight. Max would have only had a skeleton crew aboard the small vessel—less people to keep quiet about the kidnapping of a peer and a forced marriage to a princess. She and Henry would only have a short time before the rowboat arrived, a quarter of an hour at the most, and for now, the odds were more in their favor.

"Well, hello, lovey," a voice said into her ear.

Irina didn't hesitate. She brought the rear of the pike backward in a vicious stab and connected with soft tissue. She turned swiftly to see the missing female clutching her stomach on the deck. Before Irina could silence her, the woman cried out loudly. She cracked the wooden end of the pike against the woman's temple, and her screaming ceased abruptly. But the damage was done.

Booted feet pounded on the deck behind her. Irina grabbed the pistol that had fallen from the now-unconscious woman's hand and the rapier tucked into a scabbard at her waistband. Twisting, Irina fired, catching one of the men running toward her in the leg. The other she met at the point of the sword, raking him across the arm and following with a well-placed kick to the groin. He joined his companion moaning on the floor.

The sounds of a scuffle up front reached her as she grabbed the loaded pistols from the fallen men and tucked one into the pocket slit of her riding skirt. Her breath caught in her throat when she reached the bow and took in the scene. Max lay crumpled on one end of the bow while Henry was half-obscured in the meaty arms of the giant. One of Max's men lay unmoving near where she stood.

"Henry!"

Taking careful aim, with only the guttering lamp and torchlight to see by, she fired at the giant. The bullet struck Crow's calf, enough to loosen his hold on Henry, who stumbled a few feet away, but it only seemed to make the bigger man more incensed. And Henry was still bound. With a cry, Irina discarded the spent pistol and rushed toward him, using the tip of her sword to cut the ropes at his wrists in the scant second before Crow barreled into him, crashing them both into the side of the ship.

Irina rolled out of the way and sprang to her feet. Removing the second pistol from her pocket, she aimed once more, but their writhing bodies made it difficult for her to get a clear shot. Suddenly, the gun was knocked out of her grip, and she whirled around, fingers on the hilt of her rapier. Max stood there, his own sword raised, watching her with furious eyes.

"You stupid girl," he seethed, limping toward her. "You nearly ruined everything."

Irina held her ground, lifting the rapier between them. "No, Max, the burden of that is on you."

A muscle flexed in his jaw. "You're going to fight me?"

"I've beaten you before."

Their blades clashed as they met in the air. Max had the advantage of strength and height, but his leg seemed to be injured, which made his gait slower. Within a few strikes and parries, Irina had him cornered. "Yield," she said.

"You've had it so easy, haven't you?" he spat at her, and she flinched at the look of hate on his face. "The privileged life of a princess with an endless fortune at her fingertips. Don't you see that everything I've ever done has been for you?"

"You did it for yourself," she said, swallowing the lump of misery forming in her throat.

"Enough," he snarled. "Drop the sword, or I'll have Crow snap the earl's goddamned neck, and then I'll drag you by your hair below, so help me God."

Irina suppressed her shout as she turned to see Crow holding Henry like a ragdoll around the neck. She had Max at her mercy, but Henry was at Crow's. Her arm lowered, the rapier clattering to the deck.

"Come now, Irina, it's over," Max said gently, his actions at odds with his words as he wound his hand cruelly in her loosened hair and forced her head forward. "You belong to me. Can't you see that that man will only ruin you?"

Her gaze slid to where Crow stood. Blood seeped from a wound at Henry's temple, running into his face, but his burning eyes met hers with fierce will, commanding her to remain strong. She hiked her chin. "No, he won't."

Releasing her, Max walked toward Crow and Henry, dragging his obviously injured right leg behind him. Irina felt the sudden urge to break it completely. He turned to sneer at her and ripped Henry's shirt from his shoulders.

"Is this what you truly want?" he hissed. "A man who is nothing more than a dog? Look at him!"

A tortured cry locked in her throat as Crow turned Henry around, the ends of his torn shirt gaping open and falling to his waist. Helpless tears leaked from her eyes as she took in the raw, ragged mess of scars on Henry's back. Oh sweet God, the evidence of the horror he'd endured made a surge of bile rise into her mouth. Every living part of her ached for the pain he'd suffered.

"Can't you see?" Max whispered. "He let himself be whipped like a piece of filth, and *this* is the man you choose?"

Fury replaced the sorrow as Irina straightened her spine. "Those are the scars of a man who fought. Of a man who withstood torture and survived. Can't *you* see, Max?"

"Your infatuation makes you blind," he said. "The earl

is a beast. Lady La Valse says he can't spend a night with anyone for fear of strangling them. Would you want that to be you? Murdered in your sleep?" Max turned to Henry with a scathing sneer. "Your precious lover is so haunted by the demons of his past that he's become them."

"We all have those," Irina replied softly. "Even you, Max. Otherwise, why would you have gone this far? Why would you have broken my trust if it weren't for *your* demons?"

She wound her hands in the folds of her dress, and Max smiled, noticing the obvious tell of her frustrated state. "Enough of this," he snarled to Crow. "Throw him overboard. Let the sea have him."

"No!" Irina shouted as Crow moved to obey the order.

Delving frantically into her side pocket, she palmed the fruit knife she'd tucked there. The light was weak, and her hands were shaking, but in one swift move she flung the open knife at the giant's head. And missed. She'd aimed for his eye, but the tip lodged low, beneath his ear—not enough to cause damage, but enough for him to release Henry and pitch backward. Henry didn't hesitate and used the motion of the boat along with the man's momentum to toss him over the side. Crow's body entered the teeming water below with a loud splash.

Irina didn't move a muscle, though all she wanted was to hurl herself into Henry's arms. But Max still stood there between them, weapon in hand. With a shout of rage, he lunged at Henry, but Henry ducked, wheeling out of the way. The two men circled each other. Even with the blood coating Henry's face and the horror of his back, it was clear that they were not evenly matched. Henry was like some sort of savage jungle animal, his muscles bunched and ready, while Max, by contrast, seemed out of his depth. The expression on Henry's face left Irina in no doubt that he would tear Max to pieces, even though Max was the one who held the sword.

"Max, please. It's over. It doesn't have to end like this."

"You're right, it doesn't." Pausing, Max eyed her and swallowed, his throat bobbing wildly, before he threw himself over the side. Irina rushed to the edge, watching as his head appeared and he swam for the approaching rowboat. Despite his betrayal, she felt relief as he was rescued, pulled to safety by Durand and his men.

Henry wrapped his arms around her from behind. She slumped against him before twisting around to search his face for wounds. "Oh God, Henry, I thought I'd lost you."

"You'll never lose me." His thumb stroked her cheek before his lips covered hers. She couldn't get enough of him, scraping her fingers against the stubble of his cheeks as his mouth took hers with a driving intensity that left her limp. Irina kissed him back just as fiercely, their mouths grinding together as she dragged his face toward hers, losing herself in the taste and feel of him. She never wanted to let him go. But the sounds of men boarding the ship pushed them apart. She turned to see a man climbing on deck. Henry shoved Irina behind him, eyeing the pistols the man held.

"Whatever Remisov has agreed to pay you, I'll double it," Henry growled. He hooked a thumb toward the other rowboats heading toward the ship, likely drawn by the sound of the earlier gunfire. "You don't have much time to decide. I'm the Earl of Lang—"

The man nodded. "I know who you are. There are people here who will pay a hefty sum of livres for your head."

This man must have been the one Max had called Durand.

"If you know of me, then you also know what I am capable of," Henry replied softly. Irina noticed the man lift his chin and then slowly nod in acknowledgment. "But in the interests of everyone here, I'll double that amount, too."

Durand was a smuggler of some sort, Irina also realized, and Henry was negotiating in the currency that men like him understood best. "Agreed, then," Durand said, his eyes lighting at the offer. "Ten thousand."

Irina gasped at the staggering sum, but Henry did not bat an eye. He removed the signet ring on his finger and handed it to Durand. "Done. Give this to the man I send in exchange for the sum. I will have it delivered within the week."

"And what of him?" Durand asked, jerking his head to Remisov, who remained restrained in the rowboat.

Henry's eyes flicked back to Irina's for a brief moment. She knew her answer was clear in them, and Henry nodded. "Have him cool his heels until you receive the money, then he's to be released as long as he agrees to remain here in France." He wrapped one arm around Irina, pulling her close. "One more thing, I will require transport once we dock. And a shirt."

Durand smiled. "Of course, my lord."

Chapter Twenty-Three

Night was falling by the time Henry had sorted everything out with the harbormaster and secured the carriage, as promised, from Durand. Henry didn't trust the man, but money was the reigning monarch here, and ten thousand pounds was a paltry sum to pay for Irina's safety. He'd also made sure to send a message to Lord Bradburne, conveying that both he and the princess were safe and would return to London on the following day. Though it was scandalous that Irina was without a proper chaperone, Hawk knew of his intentions. And soon Irina would, as well.

Henry glanced down at the woman tucked against him in the coach, her eyelids drooping sleepily. Watching her now as she curled trustingly against him was so at odds with the fierce virago who had fended off men double her size on board the cutter. It made him smile. Irina had been magnificent and fearless in the face of overwhelming odds. His heart had stuttered when he'd seen her standing there on the deck, pistol and sword in hand like some kind of avenging pirate warrior. No other woman could have done what she did.

With a soft exhalation, Henry's fingers brushed the hair out of her face.

"Where are we going?" she asked softly, favoring him with a smile that made his chest feel tight.

"To a country house I own near here in Escalles."

"Oh."

His fingers threaded through her hair, and she turned her face into his hand, rubbing her cheek against his palm. "It's not far, don't worry. You must be exhausted."

"I'm well now that I'm with you," she said, staring up at him.

He kissed her brow, though he wanted to do far more than that at her words and the languid look in those violet eyes. "You'll have a bath and a meal, and you will feel a hundred times better."

Despite the late hour, Henry had sent a man from the public stables near the harbor ahead to alert the small resident staff to his imminent arrival. It had been years since he had stayed at the manor, but it had been his home for a long while during his time in France. Henry didn't know why he hadn't sold the estate after he'd escaped Paris. Perhaps it was sentimentality. It was here on the coast, tucked away in this tiny little sea village, that he had recovered and found the strength after his ordeal to return to England. He sucked in a sharp breath as the coach rounded the last hill and the rambling manor came into view. It was not fancy in the least, nor worth a fraction of the cost of some of his other estates, but the sight of it made heat rush to his eyes.

"My Lord Langlevit," a woman with streaked gray-and-black hair greeted in a warm voice as he stepped out into the courtyard, reaching inside the carriage to assist Irina. "Bienvenue, my lord, welcome home. It has been such a long time."

"Bonsoir, Madame Renaud," he said, smiling at his

longtime housekeeper and then drawing Irina forward. "This is Princess Irina Volkonsky. She will also be staying with us. Please escort her to a chamber in the guest wing and prepare her a bath."

Madame Renaud's eyes widened, and she curtsied. "Your Highness," she said. "Of course, my lord. Monsieur Renaud will see to it, and Helene can assist Her Highness with her needs."

She gestured to the tall young woman who had been standing silently beside her. Henry barely recognized Madame Renaud's daughter, who he knew would now be sixteen. She'd grown at least six inches since he'd seen her last. The young girl bobbed a curtsy, smiling in shy awe at Irina. "I'm 'appy to 'elp you, mademoiselle," Helene said in a thick French accent.

Smiling reassuringly, he squeezed Irina's fingers, watching as Helene led her up the stairs. Irina hadn't said much, but Henry was certain that weariness would undoubtedly be settling in. A hot bath and then a meal was what she needed before a full night's rest.

By the time he had taken his own bath and changed into clean clothing, the manor was ablaze with light, and a hearty fire burned in the hearth. Monsieur Renaud had seen to the shallow wounds on his face, cleaning them and making sure there was no sign of infection. He was also the man who had tended to the larger ones on Henry's back years before. The thought of his scars brought with it a curious feeling. Irina had seen them. She had seen the brutal evidence of his shame—that, in fact, he *had* been whipped like a dog. Though she hadn't reacted outwardly on the ship, he knew that she'd been affected by them. But Henry didn't want her pity. He wanted something else from her.

"There, my lord," Monsieur Renaud said, dabbing the last of his wounds with his own homemade healing salve of egg whites, aloe, balsam, and God knew what else. Henry trusted the old man like no other, and having him tend to him now after so much time made Henry's insides twist into nostalgic knots. He owed this family so much...for their loyalty, their service, and their discretion. Perhaps that was why he'd kept the estate for so long. It had been the Renauds' home for more than a decade, and it would continue to be, for as long as he drew breath.

Despite the short notice, Madame Renaud had a feast laid out upon the dining room table, including a selection of meats, bread, cheeses, and fruit. Irina had not yet come downstairs. Henry waited, pouring himself a healthy serving of whiskey while he sat in an armchair near the fire and stared at the flames.

"My lord," a soft voice said. He rose, the tight feeling in his chest returning at the sight of her. Irina stood there, dressed in a simple cotton gown. Her hair was uncovered. Her feet were bare. "It's Helene's," she said with a small laugh, seeing his stare. "And far too short."

"I'll send someone to the village in the morning," he said, trying futilely not to notice the tantalizing display of a well-turned ankle as she walked toward him.

"Thank you," she said and reached for his glass. "May I?"

"Of course."

Henry watched as she turned the rim to where he'd sipped last and placed her mouth to it. Amusement twinkled in her eyes when she sipped, watching him with a knowing grin over the rim. "Do you remember when I did this the last time?" She ran her tongue along the edge.

"As if I could forget. You are a temptress," he said in a choked voice, taking the glass from her hands and pulling her to him as if she were the banquet instead of the food waiting upon the table.

Henry kissed her, savoring the whiskey on her lips and

tongue and wanting to devour her. He wanted to lick whiskey from her throat, from her breasts, lap it from her smooth, bare stomach. He wanted to bathe her in it and feast from her body. His hand fisted at her hip, winding into the material of her dress as he explored the interior of her mouth, the combination of her intoxicating taste and his lewd thoughts making him senseless.

With a reluctant sigh, Irina pushed him away and drew a breath. "Henry, wait. I need to tell you something. Before everything happened, I went to your residence. I wanted to tell you that I'd decided not to marry Max."

He reached for her. "I know."

"No, there's more," she said, stalling him. "I…don't want there to be any more secrets between us. It's about the wagers." Flushing with shame, she turned away from him, and something slithered uneasily in his gut. Had she done something? Had Remisov done something? Had she done something *with* Remisov? Jealousy reared its ugly head inside of him while he waited in a numb state for her to continue. "I told Max to start the wagers. It was all my idea."

Relief flooded him. "I know."

"You know?"

"Remisov told me as much."

Irina wrung her hands. "And the idea of getting married, that was mine. I didn't think you…" she trailed off, swallowing, "that you wanted me."

"Irina, I have wanted you from the first day you touched your lips to my whiskey glass," Henry said, gathering her into his arms with a groan.

"I meant in marriage."

"I didn't think I was…suitable."

Irina stared at him. "Is it because of what Max said… about your demons?" She faltered, nervous fingers twining into the linen of his shirt. "And not being able to stay the night with anyone?"

Henry nodded and swallowed, stung by shame. "Remisov was right about that. Being touched in my sleep seems to bring back awful memories, ones my body has yet to forget. At night, I'm consumed by dreams brought on by the devil himself, and I lash out. I nearly hurt someone once. A courtesan. And I vowed never to put anyone in such danger from me again." His knuckles skimmed her cheek. "I would never want to hurt you."

"You won't hurt me, Henry," she said.

He drew a measured breath and realized something. Weeks had passed since his last night terror. He could not recall the last time he'd woken in a demented panic, though he was positive it had been before Irina had returned to London.

She blinked up at him as if worried by his silence. "You can't truly believe you will hurt me."

"No." Henry shook his head, a sense of wonder filling him. "You are right. I don't believe I will. You calm me, Irina. I don't know what it is about you, but my body, my mind…you speak to me, you lure me from the edge, even when you say nothing at all."

He trailed his fingers down the elegant curve of her throat. "I've never thought about anyone as much as I've thought about you. You're so ingrained in my thoughts that, lately at least, when I do manage to sleep, somehow the terrors remain at bay." A wicked grin curved his lips. "Though I haven't woken up with torn bedding, I do tend to find myself in a very *uncomfortable* state."

"Uncomfortable?"

"Aroused, then." His smile turned wolfish, and a becoming blush flooded her cheeks.

"Oh."

"Though that is vastly preferable to the alternative, I assure you," he said with a laugh as he took her lips in a sweet, swift kiss. She met him as she always had, with urgency and passion, and with complete honesty. No wilting wallflower, his Irina.

His Irina.

Drawing away, Henry sobered as his eyes drank in her features. Her dark, glossy hair fell in cascading waves around her face, and her eyes were a blue so deep, a man could happily float in them for eternity. Her cheeks remained flushed from his teasing and his kiss, and her lips were plump and rosy. It made him want to devour her again. Want to haul her up against him and never let go. To think of how close he'd come to losing her on that ship. The realization had loosened something buried deep…he wanted more time with her. He *needed* it. He wanted to make her laugh, to see her skill with a sword, to bask in her sparkling wit and curiosity. But most of all, he wanted to please her with a desperation that he'd never felt before. Not for anyone. And not since France, when the monsters inside had chased anything good in him away.

Irina's courage was humbling, and her faith in him was staggering. It buoyed him and terrified him at the same time. He did not deserve her. He could never deserve someone so perfect.

"I still think I'm not the man for you."

Irina's hands reached up to cup his face, her eyes sparking with anger or passion, or some fiery combination of the two. "You are the *only* one for me," she whispered fiercely. "That was what I was coming to tell you in London. That I didn't care if you didn't want to marry me, but *I* couldn't marry anyone else knowing what I feel."

"And why is that?" Henry rasped, an aching feeling taking hold of him.

"Because I love you, and I always will," she said with a shy laugh. "You've ruined me for any other man."

"Irina—"

She shook her head as if anticipating his response and smiled brightly at him. "No, don't say it. I can't bear any of your reasons why you think we won't suit or why you are somehow not good enough for me. For now, for *this* moment, I just want to enjoy your company. Will you please allow me that? And then we can return to life as we know it, where you are a cantankerous, unlovable earl and I am a foolhardy, frigid ice princess."

A tentative knock on the slightly ajar door drew their attention, and Madame Renaud entered. "May I serve the supper, my lord?"

Henry stared down at Irina at a complete loss for a response before nodding to the housekeeper. He had so much he wanted to say to Irina, but words failed him. Exhaling softly, he escorted her to her chair, and then took the one at the head of the table.

They ate in silence, though he could feel her glances settling upon him from time to time. It was a companionable silence, and one which Henry strangely seemed to enjoy. Just the feeling of having her near set him at ease. He delighted in watching her delicate hands rise to her mouth, seeing the look of decadence on her face as she tasted one of the cheeses, hearing her soft sigh of satisfaction as the meal ended. He could stare at her forever, he decided, watching her do any mundane thing. She brought so much grace and joy to the simplest of tasks.

After Madame Renaud had cleared the plates, Henry offered Irina a glass of sherry. "Whiskey, please," she said, and he grinned. He should have known.

"Would you like to sit on the terrace?" he asked, handing her the glass.

"The terrace?"

With a smile, he opened the French doors and taking a crocheted lap blanket from the back of a chair, wrapped it around her shoulders. Irina gasped at the sight that greeted them. A clear expanse of rolling ocean lay below, spread beneath the pale white glow of the moon. Foamy, silvery-topped waves lapped at the shore, lending a magical air to the view.

"It's beautiful," she said, tucking the blanket around her.

"Yes," Henry said, but he was not looking at the sea. He was looking at her. Holding her gaze, he closed the foot of space between them and reached down to grasp her hand in his, but the right words were still elusive. "You're not a frigid ice princess."

"I'm not?" she whispered.

"Not to the right man."

Something like hope bloomed in her moonlit eyes. "And who is that?"

Henry stared at the woman who carried his heart in hers. Suddenly, he was not afraid anymore. He knew he would never be, not when she was at his side.

"I have something to say to you," he said softly, "and I want you to listen."

The expression in her eyes shifted to one of uncertainty. "Very well."

"You told me once you wanted me to be happy, and this is when I am happy. When I am with you. Tonight, on that ship in the midst of it all, I felt more grounded than I have in years, and I realized it was because of you. *You* were my anchor in that storm. I am flawed in so many ways, Irina. Stubborn. Unyielding. Cantankerous, at best." Her eyes were damp already. So were his, he suspected, but Henry smiled at her, taking their glasses and placing them upon a small stone table before resuming his hold on her fingers.

"Any cracking noise will bring back memories I never want to relive. I will run my course for hours, running from nightmares that will never end. I will no doubt be unable to love you as you deserve, but I find myself out of excuses, out of reasons not to take a chance."

He pressed her knuckles to his mouth, drawing his lips back and forth over her lavender-scented skin. "God knows I've done this all wrong. I should have asked your sister and North properly for your hand in marriage. I haven't even told my own mother, but I can't wait anymore when the one I want is standing here right in front of me."

"The one you want."

"The one I love." With an inarticulate sound, he dropped to one knee, still holding her cool, trembling palm in his. "I want to marry you. Will you take me as your husband, Irina?"

Wide-eyed, she stood there, staring down at him for an endless moment, a single tear trekking down her cheek. She lifted her fingers to touch the hair at his temple, as if to determine whether he was real. Henry turned his face into her hand, kissing the heart of her palm.

"You love me?" she whispered, and Henry nodded. "You want to marry *me*?"

"With all my heart. Will you give me your answer, my love?"

"Yes, oh *yes*," she cried, dropping to her knees beside him and throwing her arms around his neck. Henry kissed her then, gently, his lips sealing the promise he had just made.

They broke apart to clapping and turned to see Madame and Monsieur Renaud standing behind the windowpanes, their cheeks wet with tears. Smiling as he rose, Henry drew his bride-to-be to his chest and held her there, staring out at the sea and feeling like he had finally come home. They stood in silence for what seemed like an eternity, holding each other, until Irina stirred in his arms, her eyes finding his.

"I'm wondering when I will wake and realize that this is all a dream."

"It's no dream, my love."

Irina laughed. "I also don't think I'll ever get used to you saying that."

"One day you might become bored with me," he teased.

"Never," she said, poking him in the ribs.

Smiling, Henry kissed the tip of her nose and then her lips, because they looked so soft and inviting. It was some time before he escorted her back inside and saw her to her chamber. The Renauds had already retired, but Madame Renaud had left a light burning near Irina's bedside. At the sight of the bed, his fantasies took flight, but Henry sighed, steeling his desires. The hour was already late enough, and his bride-to-be needed to sleep.

He, however, needed an ice-cold bath or a dip in the frigid waters of the Channel.

"Rest well," he told her at the entrance to her room.

"Wait." Irina placed a hand on his chest, stalling his departure. His muscles leaped reflexively beneath it as his breath rolled to a pained stop in his lungs. Irina's eyes met his, and the unconcealed desire he saw there nearly drove him to his knees. "I don't want you to go."

Henry huffed a laugh. Irina had never been shy about what she wanted.

He licked his lips. "Irina—"

"Stay."

"You don't know what you're asking."

Her palm slid down to his stomach. Henry sucked in a sharp breath as her finger slid in between his waistband and his shirt. "Yes, I do."

"But…what if I *do* hurt you?" he asked, a beat of panic struggling to take shape within him.

"You won't. We have already agreed upon it," she said, then blushing wildly, "Besides, I don't plan to fall asleep for quite some time. I know exactly what I'm asking, Henry. I want you to stay here. With me. Tonight."

The whispered words were his undoing. With a strangled groan, Henry took her lips as her hands wound up around his neck. Her mouth opened eagerly to him, her tongue boldly stroking against his, and Henry was lost. He kicked the door shut behind him as his hands roamed over her back, plying her against his full length and leaving her in no doubt of the state of his arousal. A gasp escaped her lips, but she arched against him, erasing what little space remained between their bodies.

"Oh God, Irina," Henry muttered as he swelled even more. He wanted nothing more than to bury himself in the heat of her, feel her body undulate around him, but he forced himself to slow. He would take his time, even if it killed him.

Henry drew small kisses along the column of her throat, his fingers inching down toward the simple neckline of the gown. His mouth followed their path, nudging and nibbling her skin and making her moan. Her head fell back, and he supported her with one hand as his mouth devoured the swelling rise of her breasts. He pulled her bodice low, exposing one crest to his greedy gaze, and then the other.

"You are perfect," he said, kneading the rounded flesh gently and taking one peak into his mouth. Her fingers tangled in his hair as he suckled, his tongue curling over her taut nipple. Irina whimpered as he turned his attention to her other breast, his own blood turning to fire in his veins.

Lifting his mouth, Henry eased the dress down over her hips until it fell into a pool at her feet. He pulled back slightly to look his fill. A radiant flush suffused her body as she stood there in plain cotton drawers, her eyes never leaving his. Henry decided that she had never looked lovelier. She was breathtaking. And she was his.

"I do not know how I managed to resist the sight of you unclothed for so long," he murmured. "You are the most beautiful woman I've ever seen."

Irina blushed and laughed. "Surely not the most beautiful? You flatter me with poetic words, my lord. But I am far too lean, my breasts are too small, and I have muscle where most women should have softness."

Henry shook his head. She was perfect from the top of her head to her pert breasts and narrow waist, to those long slender legs that he'd obsessed about for hours on end.

"Your breasts are perfect to me." To prove his point, he bent forward, lingering over each of them, making her gasp as he scraped his teeth over each of her nipples. "I love every inch of your trim, firm body."

Kneeling, he kissed a path down the center of her flat belly and dipped his tongue into her navel, making her fingers dig into his shoulders. Henry's hands wandered down her rib cage, sliding over her hips and over the sides of her thighs. "And these legs were made to bring a man to heaven." His hot breath fanned against the embroidered edge of her drawers as he drew his tongue along its length, tugging at its ties with his teeth.

Growling low in his throat, Henry stood and in one smooth motion, hooked an arm beneath her knees and lifted her, carrying her to the bed and pulling back the bedclothes. He moved to snuff out the light, but she stopped him. "Leave it. I want to see you, too."

"Irina—" he began, his usual self-consciousness rising.

She sat up, clutching the edge of the sheet to her breasts. "You have nothing to hide from me, Henry. No more secrets, remember?"

After a moment, he nodded. She would be his wife, and he knew he could trust her. He pulled the shirt over his head. Though he was careful to keep his back away from her, he joined her on the bed, the mattress dipping beneath his weight. She moved to touch him, her hands sliding along the bunched muscles of his torso, and Henry exhaled sharply.

"You're beautiful, too," she murmured. "So strong. So powerful. When I see you like this, I think of a lion. Long and lean and dangerous."

"Lie back," he told her, pushing her hands gently above her head. She wouldn't think he was so beautiful if she got a close-up eyeful of the ugly scar tissue on his back. In his experience, most women's reactions ranged from pity to disgust to horror. And though he trusted her, and though Irina had already seen him on the ship, Henry did not want her scrutinizing him and ruining the moment.

Untying the threads of her drawers, he inched the serviceable material over her hips until she was fully exposed to him. His body flexed uncontrollably at the creamy expanse of satiny skin and the thatch of dark hair that hid the most secret part of her…the very part he was, at the moment, most interested in.

"What are you doing?" Irina asked, her eyes going wide as he settled himself between her thighs.

"Putting an end to this frigidity nonsense, and also doing what I've dreamed of doing since the Yardley."

Her cheeks burned red as she bit her lips. Henry grinned, and kissed her stomach. "Relax."

"It isn't proper," she whispered, her face flaming.

"Did it feel good?" Biting her lips harder, she nodded. Henry chuckled as he blew against her womanhood. "It felt good to me, too."

Irina's back arched like a bow as he put his lips to her core, effectively silencing any other protest. His tongue traced a hot path through her curls and the soft folds beneath them. Sighing at the honeyed taste of her, Henry nipped, licked, and swirled his tongue against her, delighting in the little moans she made, telling him what she liked and what she loved. Like when he scraped his teeth against her tiny nub, or when he flicked his tongue just so. Her fingers fisted into the sheets and then shifted to wind tightly into his hair as her breathing flattened and shortened, the muscles in her legs clamping about his shoulders.

"Henry, *Henry*…"

Acquiescing to her tortured pleas, Henry didn't slow his pace, his mouth worshipping her as Irina's entire body tensed. Her hands stilled for an infinitesimal moment before she whimpered his name and then cried out from the force of the pleasure rocking through her. She hadn't stopped trembling when Henry eased himself up her frame, kissing his way along her stomach and breasts, to hold her quivering body in his arms.

"You are indecently wicked," she said to him, burying her heated face against his chest. "My utterly cankerous, shamelessly wicked earl."

"I fear that's just the start of it, my love."

With a wicked grin of her own, Irina's hand wandered down the hard planes of his chest, skipping past his stomach to the rigid bulge in his trousers. He sucked in a sharp breath as she stroked him boldly through the material. "Surely there's not more?"

Henry laughed as he nuzzled her throat, lifting her so that she was half draped over him. "As you have discovered, there is much, *much* more."

• • •

Irina wasn't afraid. Not truly. But that did not mean she wasn't a little apprehensive, especially as she felt the length of him through his trousers. She squirmed against the tide of longing deep inside of her, in the very places Henry had just created a raging tempest. It had been a storm of pleasure, his mouth and tongue and teeth tossing her upward on ever-rising crests. From those few moments of shocked thrill at the Yardley, when he'd first set his mouth to her body, she had known it would feel exquisite to have him make love to her in such a way. But she had not anticipated the feeling of leaving the world behind and only existing right now, only for him, only for this.

She stroked Henry again and swelled with pride at the sound of his shuddering exhale. She loved knowing that her touch affected him as much as his affected her. It made her feel powerful. And emboldened. Watching him carefully, she closed her fingers around him through the material, marveling at the hard feel of him. But then again, Henry was hard everywhere—his chest, his shoulders, his stomach, and now *here*. Her fingers continued their soft exploration until he made a sound that was half growl, half laugh.

"Stop, my love," he whispered, covering her hand with his and gently removing it from his erection. "Any more of that and I won't last much longer."

Though Irina wasn't quite clear, she thought she knew what that meant. She simply had to touch him, though. Her fingers skipped up his side, counting each rib, circling his flat male nipple, and making him utter a small rumble of pleasure.

"I like touching you," she said softly, leaning forward to press her lips to it. Irina could feel his pulse leaping beneath her touch, and she smiled. "Do you like it when I do this?"

His voice was a rasp, his fingers tightening on her arms. "Yes."

She nibbled her way across his chest to the other side, her tongue flicking across its twin. "What about when I do this?"

He inhaled sharply. "Easy, my little seductress."

"You don't like it?" she asked, hiding her smile.

"You know I do."

Henry groaned, rolling her over to her back and raising up onto his elbows to stare at her. Irina did the same, memorizing the angular planes of his face. Her fingers wandered over his jaw. He hadn't shaved, and his chin and cheeks were covered in golden stubble. It gave him a raffish look that she found extraordinarily appealing.

Henry was so handsome, it made her heart hurt. Irina loved everything about him—his wide brow, his straight nose, his seductive and exceedingly talented mouth. She blushed at the thought of where that mouth had just been, and felt a new rush of heat settle between her thighs. Sweet Lord, she wanted him to touch her again…coax her to the edge and toss her over. But this time she wanted to take him with her.

As if he could read her wanton thoughts, Henry's eyes turned the color of warmed honey and gleamed with a mixture of desire and amusement. Blushing furiously, she lowered her eyes, though her palms continued their slow expedition, skimming over his hips and up the small of his back, over hard muscle and smooth skin. A small purr of pleasure escaped his lips. But then, moving higher, she felt the sudden change in texture. A coarse stretch of scar tissue. Irina lifted her fingers, pulling away, though reluctant.

Henry, his mouth nuzzling her neck, tensed above her. "I understand if you don't want to touch me there."

His voice was so soft, and though she knew he would hate it, vulnerable.

"It's not that," she said, feeling awful that she'd flinched. It hadn't been for the reason he likely imagined. "I see the way you walk and sit sometimes…you're stiff, like it pains you." Irina kissed the lobe of his ear. "I don't want to hurt you."

With a laughing growl, Henry angled his head closer to kiss her mouth. His teeth gently nipped her bottom lip. "It only hurts when you don't touch me."

Irina settled her hands back upon his skin. "So this…feels good?"

"Your bare skin against my bare skin, anywhere, feels better than good, Irina." He kissed her again, this time pushing into her mouth with his tongue, searching for hers and claiming it.

Irina flattened her hands against his back, feeling an openness between them that not only made her heart throb and swell, but also caused a flood of heat lower, in the most private part of her. She worked her fingers over his shoulders, feeling the intermittent patches of smooth skin and rough, places that had been terrorized that she now only wanted to pay reverence to. He had been through such darkness and pain, and even now the past haunted him. Tried to pull him back and finish what it had started.

Irina wouldn't let it. She wouldn't lose him.

Wriggling her body out from beneath his, she rolled upward, her eyes falling to where her hand rested against his side. The glimpse from a few feet away on the ship in flickering gaslight was nothing compared to the gruesome canvas of pain and torture that she saw now. Irina did not make a sound, studying the undulating, shiny swatches of pink and red scar tissue. Some scars were raised and others were deep gouges. Some were so dark, they still looked bruised, as if they'd been lacerated again and again. Irina's heart ached with compassion for the agony he'd endured.

Henry shifted instinctively as if to conceal himself, but she stalled him.

"Please don't," she whispered, meeting his eyes and seeing the pain and shame there. Her voice broke on a stifled sob. "Don't you know how beautiful you are, Henry? These scars are part of that beauty. And your strength. Every one of them is a sign of the remarkable man you are. Without them, you wouldn't have survived and you wouldn't be here, in my arms."

Irina placed her lips to the center of a livid scar that ran from his right shoulder to his spine. He stiffened under her touch, but did not pull away. She moved her mouth to another and then another, accepting each of them, loving each of them. She wanted him to know that she loved *every* part of him. Even the parts that carried hurt and sorrow. She only sought to take it away…to erase…to heal.

"I love you so much," she whispered, kissing her way to his shoulder. "And I'm so sorry for every second of pain you felt. If I could take it away, I would."

"You already have," he rasped.

Irina rained kisses over his cheek and rejoined her lips to his. The kiss started out gentle but then shifted into something more impassioned, more volatile. There were no barriers between them now. No secrets, no fear. Only love.

Henry moaned his pleasure into her mouth and she took it, making it a part of her own. This would not stop—*they* would not stop—until they had come together in the most human and intimate way. Irina knew this, and as she felt the heavy weight of his body against hers, she was ready.

Swiftly, Henry rose from the bed, standing to discard his trousers and smalls. Irina caught a healthy glimpse of the places she'd explored with her fingertips before he returned to her, and her breath fizzled deliciously in her throat. Every magnificent inch of him rippled with lean muscle and sinew. Bolts of heat shot through her limbs, making them tremble as Henry prowled toward her from the foot of the bed, kissing a burning trail up one leg and then the other.

"I love these long, gorgeous legs," he told her in a hoarse whisper. "For weeks I've imagined them wrapped around me, holding me close when I'm deep inside you. When I'm part of you."

His provocative words made everything inside her dissolve, and by the time Henry had climbed his way to her mouth, every nerve ending was on fire and Irina was a writhing mass of need.

"Henry," she whispered as he hovered over her to lick a

path down her throat. Again, he took one hardened nipple between his teeth. His tongue suckled and soothed while his teeth pinched with just enough pressure to make Irina arch her back and gasp.

"Now," she managed to say. His hand dropped to the hot, aching crux of her.

"Are you ready, my heart?" he asked. His clever fingers moved skillfully against her, making her center feel liquid. She thrust her hips against his hand, wanting more of him, wanting all of him, and through her heavy lids she saw him grinning rakishly. "Yes, I believe you are."

"And are you?" she returned, feeling bold.

Henry gripped the back of her thigh and hitched it up against his hip. He moved forward, nudging her legs apart and opening her to him.

"That is a question you need never ask again," he said, the hard tip of his arousal pressing against her nub. A tingling shock branched out, lightning arcing through her.

"I will want you, in every possible way, until my last breath," he said, his voice pulling lower as he angled himself at her entrance.

At his first true push, even as patient and hesitant as it was, Irina tensed. Of course, she knew the basic steps, knew that he would seat himself inside of her, but…then what?

"Stop thinking," he said, bracing himself over her, one hand settling over the pulse at her throat. "Just feel."

His thumb caressed her there, his fingers softly kneading the back of her nape. He looked directly into her eyes. He was so close, he could have kissed her, but he didn't. Irina nodded and relaxed her muscles. She trusted Henry more than anyone, and though he wasn't the paragon she'd once imagined him to be in her fantasies, she'd come to learn he was better. He wasn't a fantasy. He was real. He was her truth. And he was *hers*.

Henry edged forward, never taking his eyes from hers as he pushed inside, thrust by gentle thrust, easing himself into her welcoming heat. His lids grew heavy with passion, the muscles along his jaw jumping as he held himself still within her.

"I…" Irina said, the pressure filling her and making it hard to breathe. She couldn't fathom taking another inch of him inside. She thought of her earlier question and wanted to laugh at the incongruity. With a breathless giggle, she asked it again. "Surely there's not more?"

Henry's serious expression broke, and his mouth twitched into an arrogant grin. "A bit more, my sweet, but I want to be certain you're ready."

Laughing softly, she wrapped her hands around the back of his neck and pulled his lips to hers. As she kissed away that infuriating grin, Henry thrust forward again. Irina yelped into his mouth as bright pain lanced through her lower abdomen. *Oh.* That was what he meant by ready.

Henry held himself still again, and this time when he spoke, it wasn't with playful arrogance. "Is it too much?" He was gritting his teeth against some anguish.

Irina winced against the discomfort, but hoped it wouldn't last. Already she could feel the throb of something more insistent beginning to take over.

"No," she whispered.

"God, Irina, you're so small and tight. I don't want to hurt you," he breathed, starting to withdraw.

She clutched at his hips to halt him. "Don't. It doesn't hurt, not really. Please, Henry, don't stop."

But Henry continued to withdraw, and Irina nearly wept with fury at the loss of him—until he thrust back inside of her, sending a shockwave of relief, and a little pain, through her body. Much less pain, though, and as he withdrew once more, it extinguished completely. Again, he plunged back in, then withdrew, and returned again, each thrust reaching deeper, possessing her, marking her as his and only his. Their bodies glided together and apart, Henry's mouth ravaging hers, his tongue diving and receding in the same erotic motion as his hips.

The bed, the room, the entire house, disappeared, and it was only she and Henry and the sensual friction of their bodies. She could barely breathe, but the only parts of her body that seemed to matter were the ones he was ravishing. Anything could have happened right then and it wouldn't have concerned her. In that moment, Irina's sole purpose in life was Henry and his love and the increasingly frantic motion of his body against hers.

He was bringing her up again, back onto that crest, and she felt it coming…that perfect moment of undiluted bliss, just out of reach. She grasped for it, rocking against Henry, joining him as each controlled thrust deteriorated into something more frenzied and wild. Clasping her to him, he growled her name, muttering insensible love words against her throat.

"Oh God, Henry," she cried, knowing she was too loud and vulgar, and yet not caring at all.

"Hold on, love."

But she couldn't, not for another second. Pleasure spiraled and broke through her then, coursing against every nerve ending, loosening every muscle. Irina tightened her legs around his hips as she threw her head back and dragged in a deep breath, the cool sea air from one of the bedroom's open windows rushing over her damp skin. Henry drove forward once, twice, three more times and then, with a long groan of satisfaction, went still.

They breathed into one another's necks as the rest of the world slowly filtered back in around them. Outside the window, Irina could hear the crash of the waves upon the rocks below, the small, incessant chime of a bell somewhere.

Henry kissed her temple and rolled onto his back, pulling her with him until she lay flat on his chest and stomach.

"My brazen, beautiful princess," he said, breathless from exertion. Irina's hair had come completely free and now hung in dark locks around her face. He pushed a few back, behind her ear, and smiled up at her.

"My handsome, wicked earl," she replied, her own breathing just as choppy as the waters of the channel outside.

Something changed in his expression, a slight lift of his brow as a thought seemed to strike him. "I'll be calling you my beautiful countess, soon," he said, that roguish smile returning.

She matched it. She would be his wife. And they would make love like this whenever they pleased. Already feeling the stirrings of desire again, even as her body thrummed with loose, languid release, Irina imagined they would be spending great amounts of time wrapped together like this, limbs sweaty and tangled, and utterly satisfied.

"You will call me princess," she commanded with as imperious a tone as possible. She kissed him, playfully nipping his bottom lip the same way he'd done to hers.

His tongue teased the inside of her lip, making her shiver. "I shall call you anything you like, as long as I call you mine."

"I've always been yours, Henry." Irina's amusement shifted into something deeply profound as she stared down at the man she loved more than life itself. She sealed her lips to his. "I will love you forever."

Chapter Twenty-Four

Leaving Henry's side early the next morning had been one of the most difficult tasks ever presented to Irina. She'd wanted to stay cocooned in those soft, white sheets, with the sea air blowing through the window in easy, random gusts all day. They'd slept on and off the night before, wrapped in one another's arms, waking every few hours to make love or, when Irina became too sore, to kiss and touch.

Despite his fears of hurting her, nothing untoward had happened during the night. Henry had slept fitfully but without incident. She'd woken at one point when he'd called out in his sleep, but she'd only had to murmur softly to soothe him. Irina had marveled at her power over Henry…that she could calm those demons that had terrorized him for so long. She supposed it was the reverse, as well. She had never felt so safe as she did with Henry. Both fractured by their pasts, they had found strength and a haven in each other.

She hadn't wanted the night to end, and as dawn had broken, lighting the room and the man lying beside her, a part of her had become anxious. Henry would be her husband. It was what she wanted, more than anything in the world, but even after last night, it felt too good to be true. Like something was going to lurch up out of nowhere and drive them apart.

Her fears were silly, though, she knew, so she'd kept them to herself and had gotten on with the day. There had been much to do to prepare their return to England, and as Irina had dressed in a simple gown that had likely been found overnight by Helene and Madame Renaud, Henry had seen to securing passage on a packet ship back to Dover. Travel being entirely dependent upon the tides, they'd had to rush to the docks in order to catch the first ship out, or be stuck waiting the whole of the day until the next tide came in. Not that Irina would have minded more time with Henry at his estate, with no prying eyes or judging stares. But the idea that Max could possibly still be close by, in Calais, weighed on her. She hoped he'd left for Paris. He had friends there. Benefactors. And now that she knew how and why they funded him, she felt sick. Heartbroken. If only he'd trusted her. But Escalles was gorgeous, and she didn't want to think of Max anymore. They would go back there, she decided, after they were married, and stay for as long as they wished.

It was thoughts like these that swept away her anxiety as the packet ship cut across the Channel, toward Dover. She and Henry stood on deck, preferring the salty air and buffeting winds to the enclosed quarters belowdecks.

"Do we go to London, then," he asked, stepping up behind her at the railing as the shores of Dover came into view, "to put all that betting nonsense to rest, or straight to Essex to see your family and my mother?"

The mention of the book at White's didn't bother her now. No gentleman would be winning another shilling, of that she was certain.

"To Essex," she said as his hands settled on her hips, and they stared out into the water together. "You have a stipulation to fulfill, Lord Langlevit," she added, leaning backward against him.

"Ah yes, duty first," he said with mock pomposity. Then, brushing his lips to her ear, "I should tell you that part of King Charles's requirement on the Langlevit title includes the earl getting his wife with an heir as soon as possible."

Her body trembled as a wave of heat rose into her cheeks. "I shall look forward to fulfilling my duties, my lord," she replied demurely, turning to look up at him.

Henry laughed and swiftly kissed her lips, holding her close until they neared the port. Loud voices from the harbor reached them, noises from other ships and from the pier filling the air. Suddenly, Irina had the strangest feeling of wanting to turn around and head back to Escalles. Returning to England seemed to bring with it a cold measure of reality, making it seem as if what had happened between her and Henry was part of some quickly fading dream. She clutched the arms that were wrapped around her waist, trying to calm her rapid breathing.

"Are you well?" Henry asked as if sensing her unease.

Irina nodded, turning in his arms to reassure him. "Yes, of course." She lowered her voice, her lips brushing his ear. "Though I'd rather still be naked in bed with you."

"*Christ*, Irina, don't say such things to me in public," he said with a laughing groan, holding her close to nuzzle her head before releasing her. "But soon, love, you have my promise."

A short while later they descended toward the familiar carriage that awaited them. Henry's message to Lord Bradburne had been delivered, and it seemed the duke had sent the earl's carriage to meet them in Dover. Henry deposited Irina next to the coach while he went to finalize some business with the ship's captain.

"Hello, Billings," she said, recognizing Henry's driver,

who stood at stiff attention. A young footman stood near the horses.

"Your Highness," Billings said with a short bow. "May I?" he asked, extending his arm to seat her in the conveyance.

Eying the inside of the dark box, Irina shook her head, preferring to stay outside until the very last moment. "I would rather wait for his lordship, thank you, Billings."

Henry remained deep in conversation with the harbormaster and an official-looking man dressed in a dark tweed suit. The shorter, weasel-faced man looked agitated, his hands gesturing impatiently, but Henry didn't seem too bothered by the discussion. Irina glanced into the carriage, at the box beneath the seat that held the bourdaloue. She had no maid or traveling companion for the return journey, and the thought of relieving herself in front of Henry, despite their recent intimacy, made her blush.

It seemed as though he would be a while, so she decided to make a quick stop in the nearby coaching inn prior to the long journey. "I'll be back shortly," she said to Billings. "I don't wish to disturb Lord Langlevit."

"Of course, Your Highness." He signaled the footman. "Needham will accompany you."

She felt Henry's eyes turn toward her as she crossed the cobbled courtyard, and she smiled to reassure him. He frowned but nodded. Inside, the inn was noisy, though it didn't seem to be crowded. Needham followed closely behind as she made her way to the ladies' cloakroom, where she tended to her needs while he waited. Given the amount of human traffic the inn saw, it was not the most pleasant of spaces.

Hurrying back into the corridor, she blinked, realizing that Needham wasn't where she'd left him. The narrow hallway was strangely empty. A short shriek left her lips as a hand clapped over her mouth and she was dragged backward and through a door, into a smaller side courtyard. Irina struggled wildly, though she was no match for her captor's strength. She was bundled roughly into a waiting carriage.

As the door was shut behind her, she stared into the calm face of a well-dressed, well-groomed Max. He looked a far cry from the bedraggled man she'd seen last, in Calais. But despite his peaceful countenance, a hint of madness glinted in his eyes. He held a pistol pointed at her.

"What are you doing, Max? Henry will kill you."

His lips flattened, but then he smiled. "No hellos? No 'I've missed you, Max'? Sad to think you've forgotten me so quickly."

The carriage started to move, and she lurched forward reaching for the door, but a quick flick of the pistol made her freeze. "I do love you, my darling," Max said, "but I won't hesitate to use this. Not that I want to harm one hair on your head."

Irina exhaled and sat back. "Max, you must let go of this scheme. I won't marry you. It's over. Please don't make it any worse than it is." Her voice shook. "You know what Henry's capable of. He won't rest until he finds me."

"By the time he realizes you are gone, we will be far from this place." He leaned forward. "And when he does find you, *if* he does, it will be too late."

Fear gripped her as she stared at the cold, implacable face of her friend. He was deadly serious, she realized. "Why are you doing this? For money? I will gladly give you whatever you need. But don't do this, please."

Something flashed across his face. Doubt maybe. But then his expression hardened. "It isn't just about the money, Irina dear. It's about respectability. You are the answer to my father's prayers. You see, I wrote him a letter about our betrothal. And do you know what he responded with? He welcomed me back with open arms. I'll no longer be the bastard black sheep, Max Remi, but Maxim Ivan Remisov, son and heir of Count Remisov."

"You told him we were engaged?"

Max tapped the pistol thoughtfully in his palm. "Only that you had indicated an interest in a union. My father's shallow response was nothing short of predictable. Wed her, bed her, get her with an heir, and you shall be reinstated in the family fold."

Irina felt something cold and despairing slide through her.

"But you said you never wanted to go back to him. You hate him."

"I do." His jaw clenched. "And I will destroy him once my inheritance is mine. And you, my darling, are a critical piece of that process."

"Max, please…" She reached out a hand to him. "I adore you. You've been like a brother to me, but I can't. I can't marry you. I'm already betrothed to Henry. I've already accepted him." Her face flushed. "And we…we… I could already be with child."

It was entirely the wrong thing to say, and she knew it as soon as the words left her mouth. Max's expression blackened, fury making his nostrils flare. Rage glittered in his eyes before it was eclipsed by a knowing leer. "You surprising little tart. Well, at least now we won't have to worry about awkward first times. And no matter, anything that comes out of that body will be a Remisov."

Keeping the pistol trained on her, Max reached into his coat pocket for a square of linen and a small bottle. "What are you doing? What is that?" she asked, her eyes going wide.

"Ether. Delightfully fun at soirees, but even more useful for silencing uncooperative princesses."

"No, Max, no!" She fought, but as the linen settled over her nose and mouth and she inhaled the sickly sweet aroma, she felt her strength fading. Soon Max, the carriage, and the world disappeared altogether.

• • •

Henry knew something was amiss the instant Needham appeared stumbling from the coaching inn and rubbing his head. Alone.

He didn't stop to think, he just ran, shoved past Needham and burst into the inn, his eyes searching every corner, every nook, every cranny. Irina wasn't there. Henry could feel it. A heavy, deadly purposeful calm settled over him.

He strode back outside to grab Needham by the shoulder. "What happened? Tell me every single detail," he commanded through clenched teeth. "Leave nothing out."

Needham nodded, his eyes going wide at the demented expression Henry knew must be upon his face. "I took her to the privy, my lord, and waited outside. There weren't many people around. It was quiet, and then I saw a shadow of someone coming down the hallway."

"Small or large?" Henry interrupted.

"L-large, like a hulking shape. And then something hit me in the back of my head." Needham rubbed at the lump there. "And then I woke up in another room."

"Did you see anything else? Hear anything else?"

"I heard a voice talking about a carriage, but it could have been anyone." The young man stared at him, his eyes terrified, and Henry released him. "I'm so sorry, my lord."

Henry nodded. "I know. Find Billings and get me a horse."

"Yes, my lord."

Every muscle in his body ached with powerful fury. It hadn't been more than ten minutes since Irina had walked across the courtyard, smiling at him. And now she was gone. Taken. His fingers curled into fists. He could hazard a guess at exactly who had taken her.

Rage made him see red.

A crowd had gathered by that time, including the rigid head of Bow Street he'd been speaking to earlier. "Mr. Thomson," he called to the smaller man, who had ridden from London the day before to investigate leads on Henry's own apparent kidnapping. "Gather your men. I want everyone questioned. The barkeep, the barmaids, everyone inside that inn. Someone must have seen something, heard something. Pay them all off if you have to. I want a description of everyone staying here in the last two days, especially a tall blond man accompanied by a very large one with a wound in his neck. I want to know who he talked to, what he talked about, where he slept, what he ate, who he fucked. I want to know his every goddamned move."

. . .

When Irina awoke, she was no longer in a coach. Or on the road. She was in a room, on some kind of cot. She stood, wooziness making her sit down again. Swallowing hard, she stood once more and tried to get her bearings. A narrow window looked out onto overgrown, rolling fields. She was in a tower. Thick dust coated the floor. A dirty, unused tower room in a crumbling old castle. Whatever estate they were on seemed to be in disrepair, or even abandoned.

Irina blinked as another dizzying rush made her sway. That bloody bastard had *drugged* her! When she found him, she was going to wring his neck and kick him in the place he loved the most. Then she would kill him. Slowly and with pleasure. Glorying in her murderous thoughts, she tried the wooden door and found it locked.

No doubt Crow or some other servant stood outside guarding it. She'd guessed somewhere deep down that it had to have been Crow who'd picked her up like a sack of potatoes and shoved her into the carriage at the coaching inn. She wished to God that she hadn't missed and had succeeded in piercing his eye with that fruit knife on the ship to Calais.

A cup of water lay on a tray next to the cot, and Irina drank it greedily. She ate the crust of bread beside it, as well, though the hard chunks grated her throat on their way down. She knew she would need her strength and her wits about her if she planned to escape. Peering out the window, she drew back. It was a sheer drop to the bottom, with no moat to offer a softer landing. Irina growled her frustration. Her exit would have to be through that door…whenever it opened.

Resuming her seat on the edge of the bed, she waited. It wasn't long before she heard footsteps. She stood, readying herself. The minute the door cracked open, she rushed the person, stopping short of crashing into a thin young girl who stood there with some kind of gown in hand. Crow, as expected, stood behind her, his enormous size blocking the staircase. It would take a miracle for her to get past him.

"Release me," Irina snarled, but he ignored her.

A much older man entered behind the girl, carrying a pitcher of water and a length of cloth. He deposited the items without looking Irina in the eye and then hastened out. Crow stepped back onto the staircase landing and shut the door behind the old man as he left.

"His lordship said to bathe and dress you," the girl said, bobbing.

"I will do no such thing."

"Please, mum," the girl begged. "The big man said he'll hurt me if I don't."

Irina's fingers clenched into fists at her sides, but she nodded grimly. If she got the chance, she would finish what she started on that ship. Allowing the girl to strip, bathe, and dress her, she eyed the satin ivory gown in distaste. It was a wedding gown.

The girl smiled shyly as she braided Irina's hair. "His lordship seems kind."

"His lordship is a right arse," Irina muttered.

The door crashed open. "Get movin', Yer Highness," Crow said, a smile cracking his ugly face.

Obeying in silence with her head held high, Irina was acutely conscious of the young girl walking beside Crow. She would wait until an escape was possible without her being in harm's way. They descended the crumbling staircase to a large room. Max waited there with a man dressed in robes. A vicar. Fear settled into her bones. Her eyes flicked to the nearest exits, and her fingers wound in her skirts, ready to hike them and run.

"Don't even consider it, my radiant bride," Max said. "I wouldn't want to regret all the trouble I went through to get this special license."

She seethed as Crow prodded her forward, and glared at the vicar. "You are a man of the cloth. How can you do this?"

The vicar didn't answer, but Max did. "Mr. Bolden and I have a…special relationship."

Irina's heart sank. Of course, they did.

"Come, my dove, let us begin."

. . .

It didn't take long for Thomson to find the young chambermaid who confessed that she and a stableboy had both spent the night in the quarters of a Lord Ivan Maxim. Nor did it take long to determine that Lord Maxim had leased a carriage and a pair of horses, which were to be left in Canterbury. A two-hour ride by coach. Shorter by horse.

With Lady La Valse's help days before, when Henry had discreetly inquired about Max's benefactors, Thomson had been able to track down the estates of Remisov's many lovers.

Two of them were located in Canterbury.

Henry was glad he and Françoise had never spoken when they'd spent time in bed. Too many confidences seemed to be shared in pillow talk, but he was grateful that Remisov had been so loose with his own tongue, otherwise finding Irina would have been like searching for a single grain in a hayfield.

Straddling the beast Needham had procured, he and Billings took off at a grueling pace, with Thomson in close pursuit. Thomson and his men would take the southern estate, and he and Billings would take the northernmost one. It had made the most sense to divide and conquer, though Henry desperately wanted to be the one to find Remisov.

As they came upon the estate, at first glance, the rambling old castle seemed to be abandoned, but Henry noticed fresh ruts in the dirt leading up the drive. He wanted to rush inside, but too many years of war made him prudent. Instructing Billings to approach from the front, he slipped around the back and entered a door he guessed would lead to the kitchens. The room was deserted.

He crept along the corridor to the main room, where he heard muffled voices and peeked around the archway. The sight of Irina standing in a white dress with Remisov's arm firmly on her elbow nearly made all of his years of training tumble away. It took every sliver of his self-control to remain where he was and properly assess the situation. Other than a girl of about twelve and a vicar, no one else was with them. The giant Crow was nowhere in sight.

The hairs on the back of his neck rose just as the butt of a pistol tucked into his ribs. Crow smelled just as bad as he had on the packet boat. With nothing but sheer instinct taking over, Henry made a split-second decision. He fell to the ground, raising his pistol and firing upward to catch the giant right in the chest. The noise echoed like a blast into the hall. The young girl screamed and ran away as Crow collapsed into a motionless heap. Remisov, however, grabbed Irina by the arm, a pistol appearing like magic in his hand.

Discarding his pistol and stepping over Crow's dead body, Henry walked forward, scanning Irina's face and body to make sure she wasn't hurt. He raised both hands to show that he was unarmed.

"Lord Langlevit, I have to say you are as persistent as a dumb ox." Remisov gestured to the vicar. "Can't you see we're in the middle of a wedding?"

"The bride is already betrothed to me," Henry said. "Let her go and we can settle this like men."

Remisov laughed, his fingers tightening on Irina's arm. "Do you think me stupid? I am aware of your skill." He waved the gun. "No, you will remain where you are, and Mr. Bolden will complete the ceremony."

Henry nodded to Billings who had entered the far end of the hall. "Now!"

But upon entry into the hall, Billings slipped on a bit of loose gravel, losing his balance and giving Remisov the chance to point his loaded pistol right at Henry. The terrified vicar took off at a clip.

"Max, don't!" Irina screamed, but the bullet discharged from the gun in a black cloud.

For a blinding instant, Henry felt a stinging pain in his shoulder, but it was of no consequence. He leaped forward and tackled Remisov to the ground. His fists flew, pounding into the man's torso and face, and only the sound of Irina's voice made the furious haze clear.

"Stop, Henry, you'll kill him. *Please*."

He *wanted* to kill him. But Henry stopped, breathing heavily and heaving backward as his beloved threw herself into his arms. "Did he hurt you?" he asked hoarsely.

"No." Irina touched his arm. "You're bleeding."

Henry blinked at the hole in his jacket and the bullet

wound beneath. His arm throbbed, but he smiled reassuringly at her. "It's only a scratch."

"Oh, Henry," she cried. "I knew you'd find me."

Remisov stirred, moaning, and Henry frowned, his intent to commit murder not truly gone. The younger man groaned as he lifted his hands to his face and watched them come away, wet with blood. "Bloody hell, Langlevit," he wheezed. "Don't you know that these looks are my currency?"

"Not where you are going," Henry snarled. "If it were up to me, I'd send you to the devil, and trust me, he has little care for such vanity."

He half-cocked his arm back, his murderous inclinations returning in force, but felt Irina's gentle touch on his sleeve. "No, Henry. He's not worth it." Her voice lowered to a whisper so only he could hear. "Think of the demons you already fight. Don't make him one more. Don't let him destroy your soul."

"After all I've done, my love, my soul is already lost."

She shook her head. "Not to me, it isn't."

Beneath her gentle fingertips, Henry's body trembled with barely leashed fury. He wanted to eviscerate this piece of filth who'd presumed he could put his foul, grasping hands on her. He wanted this man to suffer, and the darkness in him itched to employ every vile skill he'd acquired in service to the Crown to that end. Irina's belief in him, however, made him pause. She'd always seen the best of him. For her sake, he would do as she wished. He lowered his fist. "I suppose I could hand him over to Bow Street."

Remisov whimpered, his bloodshot gaze turning toward Irina. His hand lifted slightly toward her, and Henry shifted protectively. "I would never have hurt you, Irina."

"You abducted me." Her voice shook with rage as she faced the man who had been her friend. "And threatened me. I *trusted* you, and you broke that trust. Twice!"

"You gave me your promise."

"A woman has the right to change her mind, and that doesn't give you any right to do what you did. You tried to kill a peer of the realm. You intended to force me…force me to your bed…" She broke off, a cry catching in her throat.

Henry stroked her arm, drawing her closer to his side. Max had betrayed her in ways that could never be forgiven, and Irina had no doubt arrived at that same conclusion.

"You're despicable," she whispered.

"I'm all talk, you know that, Irina," Max said, trying to crawl to his knees from where he'd been sprawled on the floor. Henry moved toward him, and Max threw his hands up in surrender. He stayed crouched where he was.

"I don't," she said softly, biting off her sob and straightening her shoulders. "I don't know that. I don't even know who you are. I doubt I ever knew the real you, Max, nor do I ever want to see you again."

Her voice was an arctic blast, her words a regal declaration. She glanced up at Henry. "What will Bow Street do to him?"

Henry sighed. She had so much compassion inside of her…even for a louse of a man who had betrayed her and planned to use her, without a qualm, for his own ends.

"His crimes will either earn him a long sentence or a short rope," he answered, and seeing the flicker of despair in her eyes, continued, "However, I can perhaps see to eliminating the possibility of the latter punishment."

If it would put Irina at ease, he would do anything within his power to make it so.

"Irina—" Max started again, panic sharpening his tone. "You can't let him do this to me. I'm your cousin. We're *family*."

"I don't think you know what that word means."

His tears came hard and fast. "Please, I'm begging you, I won't survive prison."

"Stop," she said, closing her eyes as if to ward off the sight of him. "You should have thought of that when you paid a highwayman to abduct an innocent man. At least you'll have your life." A single tear leaked from the corner of her eye. "I wish you had trusted me. I wish you had told me the truth from the start. I wish...I suppose it doesn't matter what I wish, not anymore. Not after what you've done. Good-bye, Max."

Sighing, Henry rocked back to his haunches and took a deep breath. He nodded to Billings. "Get him up and into the carriage. Inspector Thomson will be here soon, Remisov, and you'll answer to him."

Billings held a pistol on Max as he dragged him weeping from the room. Irina tucked herself against Henry's side, and he wrapped her trembling form in his arms. His shoulder ached from the bullet wound, but he refused to release her.

"You'll make sure they don't...hang him?" she whispered into his chest.

"If that is what you wish, I'll make sure of it," he answered and kissed her forehead.

Henry happened to believe in redemption, and that all men were deserving of a second chance. Or third chances, in some cases. Remisov deserved to pay for his crimes, but no, Henry also did not want to see the pathetic soul executed. Mostly for Irina's sake. It would hang over her forever.

"I should join Billings. I don't trust Remisov not to attempt an escape." Henry peered down at her. "Come. Let me take you to the kitchen. That young servant girl is about still, I'm sure, and she can get you something to drink or eat."

She quickly shook her head, clinging to him tighter. "I want to be wherever you are."

"I would not be very far." Having nearly lost her twice now, he understood her desire to stay close.

Irina only gripped him more fiercely. "Give up, my lord, I am coming with you."

He chuckled. "You should know by now that I do not give

up easily."

The first glimmer of a smile on her lips faded quickly, and Irina's gaze slid from his to Crow's motionless body at the far side of the hall. "Neither did Max," she said, the grief-stricken expression she'd worn earlier returning. "I feel so duped," she confessed. "I should have seen it. I should have seen what he wanted all along, and that I was nothing but a pawn in a sick game to regain his father's goodwill. He accused all those men of being fortune hunters when he was the worst of the lot." Her voice broke on a strangled sob. "I should want him to pay for what he's done, should be happy he'll be punished, but God, I just feel so sorry for him…so sorry for what he's become."

"My sweet love," Henry said, pulling her gently from the room where Crow lay and where Remisov had nearly forced her into marriage, and ushered her toward the front door. He only wanted to soothe her sadness away, make her happy again. "I will make no excuses for him, but it's clear he is desperate. And desperation can turn a man into a shadow of what he truly is."

Perhaps Remisov had once truly cared for Irina. He curled a few strands of the hair framing her face around his finger. "I am sure his friendship was not always a lie," Henry said. "His past simply warped him into something unrecognizable."

He drew a breath and thought of himself. Of his own past and his own twisted soul. He'd almost let who he'd become destroy him…until *her*. Until this woman, the beautiful and loving woman in his arms, had swept into his life and somehow started to mend all the broken edges within him. There was much more mending to be done, but at least she would be at his side to see it through.

"Do you think he would have…done it? Taken me?"

Henry stilled, considering his words with care for her feelings. "I'd like to think he would not have intended to, love, but I also want to be honest with you. Ultimatums can drive men to dangerous extremes." Shutting the door behind them, he pulled her close. "I'm just glad it's over and you're in my arms where you belong. You never have to think of him again."

"What if he comes back?"

"Don't worry about Remisov," Henry said, needing to put her at ease the same way she always put him at ease. "Once he has completed his sentence, I'll see to it he is returned to St. Petersburg. You'll be safe from him, Irina, I promise you."

By then, Henry realized, Irina would be Countess Langlevit. She would take comfort in the security of his name and the power of his title. And as her husband, he'd never let any harm come to her. His *wife*. The notion had him folding Irina closer against him, a pulse of joy overtaking the chaos that had surrounded them only minutes before. She wrapped her arms tightly about his torso, as if she could sense the happiness spreading through him, and raised her beautiful eyes to his.

"I love you so much," Irina whispered, lifting up onto her toes to kiss him.

"It cannot possibly be as much as I love you, my princess," he teased, winking devilishly at her and arching a challenging eyebrow. She did not disappoint.

Finally, *finally*, the love of his life grinned against his lips, her tongue darting sweetly into his mouth. "Challenge accepted, my lord."

Chapter Twenty-Five

"I believe we may be destined to do everything in an unorthodox manner," Irina said as she stood before the mirror in her room at Stanton Park. Her maid crouched at her side, carefully pinning a piece of ivory lace at the hem of the wedding gown.

Lana sat in a plush chair by the hearth, a hand resting contentedly on her burgeoning stomach. "Whatever do you mean?"

"How many earls do you know who get married in the woods?" she asked her sister through the mirror's reflection.

Lana laughed. "How many princesses, at that?"

Irina shook her head, smiling. She'd been wearing this same expression it seemed for the last several days, and oddly enough, her cheeks did not ache one bit. She supposed that only happened when a smile was forced and false. Irina had never in her life been happier than she had been over the last few weeks. And even the occasional passing thought of Max couldn't dampen her joy. As Henry had promised, he had been spared the noose and had been sentenced to a lengthy stint in a gaol in Cambridgeshire. Irina hoped his time there would be well spent in reflection and reformation, and once he completed his sentence, he'd be shipped back to his father. That was all she permitted herself to think of him. Max was a part of the past.

She and Henry had left the Canterbury estate and gone straight to Essex, though not before sending a messenger to Brighton. Lady Langlevit would still be taking the waters there, recovering from her bout of illness, and would want to know straightaway the news of her son's new betrothal. Both Irina and Henry agreed the faster the countess returned to Essex, the sooner they could marry.

"Fairy princesses," Irina sighed, and with another long look at her gown, felt such warm serenity she wanted to twirl around. She didn't, though, not with Jane still pinning some lace.

"Well, you certainly look the part of a fairy princess," Lana said.

With no modistes in Breckenham to speak of, and with no desire to return to London to visit Madame Despain at her shop on Bond Street, Irina and Lana had been left to their own devices for the creation of Irina's wedding gown.

It had given them something to focus on for the week it took for Henry's letter to reach Brighton, and for Lady Langlevit to make a surprisingly speedy return to Essex.

They had taken Lana's wedding gown, and with the help of several maids at Stanton Park and seamstresses in Breckenham, had transformed it into a completely new masterpiece. Still the same bone-ivory color, but with a high collar of sheer lace, small rose buttons from the nape of the neck to the start of the short train, and lace sleeves to the elbow. It was a simple gown, with hints of pink and rose in the new embroidery along the bodice.

"Thank you for allowing me to wear your gown," Irina

said, relieved when Jane stood and moved away. Irina picked up the sides of the skirt and inspected the new lace.

"It is our gown now," Lana replied, lifting herself from the chair. Irina moved to help her, but Lana shook her head. "I am fine. Truly. I'm feeling much better and stronger. Oh, look at me!" she cried as she saw her figure in the mirror. "To think I once fit in that gown."

She touched the buttons along Irina's spine with a sigh.

"You are beautiful," Irina told her, turning to take her sister's hands in her own. She saw the flush of pleasure in Lana's cheeks, the rosy glow of motherhood in her every motion. "I can only hope I am as lovely when I am with child," Irina whispered, knowing that she could not have spoken of such things with anyone other than Lana. Or Henry.

They had not had much opportunity over the course of the last two and a half weeks to make love again, though they had certainly made the most of one unchaperoned horseback ride, and then after a tea with Lady Langlevit the day she'd returned.

The countess had been tired from her journey and had excused herself, leaving Henry and Irina alone in the day room at Hartstone. He had stared at her from his seat, a smile creeping over his lips, before he'd jumped to his feet, taken the teacup straight out of her hand, and dragged her to the carpet behind the sofa. It had been a quick union, though no less thrilling, especially with the threat of a servant walking in on them.

However, even after only so few encounters, something was different. Irina could feel it, though nothing she could quite describe. Yesterday, she'd thought back to when she'd last had her monthly menses and had realized with a burst of elation that she should have started bleeding a week before. She was carrying Henry's child. It was still much too early to be completely sure, but she hoped for it, and a part of her *knew.*

"You will always be lovely," Lana told her now, cupping her cheek and grinning. Tears trembled in her eyes. "And I am so very happy for you and Henry. I'm not sure I could have allowed you to marry anyone else, in fact. I trust him completely, and I know how deeply he cares for you. I saw it even when we were younger and he went to such extraordinary lengths to keep us both safe." Lana kissed Irina's cheek and stepped back, blinking away her tears. "You have chosen well, sister. And so has he."

Like Lana, Irina was quite certain she couldn't have married anyone else, either. She'd been more than prepared to return to St. Petersburg alone, with no prospects and no hope. It seemed like a lifetime ago instead of only a month.

There was a knock at the door. "Are my two favorite princesses quite ready? The carriage awaits, and the sun will not slow its descent, not even for royalty."

Irina laughed at Gray's announcement. "Yet another unorthodox decision."

"Yes," Lana agreed as Jane rushed forward with a small spencer made entirely of lace and sheer silk. "Getting married at sunset does mark you as an eccentric, I'm afraid."

She opened the door. "Normal people are boring," Gray announced, extending his arm to Irina. He looked entirely handsome, even though he wasn't in full evening dress. Black kits in the woods seemed a bit much, so everyone had been invited to wear something a little less formal. Even her own wedding gown was suitable for a ceremony in a chapel in the woods.

The small stone structure sat in a clearing on a ridge, not too far from Henry's obstacle course, Irina had noted when he'd first shown her the site. It had been built by his ancestors, and though it had been kept up over time, it was not used often. Ivy had begun to creep over the stone and the stained-glass windows, but Henry had always loved the solitude of it, and when Irina had seen it, she'd fallen in love, as well.

The carriage took her, Lana, and Gray through town and onto Hartstone land, traveling as far as it could through a field to the base of a hill which was thickly covered with elms and yew trees. There, several footmen in livery waited with saddled horses and, to Irina and Lana's surprise, two covered sedan chairs, each one set on two long poles.

"These poor men have to carry me all the way up that hill?" Lana said, grimacing. Gray helped her into one of the wicker sedan chairs.

"I will carry you myself if you complain. Now sit and relax and pretend you are Cleopatra."

He kissed her quickly and then turned to help Irina, but she had already climbed into the chair. Though she could have easily climbed the hill to the chapel, the last thing she wanted was to catch the lace Jane had so painstakingly sewn onto the hem on brambles.

So, she and Lana were carried up the hill path, giggling at the ridiculousness of their modes of transport. Henry had thought of the sedan chairs, she was certain. Or perhaps Lady Langlevit. Together with Lady Dinsmore, she had thrown herself into the wedding plans the moment she'd arrived home, and considering the small guest list, the combined staffs at Stanton Park, Ferndale, and Hartstone, as well as the simple ceremony, things had come together easily and quickly.

Irina turned her face up to the dense canopy, where slivers of the brilliant sunset shone between the leaves. Henry had taken her to the chapel at this same time of day and the setting sun had come through the stained-glass windows so magnificently, Irina had decided to hold the ceremony at sunset instead of the more typical late morning or early afternoon. Now, as they approached the crest of the hill, where the trees thinned and there was a clearing of grass along the hill's ridge, her stomach twisted into knots.

She wasn't nervous; she was ready to be Henry's wife. The knots were pure excitement. Tonight, she would be able to fall asleep beside him, and if they chose to stay in bed for days on end, that would be their prerogative. This was the beginning of everything. Irina placed a hand on her stomach and felt lighter than air.

The footmen, huffing with exertion, lowered the poles and set the chairs on the grass just outside the small chapel. There were murmuring voices echoing off the arched beam ceilings inside, but only Gray was there to help both her and Lana to the doors. Gray escorted Lana in first before coming back to escort Irina to the altar. A maid from Hartstone stood ready with a bouquet of roses for Irina, and once she'd taken them and slipped her arm in Gray's, the doors to the chapel opened.

A hushed silence fell over the small crowd, and as the first notes of a single violin began to play Pachelbel's Canon in D major, Irina's eyes settled on the only man she had always loved. The only man she would *ever* love.

Henry stood tall and straight and proper at the end of the aisle, his stance at complete odds with the expression in his eyes, a heated mix of love and desire and happiness. He saw no one but her, she was certain of it. As she walked toward him, and though the half dozen pews were filled, Irina saw no one but him.

He wore a dove gray kit with a cravat that matched the ivory of her gown, and his hair, combed into tousled waves, was lit to a golden hue by the honeyed sunlight. Jewel tones of sapphire and ruby and emerald cut through the chapel, creating a kaleidoscope of halcyon light over everything it touched.

The slowly building smile upon Henry's lips coaxed her toward him, and when he finally reached for her hand,

Irina trembled. As everyone turned to face forward again, the rustling of clothing echoed off the ceilings and the violin approached the close of the wedding march.

"My radiant countess," he whispered in her ear.

"I'm not a countess quite yet, my lord."

His lips brushed her ear, and as though without a thought to the chapel filled with people, kept them there. "You are already my wife, Irina. In my heart, you are mine. This is just ceremony."

He pulled back, and she met his gaze. Even as intimate as they had been a handful of times, she had not yet seen so much passion and love in his eyes as she did now.

"In my heart, you have always been mine," she whispered as the last strains of the violin's canon ebbed.

He tucked her arm close to his ribs and turned them to face forward, toward the vicar, though his eyes remained on her. "Always," he repeated.

And then the ceremony began.

It wasn't until nearly midnight when Irina and Henry managed to escape the party at Hartstone and steal a few moments alone in the dark. There were fewer than twenty people in attendance, including their families, the Duke and Duchess of Bradburne, and the Earl and Countess of Kensington, and Irina knew they'd be noticed missing, but she doubted any of them would bother to be put out about it. They were married now, and newlyweds at that. They could slip out into the garden "for air" all they pleased.

Henry held her hand, something that he had been doing ever since they'd stood at the altar, repeating the vicar's instructed words of love and devotion and loyalty, binding themselves to one another for the rest of their lives. He'd had at least one hand on her at all times since. A palm at the small of her back or cupping her elbow, fingers threaded through hers. When they had been physically parted, Irina had always been within his sight, and those eyes had held her just as possessively as his hands had.

Now, as they breathed in the sweet, chilled air, damp with a coming rainstorm, Irina leaned against him, their arms wrapped around one another as they walked away from the French doors leading inside to the revelry.

"Is it too much to hope for that they'll all have departed by the time we return?" Henry murmured. Irina nudged him with her shoulder, but didn't reprimand him. She secretly wished for an empty house as well. Lady Langlevit had already retired to her rooms, and they would not see her until morning, when they set off for Cumbria. There, they would spend the remaining summer months, visiting the distillery and planning out and constructing a new obstacle course in the woods surrounding that estate. It was something Henry had wanted to do for a while, and Irina got a thrill when he'd asked for her help designing it.

She leaned more heavily against him. Ahead, at the labyrinth's entrance, there were wide globe lamps hanging from the same kind of poles that had carried their sedan chairs up the hill. Their feet seemed to be taking them in that direction. Perhaps it was exhaustion or pure contentedness, but Irina was surprised that her heart did not constrict with fear. She hated garden mazes or anything that reminded her of the twisting path at Henry's Cumbria estate and the terrifying day she'd been kidnapped—for the first time. But now, with him at her side and more confidence in herself and her life than ever, the mouth of the maze didn't faze her. It made her feel a bit giddy.

"I'm only glad we don't have a ballroom full of London society awaiting us back there," she said, her head resting against his shoulder.

"As am I," he said. "I can guarantee the men would all be in terrible moods."

She glanced up at him. "Why is that?"

"Because there are no fewer than thirty men who lost two thousand pounds this day, the moment you accepted me as husband."

Irina stopped and tugged him to a halt. "What do you mean? The betting…I thought you said you'd taken care of it?"

Henry had gone to London to post the banns for a few days and had returned saying he'd also "put an end" to the ridiculous wagers.

"And I did," he replied, a mischievous smile touching his lips. "Wiping the ledgers clean for the marriage pot was out of the question, but raising the stakes was not. Any man could have done it, upping the entrance from two thousand pounds to whatever sum they chose. I simply made certain no one else cared to enter the pot."

Irina gazed up at her husband, the lamplight slanting down from the globes and gilding his hair.

"What did you do?"

He shrugged lazily. "Put in five thousand pounds. Then I immediately went to my solicitor and had him draw up our contracts and post the banns."

She stared at him, dumbfounded. "You *entered* into the pot?"

"The lady had given me every indication that she was interested," he said, holding up his hands in mock innocence. "I truly thought I had a chance at winning."

And he had won. The Earl of Langlevit had won the Quest for the Queen. Irina threw her head back and laughed.

"You took their money?"

"All of it," he said with a firm nod, gathering her in his

arms. "Those fools deserved nothing less. And now the Bradburne Trust will have a princely little sum deposited straight into its coffers just as you had envisioned."

Irina pushed up onto her toes and kissed him soundly on the lips. He clutched her, pressing her breasts and hips into him. Within the hour, she hoped, there would be no clothing between their bodies, and they would be coming together in their marriage bed. She thought of her late menses, and her lips broke from the kiss in a smile. Within a few days, she would be certain. She could not wait to tell him.

"Why, Lord Langlevit, I am shocked. I clearly remember you saying more than once that you had no interest in winning any ridiculous bets."

He angled his head closer and took her lower lip between his teeth. He applied enough pressure to make her wilt against him then with a flick of his tongue, released it. "A man is allowed to change his mind. Especially when the prize is so very tempting."

She feigned insult and with a dramatic gasp pulled back. "So I am a prize to you after all?"

Henry's arms became steel and cinched her back against his chest. His eyes turned languid and serious in the golden lamplight. "You are a gift, Irina. The greatest one I have ever received."

She reached to touch his cheek. This man. Would she ever stop being stunned that he was finally hers?

"This gift wishes to be unwrapped," she whispered, and with a spark, his gaze turned from adoring to determined.

"Then let us bid our guests good night," he said. "To hell with politeness."

Henry ushered her back toward the French doors, Irina's laughter floating up into the night sky.

Epilogue

Sweat beaded his forehead and clung to both palms as Henry paced in the upstairs corridor of Marsden Hall, his Cumbria estate. Irina had been in labor for nearly a day and a half. In the last few hours, the only people entering or leaving the inner room of the lying-in chamber were Dr. Hargrove and the birthing attendants exchanging dirty linens for clean ones. Dr. Hargrove's expression had gone from calm to grim in the space of the last half day, suggesting that all was not proceeding as expected. Terror had gripped Henry then, fear for both his wife and his unborn child.

"The birth is imminent," Henry had been told a quarter of an hour earlier, and as such, he'd taken to treading a hole in the thick carpet in the hallway, wanting to damage everything in his path. His deranged mood was so obvious that the servants scurrying about had started avoiding this particular hallway, taking the long way around instead.

"My lord," a gentle voice said as a hand reached out to take hold of his sleeve. "You will make yourself ill if you continue like this."

Henry turned to see his sister-in-law standing there with a compassionate look on her face. Lana carried linens and a fresh change of clothing in her arms. "How is she?" he asked, anguished desperation clogging his throat.

"She is doing as well as can be expected," Lana said gently. "She is a fighter, as you know."

His heart stuttered in his chest. "Why does she have to fight?"

Lana drew a deep breath, worry puckering her brow for a moment. She hesitated as if trying to choose her words carefully. "Some births are more challenging than others. It won't be long now." She hurried past him. "I know it's difficult, but try to remain calm. It's the best thing you can do for the both of you."

Although Dr. Hargrove, Lady Northridge, and his own mother had insisted that such ordeals were normal, it did not help that Henry had scoured the texts in his library and had learned the staggering, nausea-inducing statistic that one in five women died in childbirth. Even Princess Charlotte had died five years before, a few hours after she'd given birth to a stillborn. She'd been in labor for over two days. That news had rocked England.

And fear of the same outcome crippled him now.

Though he knew that Irina had the best care, and that Dr. Hargrove had delivered many healthy babies, including Irina's own sister's, the knowledge had put a coil of fear in his chest that would not loosen. Nor was it alleviated by Irina's more frequent cries of pain followed by the subsequent rushing of footsteps from the outer room to the inner room and back.

But Lana was right—Irina *was* a fighter.

Even in in the beginning throes of labor, she'd been a warrior. Hours before, pale and beautiful, she had clasped his hand tightly and told him to be ready to welcome his child. *Their* child.

Henry allowed himself a tiny smile. Irina had been convinced based on her women's intuition that their baby had been conceived in Escalles. Henry wasn't as sure, given how many times he'd kept his young wife abed after their wedding, but it wasn't surprising that Irina had found herself with child in short order.

"We have a duty to fulfill," she'd reminded him, when she had boldly initiated their lovemaking one morning shortly after their arrival at Marsden Hall.

He had laughed. "You are quite determined."

"I never shy away from a challenge."

Nor had she.

Expectant motherhood had made her even more beautiful, filling out her features and making her alight from within. Henry couldn't keep his hands off her. And though he'd heard passion diminished for some during pregnancy, it had not for them. Henry never seemed to be able to get enough of her, and she'd been as insatiable as he, even up to recent weeks. When her belly became too rounded for certain positions, he pleasured her gently from behind, which she seemed to enjoy as much as he did.

Like him, Irina had delighted in the changes of her body, and he'd often found her walking the gardens of Marsden Hall, talking to the child growing within.

"What do you say to the baby?" he asked her once. "When you walk."

Irina's smile had been radiant. "I tell him or her about their wonderful father, and how much their parents will love them, and how happy we will be to meet them. I tell them that I hope they inherit their father's eyes and his strength."

"And what shall they inherit from you?" he'd asked, smiling back.

"My mule-headedness, I suppose."

"I couldn't agree more." He had kissed her indignant

laughter away then. "I happen to love that about you. You never give up in any circumstance."

Yes, his Irina was a fighter. And she was far too stubborn not to best the current challenge at hand. Henry drew a deep, calming breath and returned to the outer room where he sat and tried not to drive himself mad with irrational thoughts. He wanted to be there the minute there was any news, and regardless of the outcome, he had to be strong for Irina.

It seemed like an eternity had passed before Dr. Hargrove himself appeared.

The smile on his face immediately put Henry's tormented heart at ease, though not entirely. He wanted to see his wife for himself.

"My lord," the doctor said. "Would you like to come in and meet your family?"

Henry blinked at the odd choice of words, but supposed that Irina wanted to tell him herself the gender of their child. As he entered the room, his gaze immediately went to the love of his life, even as it swept over the birthing attendants holding an infant and cooing at the far side of the bed.

Henry was happy to be a father, but he was even happier to see his wife healthy and well. A few dark shadows hung beneath her eyes, and her brow still seemed somewhat pale, though her cheeks were flushed from the effort of the birth and her violet eyes were like jewels, gleaming in her face. Every part of him leaned in magnetic impulse toward her.

"Hello, my love," he said to her, bending to kiss her forehead. "You have never looked more beautiful."

Irina chuckled softly and turned her lips up for a proper kiss, despite the lack of privacy. He obliged with a muffled laugh. "You flatter me, my lord. I must look a fright."

"You are beautiful," he insisted.

She ran a hand over the stubble coating his jaw, her thumb tenderly stroking across his cheek. "Would you like to meet your sons?"

Dumbfounded, he stared at her. *"Sons?"*

"Twins." Irina grinned at his expression as the birthing attendants brought two swaddled shapes toward them. "An heir and a spare."

They were perfect, Henry decided as he stared down from his wife to the two tiny human beings they had created. Both boys were rosy-cheeked with peach fuzz covering their heads. One of them, a ribbon pinned to the swaddling that marked him as the firstborn, opened his mouth to emit a lusty wail, and his brother soon followed. Their cries made a fiercely protective feeling erupt in his heart. They were both already like her, Henry also decided, fighters. Warriors. And not shy about announcing their presence to the world.

Something indescribable filled him then as Henry studied his family. His *family*. It wasn't only love. It was awe and pride and incandescent happiness. He'd never thought himself capable of feeling anything so profound…to be so incredibly humbled by the gifts he'd been given. Nor had he ever thought he would be deserving of anything so precious. But he had been. Because of her.

Henry stared at Irina with all the love he felt in his heart. "You never do anything in half measures, do you?"

"No," she said, reaching for his hand and grasping it in hers, "and it seems, since this was a joint effort, neither do you, my lord." Her brilliant smile made his heart ache. "We don't tend to do things by the book, do we?"

"No," Henry agreed, his chest feeling like it would burst. "And I don't think we ever will."

As Lady Langlevit and Lady Northridge came in to welcome the arrival of the Radcliffe twins, Henry could not help feeling a surge of intense gratitude. Seeing the teary happiness on his mother's face as she welcomed her grandsons made his throat choke up. He watched his sister-in-law coo over how handsome her nephews were and hug her sister while weeping copious, happy tears. Even Dr. Hargrove seemed to be in jovial spirits, proclaiming he'd never delivered such robust twin boys.

But most of all, Henry watched his wife—his fearless, indomitable, lionhearted countess—feeling his body respond to every smile, to every word, to every laugh.

Irina was the sun in his world, the anchor in his storm, the joy in his life.

She was his heart.

Acknowledgments

Amalie Howard

Three books in the Lords of Essex series later, and I can only bow down to my fabulous co-author, Angie Morgan, who continues to inspire me with her talent. Tremendous thanks to our wonderful editor, Alethea Spiridon, and our fearless publisher, Liz Pelletier. Thank you to the entire production, design, and publicity teams at Entangled, with special thanks to Curtis Svehlak, Holly Bryant-Simpson, Riki Cleveland, Heather Riccio, Melanie Smith, Anita Orr, and Erin Dameron-Hill. A huge thank you goes out to my loyal readers, fans, and friends. Lastly, to Cameron, Connor, Noah, and Olivia—you guys are my forever loves!

Angie Morgan

With every book we write together, I find something new to admire in my co-author. Amalie, you know how to keep me smiling and motivated, and I'm so thankful we're a team! We also have an amazing team at Entangled, including Alethea Spiridon, Liz Pelletier, Curtis Svehlak, Holly Bryant-Simpson, Riki Cleveland, Melanie Smith, and Anita Orr—you're all the best! To my readers, I wish I could give all of you a big hug of thanks! And of course to my favorite people in the world: Chad, Alex, Joslin, and Willa—I love you.

About the Author

Amalie Howard's love of romance developed after she started pilfering her grandmother's novels in high school when she should have been studying. She has no regrets. A #1 Amazon bestseller and a national IPPY silver medalist, she is the author of *My Rogue, My Ruin*, the first in the Lords of Essex historical romance series, as well as several award-winning young adult novels critically acclaimed by Kirkus, Publishers Weekly, VOYA, School Library Journal, and Booklist, including *Waterfell*, *The Almost Girl*, and *Alpha Goddess*, a Kid's IndieNext pick. She currently resides in Colorado with her husband and three children. Visit her at www.amaliehoward.com.

Angie Morgan lives in New Hampshire with her husband, their three daughters, a menagerie of pets, and an extensive collection of paperback romance novels. She's the author of *My Rogue, My Ruin*, the first book in the Lords of Essex historical romance series, as well as several young adult books, including The Dispossessed series written under the name

Page Morgan. Critically acclaimed by Booklist, Publisher's Weekly, Kirkus, School Library Journal, VOYA, and The Bulletin, Angie's novels have been an *IndieNext* selection, a *Seventeen Magazine* Summer Book Club Read, and a #1 Amazon bestseller. Visit her at www.AngieMorganBooks.com.

Discover more historical romance from Entangled...

An Earl for an Archeress
a *Ladies of Scotland* novel by E. Elizabeth Watson

Lady Mariel Crawford enters an archery contest as a boy but despite her skill she loses to the very handsome Earl of Huntington. When Robert of Huntington realizes she is the runaway daughter of the Beast of Ayr and that her father conspires with the Sheriff of Nottingham, he is compelled to protect her. Even though she wants nothing to do with him, he will risk everything for the Scottish wilding who's pierced his heart.

A Dance with Seduction
a *Spy in the Ton* novel by Alyssa Alexander

Vivienne Le Fleur is a spy. When a French agent abducts her sister, she is forced to seek the help Maximilian Westwood, retired code breaker, and the one man who doesn't want her. When she sneaks into his study with a coded message, he's ready to push her away, but can't say no to a woman in trouble. They soon discover there is more between them than politics and hidden codes, but love has no place among the secrets of espionage...

ONCE A COURTESAN
a *Once Wicked* novel by Liana LeFey

Romance blossoms between Headmistress Jacqueline Trouvère and her mysterious new maths instructor, Mr. William Woodson, but both harbor deadly secrets. When danger jeopardizes the school, all will come to light, threatening to destroy their newfound love.

ONLY A DUKE WILL DO
a *To Marry a Rogue* novel by Tamara Gill

On the eve of Lady Isolde Worthingham's wedding to Merrick Mountshaw, the Duke of Moore, a scandal that rocked the ton leaves her perfectly planned future in a tangle of disgrace and heartbreak. The duke loathes the pitiful existence he hides from the *ton*. With a scandalous wife he never wanted, life is a never-ending parade of hell. When the one woman he loved and lost returns to London, he can no longer live without her. But vows and past hurts are not easily forgotten. Love may not win against the *ton* when a too proper Lord and Lady play by the rules.

Made in the USA
Middletown, DE
29 September 2023